STEPHANIE FAZIO

OPAL SMOKE

OPAL CONTAGION BOOK 1

Syafant Press

New York, New York

Cover designed by Keith Tarrier

This book is a work of fiction. Names, characters, places, and incidents either are the product of the author's imagination or are used fictionally, and any resemblance to actual persons, living or dead, business establishments, events, or locales is entirely coincidental.

Stephanie Fazio

Visit www.StephanieFazio.com

Printed in the United States of America
First Printing: June 2020

Library of Congress Control Number: 2019918526

ISBN 978-1-951572-05-1

To Sally, David, and Lizzie

PROLOGUE

1 YEAR EARLIER

Every man, woman, and child in Lagonia had turned out for the momentous occasion. Councilmen, courtiers, and soldiers emptied out of the palace. All the merchants had returned from their travels abroad in time for the celebration. Aside from the ones unlucky enough to be on duty, the men and women who made up the strongest army on the continent mingled with all the other Lagonians crowding the cobbled streets.

It was a true mark of the day's importance that everyone in the empire had been up since early morning, primping and preparing. As a rule, Lagonians were not early risers.

Everyone was dressed in their finest, with the latest fashion trends on full display. Rubies, sapphires, and emeralds gleamed at women's throats, often simultaneously. Ears and fingers sparkled from the flawless diamonds adorning them. The whisper of silk trailed in the ladies' wakes, and there was the smart clip of polished dragonhide boots that followed in the men's. Children wore garlands of fresh flowers and strings of pearls so long the gemstones dragged on the ground behind them.

Everyone was making their way to the Golden Bridge, which was, in fact, made out of solid gold. The Golden Bridge stretched across the river that served as one of the natural barriers between Lagonia and the world beyond. For generations, the only ones who made use of the bridge were the merchants who risked their lives every time they stepped onto the other side of the river, and the hundred archers who kept outsiders from setting foot on Lagonia territory.

Trumpeters on the bridge blew out clear melodies. Singing and laughter filled the streets. Children wove through the crowd, tossing lumps of silver and sapphires the size of their heads to one another as the adults scolded them good-naturedly. Neighbors greeted each other, and lovers shared secret smiles as the merry crowd was swept toward the bridge.

Not even a single cloud dared make an appearance on this day. The sun shone down from a perfectly blue sky. The air was comfortably warm, but not over-humid. It was an especially beautiful day in the only empire that was blessed with temperate weather in all seasons. The mountains on two sides of Lagonia and the ocean on another protected the empire from the extreme weather that plagued the other lands. Lagonia weather, as was the case for everything else in the empire, was idyllic.

The scent of expensive perfumes and colognes mixed with the other appealing aromas filling the streets. The promise of spiced wine, sizzling meat, and fried pastries wafted through the streets as cooks and slaves prepared for the evening's festivities. Pixies fluttered overhead, sagging under the weight of party invitations their masters had bid them deliver.

People swallowed from vials containing luminescent liquid—potions purchased from the witches and warlocks in the Insorsil Kingdom for exorbitant prices that would help them enjoy the coming festivities all the better.

After swallowing a bright purple potion, one woman's nose shrunk to half its prior size, and her short hair transformed into sleek, raven waves. A man who drank from another vial grew in height as his potbelly flickered out of existence. With his lips still stained green, he approached a woman who was too beautiful not to be under the magic of her own Insorsil illusion.

Lagonians valued beauty and pleasure above all else, and their empire was well-equipped for delivering all that was needed for both…at least, for those who could afford it.

It would be an understatement to say Lagonians were fond of celebrating. They used any excuse to throw a banquet or a dance. But not a single Lagonian alive could recall an occasion as worthy of commemorating as the event about to take place.

Today, for the first time in over a hundred years, Lagonians could travel beyond their borders without fear of contracting the deadly opal contagion.

Merchants and their families were returning from the other side of the Golden Bridge, where they had witnessed the ceremonial burning of the quarantine village. For over a hundred years, the merchants had risked their lives every time they traveled to Insorsil to trade Lagonian jewels and gold for magic. On their return to Lagonia, they had to endure a month-long quarantine to ensure they hadn't been infected with the contagion. Now, that was all over. Like death from opal contagion, the need for quarantine was a thing of the past.

For the first time, Lagonians didn't need to dread encountering one of the Extended…survivors of opal contagion. These carriers of the disease all had the defining characteristics of a strange, shimmery glow to their skin that was reminiscent of opals, orange-rimmed eyes, and burnt orange hair. And of course, no one could forget the inhuman abilities that came with these unfortunate-looking carriers of the opal contagion.

Lagonia had been protected by its geographic insulation when opal contagion first broke out. As other empires fell to the deadly disease, Lagonia continued on more or less as it had before, accumulating riches and trading them for the magic that fascinated and amused them.

But Lagonians were tired of isolation. They were tired of waiting months for the latest charms and potions to arrive from Insorsil, and for the latest furs and silks to be delivered from across the sea.

Slavers were already packing their supplies and making ready to cross the Golden Bridge as soon as darkness fell, and the guards could be convinced to look away from their illegal activities. The slavers rubbed their hands together and talked in hushed voices about the Extended they would capture and bring back to Lagonia.

All the leaders on this side of the sea had signed an anti-slavery treaty some years back, but slavers were convinced that law would more often be overlooked than enforced when it came to the Extended. There was no limit to the amount the wealthiest Lagonians would pay for Extended slaves now that no one in the empire needed to fear infection.

A joyous cry went up from the crowd as the Emperor's fire-breathing gold dragon sailed overhead. The hundred archers on the Golden Bridge shooed citizens back, clearing a place for the two-ton dragon to set down in the center of the bridge.

It was the new emperor's first public appearance since his father, the previous Emperor Jaikon, had been found murdered in his own throne room only a week ago. The murder had come as a shock, but it was the Lagonian way to look beyond tragedy and unpleasantness. The best medicine for a grieving people was feasting and revelry. Life was too short to spend it lamenting what could not be changed, as the deceased emperor no doubt would have counseled them. Thus, today would be a day to celebrate the empire's gains, rather than to shed tears over what it had lost.

Everyone waited to see how the late Emperor's son, Jaikon, Jr., would conduct himself on this day. It was customary to wait a year after an emperor's death to officially crown his successor, but the twenty-year-old standing on the bridge was by all rights the new leader of Lagonia. Jaikon, Jr. was now the ruler of the empire whose wealth exceeded that of all the other lands put together.

Jaikon dismounted from his father's—now his—dragon. No one could deny that, already, the young man looked the part of an emperor. He was adorned in black and gold, Lagonia's official colors. His gold cape was studded with black diamonds that winked in the sunlight. Jaikon's eyes, known to be a pale, icy blue, had been Insorsiled to appear as deep blue as the sky overhead. A gold circlet rested atop his head. It was a breach of tradition, which dictated that no crown be worn until the official ceremony in a year's time.

Jaikon had a reputation for being an impatient and ambitious child, and it seemed the almost-grown man was no different.

Jaikon looked nothing like his father. The previous emperor had been olive-skinned and dark-haired. His son had inherited his mother's pale skin and golden hair. He couldn't be called handsome, exactly, but there was something undeniably striking about the Emperor-to-be.

Citizens craned their necks to catch a glimpse of him. The rumor at court was that Jaikon had walked into the throne room, seen the blood from his father staining the floor, and collapsed in grief. But talk among his closest advisors was that Jaikon had called a meeting that very night to discuss changes in his father's longstanding tax laws.

Jaikon took the glowing orange stick a guard offered him, held it to his throat, and began to speak. The Emperor-to-be's voice, amplified with Insorsil magic, extended to the far reaches of the crowd.

"Citizens of Lagonia," he boomed. "Today, I am proud to announce that our collective dream of immunity to opal contagion has been achieved."

There were cheers and applause.

"I will not say more about it, as the cause of our newfound immunity is a secret known only to myself and my most trusted advisors. While I do not wish to keep secrets from my subjects, I know you all can appreciate how this particular secret is imperative."

The citizens murmured among themselves. Curiosity about the immunity ate at them, even if they knew it was prudent for their young leader to keep the knowledge quiet. After all, if the source of their people's immunity to opal contagion became known, there'd be nothing to stop Lagonia's enemies from destroying it, thereby leaving its citizens susceptible to the disease once again. There was no shortage of leaders clamoring to take control of the bountiful empire and seize the riches that belonged to its people.

Lagonians desired freedom from their confinement more than they craved satisfaction for their curiosity. Besides, Lagonians were not good secret-keepers. Gossip flowed as freely as the golden nuggets that were Lagonia's lowest denomination of currency.

It was enough to know they were finally safe from the poison that ran through the Extended people's veins. The Extended would no longer be able to terrorize the rest of the world, infecting people and using their inhuman abilities with impunity.

"Now, we can come and go as we please," Jaikon continued.

The one-hundred archers who were stationed on the Golden Bridge day and night lowered their weapons in perfect synchronization. The archers had been there to protect Lagonia from the outside world for three generations, ensuring anyone who might be infected never set foot on the bridge. They would remain to police all who entered and left Lagonia, but now, their presence was more for show than to guard against any real threat. The Lagonians were safe. They were free.

Now, the Extended would know what it was like to fear for their lives.

"We will show no mercy. We are Lagonians, and we bow to no one."

The crowd cheered as a burst of black and gold sparks erupted in the sky overhead. As everyone watched, the flaming sparks rearranged themselves in the sky, forming into letters that were alternating black and gold. When they stopped moving, "Emperor Jaikon" was written across the sky for all to see. The court advisors exchanged meaningful glances as they swatted at the wild tree fairies who had flown from the Insorsiled forest to see what all the fuss was about.

Only time would reveal what kind of a leader the Emperor-to-be would become. His tutors spoke of his cleverness and love of battles of wit. The fighting masters described his ruthlessness and unconventional techniques that compensated for his average skill with a sword. Court advisors whispered about the discord that had existed between the late Emperor and his son in all matters relating to foreign affairs.

Perhaps, under his rule, the Lagonians would see their wealth and prestige grow even beyond what had already been achieved.

The only ones who weren't smiling were Lagonia's Chief Assassin and his entourage. They stood on the Golden Bridge beside the Emperor. The three men who were always seen in the assassin's company wore the uniform of the Emperor's guard: dragonhide jackets and boots, and no fewer than a dozen weapons strapped to their person. The Chief Assassin wore simple black. There was no hint of the dragonhide that protected the rest of his soldiers from arrowheads and blades. He was also bare of weapons, except for an unadorned dagger. The four men's faces were stoic as they stared straight ahead. Their expressions revealed nothing.

Lagonia's Chief Assassin was just a boy himself—barely nineteen. He had been promoted to the role by the previous emperor. The appointment had caused quite a stir. The coveted position was outranked only by the emperor, who filled the role of Commander of the army. Convention dictated that the appointment should have gone to the emperor's heir and only legitimate son. Still, none of the emperor's advisors had questioned the decision to promote the emperor's bastard son, instead. The boy was inarguably the best candidate. His guardian, the ruthless and taciturn Master Interrogator, had taught the boy well.

In the last six months since he'd taken on his new role as Chief Assassin, Rhetteman Loniger—Rhett, as he was known to the men and women soldiers under his command—had dispatched the emperor's enemies in Lagonia with a brutal efficiency. He commanded a great deal of respect among the soldiers, and a great deal of sighing among the young ladies at court.

Now, the young assassin would have a chance to really prove his worth. He would be tested against Extended, whose superhuman talents made them more dangerous than even the giant lords he was rumored to have fought and dispatched—without assistance.

"Forward, my faithful soldiers," Jaikon called, signaling to the assassins.

The crowd parted as the small retinue of men marched toward the four saddled dragons that waited for them at the end of the bridge. They were prime specimens of the famed Lagonia army. Their strength was apparent in every flex of their muscles and stomp of their boots.

As the Chief Assassin and his men passed, women in the crowd threw flowers and silk handkerchiefs at them. Whatever thrill these men felt at being selected for this highest of honors was hidden behind faces trained to be expressionless.

"Rhetteman Loniger," the Emperor-to-be boomed. "Bring me back a dozen Extended heads."

The stoic young Chief Assassin, the deadliest man in all of Lagonia, turned and saluted his Emperor.

The crowd roared, shouting for Extended blood.

CHAPTER 1

NOW

Only Jaikon would hold an execution and an enthronement on the same day, Rhett thought.

Everything about today felt wrong, starting with his uniform. Rhett was wearing his ceremonial black-and-gold suit. It was too tight, and the black diamonds sewn into the fabric clicked together with his every movement. Rhett itched to change into the simple and silent clothes he wore as Lagonia's Chief Assassin. But his normal clothes weren't up to the pomp and circumstance of an enthronement, at least as far as the new Emperor was concerned.

Jaikon had effectively been ruling for the last year, but today, his reign would become official.

They were all standing on the cliff overlooking the glittering sea on Lagonia's northern border. The wind coming off the water smelled of salt. Jaikon's gold cape snapped behind him as he stood, flanked by his Master Interrogator on one side and Rhett on the other, and faced the executioner's platform. The councilman now climbing the stairs on wobbling legs would stand on the platform while his crimes were announced. He would be beheaded, and then his body would be tossed over the cliff to join all of Lagonia's other dead.

Rhett had seen enough bodies tossed over the cliff to know he wouldn't be able to hear the splash when the corpse hit the water. The cliff was too high and the wind too loud. There was something unsettling about not knowing when the body broke the surface. Rhett kept his breathing even as he imagined his own body's weightlessness and the crash of water against his bare skin as he himself was tossed over the cliff.

It wasn't a peaceful image…fish devouring innards and flesh, currents separating the bones one by one…. Cold, dark water.

Rhett wasn't the only one with these unpleasant thoughts. He felt Stone's tension even though they were separated by the new Emperor. No one else would have noticed. Anyone who looked at either Rhett or Stone would see Lagonia's Chief Assassin and Master Interrogator, and nothing more. But Rhett knew his mentor and former guardian better than anyone alive. Stone's wife and son had been thrown over the cliff twenty years ago, and Rhett didn't think Stone would ever be able to stand in this place without remembering their deaths.

Jaikon wanted to draw out the councilman's suffering, which was why he requested the enthronement take place before the execution.

Rhett watched as one of Emperor's advisors lowered the crown onto Jaikon's head. Jaikon spoke oaths, and the crowd whooped and applauded.

Jaikon was talking about how much his father, the previous emperor, would be missed. He was talking about how he intended to carry on his father's legacy.

Empty words, Rhett thought. Words came so cheaply to Lagonians. They said whatever they thought would serve them best in that moment. In an empire where subterfuge reigned in equal partnership with the emperor, Rhett had long ago learned to recognize the forked tongues in the bejeweled, pressed, and powdered members of the court.

A feeling of dread crept over Rhett as Jaikon continued to make promises to the citizens of Lagonia. As a rule, Rhett didn't concern himself with court gossip, but last night, Stone had told him there was talk among the councilmen that Jaikon was changing too much too quickly. He was spreading Lagonia's army too thin—a fact Rhett could personally attest to—and making enemies by disregarding trade agreements ratified by the former emperor.

Rhett could feel that unrest now, simmering beneath the glittering veneer of the councilmembers surrounding him. As deep as Rhett's loathing for the new Emperor ran, he knew if the whispering and unrest got any worse, it wouldn't bode well for the empire.

Directly in front of Rhett, a hollow-eyed Extended slave girl was writing down every word of Jaikon's speech with one hand and painting his portrait with the other. The girl, who didn't look older than ten or eleven, had shackles on her ankles.

Tiny rainbows shimmered across the slave girl's opal skin, giving her an effervescent look. Her burnt orange hair and halo of orange around her cornea were the other physical characteristics of all the Extended. Before Lagonia's immunity was bought by the previous emperor and introduced by the current one, the sight of opal skin and orange hair drove panic into Lagonians. Now, it only sparked their hatred.

The Extended, survivors of opal contagion and their offspring, were carriers of the disease that had ravaged whole continents. All the Extended were gifted—or cursed, depending on one's perspective—with special abilities. There were common Extensions like Flamers, who could set anything alight just by touching it, and Flooders, who could draw water from any source and direct it anywhere they chose. The common ones weren't very powerful. They were only able to command small flames and puddles, respectively, and wouldn't be able to turn their abilities against Lagonia. It was the reason why many of them were slaves in the palace instead of dead by Rhett's own hand.

Less common Extensions were included in the general group of Extended known as Fighters. The Fighters' muscles, flexibility, or other similar skill gave them the advantage over any normal opponent. In the last year since Jaikon distributed the immunity and re-opened Lagonia's borders, it had been Rhett's task to eradicate any Extended who might be able to threaten Lagonia. Whatever Extended Fighters remained had gone into hiding.

With the enthronement complete, all eyes turned to the executioner's platform.

Rhett stood beside the Emperor as he listened to the crimes being read against the man kneeling on the platform.

"Do you admit guilt for murdering the prior emperor, Jaikon, Sr., in cold blood?" the executioner asked. His voice was amplified with Insorsil magic.

"I do," the disgraced councilman said, bowing his head.

A woman and young girl standing at the foot of the platform clutched each other as they wept.

Rhett kept his face blank as a torrent of pity and anger swept through him. Rhett had been the one to come into the throne room at the moment when Jaikon plunged the dagger into the emperor's chest. Rhett had been too overcome to speak or even move.

"Don't just stand there," Jaikon had told him. "Clean this mess up."

And, with little other choice, he had. Rhett mopped up the blood of the emperor—his own father, even if the emperor had never acknowledged the bastard child of his mistress. When Jaikon had demanded Rhett hand over his own shirt to replace Jaikon's bloodstained one, Rhett had given it to the half-brother he loathed.

Rhett had been forced to stand by as Jaikon brought in the scapegoat for the murder—a member of the emperor's council who was universally disliked for his proposition to lower the peasants' taxes.

Jaikon had taken great pleasure in describing exactly what he'd do to the councilman's wife and daughter if the man didn't confess to the murder. The meeting had gone the same way such meetings always went. The councilman had cursed Jaikon and made empty threats. By the end of the meeting, he was weeping and begging. The inevitable conclusion came when the man agreed to every one of Jaikon's terms.

After, just for appearance's sake, Jaikon had ordered Stone, the emperor's Master Interrogator, to torture the man and force a dozen other false confessions from him.

Stone had been Rhett's guardian until he turned eighteen, and was in effect the only person who had ever treated Rhett like a son.

Rhett's mother had died in childbirth—a rarity with the abundance of Insorsil magic—and his father, the emperor, had never acknowledged Rhett as anything more than a gifted soldier in his army.

The man on the executioner's platform stopped mid-confession and looked down at his family.

"I love you," he said in a choked voice.

The woman and child cried harder, begging the Emperor for mercy.

Rhett kept his muscles relaxed and his face blank. Anyone who looked at him wouldn't see even a trace of emotion in his eyes. There would be no sign of a clenched fist or tight jaw.

Steel doesn't know love or despair. It can't be bent or broken. It needs no heart or warmth. I am steel.

Stone had taught him the mantra when he was a child, and it had been Rhett's only comfort for as long as he could remember.

The councilman about to die was a stark reminder of why Rhett kept himself aloof from everyone and everything. The woman and child crying below the platform were the reason why Rhett didn't allow himself to form attachments beyond the loyalties expected between the second-highest-ranking officer and his soldiers.

Jaikon prided himself on finding a person's weakness and exploiting it. It was a game to him. Rhett knew from years of observation that the game only ever had one winner.

Jaikon had ordered Rhett to be the councilman's executioner. Rhett had refused. He had no desire to kill a Lagonian in cold blood, especially when he knew firsthand of the man's innocence. Jaikon would have forced Rhett the same way he bent everyone else to his will, but the Emperor had no leverage over him. It was the only reason Rhett wasn't standing on the platform now with an axe in his hand. Jaikon had nothing to threaten him with.

Jaikon couldn't control Rhett, and as deep as the hatred ran between the half-brothers, Jaikon couldn't kill him. As the best assassin on the continent, Rhett had become a living symbol of the empire's power and strength. If Jaikon killed him without cause, the councilmen and soldiers would revolt. Jaikon was aware of this fact and was constantly searching for a passable reason to kill Rhett. That Rhett never gave him one made Jaikon's hatred even stronger.

As the executioner read out the long list of crimes, and the councilman accepted responsibility for each one, Rhett remembered the stickiness of his father's blood on his hands as he scrubbed the granite floor. He remembered the way Jaikon had laughed as he pulled Rhett's shirt over his head and sauntered out of the throne room.

Steel doesn't know love or despair.

The confessions were over. As the executioner raised his axe, Rhett saw Jaikon's ice blue eyes swivel away from the man about to die. They fixed on him. He felt the weight of the Emperor's gaze even as he kept his own eyes trained on the execution.

It can't be bent or broken.

Rhett could almost feel the cogs inside Jaikon's head turning as he schemed and waited for Rhett to make a mistake. Jaikon wanted a reaction—a twitch of a muscle, the tightening of a fist—anything that would help him find whatever weakness he was certain lurked just beneath the surface. Jaikon would never find it. Rhett would never give Jaikon anything that could be used as leverage to manipulate him. Rhett would never be owned.

It needs no heart or warmth.

Rhett stayed perfectly still, not allowing even the ghost of an emotion to cross his face. After so many years of practice, it was easy to keep the feelings of anger and injustice so deeply buried no one would ever know they were there.

I am steel.

The executioner's axe fell.

CHAPTER 2

Liss leaned over the warlock at the bar.

The warlock's emotions were subdued, quieted by the three drinks he'd consumed in a quarter of an hour. *Perfect.*

"So sorry." She let just enough of her drink spill onto his shirt. Not so much that he'd be angry, but not too little that she wouldn't have cause to "help" him out. She let out a little giggle and covered her mouth with her hand as she dabbed at the spill. The warlock gaped openly at her chest, muttering about how she had nothing to apologize for.

She gave him *the smile*, the one that had literally once brought a man to his knees, as she relieved the warlock of his dragonhide wallet.

Out of the corner of her eye, Liss saw Mari's small, opal-hued hand appear through the solid oak wall of the bar beneath them. Liss passed her the wallet, all while keeping the warlock's gaze otherwise occupied, and waited until both girl and wallet had disappeared. No one else in the bar noticed.

Mari was a wisp of a girl, and walking through walls aside, no one ever looked twice at her. The Insorsiled didn't notice dirty little Extended children, unless it was to call them swine and chase them away.

The Insorsiled, witches and warlocks who lived in this empire, were immune to the disease her people carried in their veins. But it didn't stop them from discriminating against the Extended, regardless. The Insorsiled saw her people as inferior because their power came from a mutated disease; the Insorsiled possessed true magic.

Liss slipped her hand inside the warlock's jacket as she continued to dab at the spill, sensing for any change in his emotions that would warn her he'd noticed her thievery. His soul was placid. *No, wait…*she froze with her hand curled around his pocket watch. His emotions were changing. He felt interest and longing.

Liss could never know for certain the reason why someone was feeling the emotions she sensed, but she'd be willing to bet the ruby-encrusted ring she'd just neatly removed from the warlock's pinky finger that she was the target of his emotions.

Gross.

Liss said her final apologies and turned to go. The warlock grabbed her wrist and leaned into her. His long, greasy hair brushed against her as his eyes fixated on her chest.

"I'll brew you a potion to give you sweet dreams for a year if you spend an hour with me."

"No, thank you," Liss replied, keeping her voice light.

The warlock's emotions shifted again. This time, they turned more sinister. There was intrigue and desire, and something like possessiveness. His soul felt slimy, dirty, and Liss wanted nothing more to do with it. She tried to slip out of the warlock's grasp, but he only tightened his hold.

This bar was one of Liss's best thieving spots in all of Insorsil, so she couldn't afford to make a scene. Instead, she leaned back and caught the eye of the boy sitting two stools down. Spence didn't even glance at her as he hopped off his stool and stumbled over to them.

"Whoops." Spence lurched, grabbing the warlock's arm to steady himself.

"Extended swine," the warlock mumbled as his hand fell away from Liss.

Spence released his hold, and the warlock slumped against the bar. He was snoring.

Liss and Spence didn't acknowledge each other as he returned to his stool. For calling Spence swine, Liss took the warlock's gold bracelet. It wasn't worth much, but it was engraved, which meant it was sentimental. She wasn't usually petty about her stealing, but she could make exceptions for people who well and truly deserved a good fleecing.

As she sauntered toward the exit, Liss felt self-consciousness and insecurity radiating off the soul of a witch sitting alone at a large table. Liss could feel unhappiness clutching at the witch's soul.

Liss had no patience for people who were dissatisfied with their lot in life but refused to do anything to change it. It was Liss's greatest frustration with her own people. They resented the way they were treated, and yet they feared to do anything to improve their bleak lives. It was one of the reasons why Liss took pleasure in stealing from Lagonia soldiers. She wasn't a fighting Extended, but that didn't mean she was defenseless against her oppressors.

Even though she'd much rather be able to kill them than just steal their correspondences and jewels, at least she was doing something. Liss couldn't abide the Extended who spent their nights huddled around their tiny cookstoves bemoaning their lot in life.

Liss went over to the witch's table and leaned over the woman, who was staring dismally into her purple, frothing drink.

"You have a lovely necklace," Liss told the witch. "I do love sapphires."

"Well thank you, thank you very much." The witch's delight came off her soul in a rush. "It's just a little trinket. I have so many others, I couldn't decide what to wear today." The witch gave a breathy little laugh.

Riiight.

Liss's Extension was soul sorting, which meant she could sense any emotion a person was feeling. She wasn't as good at detecting lies as Truthseers, but she could often identify when the words that came out of a person's mouth didn't match the emotions written across their soul. It was a convenient talent for her line of work. It helped her pick out targets who were ripe for thievery, like the warlock whose emotions were dampened from intoxication, and this witch who was desperate for attention.

Soul sorting was how she'd learned that dishonestly was the one trait that was consistent across Lagonians, Insorsiled, and Extended.

Soul Sorters were rare, especially since the Lagonia emperor had deemed it a "dangerous" Extension and had set his Chief Assassin on murdering all of them. Liss had only ever met one other Soul Sorter. He was a second-generation Extended man in his fifties, and he'd been found dead in his wagon more than a year ago. His slit throat had marked him as one of the Lagonia Chief Assassin's victims.

The Viper, Caravan Butcher, Extended Eraser, Opal Slayer…Lagonia's Chief Assassin was known by many names. All he ever left behind were slit throats and whispers about his brutality. No Extended had ever seen his face; any who got close enough ended up with their throats cut. She'd once heard the man drank his victims' blood and wore a necklace with all of their teeth.

Liss hoped the weight of all those teeth would snap the Viper's neck.

She took the witch's hand, introducing herself as she slipped the ring from the witch's finger.

Long years of practice had taught Liss exactly what to say and do to divert attention from what she was stealing. In all the time she'd been a thief, Liss had never even come close to getting caught.

Of course, it wasn't just her Extension that made her so good at what she did. Liss was pretty—pretty in a way that made shallow women want to impress her, and drew men to her like she was some kind of walking, breathing love potion.

Even though she was Extended, her wavy brown hair, blue eyes, and boringly pale skin that didn't have even a hint of opal sheen made her look Lagonian.

Liss's father had been Uninfected. He was a Lagonia merchant, and he'd fallen in love with her Extended mother. The only reason he hadn't succumbed to the disease she carried was because of a kind of Insorsiled magic that no legitimate witchdoctor practiced for good reason.

Liss had been the product of her parents' love. She had an ability like all Extended, but she didn't look like them. As far as she knew…as far as anyone in her caravan knew…she was the only Extended who didn't have the looks to match.

It set her apart from her own people, but her appearance guaranteed no Lagonian or Insorsiled ever suspected she was Extended.

The witch, still smiling at the attention, offered to buy Liss a drink. Graciously refusing, Liss backtracked toward the door. When the witch turned back to her drink, Liss tucked the sapphire necklace into her pocket.

The door swung shut behind her, and the black-and-neon sign that read "Toil and Trouble" settled back against the wood.

So far, it had been a productive afternoon. Not even counting whatever was inside the warlock's wallet, she and the kids had stolen enough to barter for the caravan's supplies for the next week. She'd trade in the necklace for more gold, which would buy grain, eggs, salted meat, bottled water, and of course, her mother's medicine. She might even have enough spare gold to get some Insorsiled magic to amuse the kids.

As long as she did the purchasing, instead of Spence, Mari, or little Jema, none of the Insorsil shop owners would charge her the gouged Extended prices. It was infuriating, but the Insorsiled discriminated against her people by charging a far higher price for Extended customers. The Insorsiled were immune to all illnesses that plagued non-magic people, including opal contagion, but it didn't stop them from treating her people like dirt under their expensive dragonhide boots.

Because the Extended were barred from the other non-magic empires for fear of the contagion, her people's only option for goods and supplies was from Insorsil. It wasn't like the Extended could take their business elsewhere, and the Insorsiled loved taking advantage of their desperate situation.

It was one of the many reasons why Liss had no qualms about stealing from them. The way she saw it, the Insorsiled stole from her people every day. She was just returning the favor.

Liss stepped out into the busy alley, pressing herself against a shop door to avoid an Insorsiled bike that zoomed past.

Liss waved away a witch who held up a crystal ball—a fake, no doubt. She shook her head at a warlock selling charms to extend one's life— definitely fake. There were other tents with displays of potions to bring luck in love, bones that could cure any minor ailment, and all manner of self-propelled flying objects.

There were Insorsiled who could do real magic, like the witchdoctors. But if there were any who could actually extend life or alter luck, they weren't offering it for three ounces of gold.

Most of the shops on this street bore the ugly "No Extended" sign. It alternately amused and disgusted Liss that she could go places the rest of her people couldn't, just because she looked "normal." Whatever that meant....

There were many theories behind the cause of the shimmery opal skin that made the Extended so easy to identify. Religious people called it the mark of the devil. Scientists said it was a genetic mutation. The Insorsiled called it a blight. Liss thought it was beautiful.

She never tired of seeing the play of light on her mother's skin, or Jema's burnt orange hair whipping in the wind, or the orange glow of Spence's eyes when they told stories in his wagon late at night. Liss sometimes wished she looked like the rest of the Extended, even if her unique parentage was more useful to her caravan than any of their Extensions.

Liss went into a shop with a "No swine, Uninfected Only" sign plastered over the front. She swallowed her anger, telling herself she'd take the man for all he was worth for his bigotry.

"I just don't understand why they keep coming 'round here to bother us," the shopkeeper was complaining to the witch at the counter. "Why don't the swine just build a farm or something? Live off the fat of the land, so to speak. Why they wheel around in those ridiculous wagons is beyond me."

Liss bit her lip until she tasted blood. There was good reason why her people lived the way they did, even if this warlock was too ignorant to know it.

Ever since the outbreak of the contagion, any person with opal skin was banned from every place where people susceptible to the disease lived. At first, some of the Extended had kept pathetic farms in the desert, but they were vulnerable to wild animals and even wilder humans who dared to attack them.

The Extended had realized early on that, if they hoped to survive, they would need to adapt. They split up into caravans and lived in wagons that stayed in one place for only a day or two at a time. It gave them some degree of safety, but it made it impossible for the Extended to provide for themselves.

Forcing her attention back on her task, Liss looked around the shop for what she should steal. The vault behind the counter was tempting, but it would be easier to empty that later with Spence's help. For now, she focused on the jewel-encrusted dagger hanging from the warlock's belt.

The decorative weapon, which Liss felt confident the warlock wouldn't know how to use if his life depended on it, could be traded for enough gold to purchase her caravan's food for weeks.

She stepped up to the counter when it was her turn to haggle with the warlock. Jema, the youngest of Liss's thieving crew, slipped into the shop as the previous patron exited.

Jema was a nine-year-old girl whose Extension gave her the ability to compress her entire body into a sphere the size of Liss's fist. By folding her arms around her chest and tucking in her chin, her entire body shrunk and rolled in on itself. She used her miniature feet and hands to roll herself wherever she wanted to go. Unless someone was looking down at the ground, no one would notice her in this form.

The warlock standing behind the counter certainly wasn't paying attention to anything except for the jewels he was loading into the vault behind him.

Liss dropped the sapphire necklace onto the counter. While the warlock's gaze and emotions were consumed with the necklace, she snatched the dagger from his belt.

She hid the weapon behind her back and then let it drop handle-first. Before it could hit the wooden floor, it connected with Jema's sphere and stared to compress. It was like the metal had turned to clay. The handle rolled in on the blade until the whole thing was a tight little spiral. Then, with a barely-audible *pop*, it was sucked into the little sphere that was Jema. Without another sound, Jema rolled out the door just as it opened for a witch to enter.

As soon as she was out on the street, Jema would find an alley out of sight, and then the little ball would unravel to reveal a normal-sized nine-year-old girl in its place.

Between Mari and Jema, there wasn't a house or shop in all of Insorsil that was off limits to their little thieving crew.

A few minutes later, Liss left the shop with her purse stuffed full of gold nuggets. She counted out the amount for her mother's medicine, and then paid two pixies to deliver the gold to the witchdoctor who made her mother's brew. She and the witchdoctor had worked out an agreement years ago, so that no matter where on the continent Liss's caravan was, her mother would still get her medicine.

Liss mentally calculated how much she'd have left after buying the caravan's necessities. Burk, her caravan leader, would want her to save the extra gold for next week when they moved away from Insorsil and deeper into the country, but what Burk didn't know wouldn't hurt him. The kids hadn't gotten any magical toys or candy in weeks. They deserved a treat.

She knew what each of them liked. Spence would want the green rock crystals that tasted so sour even the thought of them made Liss's mouth pucker. The less potent of the rock crystals made smoke come out of one's ears, while the strongest ones could levitate a skinny person a few inches off the ground. Mari favored a potion that made her opal skin disappear…at least for a few minutes. It was expensive and fleeting, but Mari so desperately longed to look like the Uninfected.

And Jema just wanted candy. Lots and lots of candy. Liss would have to hide a few pieces for herself and the other kids, or Jema would eat all of it.

The kids had been helping Liss in her thieving for the last year, and she felt a certain amount of responsibility for their happiness and welfare.

Spence, the oldest of the kids who served on Liss's thieving crew at fourteen, was growing into a lanky and somber boy. His head was a tangled mop of burnt orange, which he refused to cut because his mom had always been the one to style his hair. She'd been stabbed during a run-in with drunk Lagonia soldiers two years ago. The wound hadn't been fatal and the Insorsiled could have healed her easily, but they'd left her body in the cobbled street where she'd bled out during the night. Two days had passed before Burk heard news of her death to share with Spence and the rest of his family.

Mari, a rail-thin girl who looked younger than her eleven years, had the prettiest opal skin Liss had ever seen. Her burnt orange hair fell in tight ringlets down her back and was the envy of every Extended girl in the caravan. She used to be a giggling, bubbly child. But a year ago, slavers took both her parents and they were never heard from again. Mari didn't laugh much anymore.

Jema, the youngest of their crew at nine years of age, hadn't yet lost all of her innocence. Her parents were both still alive, but they were Energizers, which meant they worked all night long to power the caravan's wagons. They slept during the day, and Jema barely ever saw them. Jema had taken to tottering around after Liss even when they weren't out thieving. Liss didn't mind, especially since Jema's chattering broke up the silence that filled her wagon otherwise.

Spence, Mari, and Jema's stories weren't unique. Their loss was echoed in caravans all throughout the land. It was the story of the Lagonians' cruelty and the Insorsiled people's discrimination.

Liss was making her way back through the crowded street when a disturbance outside Toil and Trouble caught her attention. Liss felt the hatred, anger, and disgust radiating off the souls of the men gathered outside the bar. Not just men…Lagonia soldiers. They wore the black-and-gold armor that Liss hated more than any other sight.

She would have ducked down another alley to avoid the soldiers, but Spence was still at the bar. Whatever was happening outside Toil and Trouble, the dark emotions coming off the soldiers' souls didn't bode well for any Extended nearby.

When she saw the flash of orange hair in the midst of the circle of soldiers, Liss started to run.

Spence limped out of the circle, his face bloody, as the soldiers threw tankards and shouted insults of *swine* in his wake. Liss caught up to him, ignoring the whistling and catcalls. She helped Spence into an abandoned corner between two shops.

"What happened?" Liss demanded. "What did they do to you?" She was already thinking about which Insorsiled medicines would make Spence's pain—at least his physical pain—disappear within the hour. She felt the hurt, fear, and anger radiating off Spence's soul. Her own emotions rose to match as he told her about how the soldiers had grabbed him from the bar and beat him for the simple crime of being Extended.

Liss wrapped her arms around Spence and squeezed him. Spence was at the age where he thought he was too old for affection of any kind, but if she let go of him, she'd go kill every one of those soldiers. And then she'd have to suffer through yet another of Burk's lectures about how her impulsivity and recklessness put their caravan in danger.

"Spence!" Mari appeared through the solid stone wall of a shop and crouched beside Liss.

Jema came next, her chin wobbling when she caught sight of Spence. "What happened, Lissy?" she asked, her orange-rimmed eyes huge.

"They call *us* the swine," Spence mumbled, pressing a hand to his swollen lip.

There was fear and confusion rising from the kids' souls.

"I don't get why they do this." Mari gestured at Spence's bloody face. "Opal contagion doesn't kill Lagonians anymore. Why do they still hate us?"

Liss didn't have a good answer to that.

Caravans that could scrape together enough gold paid a monthly tax to Lagonia's Emperor, which made them more or less off-limits to the slavers who roamed the countryside. But the tax didn't keep the Extended safe when they encountered a vicious Lagonia soldier in an Insorsil bar, or when the Chief Assassin decided one of them was a threat to the empire.

"I wish someone would figure out what was giving the Lagonians their immunity," Spence said. "I'd go there and destroy it. And then I'd infect every last one of them."

Liss couldn't agree more. The mysterious immunity that allowed Lagonians to come into contact with Extended, without getting the contagion, also enabled slavers and soldiers to terrorize her people without consequences.

Spence looked at Liss. There was hatred in his soul, and she didn't blame him. She felt it, too.

"They said if a slaver showed up and took me away, they wouldn't do anything to stop it," Spence said.

Liss stood up. Her blood was boiling.

"Jema, get Spence some quick-heal," she said, handing her purse to the little girl. It was an effort to keep her voice calm, but somehow, she managed it. "There's a witchdoctor on the corner of Bashwell and Honey Pot that serves Extended. Spence'll also need numbing crystals and an Insorsiled bandage for the cut on his leg."

Liss shoved the list of the caravan's supplies back into her pocket. Those could wait.

She turned to Mari. "Stay with Spence. I'll meet you all back at the caravan."

Liss made her way back down the street, keeping a slight distance from the soldiers as she followed them. She read the emotions playing across their souls as her own anger and hatred simmered deep inside her.

There was one soldier whose soul was filled with self-importance and arrogance. He kept moving his hand to the breast pocket of his overcoat, and then feeling satisfied at whatever he felt.

Got you.

Liss slipped between two warlocks haggling over a foul-smelling brew. Turning so her face was hidden from both of them, she shoulder-bumped the one on the right. With a curse, he stumbled into the soldier.

The soldier whipped around. Liss ducked behind the other warlock, using his body to block her from view.

"What in the—"

"My apologies, good sir," the warlock said.

Liss slipped around so she was standing just behind the soldier and could reach into his pocket.

"You should watch your step, warlock. I'm an emissary of the Emperor himself," the soldier replied.

"Can I offer you something for your troubles? I'm rather gifted with strength spells," the warlock offered.

Right, Liss thought, stopping herself before she rolled her eyes.

Everyone with a brain knew strength spells were just illusion, and bad illusion at that. But Lagonians' fascination with magic, coupled with their simple minds, made them easy targets for any of the Insorsiled who had the stomach to haggle with them.

"You don't say?"

The soldier allowed the warlock to steer him away from his companions and toward a shop at the end of the alley.

Smiling to herself, Liss tucked the thick envelope she'd stolen under her arm and hurried in the opposite direction.

CHAPTER 3

Rhett pushed through the gaggle of courtiers and advisors milling around the throne room.

They were wearing the latest fashions from across the sea and playing with the newest magical toys out of Insorsil. The councilmen were applauding the Emperor's most recent trade deals, even as they schemed about how to undermine the agreements to weaken Jaikon's position and strengthen their own.

Boredom, and too much money and security, made Lagonians the type of people who would smile to your face and then shove a dagger in your back.

Rhett loathed the politics of court and avoided them like opal contagion.

"More taxes from the Extended would give the Emperor's coffers better padding," one councilman was saying to another. "I, for one, think the army should be sent to track down those wagons and squeeze the swine for all they're worth."

Only a lifetime of training to keep his face impassive kept Rhett from rolling his eyes. If these courtiers were less ignorant, they'd know the Extended didn't have anything else that could be squeezed from them. But the concept of poverty was as foreign to most Lagonians as the notion that the casualties in the Emperor's popular trade wars included their own countrymen. Rhett had fought in those wars…watched friends and soldiers under his command die in them.

Ciago, one of the only people Rhett called a friend, touched his elbow. "Emperor wants to see you in his private quarters."

Rhett could read Ciago's every expression, and the look on his friend's face immediately put him on guard. Without a word, Rhett left the throne room and strode through a hall paneled with black diamond mirrors. He nodded in greeting to the men and women standing guard in the hallway.

Rhett knocked, and then he opened the gold-plated door to the Emperor's bedchamber. It was a strange place to be meeting, but as soon as Rhett stepped into the room, he understood the Emperor's game.

Jaikon was reclining against the headboard and was clad only in a night robe. A woman was limping across the main part of the chamber. There was blood at the corner of her mouth and her eye was already swelling.

Rhett's fists wanted to clench, but Jaikon would notice even that slight reaction and use it to his advantage. Rhett forced his posture to stay relaxed and his face to remain blank. He fixed his steady, expressionless gaze on the Emperor.

I am steel.

"Ah, Rhetteman. Come forward." The Emperor's gaze scrutinized him. He wanted Rhett to react, to show some emotion, to prove he cared.

It was a deadly game, one Jaikon had been baiting him with since they were kids. Even then, Jaikon had been a master at unearthing people's weaknesses and exploiting them. Rhett would never give the Emperor that kind of power over him.

It can't be bent or broken.

The woman stumbled as she passed Rhett. He reached out a hand to steady her but didn't spare her a glance.

It needs no heart or warmth.

"You know you are welcome to any woman in my harem," Jaikon said pleasantly as the door shut, leaving them alone. "There are some real beauties among them."

"I'm not interested in your women." Rhett kept his voice cold and neutral.

"I knew you'd say that," Jaikon said, dismissing the subject with a careless wave of his hand. "There's been some ugliness along the slavers' routes. I need you to round up the slaves and kill the ones who are holding up trade."

"I'm not a slaver," Rhett replied.

"Why must you always be so difficult?" Jaikon crossed his arms. "Are you refusing to carry out my order?"

"Yes."

Jaikon let out a low, dangerous laugh. "I knew you'd say that, too. You're so boring and predictable."

Untouchable, you mean.

Jaikon raised one blonde eyebrow. "You do realize the irony of having a code of honor when you're Lagonia's Chief Assassin, don't you?"

Rhett ignored the barb. "Is there anything else…anything that falls within the bounds of my appointed role?"

Jaikon's ice blue eyes narrowed. Rhett had seen men falter under the scrutiny of that gaze. Rhett didn't blink.

"I will find your weakness," Jaikon said in a voice so soft it was barely audible. "Someday, there will be something or someone you care about. And when I discover what it is, any shreds of free will you thought you had will be nothing more than a memory."

"I have no weaknesses," Rhett replied. "I care for nothing except my duty and Lagonia's soldiers."

Jaikon offered a crocodile grin as his only response.

Most of the time, Rhett tried to forget he and the Emperor shared the same father. They'd never in their lives acknowledged each other as half-brothers, even though they'd grown up in the palace together. They didn't even look alike. Jaikon had the light complexion and softer features of his mother, while Rhett looked like the former Emperor.

At twenty-one, Jaikon was only a year Rhett's senior, but he looked much older. It was probably the beard.

For as much as Rhett tried to forget about the blood they shared, Jaikon couldn't look at Rhett without seeing his undeniable resemblance to their dead father. He had the same dark hair and eyes. He was even built like their father, dwarfing every man around save Wilsean and Ciago. Their likeness made it impossible for anyone in the palace to forget whose son Rhett was, which made his situation even more perilous.

Jaikon hated Rhett all the more because of the blood they shared. The feeling was mutual, although Rhett didn't have the luxury of showing it. Jaikon would have had Rhett killed years ago if it hadn't been for the simple fact that he couldn't…not unless he wanted to turn every soldier and councilmember in the empire against him. Even the Emperor had his limitations, and killing the second-most-powerful man in Lagonia without cause would incite a rebellion. Members of the council were looking for any excuse to strip Jaikon's power, just like Jaikon was looking for any excuse to have Rhett killed.

Stone had turned Rhett into the single most lethal person on the continent. Probably on any continent. Rhett's entire life had been an exercise in becoming invaluable to the Emperor so his life would be safe, or at least, as safe as it could be given the nature of his position.

"Is there anything else you wish me to do?" Rhett asked. *Besides see how you beat your women and listen to your threats….*

"Yes." Jaikon was still giving him that appraising look. "The Extended spy has struck again. This time, he stole slave routes from one of my emissaries."

Clever man. The emissaries weren't known for their intelligence, but they were careful and suspicious as a rule.

"I want you to find the spy and dispose of him," Jaikon continued.

"What can you tell me about him?" Rhett asked.

"Very little." Jaikon shrugged. "The emissary believes his papers were stolen outside a bar in northwest Insorsil."

There were no fewer than a hundred bars in northwest Insorsil.

"Any idea which bar? Did the emissary get a look at the man?"

"Toil and Trouble, and no," Jaikon replied. A look of irritation crossed his face. "Some are calling the spy Opal Smoke. It's believed his Extension is invisibility or turning into vapor."

Rhett nodded. He'd heard the rumors, too.

"I want him dead, Rhetteman. I expect you'll have this mess cleaned up as soon as possible." The emperor smiled. "You've always been good at cleaning up messes."

Rhett tamped down his rage before it showed on his face. He felt the slickness of his father's blood covering the marble floor and soaking through his pants.

"Bring me his head," the Emperor said. "I fear this Extended spy is after our greatest secret. I'll have every Extended slaughtered before it's revealed."

Rhett didn't doubt the Emperor's words. If the Extended discovered their secret and destroyed their immunity, there would be countless deaths.

"It will be done, Your Majesty." Rhett turned and strode toward the door.

"Oh, and Rhetteman."

Rhett turned back, waiting.

"Every man has a weakness. And I promise you, I'll find yours."

Rhett left the room with Jaikon's soft laughter ringing in his ears.

CHAPTER 4

Liss had struck gold. Not literal gold, but something even better. She knew what she was looking at the moment she opened the envelope and the maps spilled out. They were trade routes—specifically, slaver trade routes. Roads and outposts were clearly marked.

Liss ran all the way back to the caravan.

Her first stop was the second wagon. It belonged to Mari's family. Mari might be tiny, but her four brothers weren't. There were huge, in fact. All it took was one glance to know they were all Extended with strength.

Liss handed over the maps and stayed to listen as the brothers poured over them. They were discussing how to get messages to other fighting Extended who had already gone into hiding, and where to intercept the slavers.

Liss listened to their planning, wishing she could go with them. Not that soul sorting would be useful in a real fight, but she would love to see the look on those slavers' faces right before Mari's brothers killed them.

"We could use Burk's phoenix," Mari piped up from the corner of the wagon where she was stirring a pot of oatmeal.

When her brothers agreed, Liss groaned.

"Do we really need to tell Burk?" she asked.

Mari's oldest brother grinned. "He probably already knows." He inclined his head, and then in a louder voice said, "Burk, if you're listening, this was all Liss's idea."

Liss slapped her palm to her forehead.

Their caravan leader's Extension was impossibly good hearing. If he was anywhere in the vicinity of the caravan, there was no doubt he already knew what Liss had done.

"Burk is going to kill me," Liss complained.

Burk had been very clear that Liss was not to approach Lagonia soldiers under any circumstances. The last few times she'd disobeyed him, she'd gotten a stern lecture. She didn't expect to get off so easily this time.

One of Mari's brothers patted Liss on the back. "It's been nice knowing you, friend."

She scowled. "Just make sure my sacrifice is put to good use."

All of their faces sobered.

"We'll get them," Mari's oldest brother promised. "This is going to help our people. Well done, Liss."

Instead of feeling pleased by his words, all Liss felt was her own growing irritation that she couldn't do more.

By the time she'd said her goodbyes and returned to her own wagon, the last one in the caravan, the sun was setting.

The wagons stayed in place by day while Liss and the other Extended went about their business. By night, the wagons moved. When they woke up the next day, they would be in a new place.

Every caravan had at least two Energizers, whose Extension allowed them to animate the inanimate. Their ability would let them do far more interesting things if they'd had the strength and time to spare, but since Lagonia became immune, the Energizers had needed every ounce of their strength to keep the caravans moving. It was all that prevented Lagonia's Chief Assassin from swooping in and wiping them out of existence.

Liss was careful not to let the wagon door slam in case her mother was asleep. She kept her footsteps soft as she walked through the tiny kitchen, which was really just a stove and an ice box. It took six more steps to bring her through the living area where she slept on the narrow couch. She pushed aside the curtain that separated the small space that served as her mother's bedroom. She braced herself for the sadness and longing that filled her mother's soul.

Liss stepped up to the bed piled high with blankets. It had been a warm, early-fall day, but her mother was shivering under the covers.

"Hi, Mom," Liss said, trying to keep her voice soft and also bright.

Slowly, her mom turned her head to look at her. "My Liss."

The ghost of a smile passed across her mom's cracked lips. Her dull opal cheeks were sunken, and her orange eyes were bloodshot.

Liss stroked her mother's thinning hair back from her face. It had been more gray than orange since Liss could remember, even though her mom was in her early forties. Her opal skin was lined and shriveled from malnutrition. As much as Liss begged and pleaded, her mother had no appetite, and every mouthful Liss convinced her to take was a battle.

Liss knew her mother used to be beautiful and strong. She was an Extended Huntress, and Liss had heard from older members of the caravan that her arrows never missed a target. She used to track and hunt with more skill than any predator.

When Liss's mother and father left their respective people and went to live in the Insorsiled forest, her mother's survival skills had kept them both alive. But all that was before Liss's time. Liss had never seen her mother hunt or so much as touch a bow and arrow. She'd rarely even seen her mom out of bed.

Sometimes, Liss hated the father she had never known for being the cause of her mother's failing health. She knew it was illogical, especially since she wouldn't exist if it hadn't been for her father, but it hurt Liss's own soul to sense her mom's constant pain and be unable to ease it.

Liss often wished for an Extension more like her mother's than her own—an Extension of doing rather than feeling. Her life would be so much easier, and far more satisfying, if she could just go beat up a Lagonian with fists made of steel. Or hunt them from afar with a bow and arrows, the way her mother had used to hunt game.

Unfortunately for Liss, Extensions didn't pass neatly from parents to children. Extended parents had Extended children without exception, but it was always something of a mystery which Extension a child would have until she started to display her abilities.

Liss's Extension allowed her to see any and every emotion on a person's soul, but she couldn't alter them. It made her feel utterly helpless to only be able to stand by and see her mother's suffering when she could do nothing about it.

"Did Mari bring you your medicine?" Liss asked.

Her mom nodded once.

There was no name for the illness that had plagued her mother for Liss's entire life. It wasn't like opal contagion or any of the other diseases that were common among the non-Insorsiled.

Physically, she was weak, but Liss was sure her body could begin to repair itself if only her mother had the will for it. But there was no potion to cure her mother of the crippling sadness that came the day her husband died. The constant strain of those emotions made it impossible for her to fight the disease that ravished her body.

Liss's father died shortly after she was born and had been dead for twenty years. As much as Liss tried to banish the thoughts whenever she felt them sneaking across her soul, she felt a twinge of frustration with her mother. All the Extended had lost loved ones, and yet all the others still had their will to live.

Liss knew the sadness was beyond her mom's control, but she sometimes had an urge to grab her mom, shake her, and yell at her to snap out of it. She never succumbed to that urge, of course. All Liss could do was care for both of them, and swear to herself she'd never end up like her mom. She loved her mother and the kids in her thieving crew, but she was careful never to rest her happiness on any of them.

"Your eyes are beautiful in this light," Liss's mom said, reaching out a frail, cold hand to stroke her cheek. "They remind me so much of your father's."

Liss had no memory of her father, but since he was her mom's favorite subject, she felt like she knew him.

"Did I ever tell you about the first time I saw your father?" her mom asked.

"You may have mentioned it a time or two," Liss said.

Her mom missed the sarcasm. Her eyes took on that dreamy, glazed-over expression she got whenever she was talking about Liss's father.

"I was tracking a deer in the Insorsiled forest," her mother continued. "And I saw a pair of the bluest eyes I'd ever seen. It was your father."

"You don't say," Liss replied dryly, before feeling guilty. She shut her mouth and sat down in the chair next to her mother's bed.

"Even with the mask and body suit he was wearing, I could tell how handsome he was. I think I fell in love with him right then and there." Her mother smiled at the memory.

Liss had heard this story no fewer than a million times. Her dad, a Lagonia merchant, had been on his way to pick up some rare melon seedlings that only grew on the far west of the continent. Since he needed to travel through Extended territory to get there, he had been dressed from head to foot in anti-contagion gear.

Her mom had been out hunting game for her caravan. They'd taken one look at each other and fallen in love.

Since they couldn't even hold each other's hands without her dad's protective gloves and body suit between them, her mom had refused to rest until she found a solution. She went to an Insorsil witchdoctor and begged for something that would prevent her from passing on the contagion to her love.

The witchdoctor had taken all of her mom's gold, claiming he could cast a spell to make it safe for her dad to be with her mom. The spell worked, but the magic backfired, leaving her mom physically weak and susceptible to a myriad of diseases that didn't usually affect Extended. Still, Liss's mom hadn't cared about the permanent damage that had been done to her health as long as it kept the man she loved safe.

They married, in spite of the advice of everyone on both sides. Even after what Liss's mom had done to protect her husband from opal contagion, he was still at risk from any other Extended. So, Liss's mother left the Extended, and he abandoned his empire. They carved out a place for themselves in the Insorsiled forest.

The forest was a dangerous place for most, but Liss's mother could hunt down anything—animal or human—that threatened them. Liss's father built a small cottage, and Liss's mother hunted game and tended a vegetable garden. Liss was born a year later. Even though her mom wasn't as strong as she had once been and fell ill from time to time, they were blissfully happy.

And then, one day, while her mother was out hunting, a group of Extended passed through their part of the forest. Liss's father contracted opal contagion. Two days later, he was dead.

Overcome with grief and weak from the permanent damage the witchdoctor's magic had done to her body, Liss's mother had known she couldn't care for herself and her baby on her own. She was forced to return to her caravan so her infant didn't perish. But she never recovered from the loss of her husband, and she continued to grow weaker rather than stronger.

"I wish I remembered him," Liss said.

"I wish he was still here," her mom whispered, her eyes brimming with unshed tears.

"Oh, Mom," Liss began, reaching for the napkins she kept beside the bed for just this reason.

Her mom turned away from her as her shoulders shook with silent sobs. Liss wanted to stay and comfort her, but she could sense from her mom's emotions that she just wanted to be alone. Sighing, Liss tiptoed out of the bedroom and pulled the curtain shut behind her.

Liss loved her mother, she really did. But seeing her mother's constant heartache, and feeling the same pain and hopelessness dragging at her soul day after day, was difficult to bear. Liss had taught herself how *not* to read a person's soul just so she didn't have to feel her mom's sadness every second she was in the wagon.

Several years ago, Liss had stolen a veritable fortune from a traveling merchant, and she'd used it to get a renowned Insorsil witchdoctor to examine her mom. The witchdoctor had determined that her mom's health was permanently damaged from the spell the previous one had cast.

The witchdoctor brewed a potion for Liss's mom, which her mom had to take daily. It would have been more helpful if her mom had the will to fight and get healthy. As it was, the potion kept her alive, but not much more than that.

The potion was necessary, but it was also very expensive. And since the witchdoctor was the only one who knew how to make it, Liss had to purchase it legitimately.

"I'll bring you some bread and butter," Liss called to her mother from the kitchen. "It'll make you feel better if you eat something."

"I'm not hungry," came her mother's soft reply.

Shaking her head, Liss moved to the kitchen.

A knock came at the wagon door. She opened it to find the caravan's Flamer and Flooder standing on the steps. They were brothers and looked almost identical. Truth be told, Liss had trouble telling them apart even though she'd known them her whole life. It was awkward because the Flooder had been smitten with her a while back, and every time she saw one of them, she wasn't sure if it was the brother who was going to try and ask her out or the one who just wanted to light her lamps.

Even if she had been able to distinguish him from his brother and was attracted to him (which she couldn't, and she wasn't), she never would have given him a chance. She'd spent her life watching her mother slowly waste away from an illness Liss was sure she could conquer if it weren't for her debilitating grief. Liss didn't know if that kind of love and dependence of one soul on another was an inheritable trait, but she never intended to find out.

It was why she never dated, even though there were plenty of Extended men who had tried. She would never rest all of her heart so completely on another person that losing him would destroy her. She would never drown in a sadness of her own making.

Her soul would never belong to anyone but herself.

When she'd tried to explain to the Flooder that there was never going to be anything romantic between them, he hadn't taken it well. He'd made Liss's toilet overflow every night for a month until Burk finally told him to knock it off.

"Come on in," she told them, squeezing herself against the side of the wagon to give the men room to enter.

"Evening, Liss." The Flamer touched his fingertip to her stove, and a bright blue flame immediately came to life. He did the same for the lamps scattered around the wagon until the space was lit with a warm glow.

The Flooder didn't look at her as he filled the bathtub while his brother heated the water. He moved on to the water pitcher, drawing water up through cracks in the wagon's floor boards and shooting it across the room without spilling a drop.

"Have a pleasant evening," the Flamer said as he and his brother left the wagon.

Liss stood by the window as she ate the bread her mom had refused. Liss should cook something, but she just couldn't be bothered when she knew she'd be the only one to eat it.

Liss stared out the window—the only one in the wagon—as she watched the sun set over the rolling green hills. If the Extended weren't always on the run, they could stop the wagons and make a permanent home for themselves. They could plant crops and use timber from the surrounding forest to build houses. Liss wouldn't need to steal because they'd be able to grow what they needed. But that wasn't how things worked.

Liss put the butter back in the ice box and wiped the crumbs off the table. She busied herself with menial tasks to stave off the thoughts that occupied her soul in the dark, lonely hours of night.

She wanted to hurt every one of those soldiers who had made Spence bleed. She wanted to hurt every Lagonian for making him and Mari orphans, and for forcing her people to be constantly on the run...like animals. No matter how much she stole, or how much mayhem she caused the Lagonians who crossed her path, it was never enough. The Lagonians ruined lives, and they got away with it. The unfairness of it all settled around her soul like a dense storm cloud. Or a noose.

A year ago, when Lagonia opened their empire back up to the outside world, there had been excitement and hope among her people. Everyone thought immunity to the contagion would bring an end to the hatred, fear, and bigotry that had led to the isolation of her people for three generations.

The Extended thought trade would open back up, and they would finally be given a slice of Lagonia's overflowing pie.

Instead of the warm welcome back into society her people had hoped for, life had gotten worse. Much worse. Without any fear of the contagion, the Lagonia emperor had looked the other way when slavers attacked her people in broad daylight and sold them off to the highest bidder.

The only way to keep the slavers at bay was to pay exorbitant taxes…taxes that only a few of the caravans could afford. The emperor called them taxes for the use of lands that had once belonged to Lagonia. *Taxes for existing,* more like.

The emperor had already raised the tax twice, causing Burk's orange hair to turn gray and driving Liss and the children into Insorsil to steal more.

But the taxes didn't keep the Viper away. Once he set his sights on a target, nothing could save them.

Liss shuddered.

She was just thinking she'd go over to Spence's wagon to see how he was feeling when the door to her wagon flew open. Burk stormed in.

Their caravan leader was a tall and reedy man, and he had to bend to keep from hitting his head on the wagon's ceiling. There were beads of sweat on his brow, which made his opal skin shimmer and dance in the firelight. It was almost enough to distract her from the look on his face.

Liss didn't need to be a Soul Sorter to know her caravan leader was furious.

"Are you deaf?" Burk demanded in a near-whisper.

"Compared to you?" Liss asked.

Burk's Extension was hearing. He could be in his wagon at the front of the caravan and hear a fly buzzing in hers, twenty wagons back. He spoke in barely-audible tones, probably because it must sound to him like everyone else was always yelling. Burk never raised his voice, not even when he was angry, like he was now.

"No, really. Are you deaf? Because I know I told you *not to steal* from Lagonia soldiers, and next thing I know, Mati is asking to borrow my phoenix to send a message about maps you *stole from Lagonia soldiers!*"

Somehow, the fact that he managed to convey his fury in a whisper made his anger more, rather than less, palpable. Fury and fear radiated off Burk's soul. The orange in his eyes flashed as he glared at Liss.

Liss sighed. "They were slave routes, Burk. And the guy hit Spence! I'm not going to apologize for—"

"Do you have any idea what you've done?" Burk hissed.

"Um, saved a bunch of Extended from a life of servitude in Lagonia?" she ventured.

"You made the entire caravan a target!" Burk's voice was still barely audible, but his lips had turned white with the fury she saw written across his soul.

"Please, Burk." Liss rolled her eyes. "We're Extended. We were already a target."

"You're foolish and reckless, and you're going to get us all killed." Burk jabbed one of his long fingers in her direction. "How many times have I told you your actions have consequences? Now, we're all going to pay the price for your impulsivity."

Liss winced. It wasn't the first time Burk had chewed her out for decisions she'd made in the heat of the moment. But she was a thief…it was a necessity of the job to deal with problems as they came and not before.

Liss knew she was impulsive, but the truth of the matter was that Liss rarely encountered a situation that deserved deliberation. Things in their world were simple: scurry past the Lagonia soldiers like a rat in the gutter, or fight back in any way she could; accept that the Extended would always be nomads racing to stay a few steps ahead of the Caravan Butcher, or bring the attack to Lagonia.

Liss saw the world in black and white. She had never once found evidence to contradict the simple truths she had come to understand about people. The Insorsiled were manipulators and bullies. Lagonians were murderers and oppressors. These were the facts. Liss didn't see why every decision should involve painful deliberations when, to her, there was only ever a single acceptable option.

"I'm sorry," she said.

She wasn't.

"I won't do it again."

She would.

She understood the risks Burk was so afraid of, but she also knew the Lagonia soldiers and slavers couldn't be allowed to keep terrorizing her people. If she could make them afraid, if she could make them pay for their crimes, then it might make other Extended want to start little rebellions of their own. Eventually, enough small rebellions would make for one big one. Or, at least, that was what Liss fantasized about in her more hopeful moments.

Burk shook his head, like he was the Soul Sorter and could read the duplicity in her emotions. "You don't get it, but you will."

Liss didn't like the sound of that.

Burk continued, "The soldier you stole from sent a pixie back to the Emperor."

It wasn't the first time there'd been talk of the *Extended spy*. Liss was actually kind of flattered that news of her had made it all the way to Lagonia.

"I've heard rumors," Burk said. "They're calling you Opal Smoke. They think your Extension is turning into vapor or some such nonsense."

Now, Liss was really flattered.

"It's not the first time there have been rumors about me," Liss pointed out, before realizing it would have been better *not* to remind Burk of the other secrets she'd stolen from Lagonia soldiers.

"That's right," Burk agreed, and that's when Liss knew bad news was coming.

"But this time, the Emperor has decided to take action. He's sending the Opal Slayer to kill you."

All the air went out of Liss's lungs.

"What?"

"That's right," Burk said in a near-whisper. "You've screwed up before, but this time, your carelessness has put the rest of us at risk. Lagonia's Chief Assassin might decide to kill the rest of our caravan for the crime of knowing you."

Liss's mind was spinning. Burk was right. It was one thing for her to take risks for herself, but to endanger the rest of the caravan….

"Change course," Liss said. "The Energizers can pick up the pace. We'll just have to stay ahead of him. He'll give up eventually." The Energizers whose Extension powered their wagons wouldn't be pleased about the extra strain, but they could handle it.

"We can't outrun the Viper! You've heard the stories."

She certainly had. He was the most feared soldier in all the lands. Every enemy of Lagonia had cause to fear him, and none more than the Extended. It didn't matter if caravans set up traps or held watches or had fighting Extended who could take on ten regular Lagonia soldiers. No one ever saw the Opal Slayer coming, and he never failed. The only evidence he left behind was a pile of Extended bodies with their throats slit.

Liss felt sick.

She hadn't been thinking about that when she'd stolen those slaver routes. She'd been thinking about the Extended children who would be bound and dragged along those routes on their way to be sold in Lagonia.

That was her problem, though. Her mantra was *Deal with today's problems now, and tomorrow's problems later.* It had always worked just fine for her. But now, because of choices she'd made, the Viper was after her. She had put every person she cared about at risk.

Her thoughts were scattered, panicked. What should she do? She couldn't stay here, but where else could she go?

She started to pace, which was supremely unsatisfying in the tiny room.

What had she done?

"I need to think," Liss muttered. If she let the panic overwhelm her, she'd be worse than useless.

Make a decision. Find an answer. Do something.

But what could she do?

"If it wasn't for this stupid immunity, he'd never be able to come after me."

"Well, they have the immunity, and he is coming after you," Burk retorted. "The Lagonians have nothing to fear from us. We're defenseless."

Liss stopped pacing and stared at Burk. The solution was so simple, she couldn't believe she hadn't thought of it before.

"We need to find out what's giving the Lagonians their immunity and destroy it."

Burk let out a low, bitter laugh. "That's a brilliant idea, Liss. And how do you propose doing that?"

Liss's heart was hammering in her chest.

"I'll do it."

Burk waved a dismissive hand. "No one gets into Lagonia unless it's in the slavers' cuffs. You know that."

Liss's mind was already speeding through possibilities the way it always did when she was faced with a particularly challenging theft. This was, in a sense, no different from any other thieving she'd ever done. It was just more dangerous.

"I look Lagonian," Liss said, her mind still racing through the options. "No one would ever guess I'm Extended."

"And you think they'll just let you walk right across the Golden Bridge as one of their own?" Burk asked.

"They might, if I play it right."

Burk scoffed.

With this new possibility taking shape in her mind, some of Liss's panic withdrew.

The more she thought about it, the more she thought she might actually be able to pull off this deception.

Liss knew plenty about Lagonia. The only subject her mom ever expended more than a few words to talk about was her father, and since he was from Lagonia, Liss's mom had recounted hundreds of stories he had told her about his empire. Liss knew enough that she could fit in. She could get work in one of the shops in town....

But she'd never gain access to the palace that way, and from what she'd heard about the new Emperor, he wouldn't let such an important secret outside the palace walls.

"I'll have to get work as a servant in the palace," she decided.

Burk was shaking his head. "I give you one hour in Lagonia—if you get in at all—before your head is on a spike."

Liss made a dismissive noise. She'd been using and abandoning disguises every day for the last year. True, she'd never had to hold onto a disguise for more than a few minutes. She'd just need a really, really convincing one. It had to be something simple enough that she could keep it up for weeks without giving herself away. It had to be believable.

"I'll figure out the details," Liss told Burk. "You just get the Energizers to speed up the caravan for now. I'll find out what's causing the Lagonians' immunity, and then we can destroy it. Then, they'll have no choice but to leave us alone."

Liss heard the desperation in her own voice. She knew how crazy this plan sounded. Still, it was the only one she had.

I can do this, she told herself. *I have to.*

"If you're discovered, you'll be killed," Burk said, apprehension radiating from his soul.

"The Viper's coming after me either way," Liss shot back. "At least this way, he won't find me cowering in the corner of the wagon. At least this way, if I fail, I'll go down fighting."

"Liss, you don't understand—"

"There's no other option."

Liss didn't want to think too hard about this foolhardy plan. It was her only choice, her only chance of bringing the fight to Lagonia. She wouldn't stay here for the Opal Slayer to find her. She wouldn't be another victim of Lagonia's cruelty.

She'd be its downfall.

Burk was still giving her a skeptical look, so she said, "I'm doing this. If you try to stop me, you know I'll just find another way."

Burk heaved a sigh.

"This is going to work," she said, her confident words belying the uncertainty and terror hovering just beneath the surface. "Just—" she swallowed, her gaze shifting to the back of the wagon. "Will you make sure my mom is taken care of?"

Burk held her gaze for a long moment. Liss felt the answer on his soul before he nodded.

"If I truly can't stop you from this insane mission, then I'll see to it that Nya gets her brew every day. And anything else she requires."

"It's expensive," Liss said, even though Burk already knew how much it cost. He knew everything that went on in the caravan.

"I'll take care of it," Burk replied. "It'll be the least I can do."

"She won't eat unless you bring her food," Liss continued, worrying at the frayed sleeve of her shirt. "And I usually read to her at night. I don't know if she cares or not, but I think the company is good for her."

Burk nodded again. "I'll personally see to it that Nya wants for nothing while you're gone."

Liss felt a strange tightness in her throat. "Thank you."

Burk adjusted the collar of his coat. It was of Insorsil make, and the fabric was much finer than the homespun concoctions most of the Extended wore. Liss had been inside her caravan leader's wagon on several occasions, and each time, she had been amazed at the comparative opulence of Burk's living space.

There were two types of Extended: those who accepted their lot in life and carried on with their heads down, and those who didn't. Liss and Burk both fell into the latter category. For Liss, stealing was her way of getting back at their oppressors. For Burk, it was to accumulate possessions of value. Liss thought he did it in part so he could feel like he lived in a stable home rather than a wagon.

Burk sighed. "We'll need to work out logistics, but you should leave as soon as can be arranged."

"Tomorrow," Liss said with a certainty she didn't feel.

Burk reached into his pocket. He pulled out two onyx stones and held them in the palm of his hand. He gave one to Liss, keeping the other for himself.

Burk brought the stone in his hand to his mouth and whispered to it.

The stone in Liss's hand grew warm. Its black surface began to glow and emit its own light. The words "Be careful," appeared in silver.

"I bought these off a witch years ago," Burk explained. "Whatever you say to yours will appear on mine. We'll use them to communicate while you're in Lagonia."

Liss could only nod in silence as she tried to comprehend the magnitude of what she was doing. Her mind raced ahead to the coming days and weeks.

She would no longer be a thief whose exploits had sparked rumors about an Extended spy. She *would* be the spy.

* * *

Burk returned to his wagon at the front of the caravan, shutting the door softly. The way people were always slamming doors and generally making a ruckus for no reason grated on his nerves. It gave him a near-constant headache.

The Flamer had lit all twelve of the ornate lamps spread throughout his wagon, bathing the small rooms in a warm light.

He sat on the velvet chair, which occupied the greater part of his living room area. He looked at the trinkets stacked on the small bookshelf and the collectibles he had scattered around. For years, accumulating these odds and ends had been his way of clinging to some sense of control and civility in a world where he was afforded so little of either.

It wasn't enough. This damn wagon wasn't a home. It was a cage.

But what to do? His conversation with Liss had brought on a host of new anxieties, but it had also reminded him of something he had left behind in his youth: a belief in the possibility of something beyond this grim existence. Liss, for all her foolish impulsivity, had shown admirable courage in the face of near-certain death. She had refused to sit around and wait for the Opal Slayer to come to her. She wanted to act.

Even as a caravan leader, Burk had existed in a state of helplessness and powerlessness for so long it hadn't occurred to him there was any alternative. Liss, with her rash and likely-suicidal bravery, had reminded him that he would go on living in this purgatory for the rest of his miserable life unless he did something to change his fate.

Still considering, Burk reached for the leather-bound book resting on the small end table. He opened the book and carefully tore out one of the thick pages. Leaning over the small table, he paused for only a moment. Then, he began to write.

CHAPTER 5

Rhett and his men left the palace at dawn. It was the time of day when the more unpleasant of Lagonian business was conducted, so it wouldn't be witnessed by the citizens who slept until late morning.

A slaver passed them along the road, not even bothering to disguise who he was and what he was doing as he yanked a hollow-eyed Extended man behind him. The slave's chains clanked with every step.

Rhett forced his tense muscles to relax. He made his jaw and fists unclench. He stilled, letting his practiced mask settle into place. *Steel doesn't know love or despair. It needs no heart or warmth. I am steel.*

"Nothing to be done," Stone said in his gravelly voice.

Even though Rhett had mastered his reaction almost instantly, Stone could tell what he was thinking.

"But do they have to be so brazen about it?" Wilsean asked, his own face tight with disgust. "Slavery is illegal. And we're supposed to be the pinnacle of civilized society."

Ciago snorted. "We're phenomenal at the illusion of civility. Maybe we could bottle it up and sell it for Insorsil prices."

"Watch your tongue," Stone hissed. "This empire has ears, and if you get dragged down to the torture cage, I'm not going to be the one to break you out."

Ciago rolled his eyes but didn't say anything more.

Wilsean and Ciago were sons of two of the most powerful families in Lagonia, which made them virtually beyond reproach. Most Lagonians in their position would be spoiled and lazy. Wilsean and Ciago were neither.

Rhett had grown up with the two of them, and neither age nor politics had changed the bond between them.

Even though they could have taken a cushy job on the emperor's council, Wilsean and Ciago had slogged through the mud of foreign lands and fought shoulder-to-shoulder with him. They were Rhett's most trusted soldiers, his best friends, and his brothers in arms. They'd all protected each other's backs more times than Rhett could remember. They were the only ones besides Stone who truly knew Rhett.

Four flightless silver dragons were already saddled and waiting for them when they reached the stable.

The dragons were twice the size of the horses kept in poorer empires. The layer of glistening, silver scales gave them a natural armor and made them look fearsome, even though they were actually quite tame. The silver dragons didn't have wings, but they weren't as temperamental and as likely to burn a hole through their riders as the winged gold dragons.

There was only one gold dragon this side of the sea—Jaikon had ordered the rest slaughtered to ensure his was the only one that could take to the sky. These tame and plodding silver dragons were just another reminder of all that rested in the Emperor's control…another move in Jaikon's game.

Rhett didn't mind this particular inconvenience. The longer it took them to get to Insorsil, the longer it would be before he had to return to the palace. His time on the road with Stone, Wilsean, and Ciago was the closest Rhett ever came to finding some semblance of peace.

The feeling would only last until they're reached their destination, and he needed to do what he'd been doing at the Emperor's command for the last year.

They'd track the caravan that held the Extended spy. He'd slip into the wagon in the dead of night, slit the Extended man's throat, and disappear again before anyone saw so much as his shadow.

Rhett gave Silverbird a pat on the nose as the dragon nuzzled him. He took a handful of gold nuggets from his pocket and offered them to the dragon, who lapped them up with her forked tongue. The scales on the dragon's throat rippled as the gold nuggets passed down to her belly. The dragon nuzzled his arm again in thanks, but Rhett pushed her away. Like with everything else, Rhett needed to be cautious.

When he was a kid, he'd had a special love for a dragon he'd nursed after its mother had died. He'd even coaxed the dragon to breathe fire, which was a real feat for a silver dragon. As soon as Jaikon had discovered the bond that existed between them, the emperor's heir had ordered the dragon slaughtered. Jaikon had left the dragon's severed head on Rhett's pillow.

They walked their dragons down the empty cobbled street to the Golden Bridge. As they got closer, raised voices interrupted the more peaceful morning sounds of birds and fairy wings. Rhett exchanged a look with his men, his hand moving automatically to the dagger at his hip.

There was a cluster of his own soldiers, dressed in the black and gold armor of the Lagonia army, blocking the end of the bridge. As he got closer, Rhett could see there was a carriage that was attempting to cross into Lagonia. Phantom steeds were at their head, their Insorsiled images flickering in and out of view. Rhett saw the magenta and ivory cloaks that belonged to the Insorsil queen's guard.

The voices only got louder as he led Silverbird to the end of the bridge. Rhett handed his reins to Wilsean and strode forward.

"Queen Gatria," Rhett said. Neither his tone nor his face betrayed a hint of emotion as he bowed to the witch queen. "My apologies for any inconvenience you've encountered at our border." Rhett turned his cold gaze on the soldiers whose weapons were drawn. "I'm sure there's been some misunderstanding."

The queen turned away from the soldiers blocking her entrance and pierced Rhett with her silver eyes. The Insorsil queen was slipperier than any Lagonian, and ten times more dangerous. Although she had never given any indication she could do more than levitate small objects for the previous emperor's amusement, Rhett could sense something dark lying dormant inside the queen. He didn't want whatever that power was to awaken and be turned on his soldiers.

"Rhetteman Loniger," she said in her sickly-sweet voice.

The Insorsil queen had an ageless look about her, although she was rumored to be more than two-hundred years old. Three emperors had lived and died in Lagonia while Queen Gatria had continued her reign in Insorsil. Her silver hair hung down to her waist and whipped back in a breeze no one else could feel.

"Perhaps you can talk some sense into your witless soldiers." She smiled with her lips, but her silver eyes were as cold and emotionless as Rhett's.

Rhett bristled on the inside. His face still showed nothing.

"My soldiers are simply carrying out orders." He kept his words formal, respectful.

Just because Gatria had never done so before, Rhett didn't trust that she wouldn't send the bridge they were all standing on crashing into the river below with one swipe of her hand.

"Sir, I can explain."

Dannica stepped forward. She was one of Rhett's best soldiers, and she was the one standing in front of the Insorsil queen now.

Gatria made a sound of disgust. "I'll never understand how Lagonia can pride itself on being progressive when it does something as backwards as draft women into their army."

Lagonia was the only empire Rhett knew of that drafted both men and women soldiers. In his experience, it was the reason their enemies constantly underestimated them…at least, until their attackers lay defeated on the battlefield. Opposing armies expected the female soldiers to be weak and for the male soldiers to be too busy trying to defend them to wage their own battles. Neither was the case.

"The Emperor commanded that the Insorsiled leave their weapons with us," Dannica explained. "The queen is refusing."

Stupid, Jaikon, Rhett thought. Everyone knew how prideful the Insorsil queen was. Lagonia couldn't afford to make the Insorsiled their enemies.

"The previous emperor never would have insulted me with such a request," Queen Gatria said in a haughty voice. "I demand you let my retinue pass, *with* our weapons."

Queen Gatria waved a hand, her nails at least an inch long and filed into sharp points, and shouted to the phantom steeds. The illusions let out blood-curdling screams and snapped their ghostly teeth at the soldiers blocking the queen's path. The soldiers flinched even as the teeth turned to smoke and wisped away on the wind. Rhett didn't blink.

"It is our job to see Emperor Jaikon's orders carried out," Rhett told the queen. "I'll have to ask you to hand over your weapons."

"These soldiers are lying," the queen purred, her voice satiny. She reached out a hand and brushed it against Rhett's cheek. Rhett didn't react even though her touch was like ice.

"My soldiers do not lie. Either give up your weapons or leave."

Stone, Wilsean, and Ciago had come to stand on either side of Rhett. None of them spoke, but their hands resting on the hilts of their weapons was threat enough. Ciago alone could have made even the most hardened soldiers turn tail and run. He was as big as an ogre and looked as mean as one to anyone who didn't know him.

"You Lagonians think your jewels place you beyond the reach of retribution," Gatria hissed, her voice no longer pretending at pleasantness. "But mark my words, you'll come to know true suffering before my reign is ended."

Rhett didn't speak. After a pause laden with tension, the queen threw up her hands. Her guards began unbuckling their weapons belts and handing them over to Rhett's soldiers.

With another hate-filled look in their direction, the queen got back in her carriage. The phantom steeds leapt into motion, drawing the cart over the bridge. Soldiers and the queen's own guards had to press themselves against the sides of the bridge to keep from being trampled.

Rhett stayed motionless as the carriage hurtled past him with no more than a hair's breadth of space. The queen glared at Rhett out the window.

Rhett took Silverbird's reins back from Wilsean. The soldiers bowed their head to him as he passed. He waved a hand, dismissing their thanks. Rhett didn't look back as he led Silverbird into the woods.

It was only when they were surrounded by dense trees that Rhett could really breathe.

The only time he didn't have to be on his guard was when he was on the road with his mentor and two best friends. In an empire where excess was the norm, Rhett often thought trust and honesty were the rarest commodities in all of Lagonia. But Rhett trusted these men. Stone had been more of a father to him than his true one had been, and he'd grown up training and getting into constant trouble with Wilsean and Ciago.

They fell into their easy routine as the dragons plodded along. Ciago and Wilsean bantered, and Stone grumbled. Even as his friends slouched in their saddles and tossed a giant ruby back and forth between them, Rhett knew a single snap of a branch would transform them into the lethal soldiers they were.

Wilsean was the best bowman in Lagonia, possibly in all of the lands. He also kept no fewer than a dozen throwing knives in the various pockets of his dragonhide jacket. Ciago's weapon was his sword. When that failed, which it almost never did, his fists were almost as lethal. Stone carried his case of scalpels. While none of them appeared deadly, they always proved to be greater motivation than any normal weapon.

Rhett had only his dagger at his hip. He forsook the dragonhide jacket and pants the rest of the men wore for plain black that made him inconspicuous, silent, and nearly invisible in the dark. He wore no insignia to identify himself. Anyone who passed him on the road would undoubtedly have heard tales of Lagonia's Chief Assassin—some of them true, most of them wildly false—but there were few outside of Lagonia who could match his face to those stories. No one would suspect a man in simple black garb to be the Chief Assassin of the most powerful army on the continent. And that was how Rhett wanted to keep it.

"I'm telling you," Ciago said, continuing an argument he and Wilsean had been having for most of the trip. "The only reason you beat me at cards last week was because I was distracted."

"I beat you because I'm the better card player," Wilsean replied, grinning at the way Ciago sputtered and huffed. "And because you can't add seven and two when you're drunk."

"I wasn't drunk," Ciago argued. "I was exhausted from taking your watch so you could spend the night with Samara."

Ciago gloated as Wilsean's cheeks darkened in embarrassment.

Ciago, pressing his advantage, turned to Rhett. "Shouldn't you have something to say about soldiers who pass their watch off onto their poor friends…using and abusing their goodwill?"

Rhett raised an eyebrow. "You mean, like the thousand times I've covered your watch so you could chase after one courtier or another?"

"I've tried to be efficient by chasing two at a time. You're welcome."

Rhett shook his head.

"Don't be jealous," Ciago told him. "You know I'd be happy to set you up with any woman in the palace."

"I appreciate it," Rhett replied, "but I'm not interested in your leftovers."

"There might be a courtier or two he hasn't been with," Wilsean mused.

"Doubtful," Ciago replied jovially.

"Rhett has the good sense to stay out of court gossip," Stone growled, "which is more than I can say for you two idiots."

"Stop acting your age, Stone," Ciago replied, refusing to wither under the older man's scowl.

Stone spurred his dragon ahead.

It took them two days by flightless dragon to reach the northwest part of Insorsil. Wilsean gave a handful of gold nuggets to an Insorsiled boy to tend their dragons while they continued on foot through the crowded streets.

Wilsean and Ciago's easy banter ended as their destination came into sight. Their expressions transformed from relaxed and humorous to deadly as they pulled out their weapons. Rhett pushed open the door to Toil and Trouble and stepped inside the bar.

It was late, but the bar was still packed. Rhett had to muscle his way past some very drunk warlocks and Lagonia merchants to reach the front of the bar.

If Rhett had come into the bar alone, his size might have turned some heads, but next to Ciago, he was easy to ignore. Those who weren't staring up at Ciago, mouths agape, turned their attention to Wilsean. His dark skin made him almost invisible against the deep brown wood as he stood against the wall, but the bow strapped to his back and throwing knives gleaming in the light of the Insorsiled lamps made everyone in the bar give him space.

Rhett stayed close to Stone, who wore the embellished black and gold armor that identified him as a high-ranking member of the Lagonia army. Anyone who did notice Rhett would think him nothing more than hired muscle to watch Stone's back.

Stone waved his hand at a patron sitting at the bar. The warlock jumped to his feet and gave up his stool for Stone. Rhett stood just behind, his arms crossed over his chest, as he scanned the bar.

A hush had fallen over the patrons. Rhett's gaze roamed over them, memorizing faces and searching for orange hair and opal skin.

He hadn't really expected Opal Smoke to be sitting around just waiting for him, and sure enough, there wasn't a single Extended in the place.

As Stone questioned the barmaid, Rhett watched her face for any sign of deception. It was obvious she didn't know anything useful.

Stone placed some gold nuggets on the bar, having reached the same conclusion as Rhett. "Let's go," he muttered.

"But I haven't finished my drink," Ciago complained, taking a giant glug from his tankard.

Rhett tilted his head at the door. Ciago drained the tankard, swiped his hand across his mouth, and winked at a wide-eyed witch across the bar. The onlookers parted as Rhett and his men made their way back through the crowd to the door.

"Well, that was a waste of time," Wilsean said as soon as they were back out on the crowded street.

"Not a complete waste of time." Ciago was eyeing two witches who looked to be about their age, who were giggling and pointing at them.

"If the Insorsiled weren't so busy with their illusions, they might pay attention to what's right in front of their faces," Stone growled, rubbing a hand over his bald head.

"Where else might our Opal Smoke have wisped off to?" Wilsean asked, hooking his knives back into his jacket.

"You two track down any Lagonia soldiers staying in this part of Insorsil," Rhett told Ciago and Wilsean. "Find out if they can tell us anything about this Extended spy."

To Stone, he said, "Keep a watch around here. Question any Extended you see. I'll meet you all back at camp at daybreak."

"And where are you going?" Ciago demanded.

"To find the caravan," he replied.

CHAPTER 6

Liss passed Toil and Trouble as she made her way down the crowded alley. She was hungry, tired, and annoyed. It had been two days since she'd told Burk she would sneak into Lagonia and discover the secret to their immunity…two days she'd been waiting to cross paths with a Lagonian servant whose clothes she could purchase. But not only did no such servant appear, she wasn't even sure she'd be able to convince said servant to sell her their clothes. The disguise should have been the easiest part of her deception, and yet, it was proving to be all but impossible.

What have I gotten myself into? she asked herself, not for the first time that day.

A group of Lagonia soldiers, stumbling out of a nearby bar with "Uninfected Only" written in block lettering across the door, made their way onto the street in front of her.

Her lack of success made Liss's hatred for the Lagonians flare hotter than usual. She might not have her disguise, but today didn't have to be a total loss. Liss let out a little yelp and let herself fall into a soldier with a diamond pinky ring.

The man grabbed her out of instinct, his grip loosening when he turned and saw her.

"Alri'?" the man slurred as he set Liss back on her feet.

"Fine." Liss glared at a warlock haggling over potions under the awning beside her, like he had been to blame for bumping her. "Thank you."

She widened her blue eyes, the ones Lagonians went crazy over, and batted her eyelashes.

The soldier leaned into her, his eyes moving from her face to her chest. "You're very welcome," the soldier told her chest.

And they called her people swine.

This soldier's reaction was one Liss was familiar with, even if the disgust she felt never lessened. All of Liss's shirts pulled too tight across her chest in spite of her best efforts to keep everything hidden. Her body was naturally made like the Insorsiled illusions that danced in the windows of bars in the less savory parts of town. She couldn't deny her…assets…had come to her aid on more than one occasion when she was stealing from a simple-minded man. And the Lagonians were all simple-minded.

"Prettiest witch in Insorsil," the soldier informed her. And then he burped.

Liss pulled her hand out of her pocket where the man's thick wallet now rested comfortably and looked up at him in surprise. This man thought she was Insorsiled.

Liss was wearing a plain brown shirt and cotton pants, while the usual style for Insorsiled witches included long, colorful dresses. Both witches and warlocks favored brightly-colored, flowing cloaks when they were traveling about town. She had neither the dress nor the cloak, and yet this soldier had assumed she was Insorsiled. It must be her hair, which had grown down to her waist simply because she was too lazy to cut it.

She had never considered trying to enter Lagonia as anyone other than a Lagonian, but maybe….

Liss took the soldier's hand in both of hers. "Thank you again for your help."

With a smile, she extricated herself from the soldier's drunken paws and sauntered away, swaying her hips just a little.

She dropped the diamond ring into her pocket, feeling it nestle into the folds of the wallet.

Liss changed course from the direction she'd been heading. A new plan was already starting to form in her mind.

There was an old Insorsil law that Empties, people born to Insorsiled parents but who never developed their own magical abilities, were kicked out of their homes at the age of eighteen. Some of the wealthier or more reluctant families were able to hold onto their Empties until nineteen or twenty with the hope that their children were late bloomers.

Once they were banished from Insorsil, the empties either tried their luck with the wandering bandits who lived in the forest, paid a merchant to sail them across the sea, or tried to beg their way into Lagonia as servants.

It wasn't a perfect plan. Even without orange hair and opal skin, Lagonia didn't welcome strangers onto their land. But it was the only plan she had.

Liss used some of the gold nuggets in the soldier's wallet to buy an outfit that would make her look more Insorsiled. She had scowled her way through the clothes racks, discarding neon colors, flashy sequins, and a dozen other outfits that would draw far more attention than she wanted. She settled on the most muted ensemble she could find: a flowing, white satin top that came to rest just above her bellybutton, and satin periwinkle pants. They were the right size, at least, even if the bright colors and bare midriff weren't her style. The outfit came with a velvet cloak that was so brilliantly white she would just about glow in the dark.

Liss paid for the clothes, silently cursing the Insorsiled people's love of bright colors. She certainly wouldn't be able to travel unseen, but she supposed if she was going to impersonate an Insorsiled Empty, she wasn't trying to be invisible.

Besides, Insorsiled and Lagonians had a mutually agreeable relationship. The Lagonians gave the Insorsiled jewels and other riches, and the Insorsiled gave Lagonians magic. Neither feared attack from the other.

Liss's plan was simple: find a Lagonia along the road, explain her plight, and try to beg her way into the empire as a servant.

By the time she left the store, afternoon was turning into evening. If she didn't get back before dark, the wagons would already be in motion, and even she might not be able to find them.

Liss stole an Insorsiled bike from outside one of the bars. She walked it through less and less busy streets. When she reached the edge of town, she got on the bike and twisted its handle. The whole machine pulsed with magic. It kicked into gear and sped away from town.

Liss rode through fields, her long hair flying behind her, as she headed toward her caravan. She had to ditch the bike in the field, since there was no way to fit it on the wagon.

Too bad. It was a nice bike.

When she got back to her wagon, Mari and Jema were sitting on the small couch where Liss slept. The kids often hung out in her wagon to get away from the noise and hubbub of their own. It was refreshing for Liss to feel their innocent, happy souls in the wagon instead of just her mom's.

Liss gave them a smile and quick hug before going to check on her mom. As soon as she pushed back the curtain and stepped into the room, her mom raised her head.

"I don't want you to go," her mom whispered.

Liss lifted her mom's hand to her lips and kissed it. "This is important, Mom. I might be able to help all of our people if I can figure out how the Lagonians are getting their immunity and destroy it."

Her mom blinked away tears and made a choked laughing sound. "You get that streak of fearlessness from your father, you know. He was just as ready to rush into danger."

Liss squeezed her mom's hand. "I'm not rushing into danger. I'm doing something that will make our lives better."

"You're only a little girl," her mom argued with as much force as she could muster, which wasn't much.

"I'm twenty years old," Liss replied.

One part of Liss felt guilty for putting more strain on her mother's weak health. The other part was restless to be on her way.

Liss had enjoyed thieving because it was her way of hurting the ones who oppressed her people. Now, she had the chance to do more. Instead of sitting up at night and being angry at their lot in life, she could change it.

Once she figured out what was giving the Lagonians their immunity to opal contagion and destroyed it, their oppressors would have no choice but to leave them alone. The Extended wouldn't be defenseless anymore.

Liss couldn't give up that chance, no matter how much pain it caused her mother.

"Come back to me," her mother whispered. "You're all I have left in this world."

"I will," she promised.

Liss left the room only after her mom had fallen into a restless sleep. She ducked under the curtain and stepped into the main room. One look at the girls' faces, and she knew they had heard everything. Even though she and Burk had agreed it would be safer if no one else except for her mom knew where Liss was really going, these kids were as much her family as her mom. She couldn't lie to them.

Liss gathered the girls in a three-way hug.

"You'll take care of Spence for me while I'm gone?" she asked.

Jema giggled. "He's the oldest one."

"Yeah, but he's also a boy," Mari said, with great authority.

As if on cue, there was a knock on the door, and Spence squeezed into the already-crowded wagon. There was no physical sign of what had happened to him the previous day. The Insorsiled medicine had made him as good as new…at least on the outside. His soul told a different story.

The same anger and resentment Liss felt herself were buried deep in his soul.

"Heard you were going to one of the other caravans to help gather their taxes." Spence looked at the clothes she was wearing. "But now, I think maybe that's not what you're doing."

Liss nodded, and then she filled him in on what she had already told the others.

The kids took the news of where she was actually going much better than her mom had.

"We won't tell anyone, Lissy," Jema said. "We promise."

The other two nodded.

"We'll take good care of Nya while you're gone," Spence added, his orange-rimmed eyes focusing on the curtain in the back of the wagon.

"Yeah, we'll read to her and keep her company," Mari said.

"And I can share my candy," Jema offered.

Liss felt her eyes prick with tears. "Thank you."

CHAPTER 7

It was his second night of tracking Opal Smoke's caravan. He was close. He'd seen the fresh tracks in the soil from the passage of many wagons, but he hadn't been able to catch up with them.

Rhett held up an Insorsiled stone, which threw a soft yellow light over the path in front of him. He had kept up a brisk jog for hours, which should have been enough to at least bring the wagons in sight. But it was clear this caravan was moving faster than they usually did.

Did they know he was coming?

It was possible. It always impressed Rhett the way the caravans could communicate among themselves when they were always on the move.

As far as Rhett could tell, the Extended wanted nothing more than to be left alone. It was a sentiment Rhett could empathize with. But he was as powerless as they were. His own life depended on him continuing to prove his value to the empire, and as long as the Extended posed a threat to Lagonians, it would continue to fall on Rhett to chip away at their hope by slaughtering the most dangerous Extended.

This caravan's Energizers must be killing themselves to keep such a grueling pace. He'd never catch them this way, and if he used Silverbird or an Insorsiled bike, any members of the caravan with Extended hearing would know he was coming a mile away. He would need to wait until the wagons came to rest at daybreak. Rhett turned around and started the long jog back to camp.

Rhett was thinking about Opal Smoke, who had eluded slavers and soldiers alike for more than a year, when he reached the edge of the road. He hadn't slept in almost two days, and he stumbled on the uneven cobblestones. He heard the laughter and quiet voices, but he didn't give either much thought as he dimmed his stone and put it back in his pocket.

It was only when Rhett felt the hair on his arms prickle that he paid attention. His hand was on the hilt of his dagger before his brain had even registered the danger. Stone had made sure Rhett's instincts were as sharp as the blade he carried. Rhett had learned long ago never to question those instincts.

There was a group of men surrounding a lump on the road. They stood just out of the light of the Insorsiled street lamp that threw pale light over the road. They would be invisible, but the blue light from the waxing moon illuminated them. They were kicking something on the ground as they laughed. Rhett heard the word *swine*.

"Move along," one of the men said, catching sight of Rhett standing on the road. "Unless you'd like to join her."

Rhett's stomach turned over as he realized the lump on the ground was a person. And she wasn't moving.

Slavers. The iron cuffs looped through their belts and the evil exuding from their every pore gave them away. There were six of them.

"Let her go," Rhett said, moving toward the men before he could think better of it.

"She's already dead," one of the slavers replied, a maniacal grin twisting his features. "So, unless you want to join her, I'd move along if I was you."

"He's seen our faces," one of them argued. "We better kill him to be safe."

Rhett smiled. "You're welcome to try."

The slavers laughed. "That little knife isn't going to help you now."

Rhett let the men surround him.

Steel doesn't know love or despair. It can't be bent or broken. It needs no heart or warmth. I am steel. His breathing steadied, even as his every muscle tightened in anticipation.

Their attack was swift.

Blood sprayed and men screamed. Rhett moved from one to the next with brutal efficiency. He used their own bodies as living shields as he slashed his blade across one throat after another.

Five down, one to go.

Rhett heard the twang of a bow. Usually, the sound meant Wilsean. But Wilsean wasn't here.

By the time he realized there was a seventh man hidden behind a tree, an arrow was already lodged in Rhett's thigh.

Rhett ignored the burn from the arrow's point as it dug into his leg. He wrenched the sixth man's curved blade from his hands and slashed it across its owner's throat. Without taking a breath, Rhett threw the blade. There was a hoarse cry as the archer fell, his bow clattering to the cobblestones.

Rhett looked down at the shaft embedded in his thigh. As he bent to inspect the wound further, he felt his leg go numb. He lifted his hands into the lamplight, only to find they were trembling.

Rhett swore. He yanked the arrow out, gasping against the pain. It was too late. He felt the poison tearing through his veins like wildfire.

Get back to camp, he commanded himself. If the poison was what he thought it was, he didn't have long before his muscles seized up, and he'd be paralyzed.

His vision was already getting hazy. He was in the wrong direction of camp and had gone too far in search of the caravan. His men would never look for him here.

Move, he thought with desperation as his legs turned to wet clay.

Rhett forced his rebelling legs into a jog. Sweat poured down his face. Every time his right foot hit the ground, an agonizing jolt traveled all the way up his leg. He held onto the arrow, using its solid weight to ground him as he pushed himself on.

He had too far to go. If he cut across the open plains, he'd get to camp faster, but it would put him out of sight of any who might be traveling on the road and stop to help him.

If Rhett had more energy, he would have laughed at that foolish notion. Even in his weakened state, he wasn't so delusional as to think anyone on the road would help him even if they did see him. That wasn't how things worked here.

Rhett stumbled off the road and tracked a path southwest across the plain. He fell to his knees on the uneven turf. He forced himself back up.

Ninety. Ninety-one. Ninety-two.

He counted his steps to give his mind something to do besides think about how every movement felt like alternating shocks of fire and ice to his veins. When he fell again, he couldn't find the strength to stand back up. He crawled on hands and knees, the arrow still clutched in his fist.

Ninety-eight. Ninety-nine.

Rhett's entire body began to convulse. His body knew it was dying, but his mind still rebelled.

Get up. He tried to say the words out loud, but his lips wouldn't move. Rhett was aware he was sprawled on his side in the middle of an empty field, but he couldn't force his body to move even another inch.

His mind was still clear, which was a particular cruelty of the poison now flooding his body. He knew now with certainty the poison was liueun root. He remembered from his training that it was of Insorsil make, and it caused total paralysis to the body while leaving the victim's thoughts intact. There was an antidote, but it was obscenely expensive and difficult to come by, and he certainly wouldn't find it growing in an open field.

The poison flooding his body wouldn't kill him. He would probably die of thirst. *An ignominious end for the great Lagonia Assassin,* he thought with all the dark humor he could muster.

Part of him regretted he couldn't at least lie on his back and see the way the clouds turned different shades of blue as they passed over the moon. The thought was stupid and sentimental, and he was neither.

Out of the corner of his eye, he could see the Insorsiled stone had come loose from his pocket. The glowing yellow stone sat beside him like a tiny ray of sunlight in a sea of darkness. He closed his eyes, the only part of his body he could still move, and tried not to think about the fire in his veins.

CHAPTER 8

Liss tripped and stumbled her way across the dark plain. She wished she still had her stolen bike, but Insorsil law forbade Empties from taking any magic with them into exile, and having it would raise too many questions. Liss didn't even dare use the Insorsiled onyx stone Burk had given her for light on the off chance someone saw her, which wasn't likely since she was in the middle of nowhere.

There was a chill breeze tonight. Fall was turning, and soon, the grass would be covered by a layer of ice that would make the going more treacherous for the wagons. The Flamers would be working as hard as the Energizers, keeping stoves and lamps constantly burning so the whole caravan didn't freeze to death.

Weather was just another advantage Lagonians had over her people. Because of the natural insulation from the sea and mountains—and, Liss suspected, some priceless gift from the Insorsil queen—Lagonia's temperatures were balmy in every season. Her mom had told her that most people in the empire didn't even own a jacket, and if they did, it was for aesthetic rather than practical reasons.

As she made her way in the direction of the road, she hammered out the details of her new persona.

Her name was the first detail that would need to be changed. While the Extended all had very short names and didn't bother with middle or last names, the Insorsiled were an old people who got bogged down with tradition and history. They also had more time for ceremony, and unlike the Extended who were all just poor, there was a class system in Insorsil. Liss knew a name was enough to indicate a family's relative position in society.

She decided to go by Tamilissa Elspeth Wren, a solid, common-enough kind of name for an Insorsiled. Nice and pretentious.

She was constructing her family tree in her head when she saw a faint yellow glow in the distance. She cursed the white cloak that would let anyone out here see her a mile away.

Liss reached for the pathetic rusted knife she carried. The Insorsiled didn't usually carry weapons, since their magic was their weapon, but she'd thought a rusted knife would be a reasonable exception for an Empty. She was preparing to change course and give the light a wide berth, when she felt a soul.

Liss sucked in a breath. The soul was unlike any she'd felt before. Her feet brought her closer without her brain consciously realizing what she was doing.

She'd encountered ugly souls, unhappy souls, and kind souls. But she'd never felt one that was filled with so many complex emotions. There was plenty of darkness and unhappiness, but there was also so much more. The soul pulsed with a depth of feeling she hadn't encountered before. Usually, she could sense two or three emotions in a single soul at once. This soul had closer to a dozen, and they were all warring with each other. So much conflict should drive a person crazy, but she could sense this soul was intact.

There was regret and pain, but there was also acceptance and a composure that struck her as noble. A flash of pain across the soul made her flinch.

She should keep going and never look back. She knew that, just as she knew she wouldn't. The soul called to her.

As Liss approached, she saw the body on the ground. If she wasn't a Soul Sorter, she would have thought the man was dead, he was so still. He wasn't asleep or unconscious, either. Those people's emotions had a clouded-over kind of look to them, like Liss was seeing them through a dense fog. And this man's soul was clear as daylight.

She approached slowly, all too aware of the way the moonlight illuminated her white cloak. The man's eyes were open, but even when she got close, he didn't move.

"Are you alright?" Liss asked when she was no more than a dozen steps away.

The man didn't respond.

As she took a few more hesitant steps forward, it became clear he most definitely was not alright. She could see the sweat glistening on his face in the light of the blue moon. And was that blood smeared across his hands?

Liss approached as she would an injured animal…slowly, with one hand gripping her knife.

"Do you need help?" Liss tried again.

There was something very wrong with this man. His soul was awake and alert, but his body was too still. Even if he was badly injured, he should make some attempt to get into a less vulnerable position as she got within arm's reach of him. And still, he didn't move.

Liss crouched down in front of the man. The unmistakable smell of blood filled the air around him.

"Where are you hurt?" Liss demanded, growing irritated by the man's silence. *Did he want her help, or not?*

Aside from a slight fluttering of the man's eyelids, he didn't move.

Liss sighed. She picked up the Insorsiled stone the man had left on the ground and held it up.

Despite the light he carried, the man wasn't himself a warlock. His plain black clothes and close-shaved dark hair gave that away easily enough. He clearly wasn't Extended. If he was Lagonian, he'd be wearing more finery and have a thick wallet or purse of gold. She could tell from a quick, practiced thief's glance that he had neither. He was big and muscular, but not brutish like the humans who lived in the Giant Realm across the sea.

She put a hand to his forehead. It was cold and clammy, and aside from movement in the man's dark eyes, he didn't react to her touch. Liss held the Insorsiled stone over him, examining him for the source of the blood that scented the air. Her gaze landed first on the arrow clutched in the man's hand.

"Were you shot?"

No answer.

Carefully, she extricated the arrow from the man's grip. He didn't resist her, exactly. It was like his hand had frozen around the arrow. *Or turned to stone.*

With that thought, she knew what was wrong with him.

"Poison," she said out loud, racking her brain for the one that caused full-body paralysis while leaving the mind intact. Unbidden, a memory she had tried desperately to forget came to her.

It was right after the Lagonians had announced their immunity. A slaver had found an Extended woman from Liss's caravan as she was bathing in a pond. The slaver had tried to take her, but the Extended woman had been a Flamer, and she'd burned the slaver. The slaver shot her as she ran away. She made it back to the caravan before the poison had completely overtaken her body.

Liss had been the one to get the antidote from Insorsil. She'd brought it back, given it to Burk, and assumed everything would be alright.

But the antidote had caused the woman unbearable pain. She shook and made these horrible whimpering sounds as sweat and tears poured down her face. Liss had never felt so much agony on a soul before. It had been horrible to watch.

As soon as the paralysis lifted enough for her to move, the woman had taken Burk's knife and plunged it into her own heart.

Liss remembered the way blood had seeped between Burk's fingers as he tried to staunch the wound. It hadn't worked, and the woman had died, still screaming from the pain of the antidote.

"Liueun root," Liss said, her voice coming out hoarse.

The man's pupils widened.

"I'll take that as a yes."

Liss searched the man for the place where the arrow had pierced him. She found it in a sticky mass of fabric on his thigh. She swore.

She and the man stared at each other.

If she was going to save him, it would mean turning around and going back to Insorsil. It would take hours to find the antidote, steal it, and bring it back here. And then she'd have to administer it. If he could live through the pain of the antidote, and that was a big *if* as Liss knew only too well, the man wouldn't be able to move for at least another few days. Unless she planned to stay here and nurse him, which she had neither the interest nor the time to do, he'd probably be killed by wild animals or crushed under the wheels of a wagon.

She felt the man's understanding and acceptance in his soul. He knew what she was thinking, and he expected her to leave. She could read it plain as day in his emotions. And still, there was no resentment or blame…just acceptance. She didn't feel even a hint of fear, even though it was clear this man expected to die.

Maybe it was all her years of caring for her mother. Maybe it was the inexplicable pull she felt toward this man's soul that was fuller of complexity and contradiction than any soul she'd ever encountered. Either way, she knew her decision before she spoke the words.

Besides, it wasn't like he was a Lagonia soldier and deserved to rot alone on this plain.

"Okay," she said. "I need to go into town and get the antidote. I'll be back in a few hours."

The man's soul reacted immediately. He didn't believe her.

She shrugged. She didn't care if he believed her or not.

"It might take me a little while to find what I need. Just—" she was going to say *stay here*, but given the circumstances, that seemed cruel and unnecessary. "—try to relax," she said finally. "I'll be back as soon as I can."

✳ ✳ ✳

Liss wouldn't dare risk stealing from the witchdoctor who brewed her mother's potion, so she had gone deeper into Insorsil to find a different pharmacy to get the antidote.

It had taken her another two hours to find one that was closed for the night, break in, and sift through the unfamiliar potions and herbs strewn all over the place until she found what she needed.

It was almost dawn by the time Liss was riding back on yet another stolen bike.

Liss could only imagine what Burk would say if he knew she was wasting time helping a stranger when she should be well on her way to Lagonia. *Impulsive. Never thinking about consequences. Selfish.*

And she wouldn't be able to argue with him. Her whole life, she'd made choices in the moment and stuck with them. Her mantra of *Deal with today's problems now, and tomorrow's problems later* had kept her alive, and had kept Spence, Mari, and Jema out of the slavers' grasp, more times than she cared to remember.

But she also understood Burk's constant frustration with her. Liss didn't think about how the choices she made could make life more difficult for the rest of the caravan. She had good intentions, but her inclination to act first and think later was the reason why the Opal Slayer had set his sights on her caravan. She was the reason why her mother was now alone.

And now, once again, she was putting her people at greater risk because of decisions she was making. Worse, she didn't even know why she was helping this man. He wasn't Extended. She didn't owe him anything.

As she let the bike fall into the grass and hauled her bag of stolen goods to the man lying on the ground, she cursed herself again for not being partway to Lagonia right now.

The surprise and gratitude that radiated from the man's soul hit her like a tidal wave.

I told you I'd come back, she thought with some satisfaction.

Curiously, she still didn't sense any fear on the man's soul. Given that he was dying—would have died if she hadn't come along—she would have expected that emotion to reign above all others. But she hadn't felt it even once.

Even though her Extension let her see emotions rather than motivations, the two were interconnected enough that she could often tell what kind of person she was dealing with from peering into their soul. She saw bravery and honor in this one. There was also a great, yawning sadness that Liss could sense he'd carried for so long he probably didn't even notice it anymore.

Liss used the man's own knife to cut away his right pant leg. The dagger was unmarked and gave no indication about what land he belonged to, but the blade was sharp and well-tended. She rummaged in her bag and pulled out quick-heal, numbing crystals, and Insorsiled balms. She squinted at the label on the antidote.

"Full disclosure," Liss said as she measured out the cloudy white liquid, "I don't know what I'm doing. It's possible you're going to turn into a centaur or grow a carrot nose."

The man's face remained expressionless, but she felt the pulse of humor on his soul. She was more pleased by his reaction than she should have been.

"This is also going to hurt. A lot."

Again, the man's soul reacted. He knew it, but he wasn't afraid.

I'm going to need to lift you up so you don't choke on this stuff," she said as she moved around behind him. She braced his shoulders and tried to pull him up.

Was he made of rocks?

The man's dead weight fought against her. She tried to wrestle him into a sitting position before giving up. She braced his head against her knee so at least the antidote would have a fighting chance of going down his throat. They must have looked like a ridiculous pair, and she imagined the moon staring down and laughing at them.

She reached for the antidote and dribbled it between the man's lips. She didn't know if any of it actually managed to get into his mouth instead of just dripping down his chin, but then she felt his body shudder. Pain flashed across his soul.

"It's okay," Liss said, gently lowering him back to the ground. "You'll be okay."

Remembering the last time she'd encountered the liueun root antidote, she tossed both his dagger and her knife far out of reach. Then, she wrapped both of her hands around one of his and squeezed.

Liss could feel tremors wracking every muscle in his body. He closed his eyes, and Liss could see the way his jaw clenched. The antidote was working, but that meant the pain was getting worse.

The antidote worked fast—she remembered that. His whole body must be flooded with it now, and yet, he wasn't shrieking and begging for death the way the Flamer woman had. He bore the pain stoically. Not even his soul reflected the agony she remembered from the Flamer. Liss couldn't imagine what this man had been through that the antidote wasn't making him writhe and scream.

She sucked in a breath when the man's fingers curled around hers. His hand was bigger than hers, like the rest of him, but their hands fit together in a way that unnerved her.

"You're going to be fine," she said, using the tone she used with her mom. She mopped the sweat pouring from his face with her velvet sleeve.

Rather than pain and fear, she felt gratitude in his soul.

"Thank you."

Liss started. The words were raspy and barely more than a whisper, but she heard them.

"You're welcome," she replied.

The sun was just starting to peek up over the horizon, throwing a dim glow over the man.

Whatever else she might have said died on her tongue as she looked at his face. With all of the blood and sweat and paralysis, she hadn't noticed that this man was good looking. *Really* good looking. In the dark, he had seemed older. She could see now that he looked about her own age.

His skin was very pale, but that was probably because he'd been close to death. His shaved hair was so dark it was almost black, and his eyes weren't much lighter. There was the shadow of a beard along his well-defined jaw. The rest of him was perfectly-proportioned, making him look less big than he was. His shirt was plastered to his skin, showing off muscles that a statue would be proud to exhibit.

Not only did he have the most interesting soul she'd ever encountered, the man was gorgeous.

"Are you thirsty?" she managed, unaccountably flustered.

"Yes."

The man still couldn't move himself, and she felt more awkward than she should have as she lifted his head and helped him drink.

She turned her attention to the nasty wound on his leg. He must have been in excruciating pain from the wound and the antidote still working its way through his body, but she didn't sense the agony on his soul she expected. Instead, there was a great deal of gratitude and tenderness. There was also shame and regret, which she didn't understand.

Liss tried not to think about the intimate places she was touching as she cleaned the man's wound. She hadn't felt awkward about it before when he'd been dying and she hadn't known what he really looked like, but now….

Liss smeared the quick-heal over the deep gash. She worked efficiently, aware of the man's gaze fixed on her. As she bandaged his leg, her feeling of awkwardness shifted to something else.

She was overcome with an overwhelming sense of foreboding. She didn't know why, but some deep part of her knew with absolute certainty she'd come to regret helping this man.

CHAPTER 9

Jaikon Horowicken II, Emperor of the most powerful empire in all the lands, sat on his gilded throne and stared down at his subjects.

"Queen Gatria is in your private meeting chambers, as requested," Elouicia, his most trusted advisor, reported.

"Good." Jaikon accepted the goblet of wine a servant offered him.

"Forgive me, Your Majesty," said one of his councilmen, "but you shouldn't have ordered the queen to leave her weapons at the bridge. You risk upending the delicate peace that your father worked so hard to ensure."

"Perhaps upending that peace is *precisely* what I intend." Jaikon never raised his voice, but its sound still reached every corner of the throne room.

Jaikon let his ice blue eyes roam around the circle of his councilmen. His gaze discouraged any of his councilmen's' obvious disapproval from turning into audible murmurings.

He ran his hand over the tiny gold circlet pinned to his shirt, right above his heart. With the magic it held, which he'd obtained in Insorsil without Queen Gatria being the wiser, it wouldn't be long before he controlled Insorsil. He'd double the amount of land belonging to Lagonia and expand their assets infinitely. They would be untouchable. *He* would be untouchable.

"It's a new age, and the isolationist policies of my father no longer apply," Jaikon said.

To emphasize his point, he unfastened the pin from his shirt and held it out on the palm of his hand. The pin looked entirely common, not even worthy of the palace servants.

"I know it doesn't look like much," Jaikon said at his councilmembers' dubious looks, "but this is going to change everything."

Councilman Geriak huffed out a short laugh. "And how's that, Majesty?"

Jaikon's hand itched to strike the insufferable man. Instead, he focused on the heat radiating from the small circle of metal that warmed his hand.

"This pin is Insorsiled. You think you've seen magic, but the baubles and trinkets our merchants deliver don't even scratch the surface. The Insorsiled have been holding out on us."

As his heart beat faster, the pin in Jaikon's hand started to vibrate. He let his advisors see the blue light radiating off the pin and seeping into the creases of his palm.

"This pin was made by the most powerful warlock in Insorsil and is the only one in existence."

Seeing that he had his advisors' attention, Jaikon continued.

"I'm in the process of acquiring more of this magic. Once I have it, our army will be invincible."

"Why would the queen allow something so valuable out of Insorsil?" someone asked.

Jaikon's smile broadened. "She wouldn't…if she knew."

His advisors were quiet as they processed this new bit of information.

"What's it do?" Geriak asked, still looking more skeptical than awed as he stared at the gold pin.

Jaikon took his time as he attached the tiny pin to his shirt, right above his heart.

"For now, all you need to know is that it exists," Jaikon said, using a lofty tone that made him sound even more regal.

"We're your closest advisors," Geriak sulked. "It would be imprudent to keep us in the dark, especially when Lagonia already has too many secrets."

"The only secrets I keep are ones that are necessary to protect the empire." Jaikon froze Geriak with his stare. "And I know I'm not the only one in this room who keeps secrets."

Jaikon had the pleasure of seeing Geriak's face pale.

Yes, I know about your secret meetings. I even know about your desperate and ill-advised plot to depose me.

"We appreciate you looking into…creative ways to add strength to our army," Councilman Troulmin said more cautiously, "but I still think that sending more troops across the sea and further fracturing our army is a mistake. Rhetteman said—"

"Rhetteman is not the emperor," Jaikon snapped.

It infuriated Jaikon the way his subjects were drawn to the assassin like moths to a flame. Jaikon had spent his childhood hearing the accolades of Rhetteman Loniger, the bastard who had sullied Jaikon's majestic bloodline. And then their father had bestowed the coveted position of Chief Assassin on Rhetteman—rather than his heir, as custom dictated.

Jaikon wasn't one to wallow in self-pity. He also wasn't one to tolerate such an offense.

The truth was that patricide hadn't been part of Jaikon's plans until his father gave Rhett the role that belonged to Jaikon by birthright. He'd gone to his father to make the emperor see reason…to convince him that his son, his *real* son, deserved the position that would make him second-in-command.

One could say negotiations had broken down.

Still, it nagged at him the way the soldiers talked about the Chief Assassin with reverence, like Rhetteman was their emperor instead of Jaikon.

The doors to the throne room opened and two guards strode in. A pixie fluttered between them, her pink gossamer wings fluttering. Elouicia stepped forward and bent his head while the pixie whispered into his ear. A few moments later, Elouicia straightened up.

"Majesty, that Extended man is requesting a private audience with you again."

The advisors gave a hearty chuckle over such a preposterous request.

Elouicia grinned. "Apparently, he believes a meeting would be mutually beneficial."

Jaikon joined in with his advisors' laughter before turning to the pixie.

"Tell the presumptuous fool that if he ever comes within sight of the Golden Bridge, the hundred archers will shoot him down without any questions asked."

Jaikon felt a small shock of pleasure at the approving nods from the half-circle of men crowded around his throne.

When the pixie and guards had left, Jaikon turned back to his advisors.

"All of you are dismissed," Jaikon announced, motioning for Elouicia to stay behind.

When they were alone, Jaikon stood up and stretched.

"Doesn't Counselor Geriak have an ailing mother?" Jaikon asked, even though he already knew the answer.

While Geriak might be too important to simply execute, Jaikon had other methods of persuasion.

"Indeed, he does," Elouicia replied. "I hear he's quite fond of the old bag."

"I should like to have a conversation with her tomorrow."

A wicked grin spread across Elouicia's face, displaying the teeth he had filed into jagged points.

Jaikon rolled his shoulders. "Any word from my Chief Assassin?"

"No, Your Majesty."

Jaikon drummed his fingers on the ornate hilt of his sword.

"How difficult could it be to eliminate a single Extended?"

Elouicia cracked his knuckles in sympathy. "I long for the day when I can toss Rhetteman Loniger's body over the cliff."

Rhetteman was too visible a figure in Lagonian society for him to simply disappear without explanation. As much as Jaikon was loath to admit it, Rhetteman had become a living symbol of the empire's might. If Jaikon executed him, or even removed him without cause, the Emperor would have a rebellion on his hands.

When the Chief Assassin finally stood on the executioner's platform, he would be disgraced and dishonored, and he would die with the whole empire scorning his existence. Jaikon wouldn't risk turning the man into a martyr.

So, until he had cause to remove Rhetteman…permanently…Jaikon would settle for controlling the aloof and infuriatingly principled bastard.

"Have you found any leverage to make my Chief Assassin more amenable to my wishes?"

Elouicia shook his head, looking almost as disappointed by the news as Jaikon felt.

It was infuriating the way Rhetteman sauntered around the palace, following some orders and refusing others. It was absurd the way the bastard thought he could live by a code when he was an assassin.

Jaikon had put his most trusted men on following Rhetteman, searching his quarters, and even setting traps to catch the Chief Assassin in a compromising state. Rhetteman never spoke ill of his Emperor or engaged in treasonous activities. He'd never been to the meetings where there was talk of overthrowing the Emperor. Jaikon had even sent the most beautiful women in his harem to seduce the assassin. None of it worked.

Elouicia continued, "His only love is for the soldiers in Your Majesty's army, especially the three men who accompany him everywhere."

Wilsean, Ciago, and Stone. Wilsean and Ciago were the sons of two of the wealthiest families in all of Lagonia, which made them invulnerable. And Stone was the most gifted interrogator Lagonia had ever seen.

"I can't very well murder my own soldiers to get Rhetteman in line," Jaikon snapped.

"Rhetteman has no preferences and little regard for his own life," Elouicia said. "I believe the man has no weaknesses."

"Everyone has a weakness." Jaikon motioned for the other man to leave the room. "And I'm going to find his."

CHAPTER 10

The last time Rhett had been awake, the sun was rising. Now, it was setting. He tried moving his limbs and found that, for the first time since he collapsed, he could raise his arms a few inches off the ground. The amount of effort it took to wiggle his fingers felt like he was trying to raise the entire world.

"Oh good, you're awake. I thought you might die after all, and then all the time I've spent here would really be a waste."

"Still alive," Rhett said, his voice sounding thin and exhausted even to his own ears. "Thanks to you."

Rhett had never owed anyone a thing in his life, and now he owed everything to this Insorsiled woman. The feeling made him almost as uncomfortable as the antidote she'd forced down his throat.

The woman came to crouch by his side. He got his first look at her through eyes that weren't glazed over from the combination of poison and antidote. She was beautiful.

"You're looking less pale today, so that's good." She smiled at him, and Rhett saw she had a dimple in her left cheek.

He realized it wasn't just her beauty that was so striking; Lagonia was full of beautiful women. It was that he could tell her beauty was real. Any Lagonian would have paid for Insorsil illusion to either make the dimple disappear, or create a matching one on their other cheek. The fact that she hadn't made him think the rest of her was just as illusion-free. Her realness made her even more attractive.

"I'm Rhetteman Loniger," he said, mostly to distract himself from her hands on his upper thigh as she unwound the bandage. "Most people just call me Rhett."

She smiled again, and Rhett had an insane urge to touch her dimple. If he had more strength, he might have. The antidote must be addling his brain.

"Tamilissa Elspeth Wren," she replied.

Her long hair and ridiculous clothes had given her away before her equally pretentious name. That would also explain how she'd been able to get all of the medicines she was giving him, which were Insorsiled.

"I owe you a blood debt, Tamilissa Elspeth Wren," Rhett told her.

Saying the words out loud sparked his anger at himself. Owing other people was a weakness. Rhett didn't have weaknesses.

"Call me Liss." She looked up from his leg. "And if I'm ever dying, I'll make sure to call you to rescue me."

"Fair enough."

Humiliation coursed through Rhett as Liss had to help him raise is head enough to swallow a few mouthfuls of water.

"I need to get back to my camp," Rhett said.

He'd been gone for two days, and his men would be breaking down every door in Insorsil to find him.

"I have a bike," Liss said. "As soon as you're strong enough to ride, I can drive you wherever you need to go."

With an enormous effort, Rhett managed to raise himself into a sitting position. But as soon as he was upright, his vision swam out of focus.

He felt her arms come around him.

"Has anyone ever told you you're heavier than you look?" she grunted as she lowered his dead weight back to the ground.

"I don't let people carry me on a regular basis," he replied. Even speaking those words left him exhausted and out of breath.

"Lucky me," she muttered.

Guilt took hold of Rhett. It certainly wasn't her fault he had been stupid enough to get shot. The last person he should be griping at was the one who had saved him.

"My guess is you'll be able to stand in another day or two," Liss said.

"I'm sure spending two days with me has caused you great loss," he said apologetically.

Liss shrugged. "I generally worry about today's problems now and tomorrow's problems later. You being pretty much dead was a today problem."

In spite of her flippant words, Rhett could see real anxiety in her blue eyes. It had cost her to spend so much time caring for him…a stranger to whom she owed nothing.

"I don't have much to offer," Rhett told her honestly, "and I don't want to imply your generosity has a price, but if Lagonian jewels or coin would help—"

"Lagonian? You're Lagonian?"

Rhett tried to nod, but it took too much effort. "Yes."

Rhett wasn't an interrogator, but Stone had taught him to read a person's every expression as well as if he was one. Rhett watched as emotions passed across Liss's face in quick succession. He caught surprise, distrust, and something else. She looked from him to something in the distance, like she was considering fleeing.

"You don't need to fear me," he told her. "Not that I'm especially threatening right now."

The way her gaze cut to his convinced him he'd been right. She hadn't been afraid before, but she was now. And was that disgust he saw on her face? He looked again, but the expression was gone.

When she looked back at him, Liss said, "I'm going to Lagonia to find work."

"Why?" It was Rhett's turn to be surprised.

Insorsiled didn't leave Insorsil.

Liss looked down at Rhett, a new determination on her face. "I'm an Empty."

That explained it. She had no choice. Rhett felt pity for her, even though he was the one with his life in her hands. It was no small thing to be exiled from the only land you had ever known.

"I'm sorry," Rhett said, and then quickly added, "not that you're an Empty, just that you were exiled. That…can't have been easy."

Liss shrugged and looked away. An unfamiliar emotion went through Rhett's chest.

"I can bring you to Lagonia," he offered. "Any job you want. I'll arrange it."

"You can do that?" she asked, her voice full of a distrust that hadn't been there before.

"Yes."

He knew he was being a terrible conversationalist, but every word was an effort. He was so damn weak.

"People say it's the greatest honor to get a position working in the palace," Liss said. "Do you think that might be possible?"

"Yeah, that's what people say." Rhett heard the twinge of bitterness in his voice. He cleared his throat. "But if that's what you want, then it'll be the least I can do."

Liss turned her attention back to his wound. His leg felt like fire. The antidote had erased the numbness, leaving a fierce pain in its wake. Thanks to Stone, Rhett's tolerance for pain was probably without equal, but still, it was an effort not to grimace as she cleaned the wound.

Liss cared for him in the way of someone accustomed to tending to invalids. She gave him exactly what he needed and no more. He never saw an ounce of pity on her face, which he was grateful for. He wondered if her parents were witchdoctors. It would explain why she didn't balk at the wound. Any Lagonian woman outside of the army would have fainted just from the sight of his leg.

Rhett felt a flare of disgust for the family who had cast her out. Sometimes Rhett forgot that his empire wasn't the only one with cruel laws and an even crueler dictator.

✳ ✳ ✳

By the time night fell, Rhett could sit up and hold a bottle of water on his own. They didn't say much. Liss seemed to sense how much it exhausted him to manage even a few sentences at a time. Still, her presence was a strange comfort.

He stole glances at her as she moved around their makeshift camp. He had never given the women in Lagonia more than a passing glance, but he found it difficult to look away from Liss. There wasn't a single person in his empire who would have done what she did…stop to help a dying stranger. She fascinated him.

Rhett remembered the way Liss had first appeared to him, like a glittering white beacon in a sea of darkness. If he'd been a religious man, he'd have called her an angel or a goddess. Instead, he saw something he had even less faith in: kindness.

Rhett meant what he'd told her before. He knew he would never be able to repay the debt he owed her, but that didn't mean he wouldn't try. Rhett had survived as long as he had by taking care of himself. But he hadn't been able to take care of himself this time, and all Liss had asked for in return for saving his life was work in the palace.

While Liss caught a few hours of sleep, he tried to force the uselessness from his body. He was grateful she wasn't awake to see the way he struggled and strained just to get to his feet. When he finally managed it, he limped around in a small circle. He almost passed out from the effort, but he was done with being a burden. He clenched his jaw and forced his vision to clear.

He found the vial of antidote in Liss's bag of medicines. He knew the antidote cost a fortune, and he felt yet another wave of guilt. Her clothes suggested her family was well off, but not wealthy.

He tossed the little medicine dropper Liss had been using to administer the antidote back in the bag. He was done with the carefully measured doses Liss had been giving him every two hours. He lifted the bottle and drank.

CHAPTER 11

Liss had never needed much sleep. Between thieving, caring for her mother, and the too-narrow couch she slept on in the wagon, Liss was lucky if she managed to get more than a few hours in a night. Being such a light sleeper was the only way she could let herself relax this close to a Lagonian…that, and the fact that he was barely strong enough to move his fingers.

His soul had been full of honesty and gratitude when he'd said he owed her a blood debt, but he was still Lagonian.

Still, she couldn't bring herself to hate him the way she should. When she'd told him she was an Empty, his soul's only reaction had been pity. Every Lagonian she'd encountered in the past would have thought her weak.

If she wasn't a Soul Sorter, she would have thought Rhett only treated her differently because she'd saved his life, but she knew that wasn't the case. *He* was different.

Liss stretched and worked out the kinks in her back. When she opened her eyes, it was to the sight of Rhett sitting by the fire. He was bent over a hare, which he was cleaning with the knife Liss had confirmed was his only possession.

She couldn't figure him out.

He was Lagonian, but he didn't have a single jewel or coin on him. His clothes were utterly plain and without a stitch of finery.

He must be a servant, she decided. It was the only explanation for how he could help her get work in the palace. Except he didn't look like a servant. Maybe he was some kind of bodyguard for a wealthy councilman.

Liss didn't know if she was lucky or unlucky that he was Lagonian. She now had her way into the empire. But traveling all the way to Lagonia with this man would be dangerous. He might ask her questions about herself. Unlike every other Lagonian she'd ever met, Rhett didn't strike her as stupid. She would need to be very careful what she told him.

Still, she had managed to gain access to the most exclusive palace in all the lands. For the first time since she'd stopped to save Rhett's life, she knew she'd made the right choice…not just for Rhett, but for her people. She might have lost valuable time these last few days, but Rhett would save her weeks of trying to get inside the palace. She had hoped to take a job in town and bide her time until an opportunity to sneak into the palace presented itself. Now, she'd just walk right in.

Take that, Burk, she thought with some satisfaction. For once, it seemed like being impulsive had done more good than harm.

Rhett's gaze flicked over to her as she sat up.

"Good morning." Rhett's soul warmed, even though his face betrayed no hint of emotion.

"I see my work here is done," Liss said, going to join him by the fire. "You look well."

"I am, thanks to you."

Liss saw the empty vial of antidote sitting on the log beside him. Her eyes widened. "Did you drink all of that at once?"

He gave a short nod. There was a keen, penetrating look in his eyes that hadn't been there the day before. He was so serious, grim, even.

"Wasn't that…awful?"

"A bit," he replied, his lips quirking in the hint of a smile.

Was he insane? Liss peered at Rhett.

His skin was less pale now. The slight color in his cheeks made him even more handsome than she'd first thought. There was something distant about his good looks, though, like he was untouchable. Maybe it was how imposing he was now that he was sitting up. When he'd been dying, he hadn't seemed as huge as he did now. He was slim, but his shoulders were broad, and every ounce of him was muscle.

Liss looked away before she'd have to come to terms with the fact that she was practically drooling over a Lagonian. Even if he was just a servant, he was still one of them. She wouldn't forget he was her enemy.

"Hungry?" Rhett passed her a roasted hare.

"Starving." As she took the stick, she realized it was the first time in as long as she could remember that someone else had cooked for her.

The meat was a little burnt, but it didn't matter. Liss thought it was the most delicious meal she'd ever eaten.

Their conversation as they ate was light and trivial. The emotions she felt radiating off Rhett's soul were not.

There was relief and gratitude. There was also confusion, shame, and self-loathing. Liss was dizzy just from peering into his soul; she couldn't imagine what it must be like to live with it.

Liss realized she'd been wrong before. It wasn't that there were so many different emotions on his soul that was unusual, although there were more than most…. It was the strength of those emotions. Liss wondered how someone could feel so much and not collapse under the weight of their own feelings. And yet, as she stole a glance at Rhett, she didn't see even a hint on his face of the turmoil that lay beneath. His expression was blank, almost eerily so. Not even his eyes betrayed emotion. If she didn't know better, she'd think Rhett never felt anything at all.

"My men are camped about half an hour from here by bike," Rhett said, breaking their silence. "I'd like to get back as soon as possible."

"That's fine," Liss said carefully.

It wasn't the first time he'd said *his men*, and she didn't know what that meant. *Other servants? More bodyguards?*

Liss would rather chew glass than stay in a camp full of Lagonian men. And what were they all doing so far from the empire without their employer? Liss wanted to ask, but Rhett wasn't much of a talker to begin with, and she got the sense he guarded his secrets as carefully as she kept hers.

"I still have business in the area," Rhett said. "It shouldn't take more than a week for me to wrap up. As soon as it's done, we'll head back to Lagonia."

It was the most he'd spoken in one breath since she'd saved him. Before, Liss had thought his voice was rough from the effects of the poison, but it seemed like this was just his normal voice. His gruff, clipped way of speaking would have made her think him callous if she couldn't see beyond his inflectionless tone.

"What kind of business?" Liss asked as casually as she could.

Rhett stared at her in a way that unnerved her. There was no emotion in his gaze, but it was a penetrating look. It was like he was staring into her soul instead of the other way around.

"I have to find someone," he said after a while.

Thank you; that just clears everything up, Liss thought with a quiet huff.

Rhett continued, "Once we're back in the empire, I'll make sure you're well situated in the palace. Anything you want or need, I'll see it done."

Liss waited for the flare of dishonesty across Rhett's soul. It didn't come. Liss felt the conviction on his soul and knew he meant every word.

Liss had seen the honor inside his soul before, and it puzzled her. She had encountered plenty of Lagonians over the last year, and their souls were all soft with deception and dishonesty. *Maybe Rhett wasn't a Lagonia by birth*, she reasoned. That would explain his incongruous emotions.

She decided it was time she found out more about this strange Lagonian.

"Are you a servant in the palace?" she asked.

A faint bitterness stole across his soul, even though his face betrayed nothing. "You could say that, I guess."

Liss raised an eyebrow at him. "And what was a servant doing all alone in a field so far from home?"

He faced her then, and Liss almost couldn't hold his gaze. It was grim and fathomless.

"There's an Extended spy who has been exposing Lagonian secrets. I'm the one the Emperor sent to hunt him."

Liss felt all the blood drain from her face.

"You…you're not…." She clenched her fists at her sides to keep them from visibly shaking.

With a sudden realization that left her breathless, she understood why Rhett's name had sounded familiar.

"Lagonia's Chief Assassin," he said. There was neither pride nor embarrassment in his soul. He just stated it like it was a fact. Like it made no difference.

Impossible, her mind screamed. Liss had seen Rhett's soul, and it wasn't made of the stuff of an assassin. Maybe he was just impersonating Lagonia's assassin, the same way she was impersonating an Insorsiled Empty. Liss didn't sense any deception in Rhett's soul now, but that could just mean he was good at lying. Only a Truthseer would know for sure....

"Not everything you've heard about me is true," Rhett said, reading the shock and horror she wasn't managing to hide.

Opal Slayer. Caravan Butcher. The Viper.

And she'd saved his life. *She's saved his life.*

This was the man who had murdered countless Extended. He was the reason the Energizers in her caravan were working themselves to death. If only she'd known, she would have left his body to rot on the field. Hell, she might have used his own dagger to slit his throat, the way he'd done to so many of her people. Instead, she'd nursed him back to life.

Liss fought to keep her dinner from coming back up.

He...Lagonia's Chief Assassin...was watching her. She needed to get her emotions under control before she exposed herself.

"Whatever you've heard about me, I promise you have nothing to fear," Rhett said.

Pull it together, Liss warned herself, even as her emotions continued to torpedo out of control. Her soul railed against the idea that Rhett was the man who had killed so many of her people...the man who'd been sent to kill her.

Options, she told herself. *What are my options?*

It was too late to kill him now. Even in his weakened state, she was never going to be able to get a hold of his dagger and use it to kill him. There was nothing else in this empty field that could serve as a weapon, especially not against Lagonia's Chief Assassin.

She could get on the bike and flee. She could return to the caravan. But even as the possibility occurred to her, she discarded it.

She had been unlucky—or stupid—enough to save the life of the man sent to hunt her. She couldn't go back to the caravan and explain to Burk what she had done. She couldn't risk leading the Viper back there. She'd just have to find a way to turn this disaster to her advantage.

Liss had no idea how she'd manage it, but she didn't have much of a choice.

You have a job to do, she reminded herself. The best revenge she could take on this man was to discover the cause of his people's immunity and destroy it. She would be the reason why the Lagonians' choices…their freedom…was taken away. Just like his people had done to hers.

This revelation about Rhett changed nothing. She was here to play a part. She would use him to access the palace and for any other information she could wring from him.

It all came down to stealing, which she'd been doing for so long it was second nature. The only difference now was that the stakes were higher.

"Alright, then," Liss said as she let out a shaky breath. She put down her food, her stomach too knotted for her to manage another bite. "I'm ready whenever you are."

CHAPTER 12

Rhett felt like a drunk newborn as he crossed the short distance between their campfire and Liss's bike. Even though his leg still burned with every step and his body rebelled against being useful, Rhett forced himself to walk to the bike unassisted. He was ashamed at the sweat rolling off his skin from the effort of just walking. It was pathetic.

There was more than a little awkwardness as they both looked at the one-person seat and realized how close they would need to sit to fit on the bike together. There wasn't even a handle on the back of the bike for him to grab onto, and Rhett was having enough trouble keeping his balance when he was stationary. With a gruff apology, he clumsily got himself onto the bike behind Liss and wrapped one arm around her waist. He felt her tense against him. He uttered another terse apology, but she revved the engine and it drowned out his words.

A change had come over Liss since he'd told her who he was. It was like a door slamming shut. He hadn't seen her smile since, even though it had seemed to come so easily before. She stood ramrod straight and her eyes darted to him like he was some kind of monster who would attack if she dropped her guard for even a moment.

He wanted to tell her that whatever stories she'd heard about him were just rumors...stupid people spreading stupid gossip.... But he wasn't sure what she had heard about him. It was possible some of what she'd heard was the truth.

He felt ashamed in a way he never had before.

Rhett couldn't get his mind to quiet. Their proximity was making him feel things he never let himself feel. He had no choice but to admit to himself that he was attracted to Liss. He'd have to be dead not to be.

Alarm bells sounded in his head. He heard Stone's mantra.

Steel doesn't know love or despair. It needs no heart or warmth. I am steel.

When Rhett leaned over to tell her where to turn, Liss flinched. It was like being thrown into a freezing river.

"Sorry," he muttered, loosening his grip on her waist and leaning as far away as he could without falling off.

The bike lurched off the loamy ground and onto the cobbled road. Rhett clenched his jaw at the pain that raced through his leg with every bump.

Rhett avoided getting any closer to her for the duration of the ride. He pointed to where she should veer off the road and to the different twisted paths to follow in the Insorsiled forest.

As soon as the tents came into sight, Liss stopped the bike. She jumped off before the wheels stopped rotating.

"Liss, wait," he said.

Either she didn't hear him, or she chose not to.

He heard the bowstring being pulled taut before he saw Wilsean. Rhett scanned the trees until he found the gleam of the arrow's point. It was aimed at Liss.

"Wilsean!" Rhett called, forcing himself to move faster than he had since he was shot. "It's me."

"Rhett?!"

His friend lowered his bow and ran forward, his face awash with relief.

"Damnit, Rhett! Where the hell have you been?" Wilsean grabbed his shoulders and stared at his face. "I'm glad to see you look terrible."

"You're…glad?" Rhett raised an eyebrow.

"If we all had to be worried sick about you, you may as well have the decency to look awful." Wilsean's eyes slid to Liss. He gave Rhett a quizzical look. "Although if you spent the last three days with her, I'd expect you to look less peaked."

Rhett just shook his head. "Nice to know you were concerned."

Wilsean turned his full attention on Liss. "Who are you?"

"Tamilissa Elspeth Wren," she said. "You can call me Liss."

Rhett had always thought it was pretentious the way the Insorsiled layered names on names. *Liss* suited her much better.

"Rhett isn't used to the company of women," Wilsean told Liss, his tone all mock-apology. "You may need to go slower with him at first."

Rhett's friends had few opportunities to rag on him, so he wasn't surprised at the direction Wilsean had steered the conversation. But Rhett hadn't expected his own embarrassment and irritation.

He could only imagine how strange all of this must be for Liss, and he felt an unfamiliar urge to protect her from Wilsean's teasing. He had made her uncomfortable enough just by being who he was. They didn't need to make things worse for her by implying she and Rhett were together.

While any Lagonian woman would have blushed and pretended to take offense at Wilsean's implication, Liss just gave him an easy grin.

"I'll have to keep that in mind for the future," she replied.

"Where are Stone and Ciago?" Rhett asked, before Wilsean could cause any more trouble.

"Tearing apart Insorsil looking for you, obviously," Wilsean replied. "Seriously, though. Where have you been?"

It was then that Rhett noticed his friend's bloodshot eyes. Wilsean looked almost as drawn and haggard as Rhett felt.

Rhett felt guilt wash over him anew. Not only had he been a burden on Liss, he'd caused the only people who mattered to him to worry.

"Listen, man," he began. Rhett had about as much experience with apologies as he had with being useless. "I'm sorry—"

"I wasn't worried," Wilsean shrugged. He turned to Liss. "Do I look worried?"

"Not at all," she replied. "My eyes get all red and puffy when I'm not worried, too."

Rhett turned his face to hide his amusement. Wilsean wasn't used to getting as good as he gave. Rhett generally ignored his and Ciago's bantering, and most of the other soldiers were too impressed by their accolades and status to put them in their place.

Liss had set Wilsean straight within a few seconds of meeting him.

"Stone, on the other hand, was beside himself," Wilsean said once he stopped stuttering. "He was actually pacing and talking to himself last night."

"Stone doesn't get *beside himself.* That's what makes him Stone," Rhett replied.

"Meanwhile, did you manage to kill the spy on your little vacation?" Wilsean demanded.

"Never found him." He gave Wilsean a brief rundown of what had happened, knowing he'd have to repeat the story for Stone and Ciago. His attention was only half on the conversation. The other half was on Liss.

He felt, rather than saw, the way she stiffened as he spoke. Even though they weren't close enough to touch, it was like he could sense the way every one of her muscles seized up as soon as the conversation turned to his reason for being here.

Rhett had never been proud or ashamed to be the most famed assassin in all the lands. It just was. For some reason, though, he wanted desperately to explain himself to Liss. He had no idea what he'd say if he had the chance. He just wanted to say whatever would put her mind at ease. She couldn't possibly think he would ever be a threat to her, could she? He wasn't some mindless savage like the humans who lived in the Giant Realm.

She didn't seem afraid of him, exactly. There was something else that she was either trying to hide or he was too dim to perceive.

Rhett dug his fingers into his temple. It shouldn't matter to him one way or the other what Liss thought about him. He had never thought so much about another person's opinion of him, and it was a waste of his limited energy.

At that moment, Rhett's legs decided they'd had enough. Without warning, they gave out.

Liss caught one of his arms and Wilsean grabbed the other.

"Put him down over there," Wilsean was saying as Rhett swallowed the surge of acid that came when his wounded leg scraped against a tree. He couldn't stand being so helpless, so weak. He couldn't bear for Liss to know he couldn't even manage to stand on his own two feet.

Her opinion of him shouldn't matter one way or the other. It couldn't matter. And yet, it did.

CHAPTER 13

If Liss wasn't a Soul Sorter, everything would be so much simpler. She would be able to see Rhett as the murderer he was, rather than the man whose soul was full of honor and a kindness that couldn't possibly exist in the Viper's body.

Maybe the fact that she'd saved his life had warped her whole perception of him. She felt some connection to him because she'd brought him back from the brink of death. She'd been by his side for three straight days before she'd known who...*what* he was.

The man she had found lying in the field wasn't Lagonia's Chief Assassin. He was just a person dying from poison. Maybe once he fully recovered, the brutal murderer she'd heard so much about would surface. She had no doubt that at some point soon, Rhett's strength would return, and with it, every kindness in his soul would be replaced by the horror she expected.

She should have let him die. If she'd known who he was when she first found him, she would have. But she hadn't known. And now, here she was, in the Viper's camp, joking with his friend. It was necessary to maintain her cover, but it didn't stop her from feeling like a traitor to her own people.

At least this wouldn't all be a complete loss. She'd already decided that if she had to be in such vile company, she would make the most of it. The Opal Slayer was close to the Emperor, and his mind was full of information she could use to help her people and hurt his.

She'd repeated these words to herself their entire ride to the camp. It had kept her mind from thinking about the way his muscled chest had been pressed against her back. She repeated them now to keep from thinking about the way her body craved his nearness now that they were standing apart.

There was some part of her that still didn't believe Rhett was who he said he was. Maybe he was just *an* assassin and not *the* Assassin. Maybe his assignment to find and kill…her…was a one-time job, and the person who had murdered so many Extended was someone else….

"Poison," Rhett was saying to Wilsean. "Liueun root."

Liss had sensed the profound worry, replaced by relief, that filled Wilsean's soul. It was obvious these men had a real friendship—the kind she hadn't believed could exist in the backstabbing empire of Lagonia.

Wilsean was also unlike any Lagonian she'd ever met. He was good-natured, comfortable in his own skin, and easy to talk to. Liss had to keep reminding herself that the only reason there wasn't an arrow in her back or a slash wound across her throat was that she had brown hair instead of orange, and her skin didn't have a beautiful rainbow shimmer.

Wilsean leaned over Rhett, who was supporting himself against the trunk of an enormous tree, to say to Liss, "As you've come to learn, it's a full-time job keeping my friend alive."

Wilsean's tone was teasing, but the only emotion she felt on his soul was gratitude.

Wilsean was vaguely handsome in the way of most Lagonian men. His tight, curly black hair was short, although not as short as Rhett's. His skin was a deep chocolate brown, as were his eyes. He was taller and more willowy than Rhett, but he also had the appearance of someone she wouldn't want to take on in a fight.

He wore Lagonian black and gold, and Liss noticed the ring on his index finger had a family crest carved into the platinum band. It was a simple ring, which conversely meant that his family was an important one. In Liss's experience, the more jewels and finery, the more a Lagonian was trying to compensate for poor lineage.

"We wouldn't be having this conversation if it wasn't for Liss," Rhett said, his voice sounding even huskier and more serious compared to Wilsean's.

"Then, I'm also in your debt." Wilsean folded himself in half as he bowed to Liss.

Liss was surprised to find his words were genuine. It was one thing for a man to pledge his loyalty to the person who had saved his life. It was another for his friend to make the same promise.

"Actually, there is something you can do," Rhett said. "Liss is looking for work in the palace. She's—leaving Insorsil."

It was a kindness for Rhett not to reveal that she was an Empty. It was the greatest shame among the Insorsiled. If she really had been one, she wouldn't have wanted to talk about it. Liss felt a flash of appreciation that Rhett cared enough to guard her secret, which was followed by irritation at herself for caring that he cared.

Liss groaned inwardly. When had things gotten so complicated? Everything had made so much more sense when Lagonians ranged from fools to tormentors.

"I'm an Empty," Liss said, schooling her features to project just the right amount of shame and sadness.

She expected Wilsean's eyes to narrow in disgust. No one hated the Empties as much as the Insorsiled, but the Lagonians had no use for an Insorsiled without magic.

His reaction was the exact opposite. Wilsean's eyes lit up. "My…er…Samara is an Empty, too."

"Samara's his girlfriend," Rhett explained, which Liss had gathered.

"She isn't my girlfriend," Wilsean protested. "We're just…fooling around."

She's his girlfriend, Rhett mouthed to Liss.

Liss tamped down the immediate thrill she felt at the secret little smile he gave her. It was the first hint of emotion she'd seen on his face, and it softened his harsh features.

"*Anyway,*" Wilsean said, "you and Samara will get along fine." Wilsean gave her a sheepish grin. "Not to say that you'll get along because you're both Empties, but she's great, and if you saved Rhett, then that means you're great. You'll be great together."

"Take a breath," Rhett muttered. His face was pale and drawn, and Liss felt discomfort on his soul.

She had to stop herself from reaching out to see if his skin was feverish.

Wilsean, noticing, squatted on the ground in front of Rhett. He touched the back of his hand to Rhett's forehead as Liss almost had moments before.

"Stop touching me," Rhett commanded.

"As swoon-worthy as I've been told you are, you're not really my type," Wilsean replied as he poured water from a canteen onto a towel and pressed it to Rhett's forehead.

Liss was having a hard time remembering to hate Wilsean. His soul was kind and honorable. There was a tenderness that filled him at the mention of Samara, and a deep sense of loyalty to Rhett that she had never expected to find on a Lagonian's soul.

Wilsean pulled a glass sphere out of his pocket as he continued to dab at Rhett's face with the towel. Liss tried not to look impressed, since Tamilissa Elspeth Wren would have had one of these spheres herself before she was exiled and forced to leave all her magical possessions behind. The sphere, called a corresponder, allowed the user to contact the owner of the sister sphere. It was kind of like the Insorsiled onyx stone in Liss's pocket, except it was much better because you could hear and see the person with the other corresponder, rather than just reading the text they'd spoken. They cost a fortune.

Liss mentally calculated how much she could get for the corresponder. That one little piece of glass could feed her entire caravan—and buy her mother's potion—for a month.

Even though these men didn't advertise their wealth like every other Lagonian she'd ever encountered, there was evidence of it everywhere. From the corresponder, to the tents that were clearly of Insorsil make, to the two silver dragons munching solid gold nuggets from a makeshift trough.

The smoke inside the glass sphere started to swirl as Wilsean spoke into the corresponder. A tiny image of another man's face appeared through the smoke. He was older, bald, and had a large, hooked nose. Liss couldn't see his soul across whatever distance separated them, but the expression on his face, even in miniature form, made her want to shrink back. If Liss had ever pictured the face of the Viper, she would have imagined it to look exactly like his.

"Get over here," Wilsean said into the sphere. "Rhett's back."

Liss expected the other man to say something, but the image dissolved and the smoke settled back to the bottom of the sphere.

"That's Stone for you," Wilsean said Liss. "Man of even fewer words than our fearless leader."

They both looked at Rhett, who was leaning against the tree with his eyes closed.

He wavered in and out of consciousness as Wilsean peppered Liss with questions about the last three days. She had just finished telling him about how she'd found Rhett when the sound of two dragons crashing through the brush announced the other men's return.

The biggest, most terrifying man Liss had ever seen leapt off his dragon's back and sprinted toward them. He looked like he was made out of boulders, and someone had slapped human flesh over the top of them. Liss had never seen any of the giants who lived across the sea, but she thought this man must have some giant blood somewhere in his lineage. Muscles bunched and rippled beneath his skin with his every step. Even his neck had muscles. Still, in spite of his size, his steps were quiet and he moved with a grace that shouldn't be possible for someone of his size. He moved like a predator. Liss shuddered.

"Ciago's harmless," Rhett said.

Liss turned to see Rhett had opened his eyes and was watching her.

"I wouldn't say harmless," Wilsean said as he reached out a hand to help Rhett up. Rhett shook his head and got to his feet without assistance.

The giant—Ciago—had an enormous smile stretched across his face.

"Where've you been, man?" he demanded. "Wilsean and Stone were practically crying themselves to sleep over you."

"Like you could even see through your own tears," Wilsean replied good-naturedly. He turned to Liss and said, "Ciago's practically hero-worshipped Rhett since we were kids."

To Liss's horror, Ciago strode right up to Rhett and clapped him on the back hard enough that her own spine ached in sympathy. Liss felt a spark of annoyance. Couldn't this buffoon see Rhett was injured?

"I just spent three days saving Rhett's life," Liss told the enormous man, "and I'd appreciate you not wasting my efforts by breaking his back."

Ciago let go of Rhett and stared at Liss. His light blue eyes widened.

"Well hello, lovely." Ciago held out his giant paw to Liss. "Who might you be?"

"Liss," she replied. When she put her hand in his, his grip was surprisingly gentle as he raised her hand to his lips and kissed her knuckles.

Ciago looked from Rhett to Liss and waggled his eyebrows. "So, this is the reason you abandoned us. I forgive you." Ciago grinned and made to slap Rhett's back again, but then seemed to think better of it and dropped his enormous hand by his side. To Liss, he said, "I commend you for taking on such a daunting challenge."

"Saving his life, you mean?"

"No, spending three days with Commander Doom and Gloom." Ciago's grin widened as Rhett rolled his eyes skyward. Ciago frowned at Rhett. "You didn't scare her off with that thing you do, did you?"

"What thing?" Rhett deadpanned.

Ciago mimed Rhett's expressionless face and blank stare. Liss couldn't help herself. She laughed.

"Look, the next time you take off with Lovely Liss," Ciago turned to grin at her before scowling back at Rhett, "give us a head's up."

"The next time someone shoots me with liueun, I'll make sure to send along a message before I'm paralyzed."

"Don't be dramatic, Rhetteman." Ciago elbowed Liss in the ribs with enough force that she would have fallen over if she didn't have the tree to brace herself. "He's really milking that scratch on his leg for all it's worth, isn't he?"

The last man in the group, the older one whose face she had seen in the corresponder, had finished tying his and Ciago's dragons beside the other two and was now walking toward them. From the look of him, Liss guessed this man was somewhere in his forties or fifties. His bald head and close-cropped salt-and-pepper goatee gave him a refined and vaguely terrifying appearance. Even Wilsean and Ciago's smiles faded as the older man reached them. Rhett was the only one who didn't see intimidated.

"I heard you were worried about me," Rhett said with a tired smile.

"I expect you have a valid excuse for your extended absence," the man replied with a scowl.

He was more human-sized than Rhett, Wilsean, and especially Ciago. He wasn't much taller than Liss, but of all of the men, there was something more lethal about him. His piercing, serious eyes scanned Rhett, lingering on his torn pants and bandaged thigh, before moving to her. Liss had to fight the urge to squirm under the intensity of his gaze. Unlike Wilsean and Ciago's souls, which were open and pleasant, this man's soul was full of a dark pain that made Liss want to shudder.

"Where have you been?" Stone demanded as Rhett continued to meet his challenging gaze without blinking.

"Lay off him, Stone," Wilsean said. "He almost died."

"Stone can't help himself," Ciago said. "Once a Master Interrogator, always an interrogator."

It was only Liss's thieving instincts that kept her from reacting. She'd heard of Lagonia's Master Interrogator. Perhaps the only opinion Lagonians, Insorsiled, and Extended shared was a fear of this man. Unlike her inability…or unwillingness…to accept that Rhett could be who he said he was, Liss had no trouble imagining Stone as Lagonia's brutal interrogator.

Rhett disentangled himself from Ciago and motioned for them all to sit down. Even in his weakened state, there was something commanding about Rhett's presence. Even though Stone was old enough to be any of their fathers and had all of their respect, it was clear Rhett was in charge.

They all sat on makeshift benches around the blackened heap of an old fire. Liss expected to feel uncomfortable in the company of four Lagonian men, especially these four. But with the exception of Stone, she felt strangely at ease.

Rhett caught the two bottles of water Wilsean tossed to him. He handed one to Liss as Stone and Ciago interrogated him about what had happened.

As Rhett described the slavers on the road and the hidden archer, it took every ounce of Liss's self-control not to let her shock and amazement register on her face. Rhett…a Lagonian…had killed slavers.

All her prior experience had taught her that Lagonians approved of, and even relished, the lucrative slave trade. But she felt the anger and disgust radiating off each of the men's souls at the bare mention of slavers. And Rhett had killed seven of them.

None of the others seemed surprised by what Rhett had done on his own. Even with everything she'd heard about the Viper, Liss found it hard to imagine how a single man with no weapon other than a dagger could take down seven of them. Slavers were vicious, bloodthirsty, and had no conscience. Killing even one of them was a feat, which she knew from the few Extended who had managed it.

All eyes turned on Liss as Rhett got to the part of the story that included her. The men's praise and thanks were lavish and heartfelt. It was obvious how much they all cared for Rhett, even Stone, who said little and scowled a lot.

"Explain something to me," Stone said after Rhett had finished. He turned his glare on Liss, and she had to force herself not to wither. "How did you identify the poison so easily, and where did you acquire the antidote?"

Liss had been prepared for these questions, but if it hadn't been for all of her practice as a thief, she still would have stumbled over her responses. It wasn't hard to guess why Stone was such a good interrogator.

"My mom's a witchdoctor," she replied, keeping her voice even. "I was training to be one, too…before." She ducked her head, like she was embarrassed.

"And the antidote?" Stone demanded. "Do you mean to tell me you shelled out ten pounds of jewels for a dying stranger?"

"Oh please," Ciago said. "With Rhett's glittering personality, how could she resist?"

Rhett gave him a withering look. Ciago just chuckled.

"I got the antidote from a warlock free of charge," Liss said, looking straight at Stone. "I gave him some medicine years back when he was desperate, so he owed me."

"Do you often call in favors for strangers?" Stone persisted.

"Enough, Stone," Rhett said.

"Well, it was obvious no one else was going to help him," Liss said, feeling defensive in spite of herself. "Maybe you all should have gotten off your asses and saved him yourself so I didn't have to."

A tense look passed between her and Stone before Wilsean's laughter drew her attention away from the older man.

"You're right, Lovely Liss," Ciago said, coming around the circle to kneel in front of her. Even on his knees, he dwarfed her. "You are a true heroine."

Ciago's words were teasing, but the gratitude in his soul was real.

"Jaikon won't be pleased to hear you killed seven slavers," Stone told Rhett, still brooding.

Rhett shrugged.

"We could just leave the whole slaver part out of our report," Wilsean suggested.

"You know that isn't an option," Stone said.

"Yes, yes," Ciago said. "Duty to the empire…we live to serve…we *know*." He rolled his eyes for Liss's benefit.

"That's right," Stone growled. "And more importantly, treason will get your body tossed over the cliff."

"I'd like to see them try to lift my dead weight," Ciago said, unconcerned.

Liss felt Stone's fury, but she didn't know its cause or to whom it was directed.

"Everyone gets tossed over the cliff, eventually," Stone said, his voice quieter than it had been before. "I'm just trying to get you all to my age before it happens."

Rhett and Stone exchanged a look full of understanding. There was emotion on each of their souls that Liss didn't understand. Sometimes, it could be so frustrating to know what a person was feeling without understanding why.

"If we find and kill Opal Smoke before we go back to Lagonia," Wilsean said, "the Emperor won't care about a few slavers."

Again, it was only Liss's years as a thief that kept her from reacting.

"The caravan will be long gone by now," Ciago said. "We should go back to Lagonia and regroup while Rhett recovers."

"I'm fine," Rhett said.

"Of course, you are." Ciago gave him another bone-crunching slap on the back. Liss glared at him.

"The caravan'll resurface," Stone said. "We're not going anywhere until the job's done."

"We have no guarantees the spy is even still with them," Wilsean argued. "We've had no word about him since we got here. He might have gone into one of the Extended hideouts."

Liss did her best to appear calm. She kept her hands in her lap so no one would notice they were squeezed into fists. She wavered between terror and a desire to rain down misery on each of these men.

She didn't have many options at the moment, though. She could listen to them talk about hunting down her caravan and killing her, or she could take control of this conversation.

"I heard the Extended spy was terrorizing some slavers in the heart of Insorsil," she announced.

The others stopped talking and looked at her.

"Can you be more specific?" Stone demanded.

"No." She shrugged. "That's all I heard."

Liss had to stop herself from smirking. *The heart of Insorsil* was a big place. These men could spend a month searching inner Insorsil, which was full of twisting, tightly-packed streets and too many people.

"What else do you know about this spy?" Stone asked her.

"I've heard he's huge, and his Extension is disappearing into thin air," she said, repeating rumors she'd heard from Lagonia soldiers' lips. "And horribly ugly. A girl I know saw him once, and she said his skin was so shimmery it hurt to look at him."

The men were nodding as they absorbed the new information. Liss relaxed. This was kind of fun.

"That's not much to go on," Stone said.

"It's more than we had before," Rhett replied.

Stone sighed. "Fine. We'll get back to Insorsil tomorrow and see what we can find."

"In that case," Wilsean said, "I propose we stop talking about business for tonight." He turned to Liss, "Am I right that the only thing you've eaten in the last three days is burnt wild hare?"

Liss looked at Rhett and couldn't help smiling.

"I have my talents," Rhett said. "Cooking isn't one of them."

Liss didn't want to think about those talents. She couldn't let herself think about them or look at the dagger resting in his lap…not now, with Stone sitting across from her. The man seemed almost as good at perceiving emotions as she was. She had to play her part now, and she had to be convincing.

Liss found herself seated on the ground next to Rhett as Ciago and Stone served up dishes of steamed rice, slices of meat so tender they melted on her tongue, and buttery vegetables that were a far cry from the canned variety she was used to. Rhett nursed a bowl of broth while the rest of them ate, and Wilsean and Ciago asked Liss about her home and family in Insorsil.

She kept her history just vague enough, and her personal anecdotes just close enough to the truth, that everything fit together into a believable picture.

"Did you bring anything Insorsiled with you?" Ciago asked, his voice hopeful.

It was an effort for Liss not to roll her eyes. She would never understand Lagonians' obsession with anything and everything Insorsiled.

"Only the bike," Liss said.

"She had to leave everything behind, stupid," Wilsean said. "Empties aren't allowed to bring anything Insorsiled with them into exile."

"Samara always has Insorsiled toys," Ciago argued.

"That's because she keeps in touch with her brother and sisters," Wilsean replied. "But that's very unusual, isn't it?" he asked Liss.

Liss nodded. Admittedly, she didn't know as much about Insorsil laws as would be ideal for her new identity.

"Can you teach me the Florinatta?" Wilsean asked her after they had finished eating.

It happened to be the one Insorsiled dance she knew. Mari had gotten it in her head that she wanted to learn it, and she'd begged Liss to help her. The only problem was that Liss had practiced the warlock's part so Mari could do the fancy twists and turns meant for the witch. Liss wracked her brain, trying to remember the way little Mari's worn shoes had moved.

"And why, pray tell, do you want to learn that?" Ciago asked, batting his eyes at Wilsean.

"It just might be good to know," he replied with a careless shrug.

No one seemed fooled.

"Samara?" Liss asked, exchanging a grin with Ciago.

"Learning a dance for his non-girlfriend," Ciago confirmed.

"Precisely," Wilsean agreed. "So, how 'bout it, Liss?"

Why not? she thought. It would be an easy way to further ingratiate herself with these men, and it might help to ease the suspicion she felt in Stone's soul.

"I'll teach you the guy's part," Liss said, getting to her feet.

It turned out Wilsean was a far better dancer than she was, and he picked up the steps almost immediately.

"Good," Wilsean said as they laughed and tripped over each other. "Now, you do the girl's part so I can practice properly."

Liss faltered. The witch's part was much more complicated, and she didn't think she remembered the order of the steps.

"It seems like you've got this down," Liss said. "Why don't you teach me a Lagonian dance?"

"Alright." Wilsean made an elaborate bow and held out his hand to her. "May I have this dance, m'lady?"

Grinning, she took it. Wilsean guided her through the steps and turns, explaining the slight differentiations preferred by older and younger generations. Liss was only half-listening. She was distracted by the emotions coming from Rhett's soul as he sat against his tree and pretended to sleep. He wasn't asleep. He was jealous.

"I've had enough of this foolishness," Stone announced. "I'm going to bed. You all work out who's on first watch."

As he passed by Rhett, who appeared to be asleep even though Liss knew he wasn't, Stone put a hand on his shoulder. Liss felt a flicker of warmth and tenderness across the older man's soul that was like a ray of sun through storm clouds.

By the time their dance lesson was over, Liss was clutching her side from laughing. Wilsean and Ciago's incessant teasing made her feel like she was back with Spence, Mari, and Jema, although the men's humor had a decidedly more adult edge.

Liss decided it was best to pretend to actually like these men…especially since she'd need to maintain her cover for weeks, maybe even months. Even so, she wouldn't let herself forget they were her enemy.

This was all just one big act. She was playing off the emotions she read on their souls, just like she did whenever she was distracting a target she meant to steal from. That way, when she reached for their wallet or jewels, it was the last thing they expected from her. By the time Liss reached her hand into the pockets of Lagonia, metaphorically speaking, these men wouldn't begin to think her capable of being Opal Smoke.

Once Stone was enclosed in his tent, Liss and Wilsean returned to the fire that was now crackling merrily.

"So, tell me," Ciago said, leaning closer to Liss. "What charms did Rhett use to draw the most beautiful woman in all of Insorsil to his side?"

"Looking for tips?" Wilsean asked.

Ciago shrugged. "I can't be the only one without an Insorsiled lover."

Liss almost laughed at the embarrassment that went through Rhett, even as his expression remained impassive.

"Give it a rest, Ciago," Rhett muttered.

"It just isn't fair," Ciago pouted, which was a ridiculous look on someone so huge. "How come you get Lovely Liss, when I'm the one with all the charm?"

"She isn't mine," Rhett said, some color coming into his pale cheeks.

"Oh good." Ciago scooted closer to Liss. "Then you won't mind if I use my charms to make her fall in love with me?"

There was no malice in Ciago's soul, and for reasons she didn't care to examine too closely, she rather enjoyed the irritation she felt in Rhett's.

"Are you ready to be wooed, Lovely Liss?" Ciago batted his eyes at her.

"You're welcome to try," she replied with a laugh.

Liss noticed that Rhett had gone very still, even as the clamor of emotions in his soul grew louder.

"Okay, how about this one?" Ciago cleared his throat. "Your eyes are more beautiful than the purest sapphires in all of Lagonia."

Liss scrunched up her face. "Trying too hard," she said.

"Okay, okay. How about this one…."

"When he gets too tiresome, you have my permission to kill him," Rhett told Liss in a bored tone.

Ciago ignored Rhett. It wasn't long before Liss and Wilsean were doubled over in laughter at Ciago's increasingly ridiculous pick-up lines.

"Do any of those ever actually work?" she asked, breathless with laughter, when Ciago finished reciting a poem about the moon, stars, and blushing maidens.

Ciago huffed. "All the time."

"That says more about the women at court than your skill," Rhett pointed out.

He'd said little, but his soul was full of emotion.

Ciago gave Liss a meaningful look. "You're falling in love with me after all that. Just admit it so we can get the niceties over with and you can give me my kiss."

Liss just laughed.

"Come on, I'm breaking a sweat trying to impress you over here," Ciago complained. "Just one kiss?"

"Alright," Liss said. "Just one."

"Really?" Ciago reminded her of a giant puppy, with his wide eyes and hopeful expression.

Out of the corner of her eye, Liss saw Rhett's whole body go motionless. It was something she was starting to notice about him. The more that was going on inside his soul, the more he outwardly appeared as though he was empty of all emotions. It must have taken enormous self-control and long years of practice not to betray any hint of what he was feeling. And he was convincing. If she wasn't a Soul Sorter, she would have believed he felt nothing at all.

"You get one kiss, and then you're never going to ask for another one," Liss told Ciago. "Agreed?"

"After one kiss, you'll be the one begging for more," Ciago assured her.

Liss leaned forward. Out of the corner of her eye, she saw Rhett go as still as a statue.

Right before their lips touched, Liss raised her dinner plate. There was an audible smacking sound as Ciago's lips connected with the leftover congealed sauce.

Ciago made a choked sound of protest. Wilsean roared with laughter.

"You wound me, Lovely Liss," Ciago said, clutching at his heart with one hand as he used the other to mop the brown, sticky mess from his lips.

"Oh, sorry," Liss said with a grin. "Was that not what you wanted? You should have been more specific."

Beside her, Rhett threw his head back and laughed. It was a good laugh, deep and husky. It warmed his brown eyes and curved his lips, which she had most often seen pressed into a straight line. It made the kindness inside him visible, and Liss wondered if that was why he made a point of looking so severe.

Wilsean and Ciago were staring at Rhett like he'd just grown another leg.

"What?" Rhett asked, still chuckling.

"I can't remember the last time I heard you laugh," Wilsean said.

"It's been a long time," Ciago agreed. "Like, really long."

"That's because I spend all my time with the two of you," Rhett replied, a glimmer of mirth still in his eyes.

CHAPTER 14

Rhett relieved Ciago early from his watch. After so many days of being useless and making his friends worry, he figured it was the least he could do.

He'd offered Liss his tent, telling her he'd sleep outside, but she had refused. She had said she didn't need much sleep, but Rhett could sense the real reason was that she didn't trust him. Even with as easily as she had fit in with his friends, Liss was still wary.

Rhett sat on the large boulder at the far edge of their camp with his dagger by his side. He peered into the darkness for any sign of a threat. They were far enough off the main road that he didn't expect any trouble, but Stone had raised him to know that safety was an illusion he could never rely on.

As Rhett stared into the darkness, his mind wandered. As much as he tried to steer his thoughts toward more practical topics, like where in Insorsil they'd pick up their search for Opal Smoke, his mind kept going back to Liss.

He'd never met anyone like her. She fit in with their little group like she'd known them for years. She hadn't gotten offended by Ciago's teasing, nor had she been impressed by it. In Rhett's observation, there were two types of women in Lagonia. The first would have been appalled by Ciago's solicitations. They would have pouted and fumed until Ciago groveled for forgiveness. The other type would have offered up their beds at the first compliment, regardless of how insincere it might have been.

Liss didn't fit into either category. She also wasn't pretentious and strange like most Insorsiled he'd met over the years. She was….

"Mind if I join you?"

Rhett almost jumped out of his own skin at the sound of her voice. He turned, telling himself his heart was pounding because she had managed to sneak up on him. No one sneaked up on Lagonia's Chief Assassin. It took him several seconds to find his voice.

"I'd be grateful for the company," Rhett said. "I think I might have been dozing off."

It was the only explanation for why she had come up behind him without him hearing her. It certainly couldn't be because he'd been too busy thinking about her to be aware of what was happening right behind him. Rhett wasn't that big of a fool.

He shifted over to make room on the boulder. He kept his gaze ahead, staring into the dark woods as she settled herself beside him. Even though there was at least a foot of space separating them, Rhett felt the air between them warm.

"I like your friends," Liss said.

The statement pleased him. Rhett didn't know why it should matter to him one way or the other how she felt about them, but it did.

"They're good men," he said. "Even if they do act like idiots most of the time."

"I'm not so sure about Stone, though," she added.

"Stone is…."

Rhett thought about the wife and son Stone had once had. Jaikon, Sr. had ordered their deaths when Stone refused to kill a deserter who was just a boy. It was only a short time after their deaths that Rhett was born and Stone became his guardian.

Even though it was Rhett's own father who had murdered Stone's family, Stone never held it against Rhett. Instead, it drove his guardian's training of him. It was the source of all his hardness and strength. It was why Stone knew, better than anyone, the danger of forming attachments…of how dangerous it was to care.

Rhett had seen firsthand what happened to people in Jaikon's service who had loyalties outside of their sworn duty. Those attachments were used to manipulate and cause pain. It was the reason why Stone had taught him all his life to keep others at arm's length, both for his safety and theirs.

"Life has been tough on Stone," Rhett said finally.

"I guess I can understand that," Liss replied.

There was a hardness tinged with bitterness in her that reminded him of his own. It couldn't have been easy being an Empty. He sensed she was a survivor. Like him.

Liss pulled her long hair over her shoulder. As she did, her hand brushed against his arm. Rhett felt his pulse jump at the contact.

Stay away, his brain warned.

This beautiful, smart, tough woman made it too easy for him to forget the incalculable danger they would both face if he ever acted on his attraction.

The point was moot. He had no reason to think she'd be interested in him even if he could pursue her. Rhett was sure every man who crossed Liss's path tried to win her heart. Adding his unwanted advances to that long list would be a poor way to thank her for saving his life.

Steel doesn't know love or despair. It needs no heart or warmth. I am steel.

His attraction to Liss was just a temptation, and that was something Rhett could control. He had twenty years of experience guarding his mind and burying his emotions. He might feel something for the woman who had saved his life...*who wouldn't?*...but he'd never act on those feelings.

Liss pulled her cloak tighter around her. Rhett saw how the once-white material was now covered in mud and his dried blood.

"I'm sorry for ruining your cloak," Rhett told her. "I'll replace it once we're back in the empire."

"I'll have no need for Insorsiled clothes once I'm in Lagonia," she said, shrugging. "Besides, I've never been a fan of Insorsil finery."

"I've never been a fan of Lagonian finery," he said, trying not to smile.

Damn. Why was she so easy to talk to?

She wasn't angry, the way most people would be in her position. But she wasn't one of those sunshine-and-unicorns types that irritated him, either. He had seen the way she looked at his paralyzed and bloody body without fear. Liss was no stranger to life's ugly side. He'd glimpsed that again when he talked about the slavers. Rhett had seen a murderous kind of anger in her eyes then, and it had strangely comforted him.

Liss shivered. Rhett, whose fever was sending prickles of heat all along his body, was wearing only his thin shirt. He reached down for the Insorsiled thermos sitting on the ground. He handed it to her wordlessly.

She hesitated for only a second before taking it. "Whiskey?" she guessed.

"Do I look like I've been drinking?" he asked, before realizing he probably did. His fever was burning in his cheeks, and he could feel a sheen of sweat on his brow. He must look like hell.

Liss opened the thermos. She took a sip, screwed up her face, and then spit it out onto the ground.

"What is *that*?" she demanded, wiping her mouth on her sleeve.

"It's coffee," Rhett said, puzzled. "I'm pretty sure they have that where you come from?" He raised an eyebrow at her.

"Ever heard of sugar?" she retorted. "I'm pretty sure they have that where *you* come from."

Rhett smirked as she pushed the thermos back into his hands like it was as repulsive as liueun.

"I've never cared much for sweets," Rhett said.

Liss gave him a dark look. "I didn't take you for insane, but now I know the truth."

"My cover is blown," he replied dryly.

They were both quiet after that. It was a comfortable kind of silence. Most Lagonians filled the air simply because they loved the sound of their own voices. It was refreshing to be with someone besides his close friends who didn't feel the need to drown out the silence with pointless chatter.

Rhett glanced at her, only to find her eyes were closed. Her neck was tilted at what looked like an uncomfortable angle.

"Liss," he said quietly, pushing down the spark of feeling that came with just saying her name.

Her eyes flew open.

"Go to sleep," he told her. "Take my tent."

He saw her whole body stiffen, like he'd said something offensive. "I'm not tired," she said. "And I don't sleep in strange men's tents."

"I told you I'd sleep outside," he said, exasperated.

"And I'm sure if you were me, surrounded by killers, you'd just curl right up in one of their tents?" Her voice was light, but Rhett saw anger darken the blue of her eyes.

Rhett stared at her. "I don't know what kind of people you dealt with in Insorsil, but my men have honor."

"Honor," she repeated, like the concept was foreign to her. Or maybe it was the concept of Lagonians having honor that was foreign to her. Rhett couldn't tell.

"Yes," he replied. "Especially after what you did for me. You're safe here."

"Maybe," she replied. "But I'd still feel more comfortable staying here where no one's going to sneak up on me."

Rhett huffed. "Suit yourself."

It was only a few minutes before she had nodded off again. This time, she tilted to the side and would have fallen off the rock if he hadn't caught her. *Enough of this*, he thought.

Liss didn't wake when he lifted her off the rock. She was small, but his body was still weak from the remnants of the poison. Still, he managed to carry her to the tent without her waking. He laid her down on top of the blankets. He considered taking off her boots and cloak, which was twisted around her, but he thought she wouldn't appreciate him touching her more than was necessary. So, he just left her like that and went back to finish his watch.

CHAPTER 15

When Liss woke, she was cozier than she'd ever been in her life. On the wagon, she always slept on the couch in the main room. The couch was itchy and the blanket thin, since she'd insisted her mom take the only decent quilt. She could have stolen a better one, but with how little sleep she usually got, she just never saw the point.

Now, though, she was surrounded by fluffy softness. The warm blankets cocooned her, and there was a feather pillow beneath her head. Liss opened her eyes.

For a moment, she was confused. She remembered sitting on that boulder with Rhett, but now she was inside a spacious bedroom. She was lying on a large mattress surrounded by pillows, cotton sheets, and a thick blanket. The ceiling was high and transparent so she could see the stars overhead. The hazy warmth of sleep lifted as she realized where she was—not inside a bedroom, but an Insorsiled tent.

How had she gotten here?

She got out of bed and went to the opening of the tent. She stepped through the zippered partition. As soon as she was on the other side, the chill night air cut through her lousy cloak. She looked back at the tent.

From the outside, it looked barely big enough for her to wriggle into. She had seen tents like this one before and knew that when it was time to break camp, the tent and everything inside it would compress into a package small and light enough to be carried on one's back.

She couldn't deny it was convenient to have all the wealth of Lagonia at her fingertips. She had to remind herself it was the taxes wrung from her people that had paid for the warm blankets she'd slept in.

The first tendrils of dawn were just starting to creep across the sky. No longer tired, Liss picked her way over to the remains of the previous night's campfire. That's where she found Rhett, asleep on his side with rocks for a pillow and what must have been Ciago's dragonhide jacket as his only blanket. He shivered a little in his sleep. Liss had to resist the urge to go get one of the blankets from his tent to cover him.

He must have been the one to bring her into his tent. She couldn't decide how she felt about that. She couldn't decide how she felt about him, period.

She still didn't see how Rhett could possibly be the same man who'd assassinated countless of her people. There was still a part of her that hoped that somehow, he wasn't that same man. Maybe he'd only been there and someone else…Stone maybe, had been the one to kill all those Extended. She didn't look too closely at her own soul for fear she'd see how much she wanted it to be someone else who had killed her people. Anyone but him.

Liss backtracked before Rhett woke up and saw her staring at him. She cut through the trees in search of a stream where she could get cleaned up before any of the men awoke. In spite of all of their promises and Rhett's assurances about their honor, a lifetime of experience had taught her never to trust a Lagonian's word. She certainly wasn't going to let any of them catch her doing something as vulnerable as bathing.

By the time she got back to camp, the others were awake.

"Lovely Liss!" Ciago called when he caught sight of her. "Now, there's a sight for sore eyes."

Rhett nodded to her but didn't say anything as he went back to talking quietly with Stone. Wilsean gave her a friendly wave. Stone ignored her.

Liss joked with Wilsean and Ciago during breakfast while keeping one ear on Stone and Rhett's conversation. When Rhett announced he and Stone would be making inquiries in town while Ciago and Wilsean went in search of the caravan, Liss schooled her features. In an offhanded sort of way, she mentioned she'd heard there were caravans heading at great speed to the southern point of the grasslands.

It was a place all the caravans avoided at this time of year because of the lowland mud that bogged down the wagons and put extra strain on the Energizers, but these men wouldn't know about that.

"Beautiful and chock full of information," Ciago said with a shake of his head. "You better hold on tight to this one," he said loudly to Rhett.

Out of the corner of her eye, Liss thought she saw a slight frown on Rhett's usually impassive face. His emotions were confused, and she couldn't make sense of them.

Rhett cleared his throat. "We'll be gone for most of the day," he told her. "You can go with Wilsean and Ciago if you want, or do whatever…." He trailed off.

Liss felt his discomfort and guessed it was because he felt awkward about returning to the place where she had supposedly been exiled from. Empties faced arrest if they were found in Insorsil after their banishment.

"I'll go with Wilsean and Ciago," she decided. It would give her a chance to pick their brains without Stone or Rhett overhearing. With any luck, she'd learn something of use that would help her once she was inside the empire.

Ciago waggled his eyebrows at her. "You can ride my dragon with me," he offered.

"She can have Silverbird," Rhett said quickly.

"Killjoy," Ciago muttered.

Silverbird turned out to be a friendly, rather simple-minded dragon. It nuzzled Rhett as he cinched up its saddle. Liss saw the way he absently stroked the dragon's nose, and it warmed her to him before she remembered she hated these men, Rhett most of all.

"See you tonight," he said without looking at her.

✱ ✱ ✱

Liss's day was about as productive as Wilsean and Ciago's, which was to say it wasn't productive at all. As entertaining as their company was, she hadn't learned anything of significance from either of them. Either they were excellent at guarding secrets, or they didn't know any more about the cause of their immunity than she did.

Liss was pleased and unsurprised when Rhett and Stone returned with nothing to show for their own search. Rhett was looking much better than he had even that morning, and when he got off the dragon he had shared with Stone, there wasn't a hint of a limp in his stride.

After a day apart, she felt a jump of emotions at their proximity. She also felt attraction. It was difficult for her to tell if the emotions belonged to his soul or hers, which was more than a little unsettling. She had never struggled to decipher which soul an emotion belonged to before.

"I hope my men weren't too irritating," Rhett said.

They were the first words he'd spoken to her since getting back to camp. His voice sounded even huskier than she remembered.

"Charming is what he means," Ciago said in his easy way. "And I held back for Liss's sake. I don't want to break her lovely heart."

"And I appreciate it," Liss replied, returning Ciago's broad smile.

Dinner was another lavish affair, with perfectly ripe fruit, bread, and cheese. Liss was more comfortable than she should have been as she sat surrounded by murderers. As she joked with Wilsean and Ciago, her hand closed around the onyx stone in her pocket. She itched to have something meaningful to share with Burk. She kept one ear on her conversation with Ciago and Wilsean and the other on what Rhett was saying to Stone.

"The trail's cold," Rhett told the older man. "We'll have to return to Lagonia and wait for him to turn up again."

"Not until you're at your full strength," Stone replied. Liss felt the fear on Stone's soul and wondered what he was afraid of.

Rhett gave Stone a short nod. It was like the two of them could speak volumes without saying anything at all. Liss could sense understanding passing between the two of them.

The same pattern of the previous night repeated itself. Stone went to bed early while the rest of them sat in easy company for several hours more. When the others started to yawn and stumble toward their tents, Rhett took the first watch. He told Liss to take his tent for the night, but she refused.

After pacing around the small campsite for close to an hour, she decided to join Rhett on his watch again. She had sought him out last night in hopes of learning something useful, although she hadn't really been surprised when nothing of value came out of their conversation. Still, if there was anyone in this company who could tell her what she needed to know, it would be Rhett. The only problem was that she couldn't just come right out and ask him. She couldn't do anything that would draw his suspicion.

Patience had never been one of Liss's strengths.

Liss hated the idea of just waiting until an elusive opportunity to broach the delicate topic of immunity presented itself. But with someone as clever as Rhett, it was her only option. Maybe tonight he'd say something that would offer some insight…give some clue…about what she would be looking for once she got inside the palace.

"Want some company?" she asked as Rhett's profile appeared in the darkness.

Rhett jumped to his feet and turned, his dagger in his hand.

"How do you do that?" he demanded, lowering his dagger.

"Do what?" Liss asked, distracted by the feelings pouring from Rhett's soul.

"Be so…silent."

Being sneaky was part of her job description. She didn't even have to think about it anymore. Keeping her footfalls quiet had become a force of habit.

"Maybe you're just used to bumbling Lagonians," Liss said. She was trying to ignore the way her pulse raced at the sight of him.

"Must be," he said, shaking his head. "You could teach my soldiers a thing or two."

My soldiers…. Because the only Lagonian who outranked Rhett was the Emperor himself.

No matter how many times she reminded herself, her soul just wouldn't accept it. She hadn't seen even a hint of violence from Rhett. There wasn't the kind of evil in his soul that would be required of a man with his reputation.

As they sat together, their shoulders not quite touching, they talked. That was another thing. She shouldn't be able to have a civilized conversation with the Viper. She had heard he only communicated with his fists and weapons. That murderer, whoever he was, wasn't the man sitting beside her and telling her about the trouble he and his friends got into as kids.

Hours passed, but the conversation never steered close enough to the topic of immunity for Liss to dare raising it herself. Still, she didn't mind as much as she should have.

Liss didn't know if it was the strange intimacy of saving Rhett's life and seeing him at his most vulnerable, or the fact she could see his emotions when no one else could, but their conversation turned personal. He had guessed that he wasn't the first person she had ever cared for, and she surprised herself by telling him a little about her mom. It turned out she could tell most of the story without giving away her real identity.

Her intention in coming here tonight was to gain Rhett's trust and try to trick him into revealing something about the immunity. If she was being honest with herself, though, that wasn't the reason she found herself confiding in him now.

One of the biggest irritations of being a Soul Sorter was that it was difficult to lie to herself.

Rhett told her about growing up as the bastard son of the emperor. His mother had died when he was born, and his father had never acted like a father. He had been forced to take care of himself from a young age, just like her.

Rhett's story surprised Liss. It was common enough for Extended to grow up without one or both parents, but the Lagonians lived a life of ease…or so she had always thought. They had the benefit of the best Insorsil medicine and endless riches to ensure they never had to know what it meant to struggle. She shouldn't have this much in common with a Lagonian…especially *this* Lagonian.

Liss began to drift off, lulled by the night insects and Rhett's solid presence. She startled awake when he spoke.

"You're nothing like the women in Lagonia," he said.

"Fewer jewels?" Liss asked, displaying her bare fingers.

Rhett chuckled. "Yes, that. But you're also honest. It's a scarce commodity in the empire."

Liss almost laughed out loud. She had begun thinking she was a much better thief than spy, but she must be more talented than she realized if Rhett believed she was honest.

It was a shock when Liss realized that, aside from the part about being an Insorsiled Empty, she really hadn't lied to Rhett. Most of what she'd told him was the truth, or at least part of the truth. It made her feel vulnerable in a way she hadn't before.

She hadn't been talking to Rhett as Tamilissa Elspeth Wren, undercover Extended spy. She'd been talking to him as herself. It felt like a betrayal of her people.

"You're not quite what I expected, either," Liss admitted.

"What did you expect?" he replied.

A man whose soul was black with cruelty.

Liss shrugged, trying to keep her expression neutral as every story she'd ever heard about the Opal Slayer filled her mind.

"I heard you've killed thousands of people."

Rhett shook his head, giving her a wry smile. "Thousands is an exaggeration."

"Alright," Liss said. Her hands had started to shake for some reason, and she clenched them into fists. "Is it true you cut off the heads of your victims and bring them to your emperor as tributes?"

Rhett grimaced. "On occasion, Jaikon has requested the head of a valuable target."

Liss shuddered.

"I don't do it unless the Emperor commands it," Rhett said hurriedly.

Liss took in a breath. "I heard you drink the blood of your victims and turn their teeth into necklaces."

Rhett laughed at that. "That's one I haven't heard before." He pulled down the collar of his shirt. "See? No teeth."

Liss gave him a quizzical look.

He rolled his eyes. "And no, I don't drink their blood. Obviously."

"I'm not sure it was so obvious," Liss grumbled, even though she felt some of her anxiety ease.

Rhett frowned. "I'm Lagonia's Chief Assassin. I kill people who are identified as threats to the empire. But I don't take pleasure in it."

His words shouldn't give her comfort. He was still the man who had murdered her people. And yet, it mattered that he killed on someone else's orders rather than his own.

A cold wind stirred her hair. Winter was coming; she could feel it on the air. She drew her cloak closer around her and drew up the hood.

"Here," Rhett said, offering her the dreaded thermos from the night before.

"No more coffee," Liss groaned. "I'd rather freeze to death."

"Wait." He bent to the ground and picked something else up. "I also brought this."

He handed her the thermos and a bowl of sugar. She was oddly touched by the gesture.

"I thought you didn't like sweets," she said.

Rhett shrugged. "I think I'll learn to."

Liss felt her heart flutter at the way he looked at her when he said those words.

Stop it, she ordered herself. She wasn't some dumb girl whose soul turned to mush at one kind gesture.

As she took the bowl of sugar from him, their fingers brushed. Liss felt the immediate shift across both of their emotions: confusion, hesitation, attraction....

For a moment, they just stared at each other. They both leaned closer. It was like there was some magnetic pull that neither of them could resist. They were close enough now that she could feel the warmth radiating from Rhett's body.

And then Liss remembered who he was...who she was. She got to her feet, almost stumbling in her haste. Rhett's soul filled with relief, making her wonder if she had just imagined the connection between them.

With some distance between them, she felt her senses return. She unscrewed the lid of the thermos and opened the sugar bowl. She ignored the way her hands shook ever so slightly.

Rhett, who was watching her every move, shook his head as she dumped in half the bowl. She swirled the thermos, took a swig, and sighed. "Much better."

She handed it back to Rhett. He took a small sip and grimaced.

"There's more sugar than coffee in there," he complained.

"Exactly," Liss replied with a grin.

A sound in the distance made them both go still. Rhett's knife was in his hand as he silently got to his feet. Liss followed.

There were voices, and they were growing louder.

Liss heard a branch snap. Whoever was out there was getting closer. She heard a cough. There was a thudding sound, and someone swore.

"Give us a little light, will ya? There's no one in this part of the woods."

Rhett grabbed Liss and pushed her behind a tree just as their part of the forest lit up.

A Flamer. Liss's heart went into her throat.

She peered around the tree to see a group of Extended boys, three of them by the looks of it. They didn't look older than Spence. And they were walking straight toward the tree where Rhett and Liss were hiding. The tree wasn't wide enough to shield them completely, and if the boys got any closer, they would definitely notice her white cloak.

What should she do?

She could shout a warning to them. The boys could separate and run away. Rhett wouldn't be able to chase them all. But if she warned them, her cover would be blown. If she did nothing, Rhett would kill them. She had no choice. She took a deep breath, buying herself a few more seconds before screaming out a warning.

Before she could utter a sound, Rhett took her hand and was leading her away from the boys. It was clear he knew this part of the forest well. He led her to a tree with a large hollow in the trunk. He pressed her into it so her white cloak was mostly hidden. Rhett's own body was close enough for her to feel the way his heart hammered in time with her own. She peered into his soul before immediately trying to forget what she had seen there. There wasn't a hint of fear. He wasn't even thinking about the Extended.

The Extended boys had stopped next to the boulder where she and Rhett had been sitting moments before. She heard their chatter without processing any of their words. Rhett was standing too close to her, and her traitorous soul was reaching for him with invisible hands. She could feel the emotions of his soul answering hers, and it only made everything worse.

Rhett was a murderer. He was her enemy. He was the Opal Slayer…the one sent to hunt her like prey.

The sound of the boys' voices and footsteps receded.

"They're gone," Rhett breathed after several long seconds had passed.

They were still standing pressed together. She could feel his chest rising and falling with each breath.

"Why didn't you fight them?" Liss asked, her voice no more than a whisper. She had to know.

"Because there was no need to," Rhett replied, his voice low and raspy. "They weren't looking for us."

"Wouldn't the Emperor have wanted you to kill them anyway?" she asked.

Liss felt a burst of resentment in Rhett's soul before he said, "Jaikon isn't here, and it's not my job to kill everyone."

His words filled her with more warmth than she could have imagined herself feeling at someone saying something so…normal.

She shouldn't be grateful to him for *not* murdering her people. Yet, he had chosen to let the boys go when he would have been praised by his emperor for killing them. If anyone ever found out he'd spared three Extended, his own life might be forfeit. It was a risk for him to let those boys go, especially when she had witnessed it.

"That's…honorable of you," she managed. She was having trouble thinking about anything except for how close they were still standing. There was no reason for it, and yet Rhett didn't back away from her, and she made no move to try to leave.

"I'm glad you think so."

His soul pulsed with emotion. There was desire and longing, but also hesitation and wariness. She was a little nettled. What reason could he have to be wary of her? Well, he would have plenty of reasons if he knew who she was, but he didn't.

Liss wanted to kiss him.

It was wrong, her brain knew that. Her soul didn't care.

Both of their souls were at war with themselves, and for a moment, she wasn't sure which way the balance would tip. She tilted up her chin just a fraction. Rhett bent down to her at almost the same time. Their lips brushed.

The touch was so soft she barely felt it. Rhett kept his hands at his sides and was already pulling away before she had even taken a breath. Liss wondered if their lips had touched at all, or if she'd just imagined it. Whatever had just happened wasn't a kiss. It felt like an apology.

Rhett backed away from her. "I'm sorry," he said, his voice gruff. "I…shouldn't have done that."

Liss didn't understand. She could feel his attraction and desire, even stronger than they had been before. But there were other emotions on his soul. There was conflict, guilt, and a desperation she couldn't make sense of. She had never felt such strong and conflicting emotions in a single soul, and she wondered with some alarm if it might be possible for a soul to split apart.

"What are you sorry for?" she asked, still trying to make sense of what had just passed between them.

"I'm no good for you," Rhett said, backing away further. "You need to stay away from me."

Liss should let this conversation die. She should let him walk away.

"Why?" she asked. "Is it because you're Lagonia's Chief Assassin?"

"Yes."

"Are you planning to kill me?"

A smile ghosted across Rhett's lips. "Not unless you're Opal Smoke."

Liss gasped.

To cover up her reaction, she grabbed Rhett's hands and pulled them around her waist.

"Then I guess we don't need to worry."

This time, when they kissed, there was nothing apologetic about it. Liss felt Rhett's swirl of emotions, but now, his tenderness and desire were stronger than the guilt and hesitation.

They were both unpracticed, but it didn't matter. Their souls were in harmony in a way she never knew two souls could be. Despite their difference in size, when they were pressed together, they fit perfectly.

One of Rhett's hands came up to tangle in her hair. The other wrapped all the way around her waist, drawing her closer. Liss forgot to be self-conscious. She forgot about why this was unforgivably wrong. She wound her hands around his neck, pulling his mouth more tightly to hers.

They kissed for a long time, and yet, it wasn't enough to satisfy the ache that had started to grow inside her. When they separated, they were both breathless. Liss felt their hearts racing in time where their chests were still pressed together. Her lips felt swollen and tingly. There was a band of heat around her waist where his arm was still wound.

Liss couldn't think above the clamor of their souls. Almost like she was in a trance, Liss reached up to touch his cheek. His jaw was rough with stubble, and she liked the feel of it along her fingertips. Rhett leaned into her touch. He caught her hand before she lowered it, turning his head to kiss her palm.

"Rhett?" Wilsean's voice came from the direction of the boulder.

They sprang apart, and it was only as the cold night air took the place of Rhett's body that reality came back to strangle Liss. *What had they…what had she just done?* She mumbled out some excuse, and then she fled.

CHAPTER 16

Liss had never before felt betrayed by her own soul. She had also never hated her Extension the way she did now.

There had been plenty of times when Liss had wished for a different Extension, one that didn't let her see the parts of people they hid from everyone else. But she'd never hated being a Soul Sorter before. She didn't want to see those feelings on Rhett's soul. She didn't want to feel the warmth, longing, and conflict he felt in her presence.

And then, there was the problem of her own soul. The kiss was supposed to keep him from noticing her strange reaction when he mentioned Opal Smoke. It wasn't supposed to mean anything.

Liss was desperate to believe she wanted nothing more from Rhett than the answer to Lagonia's immunity. If she wasn't constantly surrounded by her emotions, and his, it would be easier to believe her own lie.

She had kissed the Viper. She had put her arms around the man who murdered her people. The kiss might have started out as a quick solution to her blunder, but it had quickly transformed into something entirely beyond her control. She had wanted it…wanted him. Some part of her still did.

She hadn't even gotten to Lagonia, and already, she had messed up everything. It was one thing to have saved Rhett's life before she had any idea who he was. It was another to touch him…to let him touch her…now that she knew.

And yet, there was still some part of her that refused to accept that Rhett and the Opal Slayer were the same person. He'd let those Extended boys pass through the woods without trying to hurt them. She hadn't sensed even a shred of violence or bloodlust on his soul.

Liss splashed more cold water from the stream on her face.

Everything used to be so simple. Now, she didn't know what to think. She felt sick with shame. Liss was worn out and aching from the confusion that plagued her soul. She finally fell asleep a little before dawn, with her back propped against a tree.

She woke in Rhett's tent without any memory of how she'd gotten there, even though it didn't take a genius to know *he'd* carried her. He must have also been the one who took off her shoes and pulled the blanket over her. A shiver went through her. She couldn't tell whether it was a shiver of disgust or desire. She put her fingers to her lips, remembering the way it had felt to kiss him.

The sound of metal against metal drove her out of the memory. She yanked on her shoes and slipped out of the tent.

An unexpected sight greeted her when she approached the source of the noise. Rhett was fighting Ciago and Wilsean, although Liss could tell from the way they were talking and joking that it wasn't a real fight.

Rhett held nothing but a wooden pole, and the other two were assaulting him with blows from their swords. Rhett was also shirtless. She covered her mouth as a choked sound of horror escaped her lips.

Rhett's back and chest were covered in hideous scars. There were so many that they crisscrossed and overlapped. She could see long, jagged lines where his skin had knit back together from what must have been gaping wounds. Some of the scars were black and raised, while others were white and smooth. They all bore the memory of terrible pain.

Liss didn't need to be an expert in torture to know he'd been whipped…over and over again.

There were scars that snaked around his sides and even went down his arms, like the whip had curled around his body, tearing away flesh everywhere it touched. They tracked a gruesome path down his back and disappeared beneath the waist of his pants. There was one uninterrupted scar that went from his collarbone all the way down to his chiseled abs.

Liss felt her rage bubble up to the surface. *What kind of a monster did this to him?* If she ever found out, she'd strangle him with her bare hands.

In spite of the ugly scars, she couldn't look away. She had only known Rhett when his veins were full of poison and an almost equally-debilitating antidote, so she was used to his every move being an enormous effort. That wasn't the case anymore.

Despite the obvious skill of Wilsean and Ciago, Rhett was having no trouble fending them off. His pole moved so fast it was a blur. His movements were quick and elegant, like his hands and feet knew what to do without him even needing to think about it. When Ciago's sword nicked Rhett's arm, Liss gasped. She could see blood dripping from the shallow cut, but Rhett didn't even flinch. Instead, he went on the offensive.

If Liss had thought he was fast before, it was nothing compared to the way his pole flew now. He pressed Ciago and Wilsean back as though they were the ones who were at a disadvantage in this fight rather than he.

There was a deadly grace about all of them, but it was clear Ciago and Wilsean, even together, were no match for Rhett. There was a quiet sureness to his every movement as he spun and blocked and drove the others back.

The men were joking as they continued to rain blows down on each other. It was one of the most bizarre sights she had ever witnessed.

Liss stayed behind one of the tents, where she could see without being seen. She was so engrossed in the practice fight she didn't hear the footsteps behind her.

"You're not the first one to look at him like that, you know."

Liss turned to see Stone, watching her watch Rhett. A nervous little shudder went through her. She wondered how long he'd been right behind her.

She could feel Stone's dislike for her. She wanted nothing more than to be able to tell him the feeling was mutual. Last night, Rhett had told her that Stone had been his guardian and raised him until he was eighteen. Liss couldn't imagine what it must have been like to be raised by someone whose soul held so much bitterness.

"How exactly am I looking at him?" she asked.

"With longing," Stone said, his voice taking on a harsh edge. "I advise you to put whatever fantasies you have of being together out of your mind."

Instead of responding to that, Liss asked, "How did Rhett get all those scars?"

"Some are from battle. Some are from me."

"*You?*"

Liss couldn't believe it. Why hadn't she felt any hatred, or at least resentment, when Rhett talked about Stone? Why hadn't Rhett killed Stone for doing this to him?

"You were his guardian," Liss said through gritted teeth. "You were supposed to protect him."

"I did," Stone snarled in reply. "I'm the only reason that boy is still alive."

Liss felt the prickle of tears in her eyes. She just shook her head, too overcome to speak.

And she thought her mom was a negligent parent.

"It looks to me like you did everything you could to break him," she finally managed.

"That's right," Stone replied. "I taught him to be strong. Do you have any idea what would have happened to him if I hadn't made him what he is?" Stone answered his own question. "He's Jaikon's half-brother. If I hadn't turned him into the most lethal weapon on the continent, Jaikon's first decree as emperor would have been to have him killed."

"You protected him from Jaikon by beating him almost to death?" Liss asked, her voice dripping with disgust.

"I will not see his body tossed over the Lagonia cliffs," Stone said, his voice fierce in its vehemence. "His life may be hard, even unpleasant at times, but I gave him the tools to keep possession of his own mind and survive. It was the greatest gift I could give him."

"You are seriously deranged," Liss hissed, feeling her entire body tremble with rage. This man was a stark reminder of all Lagonia stood for. She couldn't imagine how Rhett could even stand the sight of him.

"You can put aside any notions you might have of saving him," Stone told her. "Rhett is damaged beyond repair, at least as far as you're concerned. He may look whole, but everything he hides on the inside is tearing him apart."

"That doesn't sound like someone who is broken to me." Liss glared at the monster standing before her. "It sounds like someone who still knows how to be kind, even though you've literally tried to beat it out of him."

"There is no place in our world for kindness. Those scars are a reminder of every unnecessary risk Rhett has ever taken."

Liss thought about how Burk was always yelling at her for taking unnecessary risks. She thought about what her skin would look like if he'd marked her the way Stone had whipped Rhett. She couldn't imagine it.

"What kind of mistakes could he have possibly made to deserve that?" she demanded.

Stone sighed, and for the first time, he looked weary instead of angry. It didn't soften Liss's feelings toward him even a little.

"Mistakes like *forgetting* to report the names of citizens who couldn't pay their taxes," Stone replied. "Or bringing medicine to a girl the Emperor had harmed." Stone was quiet for a moment. "I once caught him nursing a dragon the young Jaikon had tortured."

Liss's heart ached for that boy. She knew Rhett still had that kindness in his soul, despite everything Stone had done to destroy it. It explained why Rhett's face expressed nothing while his soul felt everything.

"If I were him, I would have killed you," she said with venom.

"Rhett understands what you, as an outsider, can never fathom," Stone replied. "Kindness is a weakness. And weaknesses are exploited."

Liss had heard enough. She was sick with everything Stone had told her. She was sick from the sight of Rhett's scars that were forever burned into her brain.

CHAPTER 17

Rhett didn't know how to act around Liss anymore. He had seen her talking to Stone. She had looked angry, and he could only image what Stone was saying to her. He'd been so busy looking at her that Ciago had managed to cut him while they sparred, a fact that his friend hadn't stopped bragging about all morning.

Something had changed in Liss. She still chatted with Ciago and Wilsean, but it wasn't the same as it had been before. Rhett kept his distance and could feel her doing the same.

He should never have kissed her. He had known it even in the moments before their lips touched, but he'd done it anyway. Rhett had hoped it would get that almost desperate pull he felt to Liss out of his system.

Kissing her had had the opposite effect. All he could think about…all he wanted…was to do it again. And again.

They had all washed and were planning to head out in search of the Extended caravan once again when Rhett's nerves started to tingle. Something wasn't right. He knew it even before the rest of his senses caught up with his instincts.

Their camp lay just off the road between Insorsil and Lagonia. At this time in the morning, he should be able to hear the loud thrum of Insorsiled bikes, the chatter of pixies, and the roar of dragons. He heard none of it.

Rhett stood up, unsheathing his dagger. The others looked at him, taking only a second to make the same observation and ready their own weapons. They spread out in formation without needing to exchange even a glance. Rhett gestured to Liss to stay behind one of the tents.

The silence was punctuated by a single scream. Something came tumbling down the steep embankment in the distance. Even from here, Rhett could tell it was a body.

They stalked forward. Silence had fallen again. No one came in pursuit of the body, which hadn't moved. Rhett reached the body first. It was a witch, her green dress now stained brown from the blood leaking from her chest. Rhett hoped Liss didn't know the woman.

The Insorsiled weren't usually murder victims. Queen Gatria had solid trade agreements with all of the empires, and her people were protected under those agreements. Rhett signaled Wilsean to cover them from higher ground as he, Stone, and Ciago continued up the embankment to the road.

As soon as he stepped onto the road, Rhett understood the situation. He counted thirty men. Their tangled beards and animal-hide pelts haphazardly sewn together into cloaks gave them away as humans who lived in the Giant Realm. These men were as ruthless as the climate in which they lived, and in Rhett's experience, twice as brutal as the giants they lived among.

These degenerate members of the human race were Lagonia's enemies. While Rhett was wearing the nondescript black clothes that let him slip into wagons and slit throats unseen and unheard, his men wore the black-and-gold livery of the Lagonia guard.

Rhett heard the savage men's feral roars as they caught sight of him, Stone, and Ciago.

Wilsean's arrows took down five of them before they descended on his army of three.

Their enemies were all muscle and brute strength. Whatever the giants fed them made even the smallest among them as big as Ciago. Rhett didn't have time to wonder at what these men were doing on this side of the sea.

His muscles burned from disuse, but all remnants of the poison were gone. It was too bad for their enemy. They were strong and furious, but they were no match for the four most lethal soldiers in Lagonia. Rhett killed half of them himself, and his men made short work of the rest.

The last body fell against the cobbled road with a thud.

"Still moving a little slow, eh?" Ciago asked Rhett. "Looks like you even broke a sweat."

"Rhett!"

He whipped around at the sound of Wilsean's voice. It took him less than an instant to take in the scene before him. Wilsean had an arrow pointed just off the road. One of the wild men had gotten away, and he held the blade of his axe against Liss's throat. For the first time in as long as he could remember, Rhett felt afraid.

Liss's captor kept shifting and dragging her with him, making it impossible for Wilsean to get a clear shot.

Fighting every instinct he had, Rhett forced himself to stay motionless and keep his face free of any expression that would give him away.

"Why don't you let her go." Ciago, who was closest, lowered his sword and took a step forward.

The man wound his hand into Liss's hair and yanked her head back, further exposing her throat to his rusted blade. Rhett's fury knew no bounds. Death would be too good for this man.

"Here's what's going to happen," Rhett said, his voice itself a brandished weapon. "I'm going to come forward so you can see my face."

He did, letting the man get a good look at him.

"I'm Lagonia's Chief Assassin," he said evenly, forcing himself to keep eye contact with the brute instead of looking at Liss. "And I'm going to give you ten seconds."

He made a show of signaling to Wilsean to lower his bow.

"You can use those ten seconds to kill the girl, or you can run. Whatever you choose, at the end of ten seconds, I'm coming after you."

Indecision flashed across the brute's face.

"Ten," called Ciago.

"Nine," yelled Wilsean.

"Eight."

The man threw Liss forward and fled in the opposite direction. Rhett twirled the dagger around in his hand, counting down in his head. He was a man of his word.

When he got to one, he threw the dagger.

CHAPTER 18

Liss's hands were shaking. Her whole body was shaking. She didn't know if it was from her near-death or from what she'd just witnessed.

Up until this morning, she had almost managed to convince herself Rhett wasn't the Opal Slayer. But she couldn't deny the truth any longer. Rhett must have killed fifteen of those men without batting an eye. He hadn't even been breathing hard after.

There had been a cold, almost inhuman look about him as he threw his dagger at least a hundred feet into the back of her captor's neck. Liss shuddered.

They were back in their camp now. Stone, Wilsean, and Ciago were cleaning the blood from their weapons and debating what business men from the Giant Realm might have had on this side of the sea. Rhett had disappeared, probably to recover his dagger.

When he returned a few minutes later, his dagger free of blood like it hadn't just been used to slaughter fifteen people, Rhett's gaze went straight to Liss. He approached her slowly, like she was a frightened animal that might spook and bolt. Part of her wanted to do just that.

"Are you alright?" he asked.

Even though she knew to expect it, she was overwhelmed by feeling as his emotions surrounded her.

"Fine," she managed.

Rhett reached out and took the cloth Wilsean had given her. The cut on her neck wasn't deep, but she could feel the blood dripping down the collar of her shirt.

He examined the wound.

Liss felt anger in his soul, even though the cut wasn't even as deep as the one Ciago had given Rhett this morning. He went over to one of their supply bags and rummaged around until he found what he was looking for. He returned with a bandaging kit and a jar of quick-heal.

Rhett knelt on the ground before her. He reached for her, but she flinched away.

"I'll do it," she said.

"Your hands are shaking," he replied gruffly. "You'll make it worse."

With little choice, Liss relented. More gently than she would have expected from someone who had just killed fifteen men, Rhett cleaned away the blood. As he dabbed the quick-heal along the cut, she shivered from the feeling of his fingers on her neck.

"Sorry," he murmured. "Almost finished."

She was distantly aware of Wilsean and Ciago making fun of Rhett for tending to her wound, and Stone glaring at her. Rhett ignored them. Liss couldn't concentrate on much besides his fingers on her neck.

Her reaction to all of this was wrong. She should be terrified of Rhett instead of missing his touch the moment he lowered his hand. *What was wrong with her?*

"Better?" Rhett asked her.

"Don't think this makes us even," Liss said with a shaky little laugh.

Rhett smiled. "Believe me, I know it doesn't."

Why was he making it so hard for her to hate him?

Rhett tore a small piece of gauze from a roll and ripped off a piece of tape. Even though he hadn't bothered to clean or dress the wound on his arm, he meticulously folded the gauze and taped it over the cut on her throat.

"I don't want that to happen to you again," Rhett said, his eyes fixed on his work. "So as soon as you're feeling up for it, I'm going to teach you how to fight."

Liss started. She hadn't been expecting that. "You're going to teach me how to kill people like you?"

The words came out with more bitterness than she'd intended.

Rhett's gaze pierced her. "This is who I am," he said.

Careful, she warned herself. Rhett might be a lot of things, but he wasn't stupid. She might be able to see the warring emotions inside his soul, but she didn't need to give him the same view into hers.

"I know," she said, forcing her tense muscles to relax. "It's just…a lot to take in."

Rhett nodded. "I can teach you how to protect yourself so you won't be vulnerable like that again." He paused. "If you'll let me."

"I guess that would be helpful," she said.

Rhett got to his feet. He took two steps before turning back.

"One other thing," Rhett said. "Your hair."

"My hair?" she asked, confused.

"I know the Insorsiled prize long hair, but it's too easy for an enemy to grab." He picked up his dagger from the ground—the dagger he'd used to kill fifteen men—and came back to her. He gave her a questioning look.

"I'm not Insorsiled anymore," Liss said, turning to give him access to her matted locks.

Liss couldn't stop the thrill that passed through her when Rhett's fingers brushed against her hair. There was regret in his soul, and Liss wondered if he was thinking about how he had held it while they kissed. Her cheeks heated at the memory.

There was no pressure or pulling as Rhett's sharp blade sliced through the strands. She saw the mass of hair fall to the ground and felt a sudden weightlessness.

Ciago whistled. "Looking good, Lovely Liss."

✳ ✳ ✳

The men decided, in part from her gentle suggestions, to return to Lagonia the following day. Liss was itching to begin her search of the palace and to find something of use that she could share with Burk. She had already exchanged several messages with him through the onyx stone, and she could sense in the curt messages his disappointment that she hadn't yet discovered anything of value. Of course, if she had mentioned where she was and who she was with, Burk might have had more to say.

While Stone and Wilsean made dinner, Liss had her first training session with Rhett. At least he kept his shirt on. She didn't think she could handle that kind of distraction when she was trying to duck away from the wooden pole she was quickly learning to loathe.

Rhett was patient, but relentless. Ciago, who was sprawled on the ground, shouted advice and encouragement to her.

"Get that pole away from Rhett and I'll let you ride back to Lagonia on my dragon," he said.

When she managed to block a single one of Rhett's strikes with her own pole, Ciago hooted.

Afterward, when Liss's arms and backside were so sore she didn't know how she'd manage to ride a dragon the next day, Ciago slung one of his giant arms over her shoulders.

"Lovely Liss," he said, "I think it's time for both of us to stop playing hard to get and just admit that we're meant to be together."

Liss snorted in response.

"I'll even forgive *the plate incident*, and we can try again. What do you say?"

Liss felt Rhett's irritation flare even though his face remained as impassive as ever.

Even though her muscles screamed in protest, Liss used one of the moves Rhett had just taught her, jabbing Ciago in the stomach with her elbow and stomping on his foot.

Ciago let out a little yelp and hopped back on his good foot.

"I told you you'd only get one kiss," Liss reminded him.

Rhett was staring at her. She made a point of not looking into his soul. She didn't want to know what he was feeling. But she couldn't stop herself from returning his smile.

Rhett was still her best chance at getting access to the palace's hidden rooms and discovering the information that would reveal Lagonia's greatest secret. Getting close to him was strategic. Once she had what she needed, she'd return to her own people. They would destroy the source of Lagonia's immunity, and then even being in her presence could be a death sentence for Rhett.

Anything they might be feeling for each other was temporary. There was no world in which whatever strange connection they had formed over the last several days could last. They could never be anything besides enemies.

The thought brought her a sense of relief.

CHAPTER 19

Rhett woke well before dawn and busied himself with packing their supplies. It wasn't that he was eager to get back to Lagonia. He was restless. Opal Smoke's trail was cold, and there was nothing more that could be done until new information surfaced. He had already gone for a run and worked out, but it wasn't enough to quiet his mind.

Once everyone else was awake, it took only a few minutes to collapse the Insorsiled tents and pack them into the larger travel bags that were strapped to the dragons' backs. As they worked, Rhett noticed how Liss made a point of keeping her distance.

He kept his attention fixed on his task, even though he could sense the moment she returned from washing her face in the stream.

"Looking good this morning, Lovely Liss!" Ciago called.

Rhett didn't need to look up to know it was true. Even with her hair shorn and the stained clothes she had worn since she saved his life, Liss was still beautiful.

Things had been awkward between them since their kiss. In the nights since, he'd found himself sitting alone during his watch, straining to hear the sound of soft footsteps that never came. And then there was the whole episode with the wild men. He couldn't get the sight of that axe held to her throat out of his mind. Rhett didn't scare easily…he couldn't even remember the last time he'd been afraid…but that image continued to haunt him.

"Better leave your bike behind," Wilsean was advising Liss. "The laws for Empties in Lagonia are the same as those in Insorsil."

"You can ride back with me," Ciago said, winking at her. "My dragon's small, so we'll have to sit *really* close together."

Rhett knew Ciago was only joking. Ciago was overly familiar with everyone, especially beautiful women. The reactions he got were mixed, but it never inspired him to change. Usually, being the son of the wealthiest and most influential family in the empire was enough to make any woman he set his gaze on giggle and preen. Liss didn't seem to care about that, though.

Rhett kept his distance as Ciago continued to bait Liss, making all kinds of insane promises if she only agreed to ride back to Lagonia on his dragon. Rhett knew his friend wasn't serious, but it didn't stop him from wanting to kill Ciago.

Rhett noticed Wilsean had piled the majority of their baggage onto his own dragon, so there was barely room for him to squeeze on. Rhett suspected Wilsean might have done that on purpose. And with the mood Stone was in this morning, Rhett didn't think Liss would want to ride with him. Rhett focused on tying up the last of their supplies while Liss deliberated.

The thought of spending two days with mere inches separating them was both a fantasy and a nightmare.

"I like Silverbird," Liss said going to stand on the dragon's opposite side.

Rhett's heart did ridiculous acrobatics in his chest.

"I'm sure you do," Stone growled as saddled his own dragon.

Silverbird blew out a puff of smoke as she nuzzled Liss's pockets.

"Here." Rhett took a fistful of gold nuggets and deposited them into Liss's hand. Their fingers brushed, and even that small touch sparked something inside him.

I am steel, he reminded himself.

"What's this for?" Liss asked, looking at the tiny fortune now sitting in her palm.

"Silverbird's snack. That's what she was looking for in your pockets."

Liss offered the handful to Silverbird. She smiled as the dragon lapped up the coins. *Damn,* there was that dimple again. He wanted to touch it. He wanted to kiss it.

Rhett cleared his throat. "Ready?" he asked her.

She was too short to reach the stirrup, so Rhett hoisted Liss onto Silverbird's back before climbing on behind her. The slope of the saddle made it so that she was practically on his lap. He felt her whole body tense against him.

"Is this okay?" he asked in a low voice so the others wouldn't hear.

His breath stirred her now short hair, and she shivered.

"Fine," she said as she gathered up the reins.

Rhett could sense Liss's nervousness. He tried to think of what to say to put her at ease, but he felt jittery himself. He hadn't been this near to her since they'd kissed, and he craved the closeness with an intensity that was difficult to fathom. He should have encouraged her to ride with Ciago…it would have been safer for them both.

They hardly talked for the first several hours. Every time one of them shifted in the saddle, it somehow brought them closer together. Rhett tried to distract himself by reviewing what he would say to Jaikon when they returned, but even that unpleasant thought wasn't enough to make him forget about her warmth pressed against him.

Liss sighed and leaned her head back against his chest. She was relaxed now, when a few minutes ago, Rhett could feel her tension. He realized she had dozed off. He wrapped one of his arms around her, making sure she wouldn't be thrown from the saddle if Silverbird tripped over the uneven ground.

Holding her felt like the most natural thing in the world.

"What the hell are you doing?" Stone demanded. He reined in his dragon to glare at Rhett.

"Would you rather I let her fall and get trampled?" Rhett retorted, keeping his voice low so he wouldn't wake her.

"Well, you don't have to look so comfortable about it."

"She saved his life," Wilsean said, coming to Rhett's defense. "The man's entitled to a little gratitude."

Stone just huffed.

As dusk fell, they reached the part of the Insorsiled forest that belonged to the tree fairies. The tiny lights of their tree dwellings blinked in the branches overhead. Liss tiled her head to stare up at the lights.

"So beautiful," she murmured.

Rhett was still watching Liss crane her neck to see the lights when Silverbird started to blow out smoke and toss her head. A swarm of tree fairy children had descended on Silverbird and were pulling on the dragon's whiskers.

"Stop it," Liss told the children.

The fairies only bared their tiny, pointed teeth and laughed. Liss pulled on the reins as the dragon started to dance in place.

"Relax," Rhett told Silverbird.

"Are you talking to me or the dragon?" Liss asked.

Silverbird shied again. Rhett felt Liss's breath catch as he wrapped his arms around her to close his hands on the reins. He murmured to Silverbird, quieting the dragon.

"Loosen your grip," Rhett told Liss.

"What?" she turned her head. He leaned back before her face collided with his.

"Oh," she said, flustered.

There was nothing Rhett could do about the pounding of his heart, and he was sure she must feel its frantic rhythm. They were too close. She was too beautiful.

The diabolical little tree fairies abandoned Silverbird's snout and started to swarm around Liss and Rhett's heads. Each one of them was about the size of Rhett's pinky finger. The buzz of their double wings was drowned out by the annoying sound they were all making.

Rhett felt Liss tense. At the same moment, he realized what noise the fairy children were making. They were zooming around Liss and Rhett's heads making kissing noises. One of the fairies got right in Liss's face and made a show of making out with a phantom lover. Rhett saw her cheeks turn scarlet.

"Get lost." Rhett swatted at them, but they just zoomed out of his reach, only to reconvene to continue with their bawdy taunts.

"Where are your parents?" Liss demanded.

"Kiss, and we'll go away," one of the fairy children said in a sing-song voice.

Rhett felt blood rush to his face. The fairies noticed, and it only incited them. The others took up the refrain as they buzzed around, cackling and continuing their gleeful provocation.

His only consolation was that the other three dragons were far enough ahead that their riders couldn't hear the taunts or witness this insanity. The last thing Rhett needed was more teasing from Ciago and more glares from Stone.

"Are they going to follow us all the way to Lagonia?" Liss asked, sounding a little distressed.

"Kiss, and we'll go away!"

Liss sighed and turned. She reached up, putting a hand on Rhett's cheek. He went stock-still as her eyes met his. He forgot about the fairies and the prancing dragon beneath them. She was all he could see. Liss planted a quick kiss on his lips that was over as quickly as it began.

Rhett had to stop himself from pulling her face back to his.

"There," she said, turning back to the children. "Now, go away."

Still cackling in amusement, they buzzed off, leaving Rhett and Liss with a storm of emotions.

* * *

It was late the following night when the Golden Bridge came into view. Rhett could just make out the outline of the hundred archers stationed on the bridge. Their black-and-gold armor gleamed in the light of the full, blue moon.

Liss saw them, too, and Rhett felt her shudder.

"Don't worry," Rhett said in her ear. "They're just for show now."

She relaxed a little. "You mean now that Lagonians can't get opal contagion?"

"That's right," Rhett replied.

"Everyone must be very grateful for whatever has given them their new freedom," Liss said.

"It's changed everything. People don't need to fear leaving the empire anymore."

Liss tilted her head, considering. "People must be curious about how it all works…the immunity, I mean."

"I suppose," he said carefully. He didn't like the direction this conversation was heading.

"Don't people ever ask you about it?" Liss persisted. "I mean, if I were Lagonian, I'd want to know what was making me safe from the Extended."

He could feel her waiting for his response.

"The penalty for even mentioning the immunity is death," he told her.

"Oh." She faltered.

Rhett was grateful she let the conversation drop and relieved she hadn't asked him point-blank.

He wasn't surprised she was curious. He had heard at least a hundred different theories about the cause of their immunity to the contagion. None of them even came close to the truth. The small group who knew the secret kept it well. Rhett couldn't even imagine the disaster that would ensue if the secret got out.

They stopped their dragons well before they reached the bridge.

Stone, who had been growing surlier the closer they got to the empire, asked, "How do you plan to deal with the girl?"

"The girl has a name," Liss replied.

Something had happened between the two of them. Rhett guessed his mentor had probably said something to try to make her stay away from Rhett. He would have been angry, but he knew Stone was only trying to protect him. Liss was everything Stone had raised him to avoid.

"You can't very well just march her across the bridge like that," Stone continued, ignoring Liss.

The thought had already occurred to Rhett.

"Send me Dannica," Rhett told Stone. "I'll take care of it."

After the others had gone on ahead, Rhett told Liss, "We're getting off here."

He wasn't going to give Jaikon's men the opportunity to witness him riding into the empire with Liss virtually in his arms. It would be dangerous for her and lethal for him. The fewer people who knew Liss even existed, the better for them both.

Rhett jumped off Silverbird first.

He helped Liss down, pulling his hands off her waist as soon as she was on the ground.

"Thanks," she mumbled.

He should say something to her.

"We're going to bring you into the palace in a way that won't cause any extra attention," he said, sticking to practical matters so he wouldn't have to think about the parts he didn't know how to deal with. "This way, you won't have to worry about a bunch of curious Lagonians poking around in your business."

"Sounds good to me," Liss said, looking relieved. She probably was as interested in telling everyone she was banished from Insorsil as he was in telling Jaikon a slaver had almost killed him.

Rhett caught sight of Dannica as she stepped off the bridge and headed toward them. She was dressed in the full regalia of the Lagonia guard, even though she wasn't on duty tonight. Her hair was pulled back in a tight braid, and her polished dragonhide boots clipped against the cobblestones.

Rhett felt a moment of hesitation as he watched one of his most trusted soldiers approach. What he was about to ask would put her at risk. He hated to involve anyone else, especially one of his soldiers, in the mess that was his lethal game with Jaikon.

"Welcome home, Rhett," Dannica said, saluting him.

Jaikon liked to loudly proclaim that a commander who allowed his soldiers to call him by his first name would never be respected, but Rhett knew better. He had never desired for anyone, least of all his soldiers, to stand on ceremony with him.

"Hey, Dannica," he replied.

"Who's the Insorsiled?" she asked, giving Liss an appraising glance.

"That's the thing," Rhett said without answering her question. "I was hoping she could borrow some of your clothes so she'll look a little less...."

"Insorsiled?" Dannica replied.

Rhett nodded.

Dannica didn't miss a beat. "We're about the same height, so my fatigues should fit well enough. I'll go get them."

Rhett felt enormous gratitude, but he was also guilty. "If you'd rather not take the risk," he began, but Dannica waved him off.

"Give me five minutes," she said, marching back toward the bridge.

Rhett gestured for Liss to stand next to Silverbird where she'd be hidden from the soldiers on the bridge.

"What's going to cause more talk," Liss began, "that I'm an Empty coming into Lagonia, or that I'm coming into Lagonia with you?"

She was more perceptive than he gave her credit for.

"There are too many bored gossip mongers in Lagonia, and there are people who would love nothing more than to cause you harm if they thought it would matter to me."

"Do I matter to you?" That dimple appeared again as she stared up at him, like she already knew the answer and just wanted to see him squirm.

"I owe you a blood debt," he said. "And now that you're in my empire, I'll do everything in my power to keep you safe."

"I see," Liss said, smirking a little.

Rhett got the feeling she saw more than he wanted her to…more than was good for either of them.

While they waited for Dannica, Rhett scanned the area. He'd sent a pixie ahead of them to tell Jaikon they were returning…without Opal Smoke's head…and he half-expected to find one of Jaikon's people waiting to escort him to the throne room. Or maybe, the executioner's platform.

Dannica returned with a black canvas bag. She walked around Silverbird so the dragon's bulk hid her from view before she started to unload the bag. Her discreetness was one of the qualities Rhett appreciated most about her. That, and her brutal efficiency on the battlefield.

Dannica handed Liss a uniform. Liss looked at him and raised her eyebrows.

"What's wrong?" he asked.

"Can I have some privacy?" Liss gave him a pointed stare.

"Oh, right." He strode several feet away, his face burning.

"Okay," she called after a minute.

Rhett gave her a quick, appraising glance. "Good enough."

Dannica stuffed Liss's old clothes into the canvas bag. "I'll dispose of these for you," she said to Liss. "Keep the uniform as long as you need."

"Thanks, Dannica," Rhett told her.

"Don't mention it." She saluted Rhett, and then she was heading back to the bridge.

"Ready?" Rhett asked Liss.

She took a deep breath and nodded.

Rhett greeted the archers with a nod and a few words. They were all bored out of their minds. Now that there was no threat of opal contagion, Lagonia had no enemies on this side of the sea. Any attack that came would approach from the port on the other side of the palace. Rhett had made the argument to Jaikon that the archers' talents were wasted on the bridge, but Jaikon had liked the optics of a hundred soldiers in black and gold regalia on the bridge, so the archers had remained.

Liss kept her head down as they crossed to the other side. Rhett handed Silverbird's reins to one of the stable boys waiting for them.

There was a strangeness to being in Lagonia with Liss. For the last week, they had been existing in what now felt like an entirely separate world from the one they were in now.

As they crossed the gemstone-studded walkway that led from the bridge to the center of town, Rhett watched Liss take in her surroundings. The opulence of Lagonia was on full display, as it was most nights. He didn't know which part of Insorsil she had lived in—he had avoided asking her about it, since he didn't want to cause her pain by reminding her of home but it must have been nothing like what she saw now.

Liss took in the floating Insorsiled lamps bobbing over the path and the tented pavilions lined up along the road. He led her over a small arch bridge. Beneath the bridge flowed a stream of molten gold. The gold was Insorsiled to stay at a precise temperature so that it would continuously flow without ever congealing, no matter the weather. Jaikon, Sr. had spent more jewels on that one bit of magic than most Lagonians made in a lifetime.

"Everything here is just so…beautiful." Liss frowned, and Rhett thought he understood what she was thinking.

"Most Lagonians value beauty and pleasure above all else," he said.

A group of dazzling, costumed dancers passed them, as though to illustrate Rhett's point. They were laughing and stumbling a little, and the scent of honeyed wine and expensive perfume followed in their wake.

"Seems like a giant waste of money to me," she commented.

Rhett shrugged. "Money isn't a concern for people around here."

Something darkened in her gaze. Maybe her family wasn't as well-off as he'd assumed.

Rhett felt an urge to explain himself. He knew about the poverty that plagued the other lands, and he hadn't meant to minimize their struggles.

They passed the small house of worship, which was probably the only building in the whole empire that wasn't adorned with precious gems and the most expensive materials. There were few who regularly worshipped the gods. More often, Lagonians maintained a casual belief in one god or multiple gods—there was disagreement on even that point. For the most part, the house of worship was empty except for women praying for suitors or merchants praying for a profitable haul.

Liss was staring at one of the street vendors, her mouth pressed in a tight line. The customer was unloading chunks of rubies onto the scale perched on the counter as the vendor handed over a cage crammed full of pixies. The pixies fluttered their wings and wrapped their fingers around the bars, hissing and cursing. The new owner struck the cage, and the pixies stopped chattering.

"Come on," Rhett said to Liss, not wanting her to see this side of Lagonia. For reasons he didn't care to examine, he wanted her first impression of Lagonia to be a favorable one.

He kept Liss far away from the side of town where the black market was located. It was run and operated by men who paid Jaikon a hefty sum to ensure soldiers looked the other way.

At this time of night, the black market would be in full swing. Courtiers would be lingering in alleys to purchase small bags of drugs or crowded around one of the underground dragon fighting dens, both of which were illegal but frequented by Lagonia's most elite. He also steered clear of the section of town that held the brothels, which were known for taking their raucous partying into the streets.

"I think you might like this part of town better," Rhett said.

Musicians stood in the street, playing their instruments for the sheer joy of it. Artists displayed their sculptures and paintings under bright, white Insorsiled lamps. Precious gems were exchanged for bolts of imported silks and small tins of deep-sea fish eggs.

Couples strolled along the street. The women's throats and ears glittered with ridiculously huge gems. They giggled and stumbled into each other and tossed gold nuggets to the peddlers on the street in exchange for flower garlands and sugared plums. The fountain in the street's center had been Insorsiled to change color to the beat of whichever musician was playing nearest.

Rhett never had cause to visit this part of town, so it felt almost as new to him as it was to Liss. Liss inhaled deeply, her dimple making its first appearance since they arrived.

"What is that smell?" she asked.

Rhett led her over to a stall with a banner hovering above it that read "Life's short…eat cake," where he exchanged the leftover nuggets he'd brought for Silverbird for a slice of Lagonia's famous gold cake. It was made with real gold ground into the flour…along with other ingredients. The vendor handed Liss the cake, along with a solid gold fork.

Liss took a bite, and her eyes bugged out.

"This is the most delicious thing I've ever tasted," she exclaimed, her words slightly garbled as she took another bite.

"I thought you'd like it." He grinned. "They say there's three different kinds of sugar in it. Probably keep you up all night."

"So worth it." She took another bite. And then, giving him a suspicious look and clutching the plate to her chest, she said, "Just so you know, I'm rather possessive when it comes to cake."

Rhett put up his hands and backed up a step, trying to hide his amusement.

There were Insorsiled potions many Lagonians—both men and women—drank after eating that would bring whatever they'd just consumed back out so they could have their dessert while maintaining their pristine figures. Liss didn't seem to care about that, even though her figure was…more than perfect. He watched, mesmerized, as she licked frosting off the fork.

She looked up at him and smiled.

Did she know how maddening she was being?

The night was balmy, especially compared to the chill air on the plains. For a second, Rhett felt almost like they were one of the couples out for a late-night stroll. It was a ridiculous, indulgent thought.

Steel doesn't know love or despair. It can't be bent or broken. It needs no heart or warmth. I am steel.

"We've wasted too much time," he said. "Let's go."

CHAPTER 20

Liss's mom had told her about Lagonia's opulence, but nothing could have prepared her for the sheer magnitude of it all.

The women looked like peacocks, with their frilly dresses and sparkling jewels. So did the men, for that matter. They preened and stuck out their chests as they loudly discussed their new land acquisitions or the next party they were throwing.

Every person they passed was more beautiful than the last. They were all using Insorsil illusion, of course, which made them look slightly unreal. It was like looking at people's reflections in a still lake rather than at the people themselves. Some of the illusions were stronger than others, and Liss could see the weaker ones flicker as aspects of the person's true appearance became visible.

Liss was disgusted by the flagrant extravagance that was possible, in part, from the taxes her people paid. But she couldn't deny the empire's appeal. Everything was color and light and beauty. It was mesmerizing.

They passed two women leaning against one of the vendor stalls. They had been kissing each other, but at the sight of Rhett, they started to giggle and make *come hither* motions at him. He ignored them.

"Wow," Liss breathed, as the palace loomed ahead. It was enormous and golden, with towering black turrets that were topped with gold and black banners. The two halves of the palace were joined by a bridge that must have been fifty feet off the ground. There were lights hovering over the bridge, and Liss could see the gleam of sapphires embedded in the railing.

Every window in the towering palace was blazing with light. It was the most magnificent and terrifying building Liss had ever seen.

"Any second thoughts?" Rhett asked.

She shook her head, but for the first time, it truly struck her what she was doing. Her breathing grew shallow.

What had she been thinking? She was a thief, not a spy. Burk had been right….

"I can imagine how…much this must all be for you," Rhett said in his low, rough voice. "If there's anything I can do to make it easier, all you need to do is say the word."

In that case, why don't you just tell me where you hide Lagonia's stash of immunity, and I'll be on my way?

But Liss knew better than to mention the immunity. When she'd brought it up in conversation earlier, she'd confirmed what she already suspected…Rhett knew the secret. When he told her the penalty for discussing the source of their immunity was death, Liss had found herself hesitant to push him any farther. Something Stone had said to her days ago about bodies being thrown over cliffs had left an impression on her.

Liss knew she should wish for the Chief Assassin's death. She should do everything she could to bring it about rather than safeguarding his life. But try as she might to make her brain see reason, her soul still just saw Rhett, the man she'd found dying in a field.

Now that they were back in his empire, she had no doubt Rhett's true colors would emerge. Then, she'd have no trouble stealing Lagonia's secret from him. She would be the reason their immunity was destroyed. Lagonia's Chief Assassin would die along with the rest of the empire. And she would go home, to her own people.

Already, their kiss felt like another lifetime ago. Or a dream.

"Liss?" Rhett asked. She felt his anxiety spike as he studied her.

"I'd like to continue our sparring lessons," she said, surprising both of them.

As soon as she spoke the words, she knew it was a good idea. It would give her a reason to see Rhett every so often, and she could use that time to lure out his secrets. Even if he wouldn't tell her about the immunity, there were thousands of other tidbits Lagonia's Chief Assassin would know. Everything she learned would be another weapon for her people to wield against his.

"Of course," was all he said. The emotions on his soul were too confused for even her to make sense of. She wondered what he was thinking.

Guards and servants crowded the palace entrance. At the sight of Rhett, everyone moved out of the way. When they first arrived in Lagonia, it had surprised Liss to sense the genuine love and respect the archers on the bridge felt toward Rhett. She encountered those same emotions in many of the guards on duty in the palace now.

Liss memorized every turn and hallway as Rhett led her deeper into the palace. It was even bigger on the inside than it had appeared on the outside, and Liss's thief eyes caught sight of at least a dozen hidden doorways and staircases nestled behind the elaborate statues and tapestries lining the walls.

Women in gowns swirled through the halls, holding glasses of champagne as they showed off the jewels glittering on their fingers. Men dressed in dark suits drank port from crystal glasses. A dense haze followed in their wake from the sweet-smelling smoke of a leaf that Liss knew came from across the sea. She'd once had the good fortune to steal a jewel-encrusted box filled with the leaves, and had been shocked to discover the value of the leaves outmatched the jewels by about a thousand-fold.

Peacocks, Liss thought.

"Keep your head down," Rhett muttered to her. It was the first he'd spoken since they entered the palace. She could feel his discomfort and embarrassment, and she wondered if it could possibly be for the same reason she felt disgusted with these people.

A group of five men dressed in gold robes were coming down the hallway toward them.

"Rhetteman," one of them called out, lifting a glass in their direction. "You've put our Emperor in a mood this time!"

Rhett kept walking, but that strange stillness that came over him whenever his emotions spiked was there now. To anyone but her, he looked like the picture of calm disinterest. It was truly impressive how he could hide so much.

"Councilmen," Rhett said in a tight greeting as he strode past. Liss had to hurry to keep up with him.

"Tomorrow we should like to speak with you," one of the councilmen called after him. "There seems to be a discrepancy in our accounts that we'll need to hammer out."

Liss felt Rhett's irritation. They turned a corner into the first empty hallway Liss had seen since entering the palace.

"Friends of yours?" Liss murmured.

"No." Rhett gave her a small, humorless smile. "I sometimes forget to have my soldiers collect taxes from the outer villages."

"How careless of you," Liss said, trying to ignore the annoying little flip her heart did. So what if he helped out a few Lagonian peasants? It hadn't helped her own people when he hunted down their caravans and slit their throats.

Rhett stopped walking. He scanned the hallway, and confirming they were alone, said, "There's something you need to understand about the empire. Deception flows here as freely as the wine." He stopped talking as a servant entered the hallway. When he had gone, Rhett continued, "People will befriend you and then try to use you. Don't let them."

Instead of feeling smug at the irony of him warning her about deception, Liss felt guilty. It was obvious Rhett had never once lied to her even though it was what she expected…was all she'd ever known…from every Lagonian she'd ever encountered. It was also clear that he hated this Lagonian quality, and here she was, the biggest deceiver of them all. Her guilt was quickly replaced by anger at herself for caring.

"You can trust Samara," Rhett said. "She's kind. There aren't many in this empire who are."

"Wilsean and Ciago are kind," Liss said.

"They are."

So are you, no matter how well you hide it, she almost said.

She faced him. "What about you?"

"What about me?" he asked, his voice a low rumble.

"Can I trust you?"

"You can."

She felt his honesty. Even though she knew she owed Rhett nothing, it still made her feel dirty about lying to him.

"You'll find that words come cheap," he said, looking at her in that intense way of his.

"Is that why you talk so much?" Liss asked, teasing a little.

She was rewarded with his small smile.

"In my experience, actions can be trusted," he said. "Words can't."

Rhett inclined his head, and they continued on. Each hallway they passed through was papered in gold leaf or studded with gemstones. Liss tried not to think about the gruel Mari's family had been cooking in their wagon and the all-but-empty icebox in hers.

The clank of chains made Liss turn her head. She sucked in a breath at the sight of an Extended man, his opal skin dull and his eyes empty. He was being dragged behind a woman in a white satin gown.

"I want a pastry," the woman whined. "Get me a pastry. Now."

The slave's arm, the one that wasn't clapped in iron, started to grow. It lengthened and stretched until it was on the floor. It continued to stretch. It reached all the way to the end of the hallway, turned the corner, and disappeared. A few moments later, a slithering sound announced the arm's return as the servant reeled it back.

The woman plucked the pastry out of her slave's hand before it had shrunken back to normal size.

"I wanted cherry, not apricot," the woman pouted. She tossed the pastry on the ground and then gave the chain binding her slave a yank, drawing him along behind her.

Liss was shaking with rage. She couldn't stand it. She had to do something.

Liss felt a hand on her back. Rhett gave her a little shake of his head.

She realized she had stopped walking. Rhett was beside her, and he was watching her. The Insorsiled hated Extended as much as Lagonians. Had she just given herself away before she'd seen even a single dawn in the empire? Panic started to worm its way through her fury, but when she looked into Rhett's soul, there was only pity and regret.

"I would do something about it if I could," Rhett said low enough that only she could hear him.

"Who's stopping you?" Liss asked, her voice wavering.

"The Emperor," was his only reply.

Liss bit her tongue to keep from saying anything more. *This was why she was here*, she reminded herself. She would find the cause of these monsters' immunity. Her people would destroy it. Then, Lagonians would be the ones terrified for their lives. She smiled at the thought.

They must have walked a mile just inside the palace. Liss was getting overwhelmed. How was she supposed to search someplace so enormous? And that was assuming the immunity was even in the palace to begin with. What if it wasn't here at all?

The hallway decorations went from pure luxury to utilitarian, and Liss realized they were in the servants' quarters. When they finally got to the right door, Rhett knocked.

The door flew open. A girl about Liss's age stood on the other side. Liss's first thought was that the girl was golden. Her skin was cream with a dash of honey. Her waist-length hair was a sleek curtain of gold that rippled with her every movement. There were even flecks of gold in her amber eyes.

"You must be Tamilissa Elspeth Wren," the girl said, holding out her hand. "I'm Samara Astrid Moonfall."

Liss remembered that Samara was an Empty—a real one—and felt her nerves spike.

"Nice to meet you," Liss began, but Samara was already looking past her.

"Rhett!" Samara beamed at him. "Wilsean told me about…your incident. I'm so glad you're alright." Her voice had a slight lilt. It sounded melodic after so many days of hearing only Rhett and his men's voices.

"Thanks, Samara," Rhett replied, giving her a tired smile.

Samara, who hadn't let go of Liss's hands, pulled her into the room. "It's so nice to meet you," she gushed, her eyes filling with the same warmth that reflected off her soul.

Liss liked her immediately.

Samara made a shooing motion at Wilsean, who was sprawled across the narrow bed. She gestured for Liss to sit on the bed. After riding Silverbird for two straight days, her backside was in bliss.

Rhett shut the door once they'd all squeezed into the small space. Everything about this room felt cozy. Soft pink Insorsiled lamps bobbed around the room, and the dresser and small bedside table were covered with colorful Insorsiled trinkets.

"What took you so long?" Wilsean asked, darting his eyes suggestively between Rhett and Liss. "Did you get lost in that tall grass before the bridge?"

It didn't help Liss's embarrassment that she felt Rhett's rise to match.

"Don't be a dolt," Samara told him placidly.

Liss didn't want to look at Rhett right at that moment, so instead, she turned her attention to the Insorsiled baubles and potions lined up on the dresser.

"I'm probably the only Empty who keeps in touch with my family," Samara explained, following Liss's gaze. "My siblings send me this stuff, and then I sell it to the Lagonians. Most of it's junk, but hey," she shrugged. "They keep coming back for more."

"Liss needs work in the palace, and I'd prefer her not to go through the usual channels," Rhett said. Clearly, he was finished with the small talk.

Samara nodded. "I can slip something in the head servant's tea that'll make her think Liss has been here all along." She got up and went to the dresser, selecting a small glass jar filled with cloudy gray crystals. She turned to Liss. "Three women in the Emperor's harem just lost the servant they shared. There's an opening to work for them, if you want it."

Liss tried not to look too pleased. If she really had been just an Empty in search of a new life, the position would have promised much work and little pay. But women talked, and these women had the Emperor's ear.

"I have some experience tending to needy women," Liss said. It wasn't a lie, even if her mother was likely a very different kind of needy from the Emperor's women.

"Thanks, Samara," Rhett said, his voice sounding even more gruff and masculine compared to Samara's. "I owe you for this."

Samara shook her head. "She saved your life, and she's an Empty." She smiled at Liss. "We're going to be great friends."

Liss thought so, too.

"I'll get your uniform and deal with the head servant in the morning," Samara said, covering her mouth to hide a yawn. "You can sleep here until you're assigned your own room."

"Thank you," Liss replied.

"Now, both of you, get out," Samara ordered the men. "It's late."

Wilsean got up from the floor and grabbed Samara's waist as she moved to pass him. He lifted her up, almost knocking over a row of vials balanced in a pyramid on the nightstand, and kissed her.

Before she could think better of it, Liss was looking past Wilsean and Samara for Rhett. He was looking back at her. She dropped her gaze, but she could still feel his dizzying array of emotions. It confused her own all the more.

"We'll give you a minute," Rhett said, even though neither Wilsean nor Samara was paying attention to them anymore.

Liss followed him out into the hall, shutting the door behind her.

She could feel the way their souls reached for each other, like invisible fingers that were desperate to intertwine. She took a step away from him.

"Are you doing okay?" Rhett asked her.

"Yeah, I am," she replied, feeling Rhett's shyness and uncertainty steal across her own soul. "Samara seems really nice."

Rhett nodded. "You'll want to get some sleep, but if you're up for sparring the day after, there's a training field out of view of the palace. As long as you don't mind waking up early."

At the quizzical look she gave him, he explained, "My soldiers are the only ones in the empire who wake before noontime, and even I can't get them up before seven. If we meet at dawn, we'll have a couple of hours without any unwelcome spectators."

"Are you embarrassed to be seen training an Empty?" Liss teased.

Rhett's soul rebelled, and she almost laughed. "Not at all," he said, his eyebrows furrowing. "It's just…people would have questions about why I'm training a servant. The attention wouldn't be good for either of us."

"Do you really think people would care?" Liss asked. She didn't know what information she was hoping to gain from this conversation, but the more she could learn about these people and the unwritten rules of their society, the better prepared she would be.

Rhett's restless gaze swept the hallway again before he leaned closer. "Jaikon has been looking for something to use against me since we were kids. If he gets the idea that I care what happens to you, it would put you in more danger than you can imagine."

Liss's breath hitched. She didn't have to ask if her cared about her. Rhett's answer was written plainly across his soul.

Someone, probably a servant by the looks of her, was coming toward them. Rhett murmured the directions of where they should meet. He barely moved his lips and never looked at her. As soon as he had finished speaking, he turned and walked away without another glance.

CHAPTER 21

Liss thought it would be weird spending the night with the sort-of girlfriend of a man she'd met only a week ago. As it turned out, it took about five seconds before Liss and Samara were sprawled out on the narrow bed chatting and laughing.

It was more than just their supposed commonality of both being Empties. Liss's best friends in the caravan were Spence and Mari, and they were far younger than she. As much as she didn't want to admit it, she'd loved that Ciago and Wilsean were like the adult versions of her Extended friends. But until now, Liss hadn't realized how much she'd been craving the company of a girl her own age.

They ate blue Insorsiled candy that made steam come out of their noses, and red candy that made their lips swell to quadruple their normal size. They acted like little kids as they made ridiculous noises that set their lips to jiggling. Before long, they were both clutching their stomachs as tears of laughter streamed down their faces.

Samara spent the better part of half an hour bemoaning Liss's haircut before getting a pair of scissors and working some semblance of style into it. They chatted like they had known each other for their entire lives, bonding over favorite Insorsil haunts Samara had frequented with her family, where Liss had snuck in with her crew to steal.

Liss did an admirable job of describing the neighborhood she was supposedly from. They laughed about the warlock with a wart the size of a grapefruit on his chin who stood on the corner of Alchem and Spleen Street peddling fake love charms.

Samara told Liss all about her three sisters and one brother, all of whom she still spoke with regularly even though it was illegal for Empties to communicate with any Insorsiled. Liss told Samara about her mother, changing the relevant details to make them fit with the identity she'd created for Tamilissa Elspeth Wren. Samara hadn't heard of Liss's family, which was no surprise because she'd made them up. She threw in a few tidbits about her grandparents on her fake father's side, the Widdlywinks. Liss had seen the name on an Insorsil shop window once and had decided she would very much like to be related to a Widdlywink.

After so many days spent in Rhett's serious company, Samara's perpetual good cheer was almost overwhelming. She laughed loudly and often, and the sound was infectious.

"This is the first time I've slept with someone besides Wilsean since I left Insorsil," Samara said with a sleepy giggle.

"How long have you two been together?" Liss asked.

"Oh, we're not together," Samara replied, her cheeks turning pink. "But we've been…something…for a while."

"It certainly looks like more than *something* to me," Liss smirked.

Samara's smile faltered.

"His father is one of the Emperor's advisors, and his mother is from one of the wealthiest families in the empire. Even if he wanted to, he could never bring someone like me home to his family."

"That's ridiculous," Liss said, feeling defensive of her new friend. "You should have seen Wilsean's face when he talked about you. He was practically glowing."

Samara just laughed, but Liss wasn't fooled by her flippancy. There were strong emotions in her soul that didn't lie. Liss wondered if Samara even knew they were there.

"Speaking of men," Samara said, arching a brow.

"What about them?" Liss asked. Her discomfort rose with the direction the conversation was headed.

"Rhett's got a reputation around the palace, you know," Samara said.

"For being an assassin? I think I've heard that one." Liss rolled her eyes.

"No." Samara's eyebrows crept even higher. "He doesn't date or…spend time with any women. Ever."

"Is that so unusual?" Liss asked.

"This is Lagonia," Samara reminded her.

"Well, then, maybe he's gay," Liss said with a shrug.

Samara snorted. "That wouldn't explain why Lagonia's Chief Assassin knocked on my door in the middle of the night asking for a favor for you."

"He owed me for saving his life," Liss said, trying to end the conversation.

"Maybe," Samara replied, refusing to let the subject drop. "But that also wouldn't explain why he was looking at you like that."

"Like I saved his life?" Liss drawled.

"Like he never wanted to look at anything else."

Liss's cheeks burned. "Whatever you say," she muttered.

"Rhett's a good man," Samara said, her teasing turning to earnestness. "Wilsean loves him like a brother. Any soldier in the Lagonia army would die for him without a second thought."

For some reason, Samara's words burrowed into Liss's soul even though she did her best to remember why they were meaningless.

"He's a murderer," Liss said.

"He's a soldier," Samara corrected, "whose duty is to his Emperor."

Liss shut up before she said or did something that would give her away.

* * *

Once Samara fell asleep, Liss got out of bed and tiptoed to the door. She grabbed the uniform Rhett's friend had leant her, which she already had plans to make good use of, and pulled it on. She eased the door shut behind her and walked purposefully back toward the main part of the palace.

On her way through the hallways earlier in the night, Liss had relied on her years as a thief to take in every relevant detail about her surroundings. She found one of the hidden stairwells she'd noticed earlier and ducked into the dark space. After making sure she was alone, she pulled the onyx stone from her pocket. As soon as she touched it, the stone grew warm and began to pulse with its own light. Words began to scrawl across the stone.

Any news to report? No Viper yet, but Energizers still working at full power. Nya is as well as can be expected. Talk soon.

Liss cupped her hands around the stone and whispered her own response. She told Burk she was in the process of searching for the immunity and that she had dropped hints to soldiers that the caravans were all heading to the southern grasslands. She didn't mention how she'd only just arrived at the palace. She also didn't say anything about meeting the Viper himself.

It was a detail Burk would want to know, and she wasn't sure why she left Rhett out of her report. When she tried to speak the words, Liss couldn't figure out a way to explain the situation to Burk without confirming every comment he'd ever made about her rashness. So, she said nothing at all.

With her report finished, Liss's real work for the night began. It was late—or early—and the halls were finally clear of revelers. It was a stroke of luck the Lagonia army employed women as well as men, and the sleepy guards posted at the ends of each hallway took no notice of her. In the black-and-gold fatigues, she must have looked just like one of them.

Samara's room was in the back of the eastern tower, which contained the servants' living quarters, kitchens, laundry, and all the other essential and unsightly parts of the palace. Knowing what she knew about Lagonians, Liss was sure that whatever she was looking for would be in the western tower where the Emperor resided.

Liss found the elegant marble staircase that led up to the Sapphire Bridge, which was in fact made entirely of sapphires. The guards at each end of the bridge gave her a terse nod without even looking at her. Liss hoped Rhett's friend didn't ask for her soldier's uniform back. This might even be easy.

She moved deeper into the western tower. From everything she knew about this new Emperor, he wouldn't be one to let his secret far from him. She'd begin her search in his quarters and move outward from there.

She found the Emperor's bedchamber without much trouble. The doors were gilded and the handles were encrusted with precious black diamonds. There was only one sleepy guard standing outside, which told Liss the Emperor wasn't in his rooms.

Perfect.

Liss took a copper coin out of her pocket and threw it at a marble statue behind her. Then, she melted into the shadows behind a glittering tower of gold nuggets and black diamonds. As soon as the guard went to investigate, Liss slipped out of the shadows and let herself into the bedroom.

She took in the ridiculously huge and lavish space. Everything in the room was black and gold. The floor was black granite and the walls papered in gold leaf. There was a giant bed on a raised platform on the far end of the room, which was as big as her entire wagon.

Liss searched the room. She checked every floorboard and wall panel for hiding places. She went through the enormous washroom and sitting room, searching every corner until she was convinced that whatever she was looking for wasn't here.

She let herself out into an empty hallway. She wanted to search more, but dawn was already creeping in through the tall bay windows. In spite of Rhett's assurances that Lagonians weren't early risers, it was easier to get caught snooping around in broad daylight than in the dead of night. Liss wasn't willing to risk being discovered now that she was here and the immunity was within her grasp.

As she made her way back to the servants' quarters, she wracked her brain for where, if not in the Emperor's private chambers, the immunity might be. It would help if she knew what she was looking for.

Was it a vaccine the palace physicians had developed in secret? *Doubtful.* The Lagonian physicians weren't as good as the witchdoctors in Insorsil.

Some creature found in the sea whose blood held immunity to the contagion? *Gross. And unlikely.*

Liss doubted it was anything from Insorsil. The Insorsiled were born immune and had never shown any interest in the contagion. And it couldn't be something that came from the Giant Realm, because the barbaric humans who lived there were still dying from opal contagion.

She blew out a frustrated breath. The palace was enormous; it could take her months to search all of it.

Maybe the immunity was stored in one of the palace vaults?

She slapped a hand to her forehead. Of course, it would be in the vaults rather than in the Emperor's bedroom. Why hadn't that occurred to her before?

Lagonia's vaults were legendary. There were dozens of them, crammed with more wealth and jewels than could be found in the whole of most continents. It would make sense to keep Lagonia's greatest treasure of all in a place built for guarding treasures.

She should have started there.

Before she let herself back into Samara's room, Liss took the Insorsiled onyx stone from her pocket. She rubbed at the smooth, black surface until it started to glow. She spoke quietly to the stone.

"Searched the Emperor's quarters tonight. No sign of immunity."

Burk's response came almost immediately.

"Keep searching. Report back tomorrow night."

Liss slipped the stone back into her pocket. Hopefully, by then, she'd have something worth sharing.

CHAPTER 22

Rhett waited in the throne room. It was all but empty so late at night. Besides him, the only other people in the room were the two guards and Elouicia, Jaikon's most trusted advisor. The man was more reptile than human. He'd even paid a witchdoctor to file his teeth into points for no discernible reason. It certainly didn't improve his looks.

Elouicia was the one who turned Rhett's bedroom upside down a few times a year in search of some weakness the Emperor could use to exploit him. The man always left something behind that his twisted brain found amusing. A small, dead animal on Rhett's pillow was Elouicia's favorite.

Rhett had been summoned over an hour ago, but Jaikon still hadn't appeared. Rhett wasn't surprised. It was another one of the Emperor's games to make people wait for him—to remind them where the balance of power lay.

When the door finally opened, Rhett turned slowly, making sure his face appeared mildly bored.

"Your Majesty."

"I don't see the spy's head," was Jaikon's only greeting.

"There was some trouble along the way," Rhett replied, keeping his voice even and expression empty.

In as few details as he could get away with, he told Jaikon about the attack. He made some minor adjustments to the story, leaving out the part about how he had killed seven slavers, and giving Stone the credit for finding him. Any mention of Liss was decidedly absent from this rendition.

"Your carelessness almost got you killed," Jaikon said when Rhett had finished. He lowered his voice so the others in the room wouldn't be able to hear him. "Perhaps it was premature for our sire to name you Chief Assassin."

Rhett didn't take the bait.

Jaikon turned to the two guards at the door.

"Come forward," he commanded.

The guards came. Their names were Brecher and Aliamu. They were good men who had fought beside Rhett in the Giant War.

"What do you think?" Jaikon asked the men. "Have you lost all respect for a soldier who can't even manage to keep himself from getting shot?"

Jaikon was putting them in an impossible position—pitting them between their Emperor and his second-in-command. It was obvious what they should say, but Rhett knew these men. He tried to give them a slight shake of his head. Aliamu saw the gesture and understood. Brecher didn't.

"Rhett is the best soldier I've ever seen," Brecher answered after a tense moment had passed.

Shut up, you fool! Rhett tried to will the man into silence, but the damage had been done.

"Really." Jaikon's ice blue eyes pinned the soldier.

Brecher stood a little taller. "I'm proud to serve under his command."

Jaikon eyed the man for another moment.

I am steel. I am steel. I am steel.

"Emperor," Rhett said, stepping forward. "We need to discuss the spy. Have you gotten any word about the caravan's location?"

Jaikon returned his attention to Rhett. Rhett didn't let his relief show on his face. He had expected some backlash for his soldier's loyalty, but Jaikon wasn't always predictable in the way he reacted. It made him more dangerous.

"There was a report from a village on the western tip of Insorsil. Five soldiers were murdered as they were collecting taxes," Jaikon said, sounding bored.

When were you going to see fit to mention this to me? Rhett wanted to demand.

"I'll go there tomorrow," he said. "Do you want me to kill the Extended responsible?"

"If they cross your path," Jaikon said, "but they're not your main concern. I want that spy found and executed."

Rhett nodded and turned to leave.

"Do you know what they're calling him?" Jaikon asked. "Viper's Bain."

Rhett turned back.

"Word has reached our enemies across the sea," Jaikon continued. "It makes me look weak that my own soldiers haven't been able to kill a single Extended man." His deadly gaze zeroed in on Rhett. "And I have no intention of being seen as weak."

"I understand," Rhett replied. "I'll find him."

Jaikon held his gaze, ice blue eyes against dark brown.

"Bring me Opal Smoke's head," Jaikon said, his voice soft and deadly, "or I'll take yours."

＊ ＊ ＊

Jaikon waited until Lagonia's Chief Assassin had left the room and the sound of his receding footsteps could no longer be heard. Then, he turned to the two guards in his throne room.

"You have a great deal of love for my Chief Assassin, don't you?"

The one who had so fiercely defended Rhett earlier spoke first.

"Yes, Your Majesty," the man replied without hesitation.

"And you?" Jaikon turned to the other.

A muscle twitched in his jaw. "All of my loyalty and respect are for my Emperor alone," he said.

The man was lying, that much was obvious to Jaikon, but the words were the right ones.

"Dismissed, both of you." Jaikon waved a hand and watched as the guards bowed and departed.

Jaikon tapped a finger on the armrest of his throne.

"Do you want them both tossed over the cliff?" Elouicia asked.

"Just the one," Jaikon replied. "Promote the other."

Elouicia bowed. "Your will is my command."

"And search Rhetteman's room again. If he's hiding anything, I want to know what it is."

"The man lives like a monk," Elouicia complained. "He possesses nothing. He cares for nothing. The man has no weaknesses." Elouicia bared his canines in frustration.

Jaikon recalled the sight of Rhett, on his knees, as he wiped up the blood of their dead father. He remembered the way pain and fury had twisted Rhett's usually-blank features.

"Every man has his weakness," Jaikon said. "And no matter what my soldiers think about him, Rhett is still just a man."

CHAPTER 23

Rhett got to the small training field before the first rays of dawn had touched the sky. If he knew what was good for either of them, he would have dropped Liss off at Samara's room and never gone looking for her again.

But he couldn't get the image of that axe at her throat out of his mind. Rhett never wanted to see that again, and he'd train Liss for as long as it took for her to learn how to protect herself. That was all this was. He'd call it a professional courtesy. She'd saved his life, and someday, the skills he taught her might be enough to save hers.

It was early enough that he didn't feel much cause for concern. Besides, the training field he was in now was one that was too small and out of the way to be useful. It was overgrown and more than a mile from the palace, which made it less than ideal for soldiers who preferred to spar within sight of the court lords and ladies. It was also completely hidden by trees the palace gardeners had given up on and wasn't accessible from the main road. Rhett hadn't seen anyone use it in years and had forgotten about it himself until he had cause to remember.

Rhett had already gone for a run, but he paced the length of the field as he waited for her. It had been more than a day since he'd seen Liss. He felt strange. Jittery. He itched for the sight of her…the sound of her voice….

"Morning."

Rhett flew around.

"Stop doing that," he demanded.

"Doing what?" Liss asked.

"Sneaking up on me. How do you even manage it?"

Liss crossed her arms. "It isn't my fault everyone you know stomps around like giants."

Rhett huffed out a breath as his pulse continued to race, even though the surprise of her appearance should have worn off. She was standing close enough for him to see the way the first rays of dawn warmed her skin.

Liss looked different. Her hair had been cut so that instead of hanging in one straight line above her shoulders, it was angled just below her chin, framing her face.

Rhett had grown used to seeing her in that white Insorsiled cloak. Now, she was dressed in the uniform of palace servants. He'd never before had cause to pay attention to the uniform. Now, he was all too aware of the way the tight black pants molded to her hips. The gold button-down top was too tight around her chest, and he forced his gaze away before she caught him staring.

He cleared his throat. "Should we get started?"

"Let's." Liss gave him a knowing smile, showing the dimple that he had thought about more than once over the last day. She grabbed one of the wooden poles leaning against the tree and took her position.

Liss was a fast learner. She'd already mastered blocking and landed some mean strikes with her pole by the end of the first hour. She didn't hold back, and she wasn't afraid of getting bruised and dirty. Rhett appreciated that about her.

"You're reacting too soon," he told her when he caught her off balance for the third time. "Be patient and wait until I move, then strike."

She blew out a frustrated breath. She lunged again.

"You're never going to get a hit in that way," he told her, stepping out of her path. "Control your impulses."

Her eyes narrowed at that. He'd struck a nerve.

Liss dug her foot into the ground, and before he could process what she was doing, he was blinded by a spray of dirt. He had just a second to realize what she had just done before her pole was connecting with his stomach.

"Who taught you that trick?" Rhett asked with a grudging respect as he wiped dirt from his eyes. He hadn't thought she would do something like that.

"I never said I was defenseless," she shot back, still holding out the wooden pole. "Are you going to tell me it was unsportsmanlike?"

"No." Rhett rubbed at his eyes. "I'm not teaching you how to fight so you can look good doing it. I'm teaching you so you can protect yourself. Although you do."

Her eyes narrowed. "Do what?"

"Look good doing it."

Liss's lips parted, but no sound came out.

Rhett took a step forward. Liss wavered, but she didn't move back. Rhett grabbed the weapon out of her hands.

"Now you're hesitating," he said. "That'll get you killed."

Irritation flashed across her pretty face. She kicked him in the knee, another dirty trick he hadn't been expecting. Then, she pounced, reaching for the wooden pole. Her momentum drove them both off balance.

Rhett broke their fall with his forearms. He felt rocks bite into his skin, which he forgot about the moment he realized he was practically lying on top of her.

His forearms kept his weight from crushing her, but their faces were only inches apart. She licked her lips, and every coherent thought fled from Rhett's mind.

"You're a hypocrite," Liss muttered.

"How so?" he managed. He forced his gaze from her mouth to her eyes.

"You're hesitating now."

Rhett let out a short breath. He felt his muscles quiver with the effort of keeping his distance from her. Every part of him ached to close the gap between them.

One more glance into her blue eyes, and Rhett was lost. He forgot why he was supposed to stay away. He rolled to the side, pulling her with him. Wrapping his arms all the way around her small frame, he kissed her.

He didn't hold back, and neither did she. Their mouths and bodies tangled together. She tasted like candy and magic.

"Have you been practicing?" she gasped when they broke apart.

He smiled against her lips. "Not exactly." He'd only repeated their first kiss in his head about a thousand times since it had happened. A thousand might even be an underestimation....

"Well, whatever you've been doing, keep doing it."

He took that as an invitation and gave in to the desperate desires his heart could no longer deny. He kissed her again.

Steel doesn't know love or despair. It can't be bent or broken. It needs no heart or warmth.

He recalled the words of the mantra that had been his comfort for as long as he could remember, but not their meaning. Rhett was aware of nothing except Liss's breath feeding his lungs, and her heart beating in time with his own.

CHAPTER 24

Where were you so early in the morning?" Samara asked Liss with a devilish grin.

"Don't look at me like that." Liss scowled. After checking to make sure no one else was in hearing distance, she lowered her voice and said, "We were just sparring."

"Sparring, eh?" Samara's grin widened. "I've never heard it called that before."

"You're impossible, you know that?" Liss huffed, unaccountably flustered.

Samara only winked at her and looped her arm through Liss's.

"Come on," Samara said. "The ladies are finishing up breakfast, and there's a garden party this afternoon. We need to organize hair, makeup, wardrobe, and jewelry." She lifted her perfectly arched brows. "And after, you're going to tell me all about sparring."

Fortunately, the servants were kept too busy for Samara to ask any more prying questions or for Liss to give her morning with Rhett much thought. Even though Liss was only responsible for tending to three of the women in the Emperor's large harem, their needs were as great as twenty of the fussiest women Liss had ever met.

Whether it was from the dissolvable crystals Samara had been plopping into servants' and ladies' tea over the past two days, or because people took no notice of the servants in general, no one seemed to realize Liss had just appeared in the palace. Even the three ladies she waited on hadn't even blinked when she first came into their rooms.

Liss's main role was running back and forth across the Sapphire Bridge that separated the ladies' chambers in the western tower from the seamstresses' in the eastern tower. She brought new gowns and shoes that would be worn once and never again. She delivered tiny sandwiches and cakes on gold trays, as well as sealed notes, all of which she opened and read before bringing to their intended recipient. By the time she re-sealed the third note pertaining to So-and-So's new Insorsiled nose, Liss gave up hoping to discover anything of use from her charges.

The most useful part of her day had been bringing the lockbox to collect the women's jewelry for the party, since it allowed her to mark the location and number of guards for each of the palace vaults. Liss kept her ears open as she passed soldiers in the hallways and at meals when she stood behind her charges' table.

She did overhear a guard mention the town outside of Insorsil where slavers were waiting for passing caravans. It wasn't the information she was here for, but it was something. At the first chance she got, she closed herself in her new bedroom across the hall from Samara's and spoke the news into her onyx stone.

Burk's response came immediately: *Any word on the immunity?*

When the three women in her charge returned to the Emperor's private quarters, Liss had been hoping to catch a few hours of sleep before spending the night searching the palace. Instead, Samara had found her and dragged her to the servants' hall for dinner.

Even for the Lagonian servants, there was more and better food than she'd ever seen in her life. Liss had never gone hungry…her thieving had been enough to prevent that. But there had been many times when she hadn't known when or from where her next meal would come. She thought of the gruel in Mari's wagon and the too-thin faces of many of the other Extended children. Like all of this empire's excess, the sight of such inequity made Liss's blood boil.

But as her stomach rumbled and the scent of the food assailed her nostrils, she put aside her anger and loaded up her plate.

There was a sideboard with three kinds of roasted meat, four kinds of fish in different sauces, still-warm bread slathered with creamy butter, thick slices of tomato dripping with freshly-pressed oil and sprinkled with herbs…. And then there was dessert. Liss bit into a chocolate tart that she officially deemed the second-most-delicious thing she'd ever tasted, after the golden cake Rhett had gotten for her. Laughing, Samara offered her a forkful of lemon cake, which was somehow as amazing as the tart.

"This chef is officially my hero," Liss said, her voice thick with cake.

"Lagonia's head chef is pretty legendary," Samara said, plucking the fork from Liss's hand and taking a dainty bite of the tart. "He takes food so seriously that he personally oversees the ingredients distributed to every province in the empire. Even the peasants make bread with flour approved by the palace chef."

"The man is a genius," Liss said in appreciation, swatting at Samara's hand as her fork swooped in for a second bite of tart.

"He's also crazy," Samara told her, finally managing to sneak a bite off Liss's plate. "He won't let anyone else near his ingredients, and even his assistant chefs aren't allowed in his pantries."

"With desserts like this, I don't care if he's a psychopath," Liss declared.

They drank mint tea and nibbled on sugar cookies as they chatted about everything and nothing until it was time to return to their duties. Samara was the servant for the most important of the Emperor's women, and from everything Samara had said about them, Liss's own charges were veritable angels in comparison.

By the time Liss had brushed out the women's hair and gotten them into bed, it was time for her to begin her real work.

It was fortunate that Liss had never needed much sleep. She had always spent her nights fitfully, even when she wasn't getting back late from stealing or tending to her mom. Strangely enough, she hadn't had any trouble sleeping the last week. She had no idea what was wrong with her that she'd been able to relax in a camp full of Lagonian men.

She had even fallen asleep on Silverbird with Rhett's chest pressed against her back. She didn't trust him…she couldn't trust him. And yet, her soul couldn't accept the danger he posed.

Still, she'd have to figure out how to get some sleep in her new routine of being a servant by day and spy by night. But that was a problem for tomorrow. Tonight's problem was getting into all twenty-two of the palace's vaults.

Opening the vaults wasn't the problem. The locks weren't overly complex and were mostly for show, probably because the Lagonians didn't expect any would-be thieves to make it past the guards. Besides, breaking into vaults was something she'd been doing for years. The Lagonia vaults were bigger and fancier than the ones in the Insorsil shops where she usually stole from, but the concept behind the lock mechanisms was the same.

Getting near enough to the vaults to actually open them was the real challenge. It would have been easier if she could flirt and flatter her way past the guards, but she couldn't risk one of them noticing how she was behaving in an un-soldier-like way and mentioning to Rhett that a new soldier was sniffing around the vaults.

By the time the night was almost done, she'd only managed to get into one of the vaults during the guards' shift change. Once she'd gotten in, she'd found nothing but priceless jewels…all of which she'd had to fight her thief's instincts to leave untouched.

The night hadn't been a total loss. She's learned the exact times of the guards' shift changes, and she'd found two secret stairwells that would shorten the distance between the servants' quarters and the vaults. Tomorrow night, she'd have an easier time of things.

It was almost dawn by the time she made it back to her room and changed out of her soldier uniform. She took out her onyx stone, where a message from Burk was waiting for her. There was more trouble with bigoted Insorsiled refusing to sell supplies to Extended, and the Energizers had been forced to move their caravan by day to a new part of Insorsil where Burk could purchase more food and other necessities. Burk said Jema's father had taken ill from the added strain on the caravan's Energizers.

Overwhelmed with resentment on her caravan's behalf, Liss spoke her report into the onyx stone. She wished she had better news to share with her caravan leader. She would find the immunity, she promised Burk and herself. She would find it, and then everything would be different.

She had just enough time to bathe and change into a clean servant's uniform before going to meet Rhett. She knew it was stupid to bother when she was just going to get sweaty and dirty sparring, but she did it anyway. She also ran a comb through her short hair and brushed her teeth. She tried not to put too much thought into her reasons for taking more care with her appearance than usual.

Liss still hadn't mentioned Rhett in any of her reports. She also hadn't asked him about the immunity again, even though she knew he might be able to tell her something that could shorten her search. *He was too smart and too secretive to reveal anything truly useful to her*, she told herself. That was why she had continued to spend her nights blindly searching the palace instead of asking him. He would be suspicious of why she wanted to know. He might even figure her out, and then she'd have to flee the empire without getting what she had come for.

She had been waiting for Rhett's real personality to surface now that they were back in his empire and the novelty of his life being saved had worn off. She waited for the brutal Chief Assassin and enemy of her people to emerge. He hadn't. It was almost infuriating the way Rhett continued to subvert her expectations through his honesty and veiled kindnesses.

There was darkness and guilt and even despair inside him, but Liss never felt any of the evil that should be on the Viper's soul.

Still, she couldn't let herself forget how Rhett spent his days. She had seen him and his friends riding off on their dragons for the last two days, in search of the spy who was known around the palace as Opal Smoke. Yesterday, she had seen the dark circles beneath his eyes and known the lengths he was going to in order to find…her. It made a confusing array of emotions fill her own soul until she felt as conflicted as he always seemed to be. Liss wasn't used to indecision and uncertainty, and it made her feel like she would either scream or go insane.

Nothing good could come from getting close to Rhett. She knew it, and yet, she couldn't stay away. Her soul called to his, and his to hers. She knew she should stop spending her mornings with him. She should use that time to sleep. She should stay the hell away from him.

All these and other logical thoughts left her when she caught sight of his dark silhouette on their training field. She didn't think. She ran to him.

This time, Rhett heard her coming. He caught her in his arms and lifted her like she weighed nothing. He spun her around, and Liss had only a moment to see how a real smile made his face even more gorgeous before he pressed his lips to hers.

The awkwardness that had been between them after their first kiss in the Insorsiled forest was long gone. There was still hesitation on both of their souls, but it was only a whisper. Their desire was a shout.

When they finally broke apart, Rhett laughed.

"Training first," he said, undermining his own words when he kissed her again. "I wasn't lying when I said I wanted you to be able to rescue yourself."

It took them several more long minutes before they tore themselves apart. When they did, Rhett became all business. They sparred, and Liss managed to get in several good whacks with her wooden pole. She was getting better at defense, too, even though it went against all of her instincts not to attack first.

Afterward, just as the sun was climbing up over the horizon, they lay in the grass together. Liss's chin was propped on Rhett's chest as he twirled a lock of her hair around his finger.

Something strange was happening with their souls. When Liss dared to look, she realized she couldn't disentangle his emotions from hers. That had never happened before, where she couldn't tell one person's emotions from another. She didn't know if it was just their physical proximity, or something far more dangerous.

Was this what had happened with her parents? Had their souls grown so dependent on each other that when her father died, her mother's was never whole again?

The thought was like a bucket of ice water being tossed over her head. She pulled away from Rhett and sat up.

"What is it?" Rhett asked, sitting up with her.

"I have to go." She tried to stand, but Rhett wrapped a hand around her wrist.

"What happened?" he asked, his dark eyes filling with concern.

Liss just shook her head. She couldn't tell him, because that would require admitting far more about her own feelings than was good for either of them.

"What are we doing, Rhett?" she asked instead. "What is this?"

Confusion filled his soul as he looked at her. "I'm not sure what you mean."

Liss was flustered and angry, and she wasn't really sure why. "Don't you have anything more important to do with your time than spend it with me…like this?" she demanded.

"No," he said slowly. "There's nothing more important."

A tingly feeling spread through her at his words before she could stop it. Her own weakness infuriated her.

"Don't you have to go find that Extended spy?" she asked, yanking her wrist from Rhett and getting to her feet.

"Yes, but—"

"Do you ever feel bad about it? About any of it?"

Liss had no idea why she'd asked him. She hadn't even realized the question was on her mind until it had spilled out of her mouth.

"What are you talking about?" he asked, standing to face her.

She should shut up now before she gave herself away. She was angry, though. All her life, she'd sworn she would never be like her mother…she would never be weak enough to rest her soul's happiness on another person. She had promised herself she would never fall in love. Now, she could feel herself doing just that, and it was with the man responsible for murdering her people. She wanted—needed—a reason to turn and walk away from Rhett.

"Do you feel bad about all the people you've killed?" And then, because she worried she'd said too much, she added, "I don't like the Extended, but they're still living, breathing people. And you just strike them down like they're—"

She cut herself off as the burn of tears tightened the back of her throat. *Get a hold of yourself before you ruin everything,* she commanded herself.

She was too overwhelmed with the feelings radiating from both of their souls to be able to sort Rhett's emotions. She didn't know what he was feeling.

"My job is to carry out the Emperor's will," Rhett said finally. "If he tells me to kill one of the Extended, it's my duty to see it done."

"But do you feel bad about it? Do you care?"

Liss was so desperate for him to say yes. At the same time, she wanted him to say no, because then she'd have to walk away from him…from this.

"They used to haunt my dreams," Rhett said, his voice so low it was barely audible. "I'd see their faces every time I closed my eyes."

She stopped backing away. Rhett was telling her something Liss could tell he'd never revealed to anyone else.

"One day, the dreams just stopped. I don't really know why." He looked at her with his piercing gaze that made it at once difficult to hold and impossible to turn away.

"I keep the kills clean so there's no pain. They never even see me coming." Rhett lifted a shoulder. "It's all I can do, and I guess it's enough for my conscience to accept."

Neither of them spoke for a long while.

"Someday, one of the Extended might be the one with a knife at my throat," Rhett said, "and I wouldn't begrudge him for it."

"You're awfully flippant about your own life," Liss said, still trying to work out how she felt about everything he was telling her.

"I prefer to think of myself as more of a realist. The life expectancy for men in my position isn't good." Rhett gave her a wan smile. "The last Chief Assassin died at twenty-one, and the one before him was dead at twenty."

"How old are you?" Liss asked.

"Twenty."

She sucked in a breath.

Rhett smiled. "Hope you weren't getting too attached to me."

Liss turned away as she tried to catch her breath.

"This isn't okay," she said. "None of this is okay."

Rhett pulled her against him. She didn't resist, even though she knew she should.

"I know," he murmured into her hair.

"What do we do?"

"Take every day as it comes. Enjoy the time we have together."

It was Liss's own philosophy…to worry about tomorrow's problems later. But for the first time, it didn't seem like enough.

CHAPTER 25

Rhett lived for the hours just after dawn. Kissing, talking, and sparring with Liss infused him with more happiness than he had ever known. Especially kissing. And yet, as the sun rose and he had to let her go, it felt like a bandage being ripped from an open wound. He knew it was all they could have…a few stolen hours while Jaikon and his spies slept, but it wasn't enough.

There were a hundred times a day when he had to stop himself from lingering in hallways where she might appear, just for the chance to see her. It wasn't worth the risk. If Elouicia or any of Jaikon's other cronies were around, they would see the way Rhett looked at Liss. He couldn't control his features around her like he could with everyone else. When he saw her, everything else disappeared.

Rhett shook himself as he strode down the hall, trying to organize his thoughts before the war council. He still hadn't made any progress with finding the Extended spy, even though he had searched everywhere this side of the sea. His soldiers were working tirelessly in Insorsil and even the Giant Realm, but none of them had turned up anything of use. Opal Smoke hadn't done anything in weeks…nothing had been stolen from Lagonia soldiers or slavers. Rhett had even posted soldiers with fake maps and documents that appeared to be of significant import in every place Opal Smoke had ever been rumored to visit. The spy hadn't taken the bait.

Rhett wasn't naïve enough to think Opal Smoke had given up. The man's absence from his usual thievery only made Rhett more unsettled. The spy was up to something, he could sense it. He just had no idea what it might be.

Jaikon and his advisors were already at the table. They looked up as he and Stone strode into the room.

"Apologies, Majesty," Stone said. "We were receiving reports from pixies just returning from across the sea."

"And?" the Emperor asked, looking at Rhett.

Rhett shook his head.

Jaikon pinned him with his gaze for another few seconds before gesturing for them to sit down.

"I want more soldiers across the sea," Jaikon said without preamble. "More of the giants' ships have been seen in neutral waters, and I want our army to be ready in case I choose to attack."

"I've already assigned more guards for our ports," Rhett said. "It'll be better to keep the soldiers here in case the giants decide to attack us."

Jaikon waved a dismissive hand. "I'm not interested in defense. If the time comes when we need to escalate this conflict, I want soldiers on the ground who can attack as soon as I give the word."

Rhett forced away his irritation before he spoke again.

"Our army is already spread too thin," he said, keeping his tone even. "With the troops already in Insorsil and all the other major ports, we don't have the numbers to protect our own borders if we're attacked."

"No one is going to attack us," Jaikon replied.

"With our army spread out the way it is, it'll be easy for our enemies to pick off our soldiers abroad if they choose. Our people are too vulnerable."

The conversation was civil, but Rhett could feel the growing discomfort of the others sitting at the table. Stone was glaring at a spot on the wall, but he said nothing. He knew Rhett was right.

"I've been recruiting," Jaikon replied. "Our numbers are better than ever before."

That much was true. More men and women were coming from the outermost reaches of Lagonia to don black-and-gold armor. Rhett hadn't been happy about it. These new recruits looked like soldiers, but they had little skill in fighting and even less discipline.

"They're too green," Rhett argued. "They need more time to train."

"So, let them train." Jaikon accepted the goblet of wine a servant offered him. "Send the ones who have been under your command across the sea."

Rhett bristled. He wasn't about to send the men and women he had fought beside for years across the sea. If disaster struck…*when* it struck…he would be able to do nothing to help them. "You can't just exchange one soldier for another," he said.

"Can't you?" Jaikon sipped his wine.

The air in the room was thick with tension.

"I'm not sending them across the sea to die for some pointless cause."

Jaikon slammed the goblet down on the table. A servant hurried to wipe away the red liquid that had sloshed over the side, but Jaikon waved him away. He leaned over the table to stare Rhett down. "Send five-hundred across the sea. Today."

Rhett gave his Emperor a tight nod. "Yes, Your Majesty."

Rhett stood and walked to the door, keeping his posture relaxed and his steps measured. He wouldn't give Jaikon the benefit of seeing how affected he was. He didn't want to send five-hundred of his soldiers across the sea where they'd be vulnerable and without access to any aid. He didn't want his soldiers to have to face an impossible, meaningless war without him.

Stone followed, shutting the door to the war council rooms softly behind them.

"Better get it over with now," Stone told him. There was a note of sympathy in the hard edges of Stone's expression, but Rhett knew that was all he'd get from his mentor.

Rhett nodded. He was about to head toward the training fields where Ciago, Wilsean, and Dannica would be leading the rest of the army in their daily drills, when he got the sense that something was wrong. He looked at the two men standing guard outside the war council room.

Brecher and Aliamu were the Emperor's personal guards. Rhett had given them the position himself, and they should be here now. Instead, they'd been replaced by two soldiers Rhett didn't know.

"Where are the Emperor's guards?" Rhett asked.

The men looked at each other and then down at the floor. A bad feeling crept down Rhett's spine. He stepped up to the men, forcing them to look up to meet his gaze.

"Where are Brecher and Aliamu?" Rhett asked again, his voice a deadly quiet.

Where had Jaikon dug up these assholes? More importantly, where were his men?

"Aliamu is now one of the Emperor's advisors," one of the men replied with some reluctance.

One of the Emperor's advisors? Soldiers weren't promoted to councilmen unless they were from one of the high families, which Aliamu wasn't.

"And Brecher?" Rhett demanded, his patience waning. He rested his hand on the hilt of his dagger. It was a threat neither of the men standing by the door would mistake.

"His body was tossed over the cliff three days ago."

Rhett's vision went hazy. *Three days ago.* He recalled his conversation with Jaikon in the throne room, as well as what Brecher had said in Rhett's defense. Rhett had thought Jaikon wouldn't pursue the matter…that he was distracted by Rhett's failure to kill Opal Smoke….

Brecher had been killed because he was loyal to Rhett.

Rhett was barely aware of what he was doing when he turned around and threw open the doors to the war council.

He didn't speak. He couldn't. But the sound of his dagger coming loose from its sheath said more than any words.

"Put it away."

It was Stone's voice. Rhett hadn't even known he'd come back into the room behind him. Rhett shrugged his mentor off without even glancing his way. Guards were converging around the Emperor.

"Jaikon!" Rhett thundered.

Jaikon looked past him to Stone. "Put your ward on a leash," he drawled.

"You killed one of my men!"

Rhett swatted aside counselors and guards like troublesome flies until he and the Emperor were standing face-to-face.

"And that is precisely why he was thrown over the cliff," Jaikon replied, his eyes glittering dangerously. "His treasonous behavior left me with no choice."

"Treason?! You call being a loyal soldier treason?"

Jaikon waved a hand. Everyone else in the room except Stone dispersed, only too eager to be out of harm's reach.

"Rhetteman," Stone growled. "The boy's dead. Let it go."

The knife was wrenched from his hand. Rhett heard Jaikon's words through the fog of his fury and grief.

"Get yourself under control," Jaikon said, "or I'll have Stone haul you down to the torture cage so I can knock some sense into you."

"You're welcome to try," Rhett snarled as Stone dragged him out of the room.

CHAPTER 26

Liss stood in the corner of the banquet hall, pretending to be attentive to her ladies' needs as she dozed on her feet. She'd been out all of the previous night and had only managed to get through three more of the twenty-two vaults. Even once she'd gotten inside, she'd found nothing but coins and more gems. But that didn't mean she wouldn't find what she was looking for in one of the other vaults. At least, that was what she kept telling herself.

She was exhausted and frustrated that she couldn't offer Burk more than her same refrain of "still searching."

Burk's messages were getting progressively more desperate. He didn't go into detail, but it was clear how much her people were depending on her. And she was failing them.

A sharp poke in her side snapped Liss out of her thoughts.

"You were snoring," Samara hissed, returning to her straight-backed posture with her arms linked behind her back.

"Was not," Liss whispered back. She shifted, and she winced as pins and needles went through her foot.

Liss glanced at the women she was responsible for caring for. They were all more than a little drunk, and Liss expected she'd have quite a time of getting them into their beds later. They giggled and gossiped, as their calculating gazes strayed to the raised pedestal at the center of the room.

There was a small table set in the middle of the pedestal. Jaikon sat at the table's head, holding court for the most important palace members.

Liss studied the men and women sitting around the table. She recognized most of the Emperor's advisors by now, even though they all looked vaguely the same in their three-piece black-and-gold outfits. Stone was at the table, too. Liss could feel anger rolling off his soul, and she wondered what he was so upset about. The chair next to the Emperor, Rhett's seat, was empty.

The chair on the Emperor's left was occupied by a heavy, dark-skinned man. He had a black handlebar moustache that curled at the corners, which he played with throughout the meal. He didn't wear the black-and-gold livery of the guard, and he didn't have the physique besides. He wasn't dressed in courtier finery, either. Instead of the capes and velvet hats of the advisors, he wore a plain white button-down shirt, which was stained in several places, and dusty black pants.

"Who is the man sitting next to the Emperor?" Liss whispered to Samara.

"The Emperor's head chef," Samara replied.

Liss squinted at the man. "And he gets to eat at the Emperor's table?"

Samara shrugged. "You've tasted his salted caramel pudding."

Liss had in fact tasted the pudding, and while she preferred his cakes, she took Samara's point. Still, it seemed strange for a chef, even one as talented as this one, to be worthy of a seat at the Emperor's table.

"I think it amuses the Emperor how insane the man is," Samara continued in a whisper. "About a year ago, someone snuck into the kitchens and stole a recipe the chef was working on for the summer banquet. The man went nuts. He's kept the kitchens padlocked whenever he isn't inside ever since."

Liss let out a quiet laugh. She was about to say something to Samara, when a conversation at the table in front of her caught her attention.

"I heard the Chief Assassin had quite the outburst today."

Liss's focus snapped to the woman at the table who had just spoken.

"Oh yeah," another replied. "Crazy man tried to kill the Emperor. I heard it took twenty men to pull him off." She took a long glug of her wine.

"Well, *I* heard the Emperor's Master Interrogator had to drag him out of the room and beat some sense into him."

"He can throw all the tantrums he wants, as far as I'm concerned," another courtier replied. "The man is better looking than God."

Liss exchanged a quick glance with Samara. Samara gave her a little shrug, telling Liss she didn't know anything more. Liss's heart was beating faster.

What had happened? Where was Rhett now?

Liss thought she might actually lose her mind as she was forced to stand in the banquet hall and watch the women drink their fourth, fifth, and sixth glasses of sugared wine before they finally retired. Liss practically threw them in their beds. They were too drunk to know the difference, anyway.

She used the hidden servants' hallways to make her way out of the eastern tower before a thought occurred to her. She made a quick detour, heading past the laundry toward the kitchens. She'd had no reason to come to this part of the palace yet, but all she had to do was follow the smell of rising bread to find the kitchens.

Since Rhett hadn't come to dinner, Liss reasoned she may as well bring him something to eat. It would also give her a reason for seeking him out when it turned out the conversation she'd overheard was nothing more than idle court gossip and she felt stupid for having worried.

When she got to the extensive network of rooms that made up the palace's kitchens, she found every entrance locked, just as Samara had said they'd be. The chef really was a crazy fool.

Instead of taking the time to pick the locks and risking the wrath of an insane chef, Liss went back to the now-abandoned banquet hall and filled up a plate from the leftovers the servants were packing away.

Liss didn't change into the soldier's uniform she usually used when she wanted to sneak around without being seen, since she didn't want Rhett to wonder why she still had it. Instead, she kept to the servants' hallways when she could and moved in the shadows when she couldn't. She pretended to be on an errand from one of her ladies as she crossed the Sapphire Bridge and entered the western tower.

She had never been to Rhett's room before, but she'd made a point of finding out where it was. Any knowledge of the palace's layout was useful to her as she searched for the immunity. She wouldn't read too deeply into the fact that she hadn't bothered to discover where Ciago, Wilsean, or any of the councilmen slept.

Luckily, there was only one guard in this hallway, and he was facing away from her. Liss supposed it would be redundant for guards to protect other guards.

She stopped outside Rhett's door and listened. There were muffled voices coming from inside. She couldn't make them out, but she recognized Ciago and Wilsean's souls. There was pity and regret on both of them, although she wasn't sure which was Ciago's and which was Wilsean's. Rhett's soul, which she'd recognize in any room no matter how crowded, was black with hatred and grief.

Liss felt her own emotions rise in response. She wanted to barge in, but the hallway was empty, so she forced herself to wait.

The food she'd managed to swipe for Rhett had gone cold by the time the door opened. Wilsean and Ciago both looked exhausted.

"Hey," she said, stepping out from the shadows.

Both men turned to her at the same time. Their eyes widened like they were twins, even though they looked nothing alike.

"What are you doing here?" Ciago whispered, giving a furtive glance up and down the hall. "Servants aren't allowed here."

"How did you even manage to get past the guard?" Wilsean asked.

Liss shrugged. "I heard—I mean, I was just coming to check…." She trailed off, realizing for the first time she hadn't thought about coming here, she'd just done it. She swallowed. "Is he okay?"

Wilsean and Ciago exchanged a look. For once, there was no trace of good humor on their faces or their souls.

"No, he isn't," Wilsean said after a long pause. "Jaikon had a soldier executed for being more loyal to Rhett than the Emperor. He's…not taking it well."

Liss's heart felt like it was going to explode with the pain she felt on Rhett's behalf. She knew how much he cared about the soldiers under his command. Rhett felt responsible for them.

"Should I," she began, not knowing what to say.

"He'll want to see you," Ciago said.

Liss had seen Ciago and Wilsean a few times since she'd started her new job in the palace. They'd chatted and joked with her as they had before, but

Ciago had stopped flirting with her. It made Liss think Rhett's friends knew how things had…progressed between them. Ciago and Wilsean certainly didn't seem surprised to see her here now.

"The guards change at midnight and then again at two," Wilsean said. "It'll be easier for you to sneak out during one of those times."

Liss already knew all of this, but she nodded like she was grateful for the information.

She eased open the door and went in. Rhett's room was bare of all furniture except for a dresser and the bed, where Rhett was sitting with his head in his hands. He didn't look up as she shut the door and crossed the floor.

"I thought you might be hungry," Liss said.

He sat up at the sound of her voice. Being so near to him and feeling so much pain from his soul was like a kick to her gut.

A dozen emotions passed through Rhett's soul before it settled on fear. "Did anyone see you?"

"Just Wilsean and Ciago," she said. "I was careful."

"You can't be here. If Jaikon finds out about you—"

"He won't," she said quickly.

"Liss," Rhett said, taking the plate she offered him and putting it on the bed without looking at it. "I can't even protect my own soldiers. If you know what's good for you, you'll run as fast and as far from me as you can."

There was raw emotion in Rhett's voice that she had never heard before. She had seen it all on his soul, but he was usually so composed on the outside that it threw her to see him like this.

"Don't worry about me," Liss said with a forced lightness. "I'm sneaky, and a decent soldier taught me how to defend myself."

Rhett didn't react. Liss wasn't even sure he had heard her.

She sat down on the bed next to him and threaded her fingers through his. Neither of them said anything. They just sat with their hands entwined.

Liss should be using this time to check out more of the vaults. Instead, she sat beside Rhett as the blue light of the moon streamed in through the glass.

"We can't do this anymore," he said.

After so much silence, it startled Liss to hear Rhett speak.

He turned to face her. His gaze was blank, and if she hadn't been what she was, she might have been convinced he didn't care. But she could feel the way his soul rebelled at every word.

"We can't be together. I can't afford to have weaknesses."

Liss would have been hurt and angry by his words if she didn't feel the truth in his soul. Rhett was afraid, and it didn't take a Truthseer to know his fear was for her sake rather than his own.

His words gave her an out, though. She could walk out of his room right now. He wouldn't chase her down or beg her to come back, and this thing between them would shrivel and die.

Liss had never felt two souls that were as in sync as theirs. For the second time, she thought of her parents. An immediate surge of panic tore through her. An image of her mother, downing her tonic with trembling hands, filled Liss's mind.

Her mother's suffering was the reason Liss never wanted to feel…*this*. She had sworn she would never find herself wasting away because the soul that sustained her wasn't her own. She would never love someone so much that losing him would end her. And she would lose Rhett. One way or another.

"I can't care about you, Liss," Rhett said. "Please, for your own sake. Let me go."

This time, Rhett couldn't keep the emotion from his face and voice. It was obvious he didn't want to be apart from her any more than she wanted it.

He's giving you an out, she told herself again. *Take it.*

She could disentangle her soul from his before it was too late.

But it was too late. Liss could no more easily rip her soul away as she could pull her fingers from where they were still laced through his. She didn't want to let him go.

Rhett glanced at her, then. The pain and grief she felt in his soul were also in his eyes. He reached up and touched her cheek in the place where her dimple appeared. Without thinking, without being able to stop herself, she leaned into his touch.

"Liss," he sighed out her name. "Why do you have to make this so impossible?"

"I think what you're afraid of has already happened," Liss said, putting her free hand over Rhett's heart. "You care about me."

She felt his heartbeat speed up at the contact.

"I do," he replied.

Liss felt Rhett's body go still in the way it always did before his emotions expanded.

"But if anything happens to you—"

"It won't," she said.

She rested her head against his shoulder, partly because she wanted to, and partly because she didn't want him to see from her face that she knew how his emotions were tearing him apart. And that she was just as conflicted.

Walk away, her logical voice commanded. *Stay*, said her soul.

Maybe there was an alternative for her.

Liss's feelings for Rhett didn't have to consume her the way they had her mother. Allowing herself to care for Rhett was far more complicated than just walking away, and yet, nothing was turning out to be what she had thought.

Before coming here, simple truths had governed her every belief and action. Lagonians were murderers and oppressors. Insorsiled were selfish and cruel.

Now, there were exceptions to those rules. Where Liss had always seen in black and white before, now, she saw gray.

"It would seem we're both fighting a losing battle," she murmured.

She felt, rather than saw, his smile. "It would seem we are."

Liss felt something ease in Rhett's soul. There was still the grief and anger, but there was also something else, and it was stronger. It was the beginnings of love.

CHAPTER 27

J aikon looked up from the reports spread out across his desk as Elouicia entered the room.

"News on Opal Smoke?" he demanded. It had been over a month, and all Rhetteman had produced were lists of caravans where the spy *wasn't*. As deep as his hatred for his Chief Assassin ran, Jaikon had never before assigned a task to his bastard half-brother that hadn't been promptly completed.

"No new reports, Majesty," Elouicia replied, bowing low. "They are searching the southern tip of the plains today and will be moving westward tomorrow. Rhetteman has assigned more men to set traps in Insorsil, but so far, there have been no bites."

Jaikon scowled. "Then get out, and don't come back until you have something useful to tell me."

"There are a few other things that require your attention, Majesty."

Jaikon could tell from the look on the other man's face he wasn't going to the like the news.

"Majesty, there are reports that more of the councilmen have been meeting in secret."

"I want names," Jaikon snapped.

"I have them," Elouicia replied. He released a pixie from the palm of his hand. Jaikon noticed with little interest that one of her wings was crushed.

"Well?" Jaikon asked the tiny creature cowering in Elouicia's palm.

As she repeated the names in her tremulous voice, Jaikon's mood soured further. They were important councilmen, and there were too many of them to execute.

"There's been talk among the soldiers, too," Elouicia added when the pixie had finished her report and wilted back onto Elouicia's palm. "Perhaps it would have been better if we had kept Brecher's death quiet."

"It would not," Jaikon snapped. "My soldiers need to know who they serve. They need to fear me."

Elouicia bowed his head, knowing better than to argue.

"Do you have any good news?" Jaikon asked, still mulling over the problem of the councilmen.

"I do." Elouicia grinned his predatory grin. "Gatria signed the agreement."

Of course, she did. The terms had been laughably favorable for Insorsil. Jaikon had counted on it…had counted on Gatria being so eager to sign the agreement she wouldn't notice what else he had been doing in Insorsil…and who else he'd been meeting with.

"Forgive me for asking," Elouicia said, "but how do you intend to hold up your end of the bargain?"

"I don't," Jaikon replied. "Obviously."

It was just one more step in his plan…one more cog in the machine that would inevitably bring all the territories on this side of the sea under his control.

"But, Your Majesty, the retribution could be dire."

"Gatria will be incensed," Jaikon said, smiling a little. "She might even break the trade agreement she made with my father."

Elouicia shook his head like a dog who didn't comprehend its owner's command.

"If Gatria breaks our trade agreement, it is the same as an act of war," Jaikon explained. "We will be within our rights to attack Insorsil."

Elouicia bared his canines as a wolfish grin spread across his face. "Insorsil doesn't even have an army."

"Precisely."

"But," Elouicia's grin faltered. "Won't Gatria kill you? She may not have an army, but she still has powerful magic."

"She'll try. I have no doubt about that." Jaikon didn't want to elaborate any more, so he didn't. In his experience, it paid to keep his own council until everything was in place.

Elouicia shook off his puzzled expression. "When do you intend to tell the councilmen of all your plans?" he asked.

"I don't intend to tell them."

The reminder of his own people's disloyalty and sheer stupidity was enough to foul Jaikon's passing good mood.

"There's something else," Elouicia said. "That same Extended sent another message."

"I thought I told you to take care of him," Jaikon replied.

"The message came by pixie."

They both looked at the little thing cowering on Elouicia's palm.

"He requests a meeting with Your Majesty," the pixie said, her one good wing fluttering, like she wanted to escape. "He says he has information to trade."

Jaikon turned back to his paperwork and waved a hand, dismissing them. The day that swine had something he wanted would be a black day indeed.

Elouicia cleared his throat.

Jaikon turned back to look at the man still waiting for his orders. "Tell my Chief Assassin that if I don't have Opal Smoke's head in exactly one month, I'll settle for his, instead."

CHAPTER 28

It was strange how quickly Liss's life in the palace took on a routine. She had finished checking each of the vaults—which held nothing but priceless artwork, historical artifacts, and more riches—and had moved on to the palace's medical wing in hopes of finding what she sought there. She had separated the palace into sections in her mind, and she spent almost the entirety of her nights systemically scouring each section for clues about the immunity.

She returned to her room a few hours before dawn and spoke her abysmal report into the onyx stone. The messages that came back from Burk were troubling her more and more.

Keep searching so you can come home.

Energizer died. Need you to find immunity ASAP.

Our people's survival depends on you. Hurry.

Every time Liss felt the stone heat in her pocket, she got a sick feeling in the pit of her stomach. She understood Burk's impatience, but there was nothing else she could do. She had searched all the places she had thought she might find the immunity. It hadn't been in any of them.

Despite her own frustration and desperation, Liss forced herself to get a couple of hours of sleep, and then she slipped out of the palace to meet Rhett.

It was the best part of her day, every day. Ever since the night she'd found out about the soldier's execution and held Rhett's hand in his room, things between them had changed. They both still had their fears and reservations, but those had been pushed to the side to make room for stronger emotions. The more their love grew, the quieter the other emotions became. Liss wasn't sure if Rhett was aware of it the same way she was. They hadn't talked about it, and Liss didn't think she was ready to. It was enough to know they had made this leap together.

Two days ago, Rhett had mentioned during their sparring session that he was going to the southern tip of the plains to search for the Extended spy. He was going with only Stone, Wilsean, and Ciago.

The plains were sparsely inhabited, mostly by Insorsiled farmers. There were few trees, and it was difficult to hide out in the open, especially on their dragons. The men would be visible long before they approached.

If Liss had told Burk, he would have sent messages to the other caravans. Any fighting Extended in hiding would have been summoned, and together, they could destroy the greatest threat to her people.

Instead, Liss had told Burk all caravans should avoid that area. She didn't say why.

It wasn't the first time she'd had an opportunity to give Burk information about Rhett and failed to do so. She knew she was betraying her own people every time she protected Rhett, but try as she might, she couldn't bring herself to say anything that would put him in danger.

Things that used to be simple now made Liss's head spin. Before she'd come to Lagonia, she'd known the empire was evil and everyone inside it was her enemy. Now, she had friends like Samara, Wilsean, and Ciago, whose souls were full of honor and kindness. Now, she had Rhett. How could she betray them?

But her love for her new friends didn't diminish the loyalty she felt to her own people. Every time she laughed with Samara or kissed Rhett, she knew she was betraying the Extended.

When had everything gotten so complicated? If only she could find the immunity source and get out of here, everything would make sense again.

But the more time passed, the more the thought of leaving her friends…of leaving Rhett…became almost as impossible as the thought of failing her people.

It had been more than a month since she entered Lagonia, and Liss was no closer to finding the cause of Lagonia's immunity than she had been when she first arrived. The night before, she'd unearthed the palace's sewer system, which she had choked and gagged her way through for nothing. There had been nothing down there except…sewage.

She was beginning to think she might have been wrong about it being in the palace after all. The thought of having to search the entire empire street by street was more than she could bear in her exhausted state.

"Hellooo."

Liss opened her eyes to see Samara waving a hand in front of her face. She had been sitting on Samara's bed, which was too warm and comfortable.

"Sorry," Liss said, ducking when her friend threw a pillow at her head. "You were saying?"

There was a knock at the door. Wilsean ambled in.

Liss felt the spike of emotions on his and Samara's souls and smiled to herself.

"You're all dirty," Samara complained to Wilsean.

He hopped onto the bed, drawing more complaints from Samara about his shoes, but Liss knew she wasn't really angry.

"How are my two favorite formerly-Insorsiled women?" Wilsean asked, stretching out and making himself comfortable.

He put his head in Samara's lap and sighed in contentment. Liss felt a momentary flash of jealousy. She would never be able to sit with Rhett like this, with the door open for anyone to see. Suddenly, the few hours she and Rhett stole in the training field didn't feel like nearly enough.

"You're so beautiful," Wilsean murmured as he closed his eyes.

"Have you been out drinking with Ciago again?" Samara asked. Her tone was flippant, but her soul radiated pleasure from the compliment.

"I'm going to bed," Liss announced, rising.

"No, no." Wilsean sat up, grinning at Liss. "I'm on watch tonight. I just came by for—"

"Here," Samara pushed a bottle into Wilsean's hands and shooed him toward the doorway. "Now, leave us alone. I'll see you later."

Wilsean held up the bottle, which was filled with a green, shimmery liquid. "What do you think, Liss? Want me to share some with Rhett?"

Samara smacked her palm to her face as her soul filled with embarrassment. It was then that Liss realized she had seen the green tonic in pharmacy windows in Insorsil. Liss felt her own cheeks heat in understanding.

It was a tonic that prevented men from impregnating women.

Wilsean cackled at the look on Liss's face as he sauntered out of the room. Samara slammed the door behind him.

"Sorry about that." Samara ran a hand through her long hair, frowning. "Honestly, sometimes I don't even know why I put up with him."

Liss just smiled at her friend before sinking back against the pillows. It was possible Samara and Wilsean didn't know the truth of their own souls, and Liss didn't think it was her place to tell them. They'd figure it out eventually.

"Are you okay?" Samara studied her. "You're looking a little peaked."

"You would be, too, if you'd had to deal with three women crying and fighting over a stupid pair of earrings," she grumbled.

Samara crossed her arms. "And the stains on your shirt? Am I to believe your charges lit you on fire?"

Liss went rigid. There was soot on her left sleeve from a chimney she had been desperate enough to search the night before.

"Who knows?" Liss said with a shrug. "Could be from anywhere."

Samara came over to the bed and sat down. "Now that you know about my sex life, it's only fair for you to tell me your secret."

"I don't have any secrets," Liss said, growing uncomfortable under the scrutiny of her friend's stare.

"Oh?" Samara asked.

"I'm an open book." Liss stretched her arms out wide as if to show Samara she wasn't hiding anything.

"Alright then." Samara settled herself on the bed across from Liss. "Then tell me who you really are, and what you're really doing in Lagonia."

Liss stuttered out something incoherent.

"Don't lie," Samara said. "I know you're not an Empty, or anything Insorsiled for that matter."

Liss sat up so fast she wacked her head against the wall. She barely noticed.

Her first thought was to deny it or call her friend delusional. But when she looked into Samara's soul, there was only certainty and determination.

"Don't worry," Samara said. "I haven't told anyone, and I'm not going to."

"How…how long have you known?" Liss asked, her voice coming out as a croak.

Samara scoffed. "I knew the first night when you talked about your Grandpa Widdlywink." She cocked her head at Liss. "My parents are good friends with the Widdlywinks, and all the men in their family have been dead for over a decade."

Of all the rotten luck. Liss cursed the Widdlywinks with all of the fervor she could muster. Real fear was taking hold of her.

"You can trust me." Samara took Liss's hands in hers. "You're my best friend here. My only friend, really. Don't you think I've earned the right to know?"

Liss swallowed. She felt her friend's sincerity, and she didn't like lying to Samara any more than Samara liked being lied to. Besides, it was getting harder and harder to keep up this ruse. She had gotten another disheartening message from Burk about the caravan's desperate situation, and she was exhausted beyond reasoning.

"Are you sure you want to know?" Liss asked, her voice barely above a whisper.

"I won't tell," Samara promised. "Whatever it is."

Liss would be a fool to tell her friend the truth. And yet, when she opened her mouth, it was exactly what she did.

When she finished, she wondered if she had just made the worst decision of her life.

"You're…Opal Smoke?" Samara asked, her eyes bugging out.

Liss nodded.

"That's…." She flailed her hands as she got up and paced across the room. "Freaking amazing!" She came back to take Liss's hands in hers. "You have the whole empire searching for an opal-skinned man who turns into vapor around every turn." Her awed expression turned to a devilish grin. "Wow."

"You aren't going to turn me in, are you?" Liss asked, anxious. She knew what she was asking of her friend to keep this secret.

Samara shook her head, and Liss could tell Samara was wrestling with her amazement at this new revelation and her desire to comfort Liss.

"Thank you for trusting me," Samara said, squeezing Liss in a tight embrace.

"You really don't hate me?" Liss asked, chewing on her lip. "I might not have opal skin, but I'm still Extended."

"I could never hate you," Samara said, pulling back, "and I'm an Empty." She grinned. "An *actual* Empty. I've been called swine myself a time or two. I don't hate the Extended. I've actually always thought of them…of you…as kindred spirits."

For no discernible reason, Liss felt her eyes fill with tears. Emotions she hadn't even known she had bubbled to the surface. Samara gathered her into her arms like she was the sister Liss had never had.

Liss could draw out tears whenever it served her purposes, most often when she was trying to distract a man she was pickpocketing, but she hadn't cried for real in as long as she could remember. Hot, ugly tears streamed down her cheeks as Samara held her.

All her life, Liss had needed to be the strong one. There wasn't enough room in the wagon for two grieving people, and so she had always pasted a smile on her face and gone on with the business of living no matter what she felt.

But with Samara's soft voice and tender embrace, Liss cried. Through her tears, she managed to tell Samara everything. She talked about her search for Lagonia's immunity and Burk's increasingly desperate messages through the onyx stone. A thought occurred to Liss, and her tears instantly evaporated.

"Do you know their secret? Has Wilsean told you anything—"

Samara shook her head. "I'm sorry," she said, her eyes and soul full of regret. "Wilsean doesn't know, and neither do I."

"No, I'm sorry." Liss wiped her eyes. "I shouldn't have even asked."

Keeping Liss's secret was already too much to ask of her friend.

"I wish I could be of more help," Samara said. "But any time you need to talk, I'll be here to listen."

Liss managed a tired smile. "Having someone to talk to will be amazing."

Samara smiled, and then, her features contorted in horror. "Oh no. Rhett—"

"—is supposed to kill me," Liss confirmed.

She realized that she had never spoken those words out loud. It sounded so much worse now than it did whenever she said them in her head.

Rhett is supposed to kill me.

Liss had been reckless and impulsive before, but this was the first time in her life she had truly messed up. She was falling in love with her people's greatest enemy.

Liss knew there were only two ways this could all end. She could finish what she'd come here to do and disappear from Rhett's life forever, or he could discover she was the Extended spy he had been hunting these past months. In the first scenario, he would die when Lagonians no longer had their immunity. In the second, it was her lover's blade that slit her throat.

Liss let herself fall face-first onto the bed. "I've made such a mess of everything," she said into the mattress.

"It's a deadly game you're playing," Samara conceded.

Liss turned her face and looked up at her friend. "I know."

CHAPTER 29

R hett sat in Toil and Trouble and listened with half an ear as yet another soldier reported that there had been no trace of the Extended spy.

"He's just…Opal Smoke," the soldier said, shaking her head.

Rhett had never heard of an Extension that could actually make a person invisible. Either the man he was searching for was dead, which Rhett didn't believe, or he had changed tactics. There had been no news of him on the southern plain, nor had any of his spies across the sea caught word of him being there.

Stone, Ciago, and Wilsean were busy marking up yet another map of Extended hideouts. They were making lists of villages that were too small to even have a name and assigning soldiers to patrol them. Rhett listened to report after report that used different words to convey the same message.

Nothing.

As the useless reports turned to a dull drone in the background, Rhett's thoughts drifted. They went to the same place they always went whenever he let his mind wander: Liss. He'd been on the road for two days, and already, he missed her the way someone might miss a lost limb. He felt like he was missing the best part of himself. The next time he saw her, he was going to—

The corner of his eye caught a flash of steel just before Stone's dagger impaled the wooden table between Rhett's index and middle finger. He wrenched his hand back.

"What'd you do that for?" Rhett demanded, glaring at his mentor.

"What's the matter with you?" Stone growled. "You're not…present."

"I'm right here," Rhett said, unsticking the knife and sending it skittering across the table where it would be out of Stone's reach.

"I'll hazard a diagnosis." Ciago got up from his seat and came around the table to peer into Rhett's face.

"Symptoms include dreamy expression, stupid grin—"

"I don't have a stupid grin," Rhett argued.

Ciago looked at Wilsean.

"The stupidest," Wilsean confirmed, getting in Rhett's face alongside Ciago. Rhett glared, but these were the only men on the continent who weren't intimidated by him.

"Is this about Liss?" Stone ground out.

Rhett gave his mentor a sharp look. "Who said anything about Liss?"

"If you don't want her, I'd be happy to pursue her myself," Ciago offered. "She has the most amazing pair of—"

"Shut your mouth or I'll cut out your tongue," Rhett warned.

"Eyes," Ciago said, giving Rhett an innocent look. "I was going to say *eyes*."

"Symptoms also include violent threats and possessive tendencies," Wilsean added, grinning.

Stone was the only one who wasn't amused. His eyes narrowed. "Have I taught you nothing?"

Rhett sighed. "Don't blame yourself, Stone." He felt his smile return as her face crystallized in his mind. "And don't bother with the lecture," he said, sensing his mentor's mounting fury. "It's too late."

"Diagnosis," Ciago said in a loud voice, "is an incurable case of smitten with the lovely Liss." He shook his head and put a hand on Rhett's shoulder, like it pained him to be the bearer of this news.

In one swift move, Stone threw off Ciago's arm and grabbed Rhett's collar. He dragged Rhett forward until they were face to face.

They had attracted the attention of patrons at other tables, who wisely abandoned their drinks and moved farther away. Rhett let Stone push him into the hallway that led to the private rooms in the back, where they were out of sight and hearing of the main part of the bar. If he fought back, they'd probably destroy the bar. The last time Rhett and Stone had sparred, it had been bloody and brutal, and neither of them had even been angry. Stone might have thirty years on him, but he was as fit and deadly as ever. Rhett wasn't sure which of them would win if they ever really fought.

"I didn't keep you alive this long so you could throw away everything on a servant girl," Stone said, breathing heavily.

The lightheartedness of a few moments ago was gone. Wilsean and Ciago stood blocking the hallway from the rest of the bar as their gazes moved from Rhett to Stone. The air was thick with tension.

"I'm not asking for your permission." Rhett met Stone's furious gaze. "And I'm telling you to save your breath. It's too late."

"Is she carrying your child?" Stone demanded, giving Rhett's collar a shake when he didn't immediately respond.

Rhett leveled a stare at him. "She isn't carrying my child."

"Only because I gave him some of my tonic," Wilsean told Ciago in a non-whisper.

Rhett chose to ignore that.

Stone let out a breath. "Then it isn't too late. Break it off."

"We're done here." Rhett pushed Stone back.

He turned and walked out of the bar.

* * *

Liss stared at the message on her onyx stone.

More slavers coming every day. Soldiers at every outpost. Running out of time.

When Liss put the onyx stone back in her pocket, her hands were trembling. She was doing everything she could. She kept her ears open during the day and tore the palace apart by night. She had even begun looking outside the palace. She'd stolen maps from Jaikon's private meeting rooms and was searching the streets and shops beyond the palace walls. But it was taking too much time…time her people didn't have.

Ask Rhett what he knows.

As her search continued to turn up nothing, she kept coming back to the same thought. And yet, she hadn't been able to bring herself to ask him.

Liss wasn't sure if it was because she feared he would figure out why she was asking, or if it was something else.

Liss sat in the corner of the opulent chamber and tried to doze inconspicuously as her three charges played with magic baubles they'd bought from Samara for an absurd price. Liss had been sleeping even less than usual, going out to search the empire just after dinner and only returning at dawn. With Rhett traveling, she'd been able to use the time they usually spent together to sleep, but somehow, it was less revitalizing than being with him.

"I'm so bored," Mizel, the youngest of Liss's charges, complained.

When she turned eighteen, Mizel's parents had essentially sold their daughter to Jaikon in exchange for a better position at court. She wasn't a mean-spirited girl, and even though Liss didn't want to care about any more Lagonians than had already wormed their way into her heart, she couldn't help but feel a tenderness toward this girl. On the mornings after Mizel's night with the Emperor and Liss found her covered in bruises, Mizel would raise her chin and command Liss to leave her pity at the door. The girl's bravery simultaneously heightened Liss's already-emphatic hatred for the Emperor and made her feel a grudging respect for the girl she had first written off as an airhead.

Jennev, who was somehow even more gorgeous than the other two, was tossing a fist-sized ruby in the air and catching it over and over again.

"I'm bored, too," she sighed. "There's never anything to do around here."

"We could play a game," Mireille said, her eyes twinkling.

Mireille was one of Jaikon's favorites. She had lived in the palace her whole life and was something of a legend among the other women in the Emperor's harem. Liss had been hopeful to learn something about the immunity from her, but the woman was as dumb as she was beautiful, which was to say *extremely*. She never said anything of value.

"What kind of game?" Jennev asked, letting her ruby fall with a thud on the carpet.

Mireille sat down on a velvet chair and adjusted her skirts. She looked like an empress holding court. Liss let her eyes close.

"Suppose you only had one night left to live, and you could spend it with any man you chose. Who would it be?"

"We'd spend it with the Emperor, of course," Mizel replied.

"That's a boring game," Jennev whined.

Mireille lowered her voice. "Any man *but* the Emperor."

Neither of the other women spoke for a moment.

"That's easy," Jennev said, returning Mireille's wicked smile. "I'd spend it with Rhetteman Loniger."

Liss's eyes flew open.

"Ooh me too," Mizel exclaimed. "He's so beautifully severe."

Liss tried not to breathe for fear of drawing the women's attention.

Mireille shook her head, a regretful look on her face. "You mean you girls haven't heard?" Her lower lip had the nerve to tremble. "It's such a shame."

"What is?" Jenney asked.

"What's wrong with him?" Mizel asked at almost the same time. Both of them scooted closer to Mireille.

Mireille leaned forward. "He doesn't work right *down there.*"

Liss choked on air. She covered her mouth as she tried to cough without drawing attention to herself.

"Really?" Mizel asked, her eyes widening.

Mireille nodded. "Laciette practically got naked in front of him once, and he didn't react at all. He just walked away. *I've* even tried to seduce him."

"If he didn't want you or Laciette," Jennev reasoned, "then he isn't a man."

"Maybe he prefers men," Mizel said, looking almost as devastated by that possibility as the former.

Mireille shook her head. "They've tried, too."

"That's so sad," Mizel said, looking like she might cry.

"Why do you think he's always going around killing people? He's got all this pent-up aggression and nothing to do with it."

There was a sharp rap on the door. Before any of the women could grant the person entry, the door opened.

Liss thought the women might actually faint when Rhett stepped into the room, and frankly, she wouldn't be far behind them.

Rhett had been gone for three days, and she'd forgotten how impossibly attractive he was. He wore his black gear, and there was stubble along his jaw. His dark eyes scanned the room once. They passed over her, but didn't linger. His blank expression didn't even change.

Liss, for her part, had to dig her nails into her palms to keep from reacting at the sight of him.

"Good afternoon, my—" Mireille began, but Rhett cut her off.

"The Emperor requires all servants to the banquet hall to prepare for tonight's feast." He spoke in a brisk, commanding tone that left no room for discussion. "Immediately."

Then, without another glance at any of them, he strode out of the room and shut the door behind him.

For several moments, no one moved.

"You heard the man," Mireille barked at Liss. "Get going."

Liss crossed the room in measured steps. She closed the door behind her and walked down the hallway slowly, trailing her hand along the emeralds embedded along the wall. She told herself the ache in her chest had nothing to do with Rhett's passing glance. It wasn't like he could have smiled at her or blown her a kiss...obviously. It was that look of nothing that hurt.

She'd been too surprised to see him to sort his emotions, but judging from the complete absence of any expression in his eyes, he hadn't been thinking about her these last few days the way she'd been thinking about him.

Maybe it was the dose of reality she needed, she told herself. The thought didn't make her feel better.

A hand snaked out from the shadows behind a gold statue. Before she could even process what was happening, she was pulled into a dark stairwell she hadn't even known was there.

Liss was too shocked to scream. And then, she couldn't scream because someone's mouth was pressed to hers.

She recognized Rhett's lips before she knew the rest of him. The familiar swirl of emotions roiling just beneath the surface came next. She opened her eyes and took him in for only a moment before he'd pressed her against the wall, and his lips were on hers again. He kissed her with an almost savage intensity.

He pulled back an inch, and the sound of their ragged breathing filled the space.

"I've thought about nothing else for three days," Rhett said, his voice a low growl. "I almost went mad."

"I missed you, too," Liss said with a little laugh. She stood on her toes to wind her hands around his neck. "Did you find the spy?"

"I don't want to talk about the spy." He gripped her waist and leaned into her. "Actually, I don't want to talk at all."

Rhett's desire was overwhelming. It was even stronger because of her own soul's desperation for him. Rhett's hands moved from her waist to her chest. Rhett covered her mouth with his, swallowing her moan.

"Did you hear what those women were saying about you?" she asked, breathless, when they came up for air a second time.

Rhett gave her a wicked grin. "And what do you think of their theory?" He pressed his body against hers.

"I—I think everything works just fine," she managed.

"Mm."

Liss fisted her hands in Rhett's shirt to keep silent as his thumbs traced light circles over her breasts. He pulled back just enough to look at her. His eyes were darker than usual, filled with emotions in a way she'd never seen them.

"Liss, I—"

Footsteps and voices came from the other end of the hall. As they neared, Rhett drew her deeper into the darkness. The footsteps came closer. Liss felt her and Rhett's hearts beating a fearsome, harmonious rhythm against each other's chests. When the voices moved on, she sighed.

Rhett took her face in his hands. Instead of kissing her, he said, "Spend the night with me."

Liss started. She hadn't been expecting that.

"We'd get caught," she said. "The guards—"

"I know a place," Rhett said. "No one will know."

She searched his emotions as he stared into her eyes with that alarming intensity. His desire overwhelmed every other emotion, but she knew his soul well enough to tease out the more hidden emotions. Beneath his desire there was also hope, uncertainty….

"Alright," Liss said after a moment.

"Yes?"

Disbelief, joy, and anticipation rolled through him.

"Yes," she said again, feeling a smile curve her lips. "What time?"

"Midnight at the change of the guards," Rhett said. "Do you want me to come get you?"

Liss laughed. "I think I can manage sneaking out."

He let out a shuddering breath as he stepped back from her. "Meet me on our field." He pressed another hard kiss to her lips, and then he was gone.

CHAPTER 30

When Liss returned to her room just before getting her charges ready for dinner, she found a new message on her onyx stone. *For every day you fail, more of our people will die. Find the immunity.* Liss had half a mind to throw the stone out her window. Instead, she stormed into Samara's room and raged. Samara listened in sympathy as Liss ranted about Burk and his unreasonable expectations. Samara pulled out her stash of Insorsiled candy as she berated Burk.

By the time she left Samara's room, Liss's tongue was stained purple and her anger had cooled. She had planned to search the empire's historic quarters tonight, but maybe she'd confine her search to the few places in the palace she still hadn't explored since she only had a couple of hours.

She could tell Rhett she'd changed her mind and use the extra hours to expand her search. But she wouldn't. Regardless of what Burk said, Liss didn't think one day would make a difference in her people's future. She hadn't taken a single night off from searching since she'd come to Lagonia. She could have tonight.

As Liss stood in her corner of the banquet hall, she tried not to look in Rhett's direction as the Emperor droned on about how Lagonia's coffers were at an all-time high.

There was a side-conversation going on that piqued her interest, though. A soldier had been invited to join the Emperor's table who wasn't usually there. He was bragging to the women sitting on either side of him that the Emperor had entrusted him with attacking Extended hideouts, since the Chief Assassin was preoccupied with other tasks. The soldier even took the list of his next targets out of his pocket to show the women, who fawned over his bravery and strength.

Fortunately for Liss, the soldier bid the women goodnight early, explaining how he'd be leaving at dawn to carry out his orders. Liss snatched a flagon of wine and went around the table to refill her women's glasses. At the moment when the soldier passed her, she let the flask drop from her hands.

She gasped and covered her mouth as she stared wide-eyed at the mess. Then, she grabbed a cloth napkin from the table and began to try to sop up the mess while she apologized profusely to the soldier. The soldier snarled at her as she tried to wipe his boots. The wine had soaked into the dragonhide leather, and Liss felt satisfied the stain would never come out.

The man kicked the flagon under the table and stalked out of the banquet hall, leaving sticky red footsteps in his wake.

"Forgive me," Liss said to no one in particular as more servants swarmed around to help clean up the mess.

When all remnants of the wine were gone, Liss sunk back into her corner, pocketing the folded paper and feeling monumentally pleased with herself. This list of names would be enough to get Burk off her back for a few days, at least. More importantly, it would save Extended lives.

As soon as she'd gotten her charges to bed, she ducked into one of the servants' stairwells, scanned the piece of paper, and communicated the entirety of it into her onyx stone. As she made her way back into the main hallway, she let the paper slip into one of the blazing fires that Flamer slaves kept lit at all hours.

She was feeling pleased enough with what she'd accomplished tonight that she decided to go back to her room and bathe instead of searching the palace's extensive art galleries. Maybe she'd even use some of the makeup Samara had offered to lend her.

Liss was so wrapped up in thinking about how she'd spend the next hour before she went to meet Rhett that she didn't notice the shadow trailing behind her. She didn't sense his soul or hear his footsteps until she was shoved from behind.

All the wind was knocked out of her as Liss hit the marble floor.

She felt fury and violence before a vicious kick to her ribs sent her sprawling. Liss got to her knees, but before she could even turn to face her assailant, she was flying backward. Her skull hit the ground. Her vision swam in and out of focus.

"What'd you do with it?"

Liss's whole body protested as she scrambled away. That was when she caught sight of the stained dragonhide boots. Her unfocused vision moved up to the rage-filled face of the soldier from the banquet hall.

The man kicked her again. Before she'd caught her breath, the soldier was kneeling beside her and raining down blows on her face.

"Please," she said, trying to cover her head.

The soldier let up, rocking back on his heels. Liss scanned the hallway through her left eye, which wasn't yet swollen shut. The hall was empty.

"Where is it?" he demanded.

"I don't know what you're talking about," Liss whimpered as she wracked her brain for what to do.

Rhett had taught her enough that she might be able to best the soldier. He was drunk and didn't expect her to put up a fight. But if a servant hit a soldier, she'd be in worse trouble than she already was. Liss decided her best option was to play innocent and behave as any other servant would in her position.

She started to cry. "I don't know what you're talking about. I'm sorry I spilled the wine."

The soldier returned to his beating. His strikes were vicious. When he paused to demand what she had done with the list, Liss could sense fear alongside anger on the man's soul. He would likely face far worse than a beating when his superiors found out he'd lost the list of his next victims.

Liss had hoped the soldier would wear himself out and go away, but his desperation to get back what he'd lost was too powerful. He'd beat her to death if she didn't do something.

When the man hauled Liss to her feet and wrapped a hand around her throat, she had no choice but to act.

Liss stomped on the man's foot. As soon as she felt his hold on her neck loosen, she spun and drove her fist into the soldier's face. Then, she ran.

* * *

Before tonight, Rhett had thought he'd been prepared to handle any kind of torture. Stone had beaten him, starved him, made him fight until he was too exhausted to hold up a sword, and put him through every interrogation technique known to man.

But nothing Stone made him suffer through had prepared him for the special torture of sitting through one of Jaikon's banquets as the minutes to midnight crawled by.

When it had finally been appropriate for him to leave without drawing suspicion, he'd gone back to his room where he'd spent longer bathing than he ever had in his life. He'd put on an absurdly expensive scented oil one of the courtier women had gifted him and which he hadn't gotten around to tossing. Then, unsure of whether Liss would like the smell, he'd bathed again to wash it off. He'd shaved and drunk the sickly-sweet tonic Wilsean had given him.

Now, he was pacing up and down the length of the practice field. He kept waiting for Liss to appear from the shadows. He still didn't know how she managed to sneak up on him.

Rhett checked the clockface on the palace's western tower again. It was half past midnight. He tried to remember if Liss had ever been late to one of their sparring sessions. He didn't think she had.

Did a guard stop her from leaving the palace? Did she run into some kind of trouble? Did she change her mind?

Rhett kept pacing, telling himself that half an hour wasn't even considered late by Lagonian standards.

When the clock struck one, and there was still no sign of Liss, he couldn't stand it anymore. He led Silverbird back to the stables, unsaddled her, and then strode back in the direction of the palace.

Logic told Rhett the most likely scenario was that Liss had changed her mind about what she wanted. Still, it didn't seem like Liss to just not show up without any explanation. He had to know if she was alright.

Rhett used the servants' halls, which were empty this late, as he made his way to the servants' quarters. He stood outside her door for only a moment. He knocked.

"Liss?"

No answer.

He took the ring of keys from his pocket that opened every room in the palace. He knocked once more, and then fitted the key into the lock.

CHAPTER 31

G o away," Liss said, trying to make her voice sound normal even though her mouth was swollen.

The only light in the room came from the blue moonlight streaming in through the window. As long as Rhett didn't come any closer, he wouldn't be able to see what a bloody mess she was.

"You didn't come, and I was worried," Rhett said, still standing in the doorway.

"I changed my mind. I don't want to be with you like that."

Fresh blood trickled down the corner of her mouth.

Rhett took another step forward.

"I said get out," she said again, this time with a hint of panic.

If Rhett found out what had happened to her, he'd go after the soldier, and then he'd find out what she stole. She had no idea how she'd explain that. It was better if she didn't have to.

"What made you change your mind?" Rhett asked, his voice carefully guarded.

He couldn't hide the disappointment on his soul. Feeling it hurt as much as any of her real wounds.

"I told you. I don't want to be with you like that."

Confusion filled his soul along with the other emotions.

"Why are you standing here in the dark?" he asked after a long pause.

"None of your business," she snapped, putting some venom into her words. "Now, get out before someone sees you loitering in my doorway."

Rhett turned away. Relief, followed by deep regret, filled her. *Keep walking*, her brain commanded. *Don't go!* her soul screamed.

She turned to the wall and waited for the sound of her door shutting. The door closed, but Rhett was still in her room.

"What are you doing?" she demanded.

"I want you to look me in the eye," Rhett said, fiddling with something by the door. "If you can tell me to my face you don't want me, I'll go."

Liss realized what Rhett was doing a moment too late.

"Don't!"

Her room flooded with light as Rhett twisted the Insorsiled lamp on her wall.

She kept her back to him and begged him to leave, even though she knew he wouldn't. She felt his hand on her shoulder. With no other option, she turned to face him.

Rhett's eyes widened. He staggered back like he'd been struck. Horror flooded his soul.

"What happened?" he gasped, like he couldn't catch his breath.

"I tripped and fell. It's not a big deal."

Rhett's chest was heaving.

"You fell on your eye?" His voice was quiet, which made him somehow more terrifying.

His hand shook as he reached up to touch her jaw, angling it toward the light. She flinched away from him.

"Where else did you *fall?*" he demanded.

"It's just a few bruises," she began.

"Where else?!"

She pressed a hand to her side where the soldier's boot had connected.

"Nothing's broken. Rhett, please."

He was beyond hearing her. He was on his knees in front of her, unbuttoning her shirt. She had a fleeting thought that this wasn't how she'd imagined him undressing her for the first time, and then she felt his horror anew as he took in the sight of her battered side.

It looked as bad as it felt. There was a smattering of blue-black welts all along her ribs. There was even the imprint of a boot across her stomach. Rhett brushed a feather-light touch over the ugly mark.

Fury was rolling off him with such intensity Liss didn't think he could form words.

He stood up.

"Who did this to you?" His voice was the calm before the storm.

She hurriedly buttoned her shirt. "I don't know."

"Who. Did. This. To. You."

"Some soldier. I don't know his name."

Rhett was starting to scare her.

He didn't say anything for a moment. "The one you spilled wine on."

Liss's lips parted in surprise. She had purposely waited until the soldier had come around to the far side of the banquet hall, where she thought they'd be out of sight of anyone sitting at the Emperor's table.

"Is he the one who did this to you?"

Liss didn't say anything, but whatever expression had crossed her face, she knew he'd read it correctly.

"I'll bring you some ice and something to help with the pain in a little while," he said, striding toward the door.

"What are you going to do to him?" she asked, hurrying after him.

"Nothing less than he deserves," Rhett growled.

"Don't kill him," she begged.

Liss was surprised by her own request. After all, it would be better for her if the soldier was dead, preferably before he could open his mouth and give her away. She realized it wasn't the soldier's life she cared about, though. It was that she didn't want Rhett killing anyone else, especially not for her sake.

"He was dead the moment he touched you," Rhett replied, his hand on the door.

"I mean it," she persisted. "Don't kill him."

"Why not?" Rhett spun around to face her.

Liss had never felt such fury on his soul before. It was murderous in its intensity. She didn't like it.

"Because you're not a savage. You're not like the rest of them." Rhett snarled.

"I'm serious," she said. "Don't kill him. I won't thank you for it."

Rhett turned without another word and stormed out of her room.

223

CHAPTER 32

Rhett broke into a jog, his heart hammering like it was going to explode right out of his chest. He didn't see where he was going. Liss's bloody face and bruised sides filled his vision. His single-minded purpose was all that kept him from being sick on the marble floor.

It had taken Rhett about five seconds to put together who had done this to her. He went straight to the soldiers' quarters, recalling who occupied each room until he found the one he sought.

He searched his memory for the soldier's name. *Mackal,* he remembered. The man was one of the new recruits from the countryside, and Rhett hadn't spoken more than a few words to him.

Rhett took only a moment to steady himself before he eased open the soldier's door and let himself inside. He shut it silently behind him, allowing his eyes to adjust to the darkness.

Mackal was asleep in his bed. Even though Rhett didn't bother to quiet his footsteps, the man didn't wake. The fool had been drinking the night before a mission. None of the soldiers Rhett had trained would ever do that.

None of his soldiers would ever beat a servant.

It was the sound of Rhett's blade coming free from its sheath that finally woke the man.

"Wha-what are you doing?" Mackal asked, sitting back against the headboard.

Rhett didn't look at him as he placed his dagger on the small table beside the bed.

"Get up," Rhett said.

"What's the meaning of this?" Mackal's fearful gaze went from the dagger to Rhett.

Rhett twisted the Insorsiled light next to the bed, flooding the room with a soft orange glow. He studied Mackal. He took in the soldier's left eye, which was swollen shut.

That's my girl, he thought with some satisfaction.

Rhett's amusement fled as his gaze moved to the soldier's right fist. The knuckles were cracked and covered in dried blood. Mackal followed the line of Rhett's gaze.

His eyes widened in understanding. "She—"

"Shh," Rhett said. "You don't get to talk anymore."

Mackal's gaze went to Rhett's knife, which was lying abandoned on the table.

Rhett smiled. "You're welcome to try for it. In fact, I'll even let you get in the first strike."

The soldier shrunk back.

"No? Well, then, I'll go first." He prowled closer, taking his time.

Rhett kept his punch slow enough that Mackal saw it coming. The man winced right before he thudded to the ground. His skull cracked against the floor.

"Get up," Rhett snarled.

"She's just a servant—"

Rhett hit the man again. This time, he felt bones crunch beneath his knuckles.

Mackal screamed.

"She's not *just a servant*," Rhett spat. "Not to me."

He punched Mackal in the throat, cutting off his howl. The man slammed backward into the wall, but Rhett caught him before he could slump to the floor.

"I didn't know she was yours," the man cried.

"She isn't *mine*," Rhett growled. "She's a free woman, and you hurt her."

Rhett stepped back just enough to give himself some space. Then, he kicked Mackal in the ribs, right in the place where those hideous welts covered Liss's skin.

"Please don't kill me," Mackal begged.

Rhett kicked him in the stomach, and then brought his boot down on the man's foot, feeling the give of bone. He gave the soldier another swift hit to the throat to silence his scream.

"I'm not going to kill you," Rhett said, kneeling beside the writhing man. "I should, and believe me, I would. But she asked me not to. You owe her your life."

He took hold of the soldier's right wrist, holding it up so Mackal could see the dried blood on his knuckles. The man made a feeble attempt to pull his hand free. Rhett tightened his grip.

"Unfortunately, my experience is in quick, clean kills. I'm less practiced at torture." He broke Mackal's index finger. "So, I'll just have to do my best."

"I'll never touch her again," the man sobbed.

Rhett broke two more fingers.

"Oh, I know you won't. I'm going to make sure of it." The man's thumb gave way to the pressure of Rhett's grip.

Tears streamed down Mackal's cheeks.

"Should I do the left hand, too, just in case you decide to hit her with that one?"

Mackal was beyond words. He was shaking his head back and forth like he was convulsing.

"I think I better," Rhett decided. "I don't like to leave a job half-finished."

Mackal passed out before Rhett had finished breaking the rest of his fingers. Rhett stayed kneeling by his side until he came to.

"I'd leave it at that, but you bruised her ribs." Rhett stood and leveled his foot at the man's side. "So, I'm going to break yours."

❋ ❋ ❋

Rhett closed the door behind him. One of his kicks had gone slightly astray, and he thought Mackal might have a collapsed lung. He sent the guard at the end of the hall to get a physician. If Mackal died, Rhett would have to explain it to Liss.

He had seen the resolve on her bruised and battered face, and he believed she wouldn't forgive him if he killed the man. Rhett had no idea why she should care if Mackal got what he deserved, but he wouldn't let this piece of trash make Liss resent him.

The physician Rhett had specifically requested was hurrying down the hall. The old man felt indebted to Rhett, who had once saved his son's life on a battleground covered in ice and snow. Rhett had never been comfortable with being praised for what he saw as nothing more than his sworn duty, but tonight, that gratitude would be useful. He could count on the physician to do his job quietly, without letting news of what Rhett had done become court gossip.

"He has to live," Rhett told the physician as they stood over Mackal's wheezing, weeping form, "but I want him to be in as much pain as you can manage."

The physician took one look at the bloody, broken mess on the floor and nodded. Rhett grabbed his unused dagger off the table and left without another glance. He still didn't trust himself not to kill Mackal.

Rhett went back to his room, where he washed the blood off his hands and changed into clothes that weren't stained red. Then, he went to the now-empty banquet hall.

There was a ridiculous ice sculpture of Jaikon that was beginning to melt. Rhett used his knife to chip away at the ice, finally cutting off the Emperor's hand, and slipped the ice into a satin napkin. He brought it, and the bag of medical supplies the physician had given him, back to Liss's room.

He chose speed over caution and used the main hallways. Liss had been alone with her injuries for too long. With the mood he was in, he almost hoped Elouicia or one of Jaikon's cronies were waiting for him. He would gladly kill any of them if they tried to keep him from Liss.

CHAPTER 33

L iss had been pacing back and forth across her room for half an hour. She clutched her Insorsiled onyx stone in her hand, but she hadn't used it. She had no idea what to say. There was nothing Burk could do to help her now.

Options, she told herself, trying to hold back the tide of panic. Her fear had been trying to overwhelm her since Rhett stepped into her room and saw her face. She was ready to lose her mind.

She could run—try to escape before the soldier told Rhett what she'd stolen and he figured out who she was. She didn't think she'd get far, though. Rhett had soldiers, spies, and pixies all over the continent. Besides, where could she go? If she went home, it would only put the rest of her caravan in more danger. And with her short hair, she would never be mistaken for an Insorsiled again. She wasn't a Huntress like her mom…she wouldn't survive alone in the forest.

She needed a convincing lie. She could tell Rhett the paper fell out of the soldier's pocket, and when she realized what it was, she'd panicked and burned it because she didn't want to get in trouble.

The lie sounded pathetic even in her own head, but it was all she had.

Liss's heart jumped into her throat when she felt Rhett's soul down the hallway. He eased the door open and came in, shutting it behind him. He stiffened at the sight of her.

"I brought you some things," he said, his voice gruff.

The emotions in his soul were a little calmer than they'd been before. She sorted through them, looking for suspicion or anything else that would give her a clue about how much he knew. The only emotions she felt were anger, regret, and pain.

"Did you kill him?"

"I wanted to," Rhett said, motioning for her to sit on the bed. "I still want to. But no, I didn't."

Liss sat, taking the napkin filled with ice he gave her. She pressed it to her side while Rhett pulled out disinfecting wipes and healing ointments. He cleaned the cuts on her face with such gentleness she barely felt the sting as the disinfectant burrowed into her wounds.

"That man will never hurt you again," Rhett promised, his gaze fixed on the cut on her lip.

Liss gave a short, jerky nod. She had no idea how she had gotten so lucky, but it was obvious from Rhett's emotions that the soldier hadn't told him what she'd stolen. She decided not to question this small bit of good fortune.

Rhett pulled a knife out of his belt. It looked like the dagger he always carried, only smaller. He handed it to her.

"Keep this on you always," Rhett said. "And if you ever need to use it, don't hesitate. I don't care who is on the other end of the blade."

"Okay."

"I mean it, Liss. No hesitating."

She cracked a small smile, and then winced as the cut on her mouth burned. "Thank you."

Rhett shook his head, a bitter twist to his mouth. "You don't have to thank me." He slumped onto the bed next to her. He looked exhausted.

"You scared me tonight," Liss said after a while.

Rhett looked at her. "You have to know I would never hurt you."

"It's not me I'm worried about," she replied.

Confusion entered Rhett's soul.

"You don't have to be like the rest of them," she said.

Rhett's expression tightened. "You've known who and what I am from the beginning."

"But you could be so much more." Liss felt the prick of tears at her eyes for no reason she could fathom. "You're kind underneath all that hardness.

You're a good person, even though you pretend not to be. You know Jaikon is evil, yet you obey his every command."

"I obey him because he's my emperor," Rhett replied, his voice taking on a hard edge. "It's my duty to serve him."

"You mean it's your duty to murder for him," Liss retorted. It was becoming more of an effort to keep her volume reasonable. "But you could be so much better, so much more."

"I have to choose the battles that are worth fighting," Rhett said, letting out a shaky breath.

"Like what you did to that soldier tonight?" she asked. "Was that one of the worthy battles?"

"Yes." His answer came without hesitation.

"And what about the women your emperor beats every night? I don't see you doing anything about that." She hurried on before Rhett could say anything. "What about all the other people in this empire who are suffering? What about—" she almost said *my people*, and cut herself off just in time.

Liss didn't know why she was angry, but she was. Her hands were shaking from it.

"I'm as much a servant as you are," Rhett said quietly. "There's nothing I can do for those people."

"That isn't true," Liss said, her voice rising. "You should care about them like you care about me."

"You want me to care about those people the same way I care about you?" Rhett raised his eyebrows.

"You know what I mean," she snapped.

"You don't have any idea how things work around here," Rhett said, his own anger rising.

Good. It was about time he showed some emotion.

"I understand perfectly," she said. "You see how messed up things are around here, and yet you're too afraid to do anything about it."

"I'm not afraid—"

"You're terrified!" Liss was on her feet now. "It's the same reason why you tried so hard not to get close to me. You're afraid of caring!"

Rhett stood, too. There was confusion and anger, but also a deep guilt and unhappiness on his soul that tugged at Liss's heart.

"Liss—"

"Get out."

She was on the brink of tears, and she was desperate for him to leave before she broke down.

Rhett didn't move for several seconds. Then, he crossed the room and opened the door. He turned back once, like he wanted to say something, but then he just shook his head. Liss listened to his heavy footsteps recede down the hall. When she could no longer sense the familiar tendrils of his emotions, she collapsed back on the bed and let her tears come.

CHAPTER 34

Jaikon loathed pandering to the councilmen, especially when he knew half of them had plans to overthrow him…albeit pathetically weak plans. The few who were loyal to him had counseled patience, encouraging Jaikon to win back the others' favor rather than going straight to tossing bodies over the cliff. While Jaikon had seen the merit of their advice, he hadn't been happy about it.

He was suffering through yet another meeting where they squabbled over meaningless laws and other matters of no import. Jaikon's eyes scanned the room as he tried to rein in his impatience. It was then that he noticed one of his new guards was missing.

"Where's Mackal?" he demanded.

The councilmen stopped arguing. The two soldiers in the room exchanged a brief glance, hesitating. Jaikon wanted to kill them then and there for the slight. His hand itched to reach for his sword.

"He has been grievously injured, Your Majesty," one of the women reported.

Jaikon's eyebrows lifted. "Was there a battle I wasn't informed of?"

"No, Majesty." The soldiers shared another look. Jaikon ground his teeth. "The Chief Assassin was the one who injured him."

From that first look the soldiers exchanged, Jaikon had known Rhetteman had something to do with this. Whenever his soldiers hesitated, it had something to do with the bastard.

"Bring Mackal," Jaikon told Elouicia before turning back to the councilmembers with a benevolent smile on his face.

"Majesty, we're discussing the merits of gifting land to the noblemen and their families to improve morale," one councilman said, filling Jaikon in on their tiresome conversation.

As though he wasn't adept enough to give orders and listen to their prattle at the same time.

Jaikon drummed his fingers on the solid gold table around which they were all seated.

"Is there a problem with morale, gentlemen?" he asked.

No one mistook the dangerous tone he used. An unsettled quiet stole over the table.

"Personally," Jaikon continued, "I think executions are much more compelling than gifts."

A few of the men swallowed and exchanged nervous looks. Jaikon took in each of their reactions, noting guilt on some and defiance on others. They would all pay. He'd make certain of it. This was his empire, and soon enough, there wouldn't be room for those who didn't obey him without question.

The doors to the chamber opened. Several of the councilmen gasped as a stretcher was brought in. Jaikon raised his eyebrows. The man on the stretcher looked more dead than alive.

An excited tingle began in Jaikon's spine. This meeting was getting interesting.

Jaikon couldn't recall a single time when the Chief Assassin had laid a finger on someone he wasn't expressly commanded to kill. Rhetteman wasn't violent by nature. The man didn't have a temper, nor did he have problems with impulse control, as did so many of the soldiers in his employ. What could this soldier have done to provoke him?

Jaikon couldn't wait to find out.

"What happened to you?" Jaikon asked without sympathy.

Mackal's eyes widened, displaying true fear. It was the right emotion, but the target of the man's fear was the wrong one. It wasn't Jaikon he feared.

"I abandoned my post," the man mumbled. His jaw had clearly been broken, along with seemingly the rest of him.

"Unless you fancy spending the rest of your life in the torture cage with my Master Interrogator, you'll tell me the truth," Jaikon replied evenly.

The man's eyes were leaking tears. It was pathetic.

"I abandoned my post," he said again.

Jaikon took note of how Mackal's wounds had been expertly stitched, and yet, no quick-heal had been used. Had Rhetteman told the physician to only tend to the mortal wounds? He must have wanted Mackal to suffer.

Jaikon pierced the man with his gaze. "You're telling me my Chief Assassin almost killed you for abandoning your post?"

The man nodded. The councilmen were watching the exchange with interest.

"I don't believe you," Jaikon said with a shrug, as though it didn't matter that the man was lying to his face.

"Majesty, please," Mackal begged.

"Toss this man over the cliff," Jaikon told Elouicia. "And then search the Chief Assassin's room again. Put some pixies on his tail, too. Let's find out what he's so upset about."

Elouicia grinned, baring his pointed teeth.

* * *

Rhett watched his soldiers on the training field without seeing them.

He knew he was living on borrowed time. Opal Smoke hadn't made an appearance in almost two months, and Jaikon hadn't been quiet about what would happen if Rhett didn't produce the man's head. There were only two weeks left before the deadline Jaikon had given him.

Rhett didn't doubt the Emperor would make good on his promise to take his head in exchange for the spy's.

At least Rhett had kept his wits about him enough to threaten Mackal against telling the Emperor why he'd beaten him. He had sworn that if Mackal said anything to Jaikon or so much as mentioned anything about Liss, Rhett would go to the village where Mackal had come from and kill every member of his family.

Rhett rubbed his eyes. In spite of the imminent danger he faced from Jaikon, he was having trouble caring about the conversation Ciago and Wilsean were now having about where else the spy might be hiding.

It was only when Wilsean needed to repeat his question to Rhett for the third time that his friends looked up at him.

"What's wrong with you?" Wilsean demanded. "You look terrible."

"Don't flatter me," Rhett replied.

"I know that look," Ciago said, giving Rhett a sympathetic nod. "Love trouble."

Rhett scowled.

"Did you two fight?" Wilsean asked.

Rhett didn't want to talk about it. He wasn't even clear on what had happened. But his friends knew him too well to believe a lie.

"It wasn't a fight, exactly," Rhett said.

"Well, whatever you do, do *not* give her flowers," Wilsean advised.

"I have it on good authority women love flowers," Ciago argued.

"All I'm saying is I got flowers for Samara the first time I pissed her off, and she threw them in my face. I was picking tiny thorns out of my skin for a week." Wilsean shuddered at the memory.

"Give her something shiny, then," Ciago suggested.

Rhett had never seen Liss wear jewelry and didn't think she cared about that sort of thing.

"You can't just buy your way into every woman's good graces," Wilsean told Ciago.

Ciago frowned. "It's always worked for me."

"That's because the women you go after aren't known for having much in the way of personality," Wilsean pointed out.

"Or brains," Rhett added.

"True," Ciago replied, not sounding particularly bothered. "But at least I'm not shackled like the two of you."

"Who's shackled?" Wilsean retorted.

His friends continued to bicker, but Rhett had stopped listening. His argument with Liss from the night before played in his head over and over again in an endless loop. Her words had burrowed deep under his skin.

All his life, Rhett had understood who and what he was. He was a survivor in an empire built on lies, false promises, and duplicity. Keeping his head down and doing his duty was the only way to preserve his life and his sanity. But after last night, and for the first time in his life, he thought he might owe the empire and himself something more than his silence.

Stone would kill him for even entertaining these thoughts.

Steel doesn't know love or despair. It can't be bent or broken. It needs no heart or warmth. I am steel.

Were those words even true anymore? Liss had told him he was kind. He didn't want to be…he couldn't be. He had spent so long living with the two halves of himself…the half that wanted to care and the half that knew he couldn't….

Was he even capable of changing now? Did he want to?

Rhett wasn't sure if the rest of what Liss had said was right, but he knew, more than anything, he wanted to be worthy of her.

A disturbance near the Golden Bridge caught his attention. There were four slavers surrounding a group of Extended, who seemed to have gotten free from their manacles. From the weak punches the Extended threw, Rhett knew they weren't Fighters. One of the slavers cracked a whip, striking the side of an Extended man's head. The man went down, and the slavers laughed.

The archers on the bridge averted their gazes, even as the Extended cried for help.

"Where are you going?" Ciago asked.

Rhett didn't answer as he took off in the direction of the bridge.

CHAPTER 35

Rhett waited outside the throne room until he was granted entry. Elouicia walked beside him, probably trying to intimidate him. Rhett kept his posture relaxed as he approached the throne.

"You wanted to see me, Your Majesty?" he asked.

Rhett was unsurprised to see that Jaikon's face was red with fury. The throne room was full of councilmen, courtiers and their families, and some of Jaikon's women. Jaikon couldn't afford to lose his temper with so many witnesses or he'd appear weak. Rhett waited patiently while the Emperor wrestled with his anger.

"Did you or did you not kill four slavers earlier today?" Jaikon demanded.

"I did, Your Majesty," Rhett replied without hesitation.

There was a murmur among the courtiers.

"And did you release the Extended they were bringing into the empire?" Jaikon demanded.

"I did."

A shocked, excited silence fell over the normally-exuberant courtiers.

"Why?" Jaikon hissed the word.

"Because the slavers were on our side of the bridge." Rhett turned to the councilmen, letting them see the mildly puzzled expression he wore for their benefit. "I'm sure I don't need to remind Your Majesty that slavery is illegal in the empire."

There were a few nervous titters in the crowd. Rhett kept his face impassive.

Jaikon's face went from red to purple. Rhett had embarrassed him in front of his subjects.

"If Your Majesty has changed your mind about the law," Rhett began.

"I haven't *changed my mind.*"

The laws about slavery had been put in place long before Jaikon's time, and weren't in his power to change. Everyone in the room was well aware of this fact.

Rhett waited in silence for Jaikon to master his emotions.

"Well done, soldier," the Emperor said, his fury disappearing behind a cold smile. "You are dismissed."

Rhett didn't miss the slight of being called *soldier* rather than his proper title. Jaikon's words were far less troublesome than the look in his eyes that promised retribution. If it wasn't for everyone in the throne room, Jaikon would probably kill him here and now. *Just as he'd done to their father.*

Rhett made his posture relax. "Thank you, Majesty." He bowed and left the throne room. He felt Jaikon's eyes boring into his back even after the doors had shut behind him.

Even though he knew there would be consequences for what he'd done, Rhett was feeling downright smug as he made his way back through the palace. For however short-lived his victory might be, Rhett had bested the Emperor.

His good mood fell away at the sight of Stone stalking toward him.

"News really does travel fast," Rhett said as his mentor shoved him inside an empty meeting chamber and slammed the door behind them.

They both scanned the room, making sure they were alone. Then, Stone shoved Rhett against the wall.

"Have you lost your mind completely?" Stone demanded, his lips white with fury.

Rhett sighed. "Not as far as I can tell."

"You did this because of *her*, didn't you?"

Rhett didn't say anything.

"*Ack*, of course you did." Stone looked at Rhett with disgust. "You used to have a head on your shoulders. You used to value your life."

"I've never valued my life more than I do now," he replied. It was the truth.

"You've got a poor way of showing it!" Stone's words were laced with fury.

"I have this under control," Rhett told his mentor.

Stone laughed at that. "You won't be able to protect her. You know that, don't you?"

Discomfort wormed into Rhett's mind. He thought of Liss's bloody face and bruised side. "We're being careful," he said. "Jaikon won't find out about her."

"You can't be this naïve," Stone growled. "I don't give a damn about her life, but I do care about yours."

If these words had come from anyone else, Rhett would have been angry. But he understood Stone's fury was rooted in fear.

"I can handle this," Rhett said, trying to give Stone something.

"If you love her, you'll walk away." Stone let go of him.

If you love her.

Love was such an inadequate word for what he felt for Liss. He'd heard men tell their wives they loved them right before they went to their mistresses. He'd heard the Emperor's women say "I love you" to servants who brought them their afternoon tea. In Lagonia, *love* was about as valuable as a decent bottle of wine.

Rhett didn't have the right words for what he felt for Liss. He didn't think there were words for it.

"Is that what you wish you had done?" Rhett asked Stone.

Stone stepped back like Rhett had hit him. They never talked about the family Stone had lost. There were deep lines of pain on Stone's normally sullen face, and Rhett felt guilty for even mentioning Stone's wife. He didn't mean to be cruel, but he wanted to know.

"Prescill wouldn't have let me go," Stone said heavily. "But I wish every single day I had made her. Maybe then, she and our son would still be alive."

The honesty of Stone's words stole the air from Rhett's lungs.

If he was a stronger man, he'd take Stone's advice and walk away from Liss. He had tried at first. He'd tried to push her away, to make her think he felt nothing. He'd tried to convince her he was the detached killer he presented to the rest of the world.

She hadn't fallen for any of it, and somewhere along the way, he had stopped trying to distance himself. He couldn't let her go.

"I'll talk to her," Rhett said. It was the best he could do.

"Do what you need to do," Stone said. "But if Jaikon orders me to arrest you, I'll do it. Even if it breaks me."

He turned away, but not before Rhett saw the raw emotion on his mentor's face. Stone strode from the room, slamming the door behind him.

CHAPTER 36

The stories had surrounded Liss all day. It was all anyone could talk about.

The Chief Assassin had killed four slavers and released the Extended slaves they were bringing into the empire. He'd even assigned two soldiers to escort the Extended back through the Insorsiled forest to make sure they weren't recaptured in their weakened state.

It took every ounce of willpower Liss possessed to go through the motions when all she wanted was to run straight to Rhett. If she knew where he was at this time of day, she might have done just that.

There was all sorts of speculation about why Lagonia's normally-predictable Chief Assassin had behaved so uncharacteristically. Liss knew why he'd done what he did, and it made her heart swell almost to the point of bursting.

While Liss's charges were at dinner, she felt the onyx stone in her pocket radiate heat. She slipped into a dark corner of a servants' hallway to read the message materializing across the stone. A bitter fear crawled down her spine at what she read.

We need to meet. 10:00am tomorrow, a mile past the Golden Bridge on the road to Insorsil.

More directions to find the meeting place scrawled across the stone's surface in silver lettering.

Questions and worries filled Liss's mind. Why would Burk want to meet in person? She'd been updating him every morning about her progress—or lack thereof. But she was close. She had to be. Why was Burk making her take the unnecessary risk of sneaking outside of the empire in broad daylight, when he could easily say whatever needed to be said through the onyx stone?

Maybe it had nothing to do with the immunity. Had something happened to her mother?

Liss went through her tasks in a haze of worry. How could Burk expect her to wait until tomorrow to know what was going on? She had sent ten messages through the onyx stone, pleading for some hint of what was going on, but he hadn't responded.

Finally, after the eleventh message, Burk had deigned to respond with only: *Nya is fine.*

When Liss saw her caravan leader tomorrow, she was going to give him an earful.

By the time she had gotten Mireille, Jennev, and Mizel to bed, it was almost midnight. Liss put on Dannica's soldier uniform, since she wasn't sure she'd get lucky enough to slip unnoticed into Rhett's room in her servants' clothes a second time. Besides, she was conspicuous enough with her bruised face.

The cuts were gone, thanks to the quick-heal Rhett had put on her two days ago, but her eye was still a little swollen. No amount of Samara's Insorsiled makeup could hide it completely. The bruises beneath her shirt were still sore and ugly, but at least no one could see those.

Liss threaded her way through the secret hallways and passages she'd learned over the last two months, making her way to the soldiers' quarters. She waited in the shadows of a gold statue until the guards left their posts and their replacements swarmed the hallway.

Liss hesitated outside Rhett's door. She hadn't seen him since the night they'd argued, and she wasn't sure he'd want to see her now. Before she lost her nerve, or a guard caught her loitering, she knocked softly.

No answer. She tried the handle, and the door gave way. She let herself into Rhett's dark room just as voices told her guards were approaching.

There was no trace of Rhett's soul, and she knew the room was empty without needing to turn on the light. Feeling like an intruder, she went over and perched on the edge of Rhett's bed, which was the only place to sit besides the floor.

The last time she'd been here, it was after she had found out one of Rhett's soldier friends had been executed. Liss had been too overwhelmed by the intensity of Rhett's emotions to pay attention to her surroundings then. Now, with nothing else to do, she gazed around. A sliver of moonlight came through the window, tinging everything in an eerie shade of blue.

The room was spacious, but it contained nothing except for the bed and a dresser. Unlike Samara's room, which was littered with trinkets and memorabilia, Rhett's was devoid of anything personal. His bed was made and the place was free of dust. If it hadn't been for the pile of clothes on the floor, Liss would have sworn she'd entered an unoccupied room.

Liss knew Rhett was coming long before she heard his footsteps outside the door. She'd grown so attuned to his soul that she could pick it out even among all the guards moving through the hallway. Her pulse sped up.

She heard him greet some of the guards by name, and then the door handle turned. Rhett came into the room and shut the door behind him. He sighed, and then twisted the Insorsiled light against the wall. The room filled with a soft yellow glow. Rhett saw Liss sitting on his bed and did a double take.

His face stayed completely blank. It was so creepy the way he could do that, especially when she knew he was filled to the brim with emotions.

"You shouldn't be here," he said, but he reached behind him to lock the door without taking his eyes off her. "And if anyone sees a servant going around in a soldier's uniform, there will be more trouble for you."

"I was careful," she replied. "No one saw." Liss could feel a smile stretch across her face at just the sight of him. It had only been a couple of days, but the time apart had made her soul feel shrunken and starved.

He took a step toward her. "I wasn't sure—" Rhett began.

"I heard about what you did." Liss crossed the room to him. "You can't know…what that meant to me." She swallowed the burn of tears in her throat.

"You were right about everything," Rhett said. He reached for her, and then drew back, like he wasn't sure if he was allowed to touch her. "I know what I did wasn't enough. I'm not going to stop trying to be better…to be more." Rhett swallowed. "I want to be worthy of you."

Liss's heart stuttered at that. "I'm no angel," she said. "I've done things. Terrible things…."

Rhett leaned forward so their foreheads were just barely touching. "So have I," he said in a low voice.

She reached up to wind her arms around him. He sighed and leaned into her. Rhett returned her embrace, but his touch was gentler than usual. He was careful to avoid the areas around her ribs and stomach where she had been hurt.

Reluctantly, she let go and stepped back.

"I better get going," she said. "I just wanted to say…thank you."

"Don't leave," Rhett said, taking her hands.

She laughed, feeling more at ease than she had in days. "I don't want to, but it'll be better to sneak back now while the guards are still moving around. If I hurry—"

"I mean don't go at all. Stay the night."

"Oh."

"I don't want to do anything," he hurried to say. "I mean, I do, obviously, but not until you're totally healed." Dark emotions passed through his soul, but they were fleeting.

Rhett laced their fingers together. "I want the luxury of just being with you for an entire night without having to let you go."

When he lowered his gaze to hers, there was unguarded emotion in his eyes. "Will you stay?"

Propriety dictated that Liss say no and go back to her side of the palace. But she and Rhett had never concerned themselves with propriety.

Liss nodded. The emotions that flared inside Rhett warmed her to her core, banishing any misgivings or embarrassment she might have felt.

"But I don't have pajamas," she said. As soon as the words had left her mouth, the preposterousness of the statement struck her. She started to giggle.

Rhett's lips curved upward. "You have my permission to sleep naked."

Liss shook her head, still grinning. "Maybe next time."

Rhett's whole face lit up at that, making him look more handsome than any man had a right to be.

"I'll hold you to that," he said as he went to the dresser. He handed her a stack of clothes that smelled like laundry soap and Rhett, pointing her to the washroom adjoining his bedroom.

The pants were far too big to even stay up, but Rhett's shirt reached down to her thigh, which she decided was sufficient coverage. When she came back out, Rhett was sitting on his bed wearing only a pair of black pants. He let out a low whistle when he caught sight of her, which made her laugh even as she felt her cheeks flush.

"You're not big on compliments, are you?" Liss asked him.

Not that she needed him to speak the words. She knew everything he was feeling. It was overwhelming how much he felt, especially when all of his emotions were for her.

"Words are cheap," he replied, his eyes tracking her every move. "Actions are more trustworthy."

"Is that why you're staring at me like that?" she asked, gloating a little.

"I'm staring because I can't take my eyes off you."

Liss felt a ripple of feeling pass across both of their souls. It made her all warm inside, even though the floor beneath her bare feet was cold.

The muscles in Rhett's chest and stomach rippled as he moved over to make room for her.

The bed was narrow, and Liss was immediately surrounded by Rhett's warmth. He gave her bruised side plenty of room as he wound one of his arms around her. She nestled against him. The awkwardness of being in Rhett's bed disappeared, and all that was left was the two of them together. It felt so…right.

She reached up and traced one of the scars that stretched from Rhett's collarbone to the hollow of his hip. Rhett shuddered under her touch.

"You're making it very difficult for me to behave," he said, his voice even gruffer than usual.

"Sorry," she grinned, moving instead to trace the scars on the safer area of his arms.

"Do they bother you?" he asked, watching her.

"It bothers me how you got them." Liss looked up at his face. "I hate Stone for doing this to you."

Rhett tightened his arm around her. "He was trying to protect me in the only way he knew how."

"I don't understand how you can defend him after what he's done to you."

Rhett reached up to tuck her hair behind her ear. Even that small touch sent a shiver through her body.

"Do you hate your family for exiling you?" he asked.

Liss stiffened. She didn't want to talk about this…she didn't want to have to lie to Rhett while she was in his arms.

She thought of the onyx stone in the pocket of the pants she'd abandoned on Rhett's floor. She thought of all the ways she'd deceived Rhett. It made her sick.

"There's a lot about my life before I came here that I haven't told you about," she said carefully. "I've had to do…things to survive."

"I want to know," Rhett said. "I want you to tell me."

Liss shook her head. She felt tears pricking her eyes and blinked them back. "I can't."

"I understand about surviving," Rhett said, indicating his scarred chest. "I'd be the last person to judge you."

"I can't tell you," she said, feeling miserable.

"Will you tell me someday?" he asked. "You can trust me, you know."

"I know," she said without answering his question.

Liss could feel the disappointment on Rhett's soul, but he didn't push her. It made her feel at once grateful and even guiltier.

"While we're on the topic of unpleasant things," Rhett said, "there's something we need to talk about."

He told her about his conversation with Stone, and about how Stone's wife and son had been murdered by the previous emperor.

Liss had never expected to feel even a shred of pity for the man who had covered Rhett in scars. She still resented Stone for what he'd done, but now, a small part of her understood. At least now she understood the darkness that lived inside his soul.

"Jaikon is far worse than the previous emperor," Rhett said, "and he hates me more than our father ever hated Stone."

It was so easy to forget Rhett was the bastard son of the emperor. At some point, he had stopped being the assassin who was hunting her. Instead, he'd become Rhett, the man she loved.

"We won't be able to hide forever," Rhett continued. "If Jaikon finds out about you, I'm not sure I'll be able to keep you safe. I'm…afraid."

He whispered those last words, and Liss wondered if he had ever said them out loud.

"You don't have to worry about me," she said.

"If anything ever happened to you—" Rhett cut himself off, like he couldn't even speak his fear out loud.

Rhett cleared his throat. "You know the danger, even if you won't admit it. You know I'm poison for you."

"You're wrong," she told him. And because he'd been so honest with her, she decided to give him as much as she could in return. She told him about her mom's grief over the death of her dad, and how that grief had turned to crippling illness.

"I never want to be like her," Liss admitted, and she was surprised to feel bitterness creep into her soul. She didn't think she felt any resentment toward her mom, just a desperate determination never to be like her. But it was there now.

"You never would be," Rhett told her as he traced the lines of her collarbone with his fingertips. "You're one of the strongest people I've ever met. There's nothing that could break you."

His words brought a tremendous relief to her soul. He was still troubled, though.

She raised her head so she could look at him. "You know, I'm guessing if anyone could ask Stone's wife if she would have done anything differently, she'd say the same thing I'm going to say to you now."

"What's that?" Rhett asked. His whole body stilled in anticipation.

"I don't want to be without you. Whatever happens, I wouldn't choose any differently."

Rhett pressed a gentle kiss to her lips. Liss felt love fill his soul until there wasn't room for anything else. He didn't say the words, but she didn't need him to. She knew.

As they lay side by side, talking and touching and holding each other, Liss felt the change that came over both of their souls. Their fears and hesitation were gone. All that was left was the all-consuming love they shared. And for the first time, she didn't feel any guilt for loving Lagonia's Chief Assassin. She wasn't afraid she'd become as dependent on Rhett's love as her mother had been on her father's. For the first time, she just let herself be happy.

CHAPTER 37

Liss woke up the next morning, feeling safer and more comfortable than she'd ever felt in her life. Both of Rhett's arms were around her, and she could feel the steady rhythm of his breathing against her back. It was only when she remembered her meeting with Burk that she forced herself to leave the warmth of Rhett's embrace. As soon as she started to move, he woke up.

"You don't have to go yet," he said, his voice deep as he nuzzled against her.

"Last night was Mizel's turn with the Emperor," Liss said. "I need to check on her."

The first part was true. Mizel always spent the day after her turn with the Emperor locked in her room, too embarrassed by the ugly bruises to let anyone except Liss come in. It was a horrible excuse for leaving Rhett, but it was the most convincing lie she could come up with.

Rhett's whole body tensed. His arms tightened around her.

"When do I get to see you again?" she asked, not wanting their perfect night to end on a somber note.

"Tomorrow, at our field," Rhett replied, watching as she pulled on her pants beneath his too-long shirt. "Unless you want some more time to recover."

"Stop trying to make excuses to get out of sparring," Liss said. "Don't think I haven't noticed how flabby you're getting." She poked at Rhett's rock-hard bicep.

"Flabby?" Rhett tried to look offended. "I'll show you flabby."

He tackled her—carefully, to avoid her bruises. He pulled her onto the bed, covering her face, her neck, her arms with kisses.

By the time she left Rhett's room, it was later than she meant to leave, but she couldn't be sorry for it. Rhett distracted the guards while she slipped into one of the hidden passages and made her way back toward the Sapphire Bridge. Instead of crossing the bridge, she went down the marble steps to the bottom level and out to the road that led away from the palace.

As soon as she was out of sight of the palace, she broke into a run. She didn't stop until she got to the Golden Bridge. Liss realized she hadn't come near the bridge or the one-hundred archers since she first entered Lagonia with Rhett months ago. Her palms began to sweat.

It was a stupid reaction, but she put a hand at her belt, feeling for the dagger Rhett had given her. *Like a dagger could do anything against a hundred arrows.*

As she felt some of the archers' eyes turn on her, Liss forced herself to slow her pace. She straightened her jacket and lifted her chin. She let extra weight go into her steps as her dragonhide boots clipped against the gold tiles of the bridge.

To Liss's overwhelming relief, the archers barely glanced at her. To them, she was just another soldier carrying out business across the bridge. Still, she didn't breathe until she was on the other side and had gone far enough along the road that she was out of range of the archers' arrows.

The meeting place Burk had set was close to the Golden Bridge, but she still needed to run the whole way to make it in time. Liss was sweaty and panting by the time she found the copse of trees Burk had described in his message. And she was annoyed.

"You're late," was Burk's greeting.

Liss's mood soured further.

"It's not as easy getting in and out of Lagonia as you might think," she replied testily.

A strange emotion went through Burk's soul at her words. It was vaguely hostile. When Liss peered a little deeper into his emotions, she also saw irritation and suspicion.

Liss didn't understand. She was also getting nervous, even though she had no reason to be.

"What's going on?" she asked. "Why did you bring me here?"

"Our Energizers can't keep going," Burk said. "They're utterly spent, and the Emperor raised our taxes again. Every piece of gold we get goes to Lagonian taxes and your mother's potion. We're out of all of our food stores except oatmeal, and even that'll be gone by month's end. Once the last of our Energizers die, we'll be sitting ducks." He gave her a hard look.

"I know." Liss shook her head, feeling the same frustration and confusion that had plagued her for weeks. "I'm trying, it's just…hard."

Something else was emerging in Burk's soul, not an emotion, just an overall sense. It made Liss uneasy.

Burk's orange eyes narrowed. He crossed his arms. "You look well," he said. "Well fed, well-muscled. There's even a brightness to your eyes. If I didn't know better, I'd think you were enjoying your time in Lagonia."

Liss scowled. "If you're referring to how I spend every day listening in on court gossip and every night searching for this damned immunity, then yeah, Burk. I'm doing just peachy."

"If you're doing all of that, then why haven't you found it?" Burk spoke so softly that his question sounded almost kind. But Liss saw the impatience filling his soul.

"I'm doing the best I can," she said through gritted teeth.

What the hell did he expect from her?

"Someone besides the Emperor knows what's giving those people their immunity. You mean to tell me you haven't managed to befriend anyone high up enough who knows?"

Liss let her irritation with Burk be the reason her cheeks flushed and her pulse sped up.

"I'm a servant, Burk."

"You need to give me something," he said, without a trace of sympathy.

Tendrils of emotions were curling through Burk's soul. Liss didn't like the feel of any of them.

"You haven't given me anything on the Viper. Where's he heading next? How do we kill him?"

Liss forced her breathing to even out before she replied. "The Chief Assassin's careful. I keep my ears open, but I haven't heard anything. I'm not you, Burk."

Burk smiled, but it was more of a sneer. Liss had never been uncomfortable around her caravan leader before, but there were emotions in his soul that she'd never felt there before.

"You know what I think?" Burk asked, his voice all the more dangerous for how quiet it was. "I think you've formed attachments. I think you know more than you're telling me because you want to protect your new friends."

"Did you fall and hit your head?" Liss replied, forcing out a bitter laugh. "I'm trying to stay alive. You won't get any information if I'm dead."

"True enough," Burk agreed. "But sometimes, people need a little extra motivation to get a job done."

"Motivation," Liss repeated. "Like not having to live in the empire that wants nothing more than to kill me and everyone I care about?"

"Nya's been asking for you," Burk said, distracting Liss with the change in subject.

Her heart squeezed.

"Is my mom okay? Have you been taking care of her?"

"You've been gone a long time," Burk said, again dodging her questions. "I've kept up my end of the bargain. I've gone to Insorsil for her potion myself. I've spent gold from my own pocket to keep your mother healthy."

"And I'm doing my part to keep all of our people alive," Liss said.

A terrible feeling was stealing across her soul. Still, Burk's next words sent an icy shock through her veins.

"That's just the thing," he said. "I don't think you are doing your part. That's why I wanted you to come here. I wanted you to see into my soul so you'd know I'm serious when I tell you that if you don't produce something of use soon, Nya will stop receiving her potion." He spoke quietly, but he annunciated each word so there was no mistaking them.

Liss gasped. "You wouldn't."

"Look into my soul and see."

Liss did.

"Why are you doing this?" she demanded, furious tears stinging her eyes.

"I told you. Our situation is desperate," Burk said. "Believe me, it gives me no pleasure to have to resort to threats."

Liss didn't believe him.

He continued, "But you have always had a problem with taking things seriously. Consider this…a reminder."

"You can go to hell, Burk," Liss said, raising her voice intentionally. She got some satisfaction when Burk winced and rubbed at his ears. "Here's an idea. Why don't *you* go to Lagonia, and I'll go back to dealing with my mom's potion? Problem solved."

"I don't think so," Burk said, his voice barely a whisper. "You will not return to the caravan until you have done what you set out to do. If you don't get the immunity by week's end, Nya will stop receiving her medicine."

Burk held up a hand to stop her furious outburst.

"And before you even think about coming back to the caravan to rescue Nya," he continued, "just know that I've made an agreement with the witchdoctor who supplies her brew. She won't sell it to anyone except me."

Liss couldn't believe Burk—her own caravan leader—was threatening to let her mom go without her medicine. Her hand itched to reach for the dagger at her hip, even though she had no idea what she'd do with it. It wasn't like she could hold it up to Burk's throat and demand he take care of her mother. He was her caravan leader. It was his responsibility to keep all of them safe, not threaten them.

"Why are you doing this?" she managed, fury and desperation at war inside her.

"The Extended have lived as paupers on the fringe of society for too long. I'm tired of being afraid and helpless. I'm tired of being like an insect on the ground…just waiting to be crushed by the ever-turning wheel of Lagonia." Burk took a step closer to Liss. "And our situation won't improve until you find that immunity."

"My mom will die without her potion. You know that, right?"

Liss could see from the regret and resolve on Burk's soul that he knew it very well.

"Give me something useful," Burk said, "and I'll make sure Nya stays healthy."

"I've told you everything I know," Liss ground out.

"I don't want to know where our caravans should avoid or which fighting Extended are targets. I want to know what's causing Lagonia's immunity. I want to know where to find the Opal Slayer."

"I don't know those things," Liss said. She was crying, but she couldn't make herself stop. "Please, just give me more time. I'm close, I know it. I just need a little more time."

Burk studied her for a long moment.

"One week," he said finally. "That's how long our Energizers will last before they drop dead from exhaustion. If I don't have answers at the end of seven days, Nya will go without her brew."

"I'll get you the immunity," Liss said, her tone full of acid. "And when I get back to the caravan, I'm going to tell everyone what you threatened me with."

"You just take some of your own advice and worry about today. Leave tomorrow's problems for another time."

Burk gave Liss a knowing smile as he threw her own motto back at her. It sounded twisted and wrong the way he said it, and she found she didn't have words to respond. She watched Burk turn and stride back to his Insorsiled bike.

Burk didn't glance back as the bike stuttered across the rocky ground and disappeared down the road.

CHAPTER 38

Liss's mind was in chaos as she raced back to the palace. She had lied to Burk. She had known where Rhett was going today. He'd told her before she left his room, and she hadn't told Burk. She hadn't said a word, not even when he'd made that despicable threat against her mom.

If Liss had told Burk where Rhett and his men would be today, Burk would have been satisfied enough to forget about her failure to identify the immunity. Rhett would probably be fine—he was the best assassin on the continent for a reason—but Liss still hadn't said anything.

What did it mean that she had let Burk threaten her own mother, and she'd done nothing to stop it because she was protecting her people's greatest enemy? *What was wrong with her?*

Liss had never thought of herself as a fool, but now she wasn't so sure.

Still, she couldn't bring herself to regret what she'd done. She knew she'd never put Rhett in harm's way, just like she would never let anything bad happen to her mom. She'd find the immunity. She'd search the palace's underbelly tonight, which she had only just discovered. If she didn't find what she sought, she'd bribe, steal, and kill to get what she needed.

With her new sense of urgency, Liss didn't wait until nightfall when she usually conducted her searches. Instead, she went to Mireille, told her she was ill, and begged for the day off. When Liss started to cough and sneeze, Mireille had relented and shooed Liss away.

Liss was so caught up in the urgency of her errand that she almost passed Samara in the hall without recognizing her. Samara grabbed Liss's shoulders and peered at her face.

"Have you been crying?" Samara demanded.

"No," Liss lied.

Samara took Liss's arm and yanked her into her bedroom, shutting the door behind them.

"What happened?" she demanded. "And more importantly, who do I need to beat up?"

Liss laughed a little at that. Her friend was many things, but Samara wasn't a soldier. Liss doubted she even knew how to throw a punch. She was about to tell Samara that everything was fine, but then, a thought occurred to her.

"Do you have an illusion potion I could use?"

Liss hated herself for asking such a favor. She knew what would happen if anyone caught her snooping around with Insorsil magic in her possession. They wouldn't need to call Stone to figure out where she'd gotten it from.

Samara had risked enough just knowing who Liss was and guarding her secret. But Liss had never been as desperate as she was now.

Just thinking about Burk's threat made Liss's stomach turn over.

Samara hesitated for only a moment before going over to her dresser and selecting a small glass vial.

"It isn't strong," Samara warned, as she handed it over. "It'll only work for two or three hours, tops."

"I'll make sure I'm back before it wears off," Liss promised.

Samara studied her, sympathy and concern on her soul. "Are you going to tell me what's going on?"

She didn't want to, but she owed her friend the truth. She spoke in a hurried whisper as she told Samara what had happened.

"That prick," Samara hissed. "How dare he threaten your mom!"

Samara's fury on her behalf made Liss feel a little better.

"My brother is good at transfiguration," Samara said. "Want me to message him to go over to your caravan and turn Burk into a toad?"

Liss's lips twitched at the thought. "Tempting."

"Just say the word," Samara said with a wink.

"Thank you." Liss clutched the vial to her chest. "Really."

"Just don't get caught," Samara said, giving Liss a quick hug.

Liss waited until she'd crossed the Sapphire Bridge and was almost all the way to the royal quarters before she swallowed the potion. She didn't feel any different, but as she passed a gilded mirror, she saw that her entire appearance had transformed. She now looked like a lanky male guard. There was even the illusion of a sword at her hip. She reached up to her cheek to feel the scratchy beard that had appeared, but she felt only her normal skin.

Weird.

She kept her steps even and precise like the rest of the guards as she headed for the secret stairwell just past the Emperor's chambers. She had discovered it last night, but had run out of time before she could see where it led.

It must be down here. It has to be.

Insorsiled lights along the wall threw off an ominous green glow as she descended the spiral stone stairs. The air was cold and musty down here, and there was the quiet *drip, drip* of water splashing onto the floor. Liss shivered.

When she reached the end of the stairs, she found herself in a narrow corridor. She had guessed the palace's underbelly would be a matrix of hallways and rooms, just like the palace above, but all she found down here was a short hallway that ended at an iron cage. Inside the cage was a man…an Extended man.

Liss hurried forward.

The prisoner's opal skin flickered dimly in the harsh Insorsiled light. His orange hair was matted and patchy, like someone had torn chunks of it from his scalp.

When the man sat up and Liss got a good look at him, she gasped. His face was bloody, and one of his eyes was swollen shut. A deep gash ran across his jaw.

"P-please," the man stammered. "I don't know where Opal Smoke is. I swear. Please, don't kill me."

"I'm not here to hurt you," Liss said quickly.

The man looked uncomprehending at her for several seconds. Liss pulled her lockpicks from her hair, where they doubled as hairpins, and started working at the lock. It was a complicated one, with six tumblers. It didn't help that her hands were numb from the cold. Everything down here was slippery with freezing condensation.

"How long have you been here?" Liss asked, fury and cold making her voice tremble.

"A week, I think." The man was still watching her warily.

Liss's voice still sounded like her own, and she could only imagine how strange it must be for the man in the cage to see a Lagonian man who spoke in a distinctly feminine voice.

"What happened?" she asked as she kept working at the lock.

"Some slavers raided our caravan when we stopped for supplies." The man shuddered. "I thought I was being taken to the empire to be sold, but then they brought me down here." Another shudder wracked his body. "They call this place the torture cage for good reason."

Liss's heart clenched with guilt and anger.

"I'll have you out of here soon," she promised as the second tumbler gave way.

"Why are you helping me?" he asked. "Who are you?"

"Better for us both if you don't know," Liss replied, focusing on her work.

"Are you Opal Smoke?" His non-swollen eye widened.

"What's your Extension?" she asked, trying to steer the conversation to a safer topic. She was concentrating on the problems of now…and those were getting this man out of this cage and out of the palace.

"I'm a Runner," he replied.

That was good news, at least. Liss only had to get him past the Golden Bridge, and then he'd be able to outrun anyone who tried to chase him down. There weren't many Runners left. Since they made it easier for the caravan leaders to exchange news, the Emperor considered them dangerous. Lagonia's Chief Assassin had killed two of them in the last year….

Rhett. Rhett had been the one to kill those two Runners. He'd slit their throats while they slept.

Liss's hand slipped and she broke one of her lockpicks. She swore.

But he'd been ordered to do it. If Rhett hadn't killed those men, someone else would have. He didn't have a choice.

Rhett was the Opal Slayer. He was searching for the Extended spy. He'd been ordered to kill her.

Liss was having trouble breathing.

"Someone's coming."

The Extended man's panicked whisper brought her back to the present. As much as it killed her to do it, Liss flipped the tumblers she had unlocked back into place and ran to the opposite end of the corridor where there was a narrow, unlit stairway. She fumbled her way down in the darkness, trying to keep her footsteps and breathing silent as boots stomped across the stone floor to the cage.

The flight of stairs where Liss was hiding led down to a door, where natural light seeped in through the grated bars overhead. Liss stayed where she was as she listened to the sound of the cage's door opening and clanging shut again.

Only when the footsteps receded did Liss dare to move. She stumbled the rest of the way down the stairs and peeked out through the grating, getting her bearings. There was one guard on the other side of the door. His eyes were closed, and his sword was sheathed at his side.

Liss ran back up the stairs and to the cage. A metal bowl of some kind of sloppy gruel had been tossed in the cage beside the Extended man.

"Get me out of here," he begged.

Liss had to start over…with one of her lockpicks broken. She tried not to panic, but it wasn't easy with the man who was pressed against the bars and pleading with her. Finally, she managed to get the cage open.

The man limped forward, and Liss saw that one of his legs was hanging at an unnatural angle.

"Can you run on a broken leg?" she asked, trying to imagine how she was going to get him across the bridge when she'd need to support him every step of the way.

To her surprise, the man grinned. "It won't be graceful, but I can move faster on one leg than you can on two."

"You're going to hop?" she asked.

"I didn't say it would be graceful."

Liss saw the illusion surrounding her flicker. She was running out of time.

"Come on," she said, leading the way down the stairs. She gave one short rap on the metal door, watching through the grate as the guard on the other side startled awake.

"Mariolo, is that you?" the guard called.

Liss didn't say anything. She heard the sound of a key grating against the lock, and then the door opened. Before the guard could reach for his sword, she reached up with the handle of her dagger and hit him across the head. With a soft *oof*, the guard slumped to the ground.

"Help me get him in here," Liss commanded.

Together, they hauled the guard inside the doorway.

"Get his clothes," Liss whispered, watching through the crack in the door to make sure they hadn't been seen. "Hurry."

The guard wasn't wearing a helmet or cap that the Runner could use to cover his orange hair, so Liss scooped up a handful of mud. She rubbed it through his hair and over his opal skin as the man zipped up the guard's jacket.

"How do I look?" he asked.

Liss winced. "Like an Extended wearing Lagonian clothes. Keep your face turned down and keep your hands in your pockets."

She flipped the collar of his jacket up to at least cover his shimmery neck. The sunlight would make it look like a thousand tiny rainbows glinted off every exposed surface of the man's skin, which would be sure to attract attention.

They stepped over the unconscious guard's figure and went out the door, leaving the horrible torture cage behind them.

Liss's illusion flickered again.

"If I tell you where to go, can you make it out of here on your own?" she asked.

"The only reason the slavers got me was because I was asleep when they raided the caravan," the Runner said. "Don't worry about me."

Liss gave him a tight smile. And then she gave him hurried instructions for reaching the bridge.

"What can I do to repay this kindness?" the Runner asked, earnestness filling his soul.

Liss was about to say nothing, but instead, she asked, "Can you deliver a message for me?"

The man listened as she explained what she wanted. When she had finished, he just nodded.

"I'll get Nya your message or die trying," he promised.

"Thank you."

Liss's illusion sputtered.

"Go," the Runner told her. "Do whatever you came here to do, and don't get killed."

Liss spared him a smile. "Same to you."

CHAPTER 39

Tell me again," Rhett commanded the guard. "And will someone bring him some goddamned clothes?"

"I heard a sound on the other side of the door. I was pulling out the key, and that's all I remember." He rubbed the bump on his head.

"Height? Weight? Age?" Stone barked questions at the dazed-looking guard. "Did you see shimmery skin? Orange hair? Orange eyes?"

"He knocked me out before I saw him," the guard said. At least he had the decency to look ashamed.

Rhett and Stone exchanged a glance.

"Opal Smoke," Ciago whispered.

Rhett didn't say anything, but it was what they were all thinking. There was no other explanation for how the Extended prisoner had gotten out of the torture cage. The Runner was too stupid and too weak to have been able to manage it himself.

There had been no reports of a break-in, no sighting of Extended Fighters, no dead soldiers left in their wake. There was only one possible explanation. The Extended spy was here, or at least, he had been. He'd been in the palace.

The spy had gotten in without a single guard seeing him, and then he'd disappeared again. Like smoke.

"Find out if any of the Extended slaves escaped or were unaccounted for this morning," Rhett told Ciago and Wilsean.

Stone pulled Rhett away from the others.

"Do you want me to post more guards around the stash?" he asked, his voice low enough that only Rhett could hear.

Rhett hesitated. "No," he said finally. "If the spy hasn't found it yet, it'll be better if we don't draw any more attention to it."

The spy would probably go straight to the vaults if he was searching for their immunity. He'd never guess where the stash was actually kept unless he had a reason to be suspicious.

Rhett turned to the three guards crowded in the hallway to the torture cage. "I don't want a single word about this—about any of this—getting out."

The councilmen were already whispering about insurrection. If they found out the Extended spy was in the palace, within arm's reach of the immunity....

The soldiers nodded in understanding.

"Do you need a physician?" he asked the guard who, thankfully, was no longer naked.

The man shook his head, unable to meet Rhett's eyes.

"Fine. Back to your posts. All of you."

"Sorry, Sir," the guard murmured, still staring at the ground.

Rhett put a hand on his shoulder as he walked past.

"Idiot," Stone growled as he and Rhett went back up the spiral staircase.

"Jaikon is going to lose his mind when he finds out," Rhett said, swatting at the irritating pixie that had been trailing him all day. Elouicia should tell his spies to at least try to be discreet.

Rhett sighed. His day had started out better than any morning he'd ever had. He guessed it was only fair that it had turned into such a disaster.

"You're thinking about this the wrong way," Stone said. "Our job just got a thousand times easier."

"How do you figure?"

"There was only one Extended who got across the Golden Bridge, and he was the Runner."

Rhett nodded slowly. "You think the spy is still in the empire."

Stone smiled. "He has to be."

"Then we'll find him." Rhett's mind was already busy with where he'd post extra guards and the traps he'd spring for the elusive Extended. The man could be vapor or smoke or altogether invisible. It wouldn't matter. Rhett was going to find him, and then he'd put an end to this nightmare.

CHAPTER 40

Since Liss was pretending to be sick, she had to spend the rest of the day in her room. It was agonizing to be idle as the hours slipped by. Samara had come in around noon to tell her there had been an increase in guards all around the palace. Liss had known this would happen when she released the Extended prisoner, but it wasn't like she had any choice. The Runner would have died if she hadn't gotten him out.

She sat on her bed, the onyx stone in her hand, and fumed. She still couldn't believe Burk had threatened her mom. And he'd meant it. She had seen it in his soul.

Liss's mind went from that, to the fact that she still had no idea where or what the immunity was, to how it would now be practically impossible to search the palace. She had hoped the immunity would be down in that torture room, but she hadn't felt any false walls or seen any places where a great store of medicine could be hidden.

Where could it be?

Liss stayed in her room all day, worrying and fretting. She knew she should at least try to get some sleep, but she couldn't get her mind to quiet.

Her stomach rumbled, and she realized she hadn't eaten anything all day. She ignored her protesting stomach for as long as she could. Finally, she couldn't take it anymore. She got up and put on her clothes. It was late enough that her charges would be asleep, so there wasn't much chance of any of the women seeing her up and about.

Liss went straight to the room where the servants' meals were served, only to find that it had already been cleaned and all leftover food had been taken back to the kitchens. She debated going to the banquet hall to swipe something to eat, but the Emperor had taken to staying there late with two or three of his women. She didn't want to risk walking in on that.

Her stomach rumbled again. Sighing, she backtracked in the direction of the palace kitchens.

She hadn't been back in this part of the palace since the night she'd tried to steal food for Rhett and found the kitchen doors padlocked shut. They were locked again tonight. Liss was considering whether she was hungry enough to risk earning the head chef's ire by breaking into his kitchen, when a prickling sensation began along the back of her neck. Her instincts, honed from years of stealing, told her there was something more to these locked doors than a chef who took his craft too seriously.

She studied the locks. At first glance, they looked ordinary, like the locks the shopkeepers in town used. It was only on closer examination that Liss realized these ones were far more complicated. She had come across these locks in Insorsil and knew from experience they were a bear to open. They also cost a fortune. It would probably cost the chef a year's salary to afford one of these locks.

No one was that crazy.

Liss stole a glance up and down the hall before pulling the fresh pair of picks from her hair and working them into the lock. It was delicate, tedious work. If her lockpicks went astray, a thin shield of glass inside the tumbler would break, and then the lock would become impossible to open. Liss was probably the only thief in the empire who had the skill to pick this lock.

She lost herself in the task of inching the picks around and listening to them scratch against the glass shield. Finally, the mechanism whined and popped open. Liss was too full of trepidation to feel any pride. She unwound the heavy metal chain and let herself into the dark kitchen.

Liss took the onyx stone out of her pocket and blew on it until it started to emit a warm glow that was enough to see by. She held up the stone, illuminating pristine white countertops and spotless black cooktops. Copper pots were hung above the enormous stove with all of their handles pointing in the same direction. Spoons were cradled in labeled containers that were the exact right size for their contents.

Liss found the giant icebox, which held balls of dough, wheels of cheese, and vegetables that had been washed and chopped with inhuman precision. Liss grabbed an apple and a small wheel of cheese she didn't think anyone would miss and set them on the countertop. She continued to search the kitchen.

The tingling feeling was still there, even though she'd found no evidence that this place was anything other than a kitchen. Still, she figured there was no harm in being thorough since she was already here.

Liss moved deeper into the kitchen, which turned out to be several rooms instead of just one. There were pantries, greenhouses that smelled like summer, and a whole room just for washing dishes. It was only when she reached the end that she knew she had found what she was looking for.

Anyone else would have missed it. It was only from stealing valuables out of Insorsiled people's houses that she knew before she laid her hands on it that the back wall was false. Liss held up her glowing onyx stone as she looked for the opening.

There was a long, framed painting of vegetables on the far end of the wall. She tested the frame, and it swiveled aside at her touch to reveal a handle cut into the wall. Liss grasped the handle and pulled.

The tingling feeling had taken over her entire body. *This is it*, she thought.

She had no idea what to expect when the wall panel slid aside. What she found were rows and rows of wooden barrels. She counted at least fifty of them, and there might be more that were out of sight. She unscrewed the lid of the nearest barrel and gasped.

Shimmery, rainbow light spilled out, flooding the room. The color was blinding, and it took Liss several moments before her eyes adjusted.

The barrel was filled to the top with tiny flowers, although they were unlike any flower she'd ever seen. The light moved and changed on each of their tiny petals, making it look like they were covered in rainbow oil.

They looked like opals.

When she picked one up, she realized the flower was dry. It crumbled in her fingers, turning into a fine, white dust that in no way resembled what it had looked like moments before.

Liss saw there were not just fifty, but hundreds, if not thousands, of identical barrels.

She continued to stare at the play of light across the flowers' petals. The color reflected onto her hands, making her skin look Extended. It was mesmerizing.

Liss finally tore her gaze away from the reflection of opal light on her hands.

Her pulse was racing. There was only one possible explanation for flowers that looked like a brighter version of her people's skin. She'd found the source of the Lagonians' immunity.

CHAPTER 41

Rhett gave Silverbird a pat as the dragon snorted and stamped her feet. A hundred pixies swarmed around her head, making the dragon nervous and him dizzy, as they delivered their reports.

"Nothing, Sir."

"No sign of him."

"Really must be smoke."

Rhett wanted to punch something. His soldiers had scoured every inch of the empire. He'd sent every man and woman at his disposal to hunt down the elusive Extended spy. He'd gotten nowhere.

He had spent the morning with Stone, Wilsean, and Ciago searching the woods just outside Lagonia for some sign of an Extended camp. They'd found nothing. When they returned to the palace, Rhett would need to tell the Emperor that, for the second day in a row, Opal Smoke had eluded him.

Today might really be the day Jaikon tossed his body over the cliff. The thought bothered him more now than it would have a few months ago. He'd always had a healthy appreciation for his own life, but aside from Stone and his friends, he'd never had anyone else to live for besides himself. But that was different now. Now, there was Liss.

When they came in sight of the Golden Bridge, Rhett knew immediately that something was wrong. The archers, who generally stood relaxed with their bows at their sides, were running back and forth like they were crazed.

Rhett urged Silverbird forward. From his vantage point, he could see the roads and fields on the other side of the Golden Bridge were filled with people. Rhett caught the scent of fire on the air, and he thought he heard screams.

He stopped his dragon at the edge of the bridge. Shopkeepers, peasants, and courtiers were fleeing toward the forest, like there was some terror chasing them. He jumped off Silverbird, knowing she would only slow him down with so many people in the way.

"What's happened?" he demanded as soon as the archers were in shouting range.

"The giants are attacking!" an archer yelled, running across the Golden Bridge toward him. "Their boats came in with the fog. Their humans took out our guards at the port so we never knew they were coming. We didn't know if we should stay at our post, or—"

"How many?" Stone interrupted.

"There's a dozen of their largest ships," the archer reported, breathless. "The giants are staying down by the water, but their humans took over the docks and came on shore. They've entered the palace—"

The archer was still speaking, but Rhett didn't hear anything else he said. *They had entered the palace. Liss was in the palace.*

He didn't wait to hear another word. He ran.

"Rhett, where are you going?"

"What are your orders?"

"Rhett!"

He didn't even glance back. He sprinted through the crowd of Lagonians running toward the bridge and away from the sea. Soldiers called to him as he raced past, but he didn't spare them a glance.

Liss.

Nothing else mattered. He had to get to her.

It was more than two miles from the Golden Bridge to the palace, and the roads were so crowded with fleeing citizens that Rhett had to keep going off the road, which added more distance.

He ran faster than he'd ever run in his life. He prayed to gods he'd never given so much as a passing thought to.

Let her be okay. Tell her to hang on. I'm coming.

As the palace came in view, Rhett felt a terror more powerful than any emotion he'd ever felt in his life. *What if he was too late?*

A battle was raging overhead on the Sapphire Bridge. He heard the clang of blades and screams. One of his soldiers went over the opulently useless balustrade. Rhett didn't hear or see when the man hit the ground. His gaze was fixed on an impossibly tiny figure on the bridge. The gold top of her servant's uniform shone in the sun. And she was battling three of the giants' humans with nothing but a dagger.

Rhett's limbs unfroze. He didn't remember getting to the stairs that would lead him up to the bridge. He took them three at a time, not pausing for a second as he raced up the fifteen flights.

Hold on, Liss. Please. Please.

Soldiers passed him on the stairs, racing in the opposite direction. Some of them called his name. He didn't so much as glance at them. He had stopped breathing by the time he reached the top.

Rhett leapt over bodies and threw open the door to the bridge, which was hanging at an angle. He inhaled just enough to keep his vision from going dark.

His eyes found Liss in an instant. He threw his dagger.

Rhett's blade hit its target, but there was no reaction from the man who was already falling forward. Liss was pulling her own weapon from the man's chest. The other two men were dead at her feet.

Liss tossed her head, the damp strands of her hair falling back into place. She wore an expression of fierce determination.

Rhett let out a long, shuddering breath. His whole body was shaking.

Liss straightened. Her eyes went straight to him, like she'd sensed his presence.

✳ ✳ ✳

Liss felt the imprint of Rhett's soul long before he stepped onto the bridge, and all she could feel was his all-consuming terror.

Was Rhett in trouble? Hurt? Dying?

She'd never felt so much fear in any soul, especially not Rhett's. It chilled her to her bones. When he appeared on the bridge and threw his only weapon at the man she'd just killed, she realized his fear had been for her.

Rhett's dark eyes, usually intentionally absent of the emotions roiling in his soul, were wild with fear. His face glistened with sweat.

"You're covered in blood," he gasped, stumbling in his haste to reach her.

"It's not mine," she said quickly.

He heard her, but the words didn't seem to penetrate the haze of his fear.

"The blood isn't mine," she said again. "I'm not hurt."

Liss felt his overwhelming terror start to recede. If they'd been alone on the bridge, she was sure Rhett would have sagged into her arms. Or crushed her into his. But there were others all around them, and they could be seen by anyone standing on the ground.

"I'm okay," she said, knowing it was what he needed to hear.

His chest was heaving, and his whole body was trembling.

"I thought—" He clutched at the railing, unable to get the words out.

Liss was overwhelmed by how worried he'd been about her. His soul was still suffering, like his brain hadn't accepted that she was no longer in any danger.

The other Lagonia soldiers on the bridge had killed their enemies, and there was no more immediate threat to any of them. She felt her own fear and adrenaline start to withdraw.

In an effort to lighten the mood, she said, "You wanted me to be able to save myself, remember? Give yourself some credit." She went over and pulled Rhett's dagger from the man's corpse, wincing at the sound it made as the blade came free. She offered Rhett the dagger. "You're a good teacher."

"Liss." His voice broke on her name.

He wrapped his arms around her. He didn't seem to care that anyone could see them, and at this moment, neither did she. She held him back, comforted by his solidness.

The emotions in his soul were transforming to gratitude and relief. And emerging from those was love. It was more powerful than even his fear from a few moments ago. Liss didn't feel the undercurrent of hesitation or the disquiet she had grown so accustomed to sensing on his soul. There was only love.

The way he was looking at her now left no doubt that every bit of it was for her. Rhett was in love with her, as completely as she was in love with him.

* * *

Jaikon was beneath the Sapphire Bridge, surrounded by his guards who were trading blows with the enemy. Elouicia pulled his sword from one of their stomachs before sinking his sharpened teeth into his enemy's neck. The man let out a scream that transformed to a gurgle.

The madness outside the palace turned to terror as a deep rumbling shook the earth.

A giant.

Jaikon shouted to his soldiers, but they were all locked in combat.

Jaikon's teeth rattled as a tremendous boom nearly knocked his sword from his hand. An enormous, hairy foot smacked into the ground, flattening three Lagonians who had been attempting to flee.

"Surround the Emperor!" Elouicia was shouting, but the too-small crowd of soldiers was already battling for their lives.

The giant looked down just as Jaikon craned his neck up to stare at the barbarian.

"Shiny!" the giant boomed, pointing a finger the size of a grown man's arm at Jaikon's crown. The brute kicked out a foot, scattering Lagonians and the giant's own men as he crossed the space between them.

The giant's smell made Jaikon gag, but he held his ground. It would be impossible to outrun this giant on foot, and his golden dragon was still in the stable. Besides, this was Jaikon's empire. He wasn't going to run.

On the periphery of his vision, Jaikon could see soldiers scrambling to get to him, to defend their Emperor. They were all moving too slowly. They were all too small and insignificant compared to the giant striding toward him.

Jaikon raised his sword, which probably looked like a needle to the giant. He braced himself as he waited for the giant to come within striking range.

Another step brought the hairy, filthy giant foot directly in front of him. Jaikon stabbed his sword into the giant's leg.

The beast let out a deafening roar. It leaned down, and with its index and forefinger, plucked the sword from Jaikon's grasp. Jaikon had only a moment to experience the fury that came with being so utterly weak and helpless before the giant turned the sword on him.

There were screams. Soldiers called his name. Jaikon didn't look away as the blade came straight for him.

The giant's aim was precise, and Jaikon felt the blade slice through his dragonhide mailcoat. But instead of the pain of his sword cutting through flesh and bone, Jaikon felt a steady vibration across his chest.

He looked down to see a blue light spreading out all around the blade, which seemed to be frozen in place. The giant was grunting and fighting with the sword as he attempted to drive it home, but there was something keeping it from entering Jaikon's heart.

The blue light continued to pulse. Energy emanated from the tiny pin Jaikon had almost forgotten he was wearing.

With one more pulse of energy, the magic in the pin fractured the sword. The blade turned into a thousand tiny shards, all of which exploded upward, embedding into the giant's fleshy knees.

The giant let out a roar of pain.

"What are you?" it thundered as its maddened eyes fixed on Jaikon.

"Someone you shouldn't have crossed," Jaikon replied, his veins still humming from the magic that had already receded back into the pin, lying dormant until it was needed again. "You tell that to your king who sent you. And you tell him that next time, it will be my soldiers on his land."

The giant's eyes widened in terror as he continued to paw at the shards of sword embedded in his legs.

"Go," Jaikon commanded. "And take the rest of your pathetic drudges with you."

The giant turned and fled back toward the sea. The other humans who served the giant were quick to follow.

"All hail the Emperor!" Elouicia called.

The cry was returned by everyone in hearing distance.

"Victory is ours!" Jaikon shouted back, feeling drunk on adrenaline and the implications of his success.

Jaikon looked up at the Sapphire Bridge overhead, where soldiers were shouting his name. He took the bloodied sword Elouicia was holding and thrust it into the air.

CHAPTER 42

With everything that happened after the attack, Liss hadn't been able to do any further investigating into the opal flowers she'd found hidden in the kitchens. She hadn't told Burk about them, since she wanted to confirm they were what she suspected before telling her caravan leader anything. She had planned to go back to the kitchens that night to see if there was anything else she had overlooked…anything that could tell her where these flowers came from or how they worked. But she never got the chance.

The Emperor had called for a great celebration to mark their victory. So, instead of learning more about the source of Lagonia's immunity, Liss found herself closed inside Mireille's chamber with her three frantic charges, no fewer than a dozen dresses, and as many harried seamstresses.

All the women could talk about, aside from what they would be wearing to the celebration, was the rumor that was spreading through the palace like wildfire. A giant had tried to stab the Emperor with his own sword, and the blade had shattered on contact. They were saying the Emperor was invincible.

Liss didn't know what had happened between the Emperor and the giant, but she was pretty sure there must be a more reasonable explanation. Luck was the more likely culprit…luck, combined with overactive Lagonian imaginations.

Liss was so busy trying to convince Jennev that the fifteenth dress she put on was *definitely the one*, that she didn't even notice when the door to the chamber opened.

The three women screeched and hurried to hide behind their silk changing screens as the Emperor and his retinue of guards stalked into the room. The women stayed behind their screens as they filled the room with noisy praise for how Jaikon had single-handedly defeated a giant. The Emperor ignored them.

Liss felt an icy fear steal over her as his eyes zeroed in on her.

"Well, aren't you a beauty, Miss—?"

"Wren," Liss managed when she'd found her voice.

Jaikon turned to the man beside him. "She's too pretty to wear a servant's uniform to the celebration tonight, wouldn't you agree?"

The man smiled, displaying canines that had been sharpened into points. He had a soul to match the horrible smile. Liss suppressed a shudder.

"I think I know of the perfect dress for you." Jaikon took a step closer, and Liss had to resist the urge to back up. "I believe it will match the radiant blue of your eyes."

Liss didn't have to look into Jaikon's soul to know his smile was false. This time, she couldn't suppress her shudder.

"Find other servants to attend my women for the celebration," Jaikon told one of his soldiers before turning back to Liss. "No work for you tonight. You will be my personal guest at the feast."

"Yes, Your Majesty," Liss whispered, hardly able to think above the terror that was swallowing up her insides.

Jaikon turned back to the door. "My guards will keep watch over you until the feast." His smile broadened. "I wouldn't want you sneaking off."

He was gone before Liss could catch her breath enough to reply.

"Lucky, lucky girl," Mireille said as soon as it was just the women and the two female guards who stood in front of the door.

"Does...does the Emperor invite servants to his parties often?" Liss asked, even though she already knew the answer.

Mizel and Jennev gave her a sour look. Mizel's soul was fully of worry, which only heightened Liss's own anxiety.

Did the Emperor know who she was? She'd been careful to put the top back on the barrel of flowers and leave everything in the kitchen the way she'd found it, but maybe she'd been seen. Or maybe this had nothing to do with her being Opal Smoke.

Another, equally terrifying thought occurred to her. *Did the Emperor know about her and Rhett?* If so, what did that mean? What would it mean for Rhett?

Liss had to get out of here. She needed to find Rhett and at least warn him. But in addition to the two guards inside the room, she could feel the souls of two more on the other side. There was nowhere she could go…nowhere to hide. She was stuck in here and at the Emperor's mercy.

"Calm yourself," Mireille ordered, even though Liss hadn't said a word. "You look like a bunny rabbit that's just seen a wolf. You should at least *act* grateful." She sniffed.

When a knock came at the door, Liss jumped.

Two seamstresses bustled in carrying a long dress box.

"Courtesy of the Emperor," one of them said in a breathless voice as she set the box on a table and started pulling out the tissue paper.

The seamstress took the dress out of the box and held it up. The other women in the room gasped.

"Will that even fit me?" Liss asked, incredulous. The dress, if it could even be called that, looked doll-sized rather than human-sized.

"Let's find out," the seamstress said in a no-nonsense way.

By the time Liss had been stuffed into the dress and forced to stand in front of the three-way mirror, she wanted to die.

The material had stretched, but it molded to the curves of her body, exaggerating her already tiny waist, curvy hips, and large breasts. There were ties that went all the way up each side of the dress. The ribbons crisscrossed so hints of bare skin were visible from her ankles to her chest. She couldn't wear a bra or underwear, which had no doubt been taken into consideration when the dress was selected. The front of the dress was a deep scoop and similarly left little to the imagination. Liss had a hard enough time concealing her chest in normal clothes. In this dress, there was no mystery.

The seamstress eyed her with pursed lips while Liss's three charges stared at her in scandalized delight.

"I can't wear this," Liss said. Panic, and the skin-tight dress, were making it difficult to breathe.

"You'll do as your Emperor commands," barked one of the soldiers at the door. "And he has requested your presence at the feast in this dress."

She looked at Mizel, the kindest of her charges, who only shrugged and gave her an apologetic smile.

Liss was trapped.

The grandfather clock in the corner of the room chimed. Mireille clapped her hands together.

"Time to go!" she chirped.

The servants who had helped Liss get ready handed her a tiny purse that was barely big enough for the tube of lipstick they insisted she bring with her. While the servants were preoccupied, and the guards were looking away, Liss quickly slipped her onyx stone from the pocket of her servants' uniform and traded it for the lipstick in her purse. She didn't want to be without it, not even for a few hours. Maybe she would learn something of value at the celebration, which would at least make her humiliation worthwhile.

The two guards opened the door and motioned to the women to exit. Their eyes stayed fixed on Liss, like they expected her to bolt. *Not that she could even manage a jog in this dress.*

Liss hesitated in the doorway.

The two guards who had been standing outside the room stepped forward. They were both men, and the look they gave her made Liss's gorge rise.

"Come," one of the guards said, a cruel smile twisting his features as he continued to sweep his gaze over her. "It will be our pleasure to escort you to the feast."

CHAPTER 43

Liss wished it was possible to actually die from embarrassment, because then she would be spared from anyone having to see her in this dress.

It was even worse now that she was surrounded by others who were wearing far more appropriate clothes. Lagonian women were anything but modest, but even among them, Liss's dress caused a stir. It was truly horrible, and she wasn't the only one to notice. She tried crossing her arms over her chest, but raising her arms meant there was more visible skin along her sides. Whispers and pointing surrounded her as she tried to melt into the crowd. If only she really were Opal Smoke and could disappear.

If it hadn't been for the guards on either side of her, Liss would have taken her chances and run. She didn't know what the Emperor knew or what he intended, but whatever it was, Liss knew it would spell disaster for her.

Thoughts passed through her mind in rapid succession, but the one that she kept coming back to was that she was stuck. The guards weren't letting her out of their sight. There was nowhere for her to go, nowhere to hide. Whatever the Emperor intended for her, there would be no escaping it.

Liss had a moment of optimism when her escorts fell away as she entered the banquet hall, but her hope vanished as soon as she saw why. Guards surrounded the room and stood on each side of every doorway. If she wanted to leave, she'd have to get past them. And in this dress, especially, there was no chance of sneaking past them unnoticed.

Liss had never hated anyone the way she hated the Emperor now.

She looked around the room, feeling her tension ease when she didn't see the Emperor among the guests. It was crowded, and even in her outfit, she might be able to avoid being spotted. Maybe the Emperor would forget about her.

Her temporary calm fled when she realized Rhett wasn't in the room, either. Was he with the Emperor? Had something happened to him?

Calm down, she commanded herself. Panicking wouldn't help anything. Rhett could handle himself. She needed to be patient and wait for an opportunity to get out of here to present itself. She needed to keep her wits about her.

The banquet hall, which was always beautiful and elegant, had been entirely transformed for the night's festivities. All the tables had been pushed against the walls. They were draped with black and gold tablecloths and topped with towers of finger sandwiches, bowls of pearly fish eggs, elaborately decorated cakes that had as many tiers as she was tall, and bowls of ruby red punch with fruit and flowers floating across its surface. Liss glanced into one of the punch bowls, looking for the opal flowers she'd found in the kitchens, but there were only orchids and rose petals floating on top of the liquid.

There was a twelve-piece band, and their music was already drawing couples onto the dance floor. Insorsiled lights bobbed overhead, throwing beams of pink and blue over the crowd. A tiny platform had been Insorsiled to hover on top of the band so the pixies could rest and eat without fear of being stepped on. The ceiling of the room had been Insorsiled to look like the night sky, complete with the constellations and a full, blue moon. It was breathtaking.

Servants moved through the room, offering up crystal flutes of champagne from golden trays. Liss looked around for Samara, wishing she was back in her servant's uniform and melting against the wall beside her friend. She saw Samara kneeling next to one of her charges, who was crying and holding up what looked like a diamond tiara.

Liss caught sight of Wilsean on the other side of the room. He was surrounded by a group of important-looking people with dark skin who she assumed were his family.

Ciago was sitting at a table nearby. There were two women sitting on his lap. One of them was trying unsuccessfully to tip a flute of champagne into his mouth, while the other was either whispering into his ear or kissing his neck…it was impossible to tell.

Liss was desperate for a friendly face, but she'd rather die than introduce herself to Wilsean's parents looking the way she did now, and she wasn't any more excited about barging in on Ciago's celebration.

Liss wandered the room, feeling more uncomfortable by the minute. She was getting back into panicking territory when she felt Rhett's soul. Liss followed the pull of his emotions and found him. He was standing near the doors and scanning the crowded room. Relief, quickly followed by humiliation, filled her own soul. She didn't want anyone to see her looking like this, but him least of all.

He, of course, looked as gorgeous as ever in fitted black pants, a gold shirt, and black tie. It was more or less the same outfit all the important men in the Emperor's employ were wearing, but Rhett still stood out like a beacon in the darkness.

Almost as if he could sense her presence the same way she sensed his, Rhett's attention swiveled on her. His eyes took in her altered appearance and widened.

Rhett pushed through the crowd to her.

"What—" he began, but Liss cut him off, breathlessly explaining what had happened.

Rhett waited until she had finished. He swore. His expression was blank, but his soul was furious.

"Come on," Rhett said, taking her hand. "We need to get you out of here." He pulled her to the nearest set of double doors.

The two guards standing on either side moved into their path, blocking the exit.

"Get out of the way," Rhett snarled.

"The Emperor gave specific orders to make sure she doesn't leave," one of them replied.

The guard didn't look apologetic, and his soul said the man was enjoying her obvious distress.

Rhett put his hand on the hilt of his dagger. "You sure about that?" he demanded.

Three more guards appeared, flanking the other two. There was fear but also resolution on their souls.

"Do you want to die tonight?" Rhett asked them, his voice low and dangerous.

More guards began to converge. People standing at the champagne fountain had taken notice and were staring, trying to discern the source of the drama.

"Come on." Liss touched Rhett's elbow. When he didn't move, she gripped him more tightly.

He let her pull him back into the crowd, away from the guards. Rhett scanned the room and swore again. "All the guards in here are Jaikon's people."

"What do we do?" she asked.

Rhett's soul was filled with a nervous kind of helplessness that was so different from the emotions she usually felt from him. It set her even more on edge than she'd been before. If she didn't do something, their combined panic would drive her insane.

"Not much we can do at the moment," he said in a low growl. "But we need to do something about your dress."

"Are you saying you don't like my outfit?" she asked, pretending to pout.

Rhett snorted, but her words had the desired effect. He relaxed ever so slightly.

His eyes, which hadn't stopped moving as people passed them, snagged on a woman standing nearby. Liss saw at once what he saw. The woman was wearing a blue dress that was a similar shade to hers, and she had a shawl draped around her shoulders.

Rhett raised an eyebrow at her.

Liss nodded.

They made their way to the woman. Rhett put a hand on her shoulder. The woman turned, saw Rhett, and fluttered her eyelashes at him. Liss almost laughed.

"Oh!" The woman puckered her lips. "Well, I have had to turn down three men already, but of course I'll dance with the famed Chief Assassin. I even—"

"I would like your shawl," Rhett cut in.

"My shawl?" she asked, confusion replacing the feelings of pride and flattery in her soul.

"Yes," Rhett replied. "Please."

"You better give it to him," Liss added. "He's crazy. If he doesn't get what he wants, he's liable to start murdering people."

The woman hurriedly removed her shawl and passed it to Rhett. Rhett gave her a tight a smile and pulled Liss away before the woman could change her mind.

"Crazy, huh?" Rhett asked as he handed her the shawl.

"You've got a reputation to uphold," Liss replied as she draped the fabric over as much of herself as possible.

"Mhm." Rhett wasn't really listening to her. He was still scanning the room. Liss didn't need to be a Truthseer to know who he was looking for.

"I didn't see the Emperor when I came in," Liss said.

"He usually arrives late, but he'll be here," Rhett replied, his eyes still roaming over the crowd.

"Alright." Liss let out a shaky breath, trying not to let Rhett's anxiety make her own any worse. "Well, since we're stuck in here, want to dance?"

"What?"

"Do you want to dance with me?" Liss asked again. "We may as well enjoy ourselves before everything goes to hell."

Rhett looked at her like he couldn't believe she would even suggest something so preposterous.

"You know, dance," Liss continued. "It's this thing two people do when they like each other and—"

"I know what dancing is." Rhett scowled. And then he shrugged. "Why not?"

"Please stop flattering me." Liss rolled her eyes. "I might start getting the wrong idea."

Rhett reached up and brushed the edges of her hair. The servants the Emperor had sent to help her get ready had complained endlessly about its length, but in the end, they'd straightened it and pinned up one of the sides to make the style look edgy rather than forced. Personally, Liss didn't think anyone would notice her hair one way or the other with the dress she had been stuffed into.

She took Rhett's hand and pulled him onto the dance floor where other couples were engaged in a preening, complicated dance Liss didn't know. They looked ridiculous.

As soon as his arms came around her, her careless, jesting attitude fell away. Rhett pulled her close enough that she could feel his rapid heartbeat. Since she'd seen his workout routine, she knew his pulse wasn't racing from the vigor of dancing. Especially since it wasn't even a fast song.

Rhett danced the way he fought: easily. He was still looking around the room, leading her so he was always facing the double doors through which the Emperor would eventually appear. But when Liss rested her head against his chest, she felt him start to relax.

She lifted her eyes to Rhett's face, only to see he was staring down at her. She felt the love from his soul somehow intensify her own.

Some part of Liss was aware they had stopped moving. It was like everything had stopped…everything except for the pull of their two souls as they reached for each other. Neither of them spoke. They didn't need to. She could tell Rhett saw her emotions in the way she looked at him, just as she read his across his soul. He leaned down at the same moment she stretched up on her toes.

"Let me be the first to apologize on behalf of my Chief Assassin."

Rhett tensed and moved back from her, but he didn't let go. Liss turned to see the Emperor leering at them.

"Sometimes he forgets he's just a bastard in fine clothes that are paid for from my coffers," Jaikon drawled. The Emperor's shrewd, cruel gaze moved between them. "I think you've stolen enough of the lady's attention for one night."

Rhett's hand tightened reflexively on her waist. Liss gave him a quick glance she hoped communicated her meaning.

"You are too pretty for such boring company." The Emperor made a come-hither gesture with his finger. *Like she was a dog.*

There was fire in Rhett's eyes. She pinched him before moving out of his arms. *Not worth it* she tried to tell him with her gaze as she stared pointedly at the guards watching them from around the room.

Liss let out a little laugh, turning all of her attention on the Emperor. "I'd be honored to dance with you, Your Majesty."

The Emperor gripped Liss's waist and pulled her against him. It took all of her will not to shove him away.

"I think my Chief Assassin fancies you," he said, his lips grazing her ear. Liss tried not to shudder.

"I think it's my dress he fancies." She smiled up at the Emperor. "Thank you, by the way. I was honored to receive your invitation."

"You're quite welcome," Jaikon said. He reached up and yanked the shawl from around her with far more force than was required. He tossed the shawl onto the ground and raked his eyes up and down her body.

Liss wanted to throw up, but she forced her features to melt into a placid expression.

Rhett was standing beside the Emperor, his hands clenched into fists. He looked angry, but if Jaikon had been able to sense Rhett's emotions the way she could, she was pretty sure the Emperor would have turned tail and run.

Liss gave Rhett another small shake of her head. She could tell from the emotions radiating off the guards' souls that they would sooner kill her and Rhett than help them. If Rhett tried anything stupid, they'd be on him in a second.

"No need to stand around waiting," Jaikon said. "I don't plan on letting this beauty go anytime soon. In fact," he smiled at Rhett. "We'll be together long past your bedtime."

Rhett watched as the Emperor settled his hands on Liss in a familiar, possessive way. And then, he turned and strode away.

It took all of Liss's self-control to keep the ridiculous smile plastered on her face and hold her attention on Jaikon. She knew it was better for Rhett if he didn't see this, but she couldn't help feeling an irrational disappointment that he had given her up so easily.

It was stupid. It would do neither of them any good if Rhett challenged the Emperor over a dance. And yet, that pathetic, ridiculous side of her wished he had fought for her…just a little.

Jaikon held her too tight. His soul was as sleezy and slippery as the rest of him. Liss felt his aggression and sense of victory, and excitement. It was disgusting.

Liss clenched her jaw as the Emperor's hand on her waist slid lower. She wished desperately she had the dagger Rhett had given her. She wouldn't have been able to use it, obviously, but it would have made her feel less helpless to know that she could. But there had been nowhere to hide a dagger…or anything else…in this dress.

Jaikon leaned closer, letting his lips brush against her ear. "I know you're my Assassin's whore."

Liss tamped down her fury before she said or did something she wouldn't be able to take back. She cleared her throat.

"I have no idea what you're talking about, Majesty."

Jaikon smiled at her in a way that made her shiver.

"Don't try to play me for the fool," he said, his lips still a hair's breadth from her ear. "I saw you on the Sapphire Bridge."

Liss's throat went dry. She was trying to think of what to say when a soldier pushed through the crowd of people toward them. His face was red, like he'd been running.

"Majesty," the man gasped. "You're needed at once."

"Can't you see I'm busy?" Jaikon demanded, barely sparing the soldier a glance.

"A ship was spotted just off the coast. Some of our men gave chase, but—"

"Giants?" Jaikon let go of Liss and turned his full attention on the soldier.

"Yes." The man sucked in a breath. "Lots of them, and most of the guards are off duty tonight."

"Have my dragon brought," Jaikon ordered. "And get every guard in this room down to the sea. I want the boats found and the giants apprehended before they touch the sand."

Jaikon used his hands to part the crowd, shouting orders to nearby guards. He left the banquet hall without a backward glance.

Liss just stood there for a moment, not quite knowing what to do. And then someone grabbed her arm. She jumped. She was about to throw off the intruder, when she realized it was Rhett.

"Are you alright? Did he hurt you?"

Rhett examined her face.

"What? No, I'm fine." Liss looked in the direction where the Emperor had disappeared. "What's going on?"

"I'm rescuing you. Come on."

CHAPTER 44

That soldier said something about giants," Liss said as Rhett pulled her out of the banquet hall. "Don't you need to…do something?"

"No." Rhett gave her a little smile.

He threaded their fingers together as he led her through the now-unguarded exit, through the empty halls, and down to the bottom level of the palace. The balmy night air was refreshing after the too-crowded banquet hall. Liss tried to take a deep breath, but the dress was too tight for her to manage it.

Liss saw Silverbird waiting just off the main road. Ciago, who had clearly been expecting them, was holding the dragon's reins in one hand and a black, zippered bag in the other.

"Hiya, Liss," Ciago said, giving her a little wave.

Liss noticed he was being careful not to look at her.

"Hey," she replied, a little overwhelmed and a lot confused.

"Thanks, man," Rhett said.

"I'm sure you'll find some way to repay me."

Rhett took the bag from Ciago. "You'll have to do this a thousand more times before we're even."

"Yeah, yeah." Ciago slung Silverbird's reins over the dragon's head. "Jealous as usual."

Rhett just chuckled. All of his anxiety and tension from before were gone, replaced by humor and anticipation.

"That emergency the Emperor was called off on…" Liss began.

"A distraction." A wicked smile played at the corner of Rhett's lips.

"But won't he figure it out?" Liss was worried.

What had Rhett done?

"Some of my soldiers are currently chasing boats that were never there. I had them shoot off a few canons for good measure. By the time Jaikon's dragon takes to the sky and his idiot guards get down to the water, all they'll be able to recover will be some driftwood," Rhett explained.

"My guess is any giants who survived the canons are settling into their watery graves," Ciago added. "Poor things aren't very smart, and they're known for being terrible swimmers."

"Okay," Liss said, her own smile spreading across his face. "But what happens when Jaikon comes back here?"

"A few off-duty soldiers saw me staggering back to my room with some courtier and a bottle of champagne," Rhett replied.

"Hm," Liss said, pretending to frown. "Was she prettier than me?" Rhett's grin widened.

"And some drunk oaf stepped on the hem of your dress," Ciago said. "It ripped, and you ran back to the servants' quarters. You were very upset."

Liss widened her eyes. "I was?"

"You were crying," Ciago confirmed. "Several of the soldiers saw you. You refused to talk to anyone and shut yourself in your room for the rest of the night."

"How very dramatic of me."

Rhett picked her up, then. His arms were solid and warm around her as he lifted her onto Silverbird's back.

"You two go on." Ciago waved a hand at them and squeezed his face into a pout. "Don't worry about me. I'll just be waiting here, alone and abandoned—"

"Good night, Ciago," Rhett said, urging Silverbird forward before Ciago could finish complaining.

"Where are you taking me?" Liss asked as soon as the palace was behind them.

"Somewhere safe. At least for tonight, until I can make more permanent arrangements. You can't go back to the palace."

"Oh," was all she could think of to say.

The only way she could manage to sit on the dragon in her too-tight gown was to perch side-saddle with her legs dangling off one side. It was impractical, and she would have slid right off as soon as Silverbird started to move if Rhett hadn't held her against him.

"I've got you," he said into her ear as Silverbird moved into a brisker pace than Liss had thought the old dragon capable of.

Silverbird loped across the large fields where the soldiers sparred. The dragon's claws ate up the miles like they were nothing, and Liss realized they were heading toward the mountain range that served as a natural border to Lagonia's east.

Liss expected the dragon to stop when they got to the mountain's base, but Silverbird found a path in the dark, which she'd clearly been to many times before. Rhett's arm tightened around her as the dragon navigated up the steep path that curved around the mountain. After what Liss guessed was more than an hour, Silverbird came to a halt.

"We're here," Rhett said.

Liss shivered a little at the way his breath tickled her skin. He helped her down, since she was pretty much immobile in the tight dress, and then gave Silverbird a pat.

"See you in the morning," Rhett told the dragon.

Silverbird snorted like she understood and then started back down the mountain path.

In response to Liss's questioning look, Rhett said, "Silverbird knows the routine. I come here to sleep sometimes when I don't want to be bothered," he smirked, "which is to say a lot."

The nearly-full moon threw blue light across the path, so Liss could see they were on a ledge that stretched out over darkness below. Rhett went to the edge of the cliff, where there was a pile of blankets and a pillow.

"You really sleep here?"

"Mhm," Rhett replied, dragging the blankets away from the edge. He grinned at her. "I don't usually move around much in my sleep, but I'm not taking any chances tonight."

Liss felt herself blush.

She looked around. "We're completely alone up here?"

"No one for miles," Rhett replied. And then, his emotions faltered. "I didn't even ask. I just assumed…. Damnit. If you're uncomfortable, we don't have to—"

"No," she said quickly. "I'm not uncomfortable."

The tension in Rhett's posture eased. He took off his tie and tossed it on the ground along with his dagger and the bag Ciago had given him.

Liss was having trouble telling which emotions were coming from his soul and which came from hers. There was so much feeling between the two of them it was making her a little drunk.

Liss took a wobbling step, but the needle-thin point of her heel caught on a rock. Without the ability to move her legs more than a few inches apart, she lurched forward. Rhett caught her in his arms and lowered her to the pile of blankets.

"Safer down here," he murmured.

"I'm not so sure about that," Liss managed as he hovered over her.

There was something strange about being here together. Liss realized it was the first time she didn't feel like one or both of them was looking over their shoulder for fear of who might be just around the corner. Even the night they had slept in Rhett's room, they'd talked quietly so no one on the other side of the door would hear them. Tonight was the first time they didn't need to hold back.

All of the emotions in Rhett's soul had narrowed. There was only love and desire, and they pulsed with such intensity there wasn't room for anything else.

When he kissed her, it felt different, too. There was no sense that they would have to pull away at the first sound of footsteps or gleam of light creeping over the horizon.

It was liberating and exhilarating.

Rhett gripped her waist as she slipped her hands beneath his shirt, running her fingers along the ridges of muscle and scars across his chest and back. He lifted his arms, making it easier for her to tug his shirt off.

Everywhere his hands and lips touched left a line of fire in their wake. Liss felt more alive than she ever had in her life.

"I need you closer," Rhett gasped.

He was practically lying on top of her, but the layers of clothes between them had become an insufferable barrier. She undid the buckle of his belt. Rhett didn't wait for her to finish, kicking off his pants before pulling her to him. His hands slid up the sides of her dress, and for the first time, she didn't curse all the places her skin was bare.

Rhett stopped kissing her, his breathing ragged.

Liss could barely breathe herself, but that might have been partially from the dress cutting off her circulation. It took her a few seconds to realize Rhett's emotions had changed. The overwhelming desire of a moment ago was tempered with confusion and uncertainty.

Liss felt the change like a punch to her gut. *He didn't want her…his old fears about caring too much had returned.…*

"What's wrong?" she asked, even though she thought she already knew.

Rhett gave her a bewildered look.

"How do I get this dress off?"

Too relieved to speak, Liss started to laugh.

Rhett wasn't amused. "So many ties. And what are these ribbon things?"

When her laughter subsided, Liss said, "All I can tell you is that it took three servants half an hour to tie me into it."

"I can't wait that long," Rhett muttered. He reached back to where his dagger lay abandoned on the rock. Blue moonlight shone across the blade.

"Do you trust me?" Rhett asked, holding the dagger loosely in his hand.

"I wouldn't be here if I didn't," she replied.

He kneeled beside her, the dagger in his hand. Liss braced herself for the feeling of cold steel against her skin. It didn't come. She heard the tearing of the fabric and then felt a tremendous relief as the ties were sliced away. She took her first deep breath since she'd been stuffed into the gown.

Rhett tossed the dagger behind him and slowly peeled away the two halves of the dress. He stared at her.

"Wow," Rhett said. "Just, wow."

Liss didn't have to be a Soul Sorter to know what he was feeling; it was all in the mesmerized, worshipping look in his eyes. It was why she didn't feel even a hint of embarrassment as he stared at her. Strangely enough, she felt less exposed now than she had when she'd been in the dress.

"We're going to have some serious explaining to do tomorrow," she breathed as Rhett tossed the shredded halves of the dress over the cliff.

"That's a problem for tomorrow," Rhett replied, repeating the words she had once said to him.

She reached for him.

"Wait." Rhett took a shuddering breath. He held her hands gently, but with enough force that she couldn't move them from her sides. "I need to know if you really want this…if you want me." He took another ragged breath, and Liss knew how much it was costing him to have this conversation right now when all he wanted to do was…not talk.

"I don't like games," he continued. "I want you more than I've ever wanted anything in my life. If you don't want me like that, say it now. Don't lie to me."

"I—" Liss swallowed. "I have lied to you."

She saw the light in Rhett's eyes die a little.

"There are things about me I can't tell you," she hurried on. "But when it comes to this, when it comes to us, I've never lied. I want to be with you. Only you."

Rhett stared into her eyes for a long moment. And then, he nodded.

"I can live with that," he said, drawing her to him.

CHAPTER 45

Burk was tired. He was tired of seeing his people's fear and living in his own. He was tired of going to bed every night and wondering if this would be the night the Caravan Butcher stole into his wagon and slit his throat. He was tired of his wagon, which was too small and had never felt like home. He was tired of existing without any real purpose. He was tired of being ignored.

Burk had long suspected that his thief-turned-spy was holding out on him. She was too intelligent and resourceful for her scant reports to be the whole of what she'd discovered.

When the last pixie he'd hired to deliver his offer to Emperor Jaikon hadn't returned, Burk decided he was finished with waiting.

He had brought three Extended from a different caravan—a Flamer, a Flyer, and a Metalsmith—and together, they'd journeyed from the southern plains to the Insorsiled forest. They'd pretended to wander into a slaver camp, allowed themselves to be captured, and were marched right across the Golden Bridge into Lagonia.

He knew he'd be searched when he was captured, so he hadn't been able to bring the contract he'd drawn up months ago. Once Jaikon agreed to his terms, he'd send for someone to collect the contract. Soon enough, he'd have a whole staff of people who would serve his needs, and he'd have to get used to delegating the more menial tasks.

Everything after that had been easy. The Metalsmith had unlocked their shackles. The Flamer had set a nearby shop ablaze, and while the slavers were distracted, the four Extended had knocked their captors unconscious and disappeared into the dark and crowded streets. Lagonians had been everywhere…drinking, laughing, and dancing as they celebrated what Burk gathered from snippets of overheard conversation was a victory against the Giant Realm.

No one paid any attention to the four men in black cloaks.

After that, it was Burk's Extension that had led them where they needed to go. Admittedly, it had been a stroke of luck that Liss had come running out of the palace hand in hand with a boy and taken off on a dragon just as he and his men were approaching. But the dragon had quickly outpaced them, and it was only because of Burk's Extended hearing that he was able to lead the others to the mountain where the dragon had gone.

They had found a nice little hideout at the base of the mountain to wait out the night. Liss didn't have his hearing—no one did—but she did have a thief's instincts, and Burk didn't want to risk her hearing or seeing them.

He only needed to be patient a little longer. Once the sun rose, the lovers would leave and he would find what he'd come for.

Burk was disappointed that Liss had betrayed him and the rest of the Extended so thoroughly, although he couldn't say he was surprised. What surprised him was that the reason for her betrayal was something as mundane as love.

Burk wondered vaguely who the boy was. As far as Burk could remember, Liss had never shown interest in any Extended man. There were several of them who had trailed after her like forlorn puppies, but she'd never so much as given them a second glance. Then again, her mother had been besotted with a Lagonian. Burk wondered if there was some genetic predisposition for that.

Burk looked with envy at his companions, who were playing cards and chatting, oblivious to what was happening high on the clifftop above them. Burk had gotten good at tuning out the more private sounds that came from the wagons in his caravan, but Liss and the boy were loud enough to wake the dead. And they were tireless.

It was just as well, he supposed, that Liss should enjoy what time she had left. Burk had given it careful consideration, and he'd come to the conclusion that Liss was a sacrifice he was willing to make to earn the life he had so long been deprived of.

When the sun rose, Burk felt certain he would find the source of the Lagonians' immunity. He would finally have the Emperor's attention and the power to bargain for what he desired.

Burk settled back against the side of the mountain.

One more night. In the morning, everything would be different. He would never again be the one begging for mercy. He'd be the one with the power to grant it.

CHAPTER 46

Liss lay in Rhett's arms as they watched the first rays of dawn peek over the horizon. They hadn't slept, not wanting to waste even a minute of their night together. She snuggled against his chest as he traced lazy circles up and down her spine. Liss felt his joy the same way she'd felt his pleasure: as acutely as she felt her own.

There were no lingering traces of doubt or uncertainty in Rhett's soul. There was only love and joy, pulsing through him in equal measures.

"Your family was wrong about you," Rhett murmured.

She stiffened at that. "Oh?"

"There's more magic in you than in all of Insorsil."

For some reason, Liss felt the burn of tears in her eyes.

"Thank you," she whispered.

He shifted so they were lying face-to-face and she could see his serious expression. "Come away with me, Liss."

"What? Where?"

"One of the empires across the sea. Anywhere you want to go, as long as it's far away from here."

"Be serious," she said with a small laugh, even though she could feel from his emotions that he was.

"I have money," he said. "I could buy us passage on the next ship out of here."

Liss was having trouble catching her breath. "You can't just leave."

"Can't I?"

She shook her head. "Lagonia's your home. You've got friends—"

"You're more important than any of that."

"Believe me, I'm not worth as much as you think," Liss replied. She was trying for levity, but she could hear a note of bitterness in her voice. She cursed herself for it.

Rhett stared at her for a long moment. "You're worth everything to me," he said.

Liss didn't know if she was grateful she could feel the truth of his words through his emotions, or if she wished she couldn't. It made all of her lies and deception so much worse.

"I'm not saying life would be easy," Rhett continued. "But you'd be safe, and we'd be together." His voice faltered on these last words. "Unless that isn't what you want." He swallowed. "I can make the arrangements for you to go without me."

"It's not that," Liss said, forcing herself to ignore the emotions passing across Rhett's soul so she could think for a second.

"If anything happened to you because of me, I couldn't bear it," Rhett said. "Do you understand that?"

Liss felt the rawness of his emotions. It made her chest ache.

She forced out the words that needed to be said. "There are things about me you don't know, and if you did, you wouldn't want me anymore. You barely know me."

Rhett took her face in his hands and stared into her eyes. "Tell me again I don't know you," he breathed, his face only inches from hers.

"You don't understand." Liss felt the prick of tears behind her eyes.

"Then help me understand," Rhett said. "Tell me. Whatever it is, you don't have to deal with it alone."

Liss felt a strange urge to laugh and cry at the same time.

"There are some…things I need to deal with first that you can't help me with. Once it's done, I'll tell you everything." She looked at him, and realized his face was blurry because of the tears swimming across her eyes. "If you still want me then, I'll go away with you."

A choked sensation gripped her as she realized that, twenty-something years ago, Liss's parents must have had a similar conversation to the one she and Rhett were having now.

The happiness that surged through Rhett's soul only made her feel worse. He smiled as he leaned in to kiss the place where her dimple always appeared.

"You're not scaring me off that easily," he said, his eyes full of warmth.

Liss sat up. Her lazy sense of peace was gone, replaced by restlessness. She wrapped one of the blankets around her and walked toward the edge of the cliff. The lightening sky seemed to stretch out forever before her. It made her feel very small.

Rhett came up behind her and wrapped his arms around her, grounding her.

"It'll take me a couple of days to arrange for our passage on one of the merchant ships," Rhett said. "It's not safe for either of us if you come back to the palace, so I'll meet you in the Insorsiled forest where we camped last time. Do you remember how to get there?"

"Yes," Liss said, feeling a little breathless at these whirlwind plans. She turned so she could look at Rhett. "But is it safe for you to go back after everything that's happened?"

"I've broken no laws, and as long as Jaikon doesn't know where you are, there's nothing he can do to control me." Rhett shrugged. "Jaikon might know about you, but as long as he can't find you, that knowledge won't do him any good."

"Okay," Liss said. She gave Rhett a hesitant smile. "Okay."

He pulled her against him, the warmth from his body and soul banishing all her nervous energy. He leaned down to kiss her, but at that moment, something caught her attention.

Liss peered down over the side of the cliff. Her heart stopped.

"What is that?"

Rhett turned to see what she was looking at.

"Do you not know?"

Stretched out before them, for as far as the eye could see, was a field. The sun had risen enough to illuminate the rows and rows of shimmering opal flowers…identical to the ones she'd found locked in the palace kitchens. The sunlight rippled and danced off their rainbow petals, making the whole field look like it was pulsing with color. It was almost blinding in its intensity. It was the most beautiful sight Liss had ever seen.

"I obviously couldn't talk about it, but I thought you might have known since—"

"Since what?"

Liss tore her gaze away from the opal flowers to look at Rhett.

"They're from your queen." He looked puzzled.

It was an effort to breathe normally. "I'm an Empty," she forced herself to say. "I wasn't privy to my queen's secret gifts."

"Oh, well, the last emperor got them in exchange for promising Gatria the support of our army."

"And these flowers…."

"Give us immunity to opal contagion," Rhett confirmed.

"I see." Liss was having trouble pretending to be calm as she stared out at the miles and miles of flowers. She had thought there were a lot of them in the barrels. But these fields looked like they went on forever. "How do they work?"

Rhett was too busy kissing her neck to notice how her world was being turned inside out.

"When they're dried and ground up, they turn into a white powder," he explained between kisses. "It's put into flour, molasses, raw meat…really any ingredient the powder can be mixed or absorbed into. All food comes into the empire through the palace. The head chef oversees the distribution of the immunity into the raw ingredients, and then it's sent to every household in the empire."

Liss's mouth had gone dry.

"And people don't know they're eating this?"

"Nope." Rhett nuzzled his face into the hollow of her neck. "We started all sorts of rumors about the head chef being obsessive, so no one ever questions why he would want to inspect all ingredients coming into the empire. We have two warlocks in the palace ready to deal with anyone who starts to suspect."

Rhett turned her around to face him. "You can't say anything to anyone."

"I understand," Liss managed. Her brain had splintered into a thousand different directions.

She needed her onyx stone. She had to tell Burk.

But if she told Burk, he'd destroy the flowers. Extended would descend on Lagonia, and the Lagonians would be powerless against the effects of the disease. People would die. Rhett would….

"We still have hours before the pickers come for the day," Rhett was saying. "There are hot springs on the other side of the field. We could go for a swim. Or we could do more of what we did last night—"

"I don't have time." Liss wouldn't be able to conceal her panic for much longer. She needed to get out of here.

Rhett's brow furrowed. "Liss—"

"I…." She looked around. "I need something to wear."

"Right." Rhett walked back to where he'd left the bag Ciago had given him the night before. "Samara packed a bag for you. She put some of her Insorsiled clothes in there, since wearing a Lagonian servant's uniform outside the empire will invite questions we don't want to answer."

Liss pulled out a bright green shirt, green pants, and a matching cloak, as well as clean underclothes.

"Blame Samara if you don't like the outfit." Rhett grinned at her. "There's also an Insorsiled tent, supplies for a fire, food, and everything else you'll need for the few days before I come for you."

"Um, thanks," she said, not knowing quite how to feel about the idea of running away with Rhett. Her mind was full of too many other problems to give thought to something that she knew could never be anything more than a fantasy. No matter what he said, once Rhett learned who she was, he wouldn't want to go anywhere with her.

"Will you break out that dimple for me if I tell you there's breakfast in there, too?" he asked.

He reached around her, pulling out small glass containers filled with her favorite pastries, nuts, and sliced fruit.

"Rhett, I don't have time for a picnic."

He looked at her, then. "What's wrong?" he asked, his light expression falling away.

Liss yanked on the clothes. "I need to get back. If I'm going to…take care of that stuff, I need to go back to Insorsil. Today."

"Is it safe for you to go back to Insorsil?" Rhett said, worry and confusion slipping into his soul along with the other emotions.

"No one's going to recognize me with short hair," Liss said. "It'll be fine."

"Let me come with you."

She shook her head, almost beyond words at this point.

Liss felt the tendrils of disappointment on Rhett's soul before his serious mask slid back into place.

"I'll work on getting us passage across the sea." He put on his pants and used an Insorsiled whistle Liss hadn't even known he had to call for Silverbird.

"Could you…." Liss swallowed. "Do you think you could get passage for three?"

Rhett looked at her. "Your mom?"

She nodded.

"Sure, yes. Whatever you want."

She didn't know why she had asked. No matter how all of this ended, she knew it wouldn't be with her and Rhett sailing away to some foreign land.

In only a few minutes, they heard the sound of rocks rolling out from under dragon feet.

"I'll go with you to the forest. As soon as I'm sure no one's seen you, you can take Silverbird to Insorsil," Rhett said. "It'll be faster, and she'll protect you in the forest if anyone finds you."

Liss could only nod. Too much was happening too quickly. She had to meet with Burk. She just had no idea what she would tell him when she saw him.

While Rhett tightened Silverbird's girth and tied Liss's bag behind the saddle, Liss whispered a message into her onyx stone. She slipped it back into her pocket before climbing onto the dragon.

Once they were back down the mountain, Silverbird's claws ate up the ground with such speed the landscape blurred around them. It felt like only minutes passed before they had crossed the Golden Bridge and the forest's trees were surrounding them.

Rhett lingered at the edge of the Insorsiled forest. Liss didn't even remember what excuses she had made, only that he was walking back toward the bridge and she was riding away from the empire.

Liss needed time to think. She figured it would take Burk hours to get to their meeting place on his Insorsiled bike, which would give her time to figure out what she was going to tell him.

As she rode, an imperfect solution began to take shape. It might be possible to destroy the immunity flowers and keep the Lagonians she cared about safe. She just had to approach it the right way. Remembering how Burk had acted the last time they met, she knew she'd have to be careful.

As her plan started to form, Liss's panic ebbed. She could do this. She could give her people freedom from the Lagonians' reign of terror. She could keep Rhett, Samara, Wilsean, and Ciago alive. Stone, too, she supposed. Even if she could never forgive him, she would protect him for Rhett's sake.

The tricky part would be her mom.

Liss hoped the Extended Runner had delivered her message and that her mom had fled the caravan like she'd asked. Her mom hadn't left the wagon…had barely left her bed…since Liss was a baby. But Liss believed her mom could be the Extended Huntress she had once been. And Liss believed she could convince her mom to cross the sea with her and Rhett.

If he still wanted her.

She couldn't let herself think about that now. Right now, she had to focus on the bargain she planned to make with Burk.

✳ ✳ ✳

Burk's pocket heated. He pulled out the onyx stone, read the message scrawled across its surface, and smiled.

When they'd gotten here last night, it had been too dark to see anything. After everything he'd overheard, Burk could barely contain his impatience.

As soon as Liss and her lover rode away on the dragon, Burk and the other Extended moved out from their hiding place.

Burk blinked as his eyes tried to make sense of what they were seeing.

"What in the hell is this?" the Flyer asked.

None of the others spoke as their eyes were assaulted with every color imaginable. The flower petals' rainbow hues shimmered and danced in the sunlight. Burk was used to his ears being overwhelmed with sound, but it was a different experience for his eyes. There was so much color it was almost painful.

Burk held up his bare hands, watching the play of sunlight on his opal-hued skin, and then he looked back out at the fields. His skin looked just like the flowers, except the flowers were even more radiant. The field was as majestic as it was terrible. It filled him with rage to see how something made in his own likeness had been the instrument of his suffering.

"What do we do now?" the Metalsmith asked.

Burk turned to the Flamer. "Burn them all."

The man's teeth flashed in a grin as both his hands exploded into flames.

It was a windy morning, and it didn't take long for the Flamer's fire to spread. It was a smokeless fire and burned with unnatural intensity. Burk felt a sweat break out across his brow, but he stayed to watch the opal fields turn to a chalky ash.

Burk reached into the leather bag strapped to his back. He pulled out a small glass jar with airholes poked in the top. He unscrewed the lid enough for only one of the pixies smacking against the glass to get out.

The pixie spilled onto his palm, looking a little dazed and lot angry.

"Let my sister out!" she squeaked.

The sound was piercing to Burk's ears, and he winced.

"I will, once you do something for me."

The pixie hissed. Burk didn't bother to hide his self-satisfied smile.

"I have a message for you to bring to the Emperor."

✳ ✳ ✳

Rhett didn't have time for one of Jaikon's temper tantrums. He was halfway down the hall, and he could hear the Emperor screaming at someone about something.

A few more days, he told himself. A few more days, and then this empire and his despicable half-brother would be far behind him. In the meantime, though, he needed to bargain for passage across the sea for himself, Liss, and her mother.

Rhett wasn't thrilled to be traveling halfway around the world with the woman who had abandoned Liss to exile, but he still understood why Liss wanted to bring her with them. Afterall, he wasn't in a position to judge when Stone was his only family.

There was so much to do. They'd all need warm clothes, which were difficult to come by since Lagonians had no use for them. Rhett needed to get the rest of his money without arousing suspicions. He needed to say goodbye to Stone and his friends.

The doors to the throne room flew open. Stone came out, his face pale. Wilsean and Ciago were behind him, looking similarly stricken.

"What's happened?" Rhett asked, immediately on his guard.

"The flower fields," Stone said, his voice tight. "They've been burned."

"That's not possible."

Rhett had been there not two hours ago. If the fields were burning, he would have noticed.

"I saw it with my own eyes," Wilsean said, grimacing. "Believe me, it's possible."

"When?" Rhett demanded.

"An hour ago," Stone replied. "The Extended Flamer who did it has been caught. He's down in the torture cage."

"There were other Extended with him," Wilsean added, "but they got away."

Rhett couldn't make sense of any of it. His mind was reeling. "How did they get into the empire? How did they find the fields?"

Ciago answered. "They snuck in during the celebration last night. The Flamer said their spy led them straight to the fields." He made a derisive noise. "Of course, he claims not to have seen the spy's face."

"He did mention the spy left the field this morning and was wearing a green cloak," Wilsean said. "Useless as that tidbit may be."

Rhett's whole body went numb. He had no idea how he stayed on his feet.

"I'm going to interrogate the Flamer and see what else can be learned," Stone said. "After the Emperor's meeting with that caravan leader, we'll know more. Arrangements will need to be made to close up the empire. The Extended slaves will need to be eliminated before the stash is depleted." He rubbed a hand over his face.

Rhett heard the words, but they sounded far away, like Rhett had his head submerged in water.

"The rest of those Extended couldn't have gotten far," Wilsean said. "If we catch them, we'll catch their spy."

"I'll get the dragons," Ciago said, already hurrying off.

Rhett stood rooted to the spot as he tried to catch his breath.

CHAPTER 47

Liss hadn't expected Burk to arrive so soon. A Flyer she'd never met before landed on the road and released Burk from his grip. It was an undignified way to travel, but an effective one.

Liss got to her feet as she tried to gather the scattered pieces of her plan.

"Good morning, Liss," Burk said.

Liss didn't answer. She didn't like the look of his soul. There was excitement and anticipation, but both emotions were tinged with an ugly hue. There was also a confidence in his emotions that hadn't been there during their last meeting. Her instincts screamed out a warning. She forced a smile on her face.

"I have some good news," she said. "But before I tell it to you, I'm going to need you to agree to a few things."

To her surprise, a malicious grin spread across her caravan leader's face.

"*You* want to bargain with *me*?" Burk asked, his whispery tone dripping with sarcasm. "After betraying me and the rest of our people?"

What did Burk know?

"I discovered their secret," Liss stammered. She kept on with the speech she had prepared. "But I have terms. I want some of the…immunity…to be preserved, and—"

Burk cut her off with a wave of his hand. "There's nothing left to preserve."

Damn Burk and his too-soft voice. She thought he'd just said—

"What?" she asked.

"Burned," Burk said. "Every last flower."

Her mouth opened, but no sound came out.

Burk sighed. "Yes, I know about the fields. And no, I'm not bluffing. Look in my soul."

Liss did, and her stomach turned over.

"Burned?" she whispered.

"Every last flower."

His soul filled with anticipation and a sense of victory.

Liss shook her head as she struggled to comprehend what he was saying.

"I knew you were holding out on me," Burk said, "so I came to investigate myself." A smile spread across Burk's usually-somber face. "Thank you for leading me straight to the source, by the way."

"No." Liss's voice came out as a croak.

Burk's opal skin gleamed with a vitality that seemed to mock her as he turned his face up to the sun. He took a timepiece from his pocket and studied it. "I'm meeting with the Emperor in an hour." He turned back to her. "You should know I'm hoping to avoid an all-out war with the Lagonians by striking a bargain with Emperor Jaikon."

"A bargain?" Liss asked, feeling desperate and furious all at the same time.

"The Emperor is bound to be…dissatisfied with the loss of their immunity. His people will start to turn on him, and he'll be less particular about who he allies with. I'll offer him something he wants in exchange for his assurance that he won't send any more assassins after our people. And he'll provide me with a home that doesn't sit atop wheels. And a position on his council." Burk ticked off each of his terms on his fingers.

"What are you going to give him in exchange?" Liss asked, even though she already guessed the answer.

"You."

There was no guilt or apology in Burk's emotions. There was only resolve.

"If I were you," he gave Liss a hard stare, "I'd start running."

Liss drew her dagger, the one Rhett had given her before they parted. She gripped it, unsure of what to do with it. The Flyer landed on the ground beside them. Burk lifted his arms, and the Flyer was pulling him into the sky and out of her reach before she could come to any kind of a decision.

"Come back here!" she screamed, finding her voice.

This couldn't be happening. This couldn't—

Rhett. She had to warn him.

Liss had no idea when the Lagonians would discover that their salvation had been destroyed. She had to tell Rhett so they could preserve what was left. With all the Extended slaves in the empire, Lagonia was already vulnerable. They would need to get the slaves out before everyone learned what had happened and started killing them. They would need to guard the remaining flowers before mass panic set in.

She ran back to Silverbird and leapt onto the dragon's back. She dug her heels into Silverbird's sides, urging her back to the palace.

CHAPTER 48

Still in a daze, Rhett sent Ciago and Wilsean to search for the runaway Extended in the Insorsiled forest. He had taken the Emperor's winged dragon and was circling the sky high enough that he could see all the way from the Golden Bridge to the crowd of buildings far in the distance that marked the beginning of outer Insorsil. Rhett looked through an Insorsiled glass that magnified everything on the ground.

He found Silverbird loping down the road, running toward Lagonia. Rhett's heart lurched.

He coaxed the temperamental dragon lower, almost getting his face burned off when the dragon turned its head to snarl at him. The dragon hit the ground right in front of Silverbird.

Liss hauled on the reins, but she was thrown from the saddle as Silverbird reared up. Rhett jumped from his own dragon. Even now that he knew who she was…what she'd done… his first reaction was still to make sure she didn't get caught beneath Silverbird's prancing claws.

"Rhett," she gasped, as soon as she was on her feet.

She looked so different from how she had only a few hours ago. This morning, she'd been all warmth and softness. Now, there was a wild look in her eyes.

It took Rhett several seconds to find his voice.

"Tell me it isn't you," he said, barely able to hear himself over the crash of his heart against his ribcage. "Tell me you aren't the spy, and I'll believe you."

Because I'm that big of a fool for you.

Liss shook her head. Tears slid down her cheeks—cheeks he had touched and kissed only a few hours earlier.

"Say it." His voice was rising, but for once, he couldn't control his emotions. "Tell me this is a coincidence."

"Rhett—"

"Tell me!"

Liss took in a slow, shuddering breath.

"I'm the spy you've been hunting for," she said, her voice wavering. "I'm Opal Smoke."

Rhett felt his throat closing.

"Please, let me explain." She came forward and took his hands. Rhett was too overcome to either pull away or close his hands around hers.

He focused on the facts, because it was the only way to retain the shreds of his sanity. Liss had the skills to be the elusive spy, he supposed, but not the motivation. She was born and raised in Insorsil, and the Insorsiled had no love for the Extended. Why would she risk…everything…for them?

"I'm not an Empty," Liss began, like she could read his mind. "I'm not even Insorsiled. I'm Extended."

Rhett managed a short, bitter laugh. "You must really think I'm a fool if you expect me to believe that."

The best illusion potions were convincing, but they needed to be taken hourly or they would fade. He gave her a meaningful look. "I don't remember you taking any breaks last night to down an illusion potion."

Besides, physical illusions were just that. He would have noticed if the way she looked and felt didn't match.

Liss shook her head, tears glistening in her blue eyes. "My mother is Extended, but my father was Lagonian." She blinked, and the tears spilled over onto her cheeks. Rhett had an insane urge to wipe them away. "I have an Extension like my mother, but I inherited my father's looks."

"You're an Extended who doesn't look like the Extended?" Rhett asked.

It was preposterous. Impossible. And that was how he knew it must be true. No one could expect him to believe something this insane unless it was the truth.

"I just wanted my people to stop dying."

Liss tried to take his hands again. This time, he stepped back, away from her.

"Your Extension," he said. Rhett kept his voice cold, distant. He'd had plenty of practice at it. "Can you really turn into smoke?"

She shook her head again. "I'm a Soul Sorter," Liss said, her voice small.

Rhett laughed, and the sound was foreign and terrible to his own ears. "Of course, you are."

He should have guessed. It explained how she could read him when no one else could. It explained why she hadn't been pushed away when he acted cold and distant. It was why she had never needed any assurances of his feelings. She had just reached inside him and taken them out.

Rhett felt sick. But then a new, even more horrible thought crossed his mind.

"Last night," he said, barely able to get the words out. "Was that just—"

"No!" Liss's voice was pleading. "I found the flowers in the kitchen, but I had no idea about the fields. I didn't know that's where you were taking me last night." She spoke quickly, like she was desperate to get it all out before he decided to stop listening and do…what? Rhett didn't even know.

"My caravan leader betrayed me. He followed us last night," she hurried on. "I didn't know he was even in the empire." Her voice had taken on a kind of urgency. "He found the flower fields and burned them. I had no idea. I swear it. I was going to make a deal with him to protect—"

"Listen to me, Liss," Rhett began, and then cut himself off. "Is that even your name?"

"Yes! Tamilissa Elspeth Wren was the one I made up." She was crying in earnest now. "I told you last night that I never lied to you about us, and it was the truth."

Rhett felt something inside him shatter. Liss, who was watching him, gasped.

"Stop it," Rhett ground out. "Get the hell out of my soul."

His pain was almost unbearable. He had no interest in Liss knowing that he stood before her, broken.

"I love you," she said, her voice full of the pain that was drowning him.

"Words are cheap, Liss," Rhett managed through gritted teeth.

Steel doesn't know love or despair. It needs no heart or warmth.

It had been months since the mantra had held any meaning for him. He clung to it now.

It can't be bent or broken.

"I never wanted to hurt you," Liss said.

He laughed, and she flinched at the sound.

"Do you think I planned for any of this?" she asked, her voice rising. "Believe me, I didn't want to fall in love with you."

"I'm sorry I was such an inconvenience," he bit back.

"No, that's not what I meant. I—"

Rhett drew the dagger from his belt and strode forward.

I am steel.

He gripped the hilt of his dagger. "Are you the Extended spy I've been searching for?" he demanded, his voice strong and full of authority.

Liss's gaze went from the dagger to his face. "Yes," she whispered.

They were standing only a foot apart, but she didn't back away from him. She had stopped crying and met his gaze with a defiance he couldn't help but respect. Somehow, even though Liss was facing down the man sent to hunt her, he was the one who was destroyed.

They stood like that for several seconds.

"You saved my life," Rhett said, sheathing his dagger. "Consider my blood debt repaid."

Liss looked at him like she suspected him of a trap.

You're the one who lied to me! he wanted to shout at her. She could probably sense the betrayal he felt, which in of itself felt like a betrayal. He was dizzy and sick with all of it. He needed to get away from her.

"I'm the only one who knows your identity," Rhett said, letting numbness sweep in to wash everything else away. "I'd guess you have a few hours before anyone else figures it out." He let a sneer twist his features. "Especially since everyone is looking for a man with opal skin."

"Rhett—"

"Silverbird will be too conspicuous," he continued, his voice monotone, "so you'll have to go on foot. I suggest getting as far from here as you can."

"Rhett, please."

"I'll cover your tracks this once," he said, letting darkness fill his heart until it was a cushion of nothingness between himself and the horror that lay beneath. "But if we ever cross paths again, don't expect me to spare you."

Liss had the gall to look heartbroken. He was grateful for the blanket of nothing around his heart, which was all that kept him standing.

"Go," Rhett said, feeling all his strength leave him at once.

She gave him an uncertain look.

"Go!"

Liss turned and fled.

CHAPTER 49

Rhett didn't remember getting back to the Insorsiled forest where Wilsean and Ciago were waiting for him. They were both talking to him, but he couldn't bring himself to make sense of their words.

The walls of darkness that had gone up in his mind were receding, and the pain of Liss's betrayal was coming back.

Rhett handed both dragons' reins to Ciago without a word and then sank down at the base of a tree. He covered his face with his hands, even as he felt his friends prodding him and demanding to know what had happened.

He couldn't have told them even if he wanted to. He couldn't speak at all.

He really was a fool. A fresh wave of shame hit him like a fist to the stomach. He'd asked her to come away with him. He'd been planning a life with her, while all along, she'd....

Liss must be having a good laugh at his expense.

Rhett had been ready to give up his duties, his home…for the sake of something that was a lie. Even his memory of last night, the happiest night of his life, was a lie.

"Rhett!" Ciago grabbed his shoulders and shook him. "What happened?"

"Nothing," Rhett managed. "I just…need a minute."

His friends were still staring at him. Rhett couldn't meet their eyes.

I am steel. I am steel. I am steel.

No matter how many times he said the words, all he heard was Liss's voice telling him she was the Extended spy. All he saw was the look on her face when she told him the truth.

"I just need a minute," he said again.

✳ ✳ ✳

Liss could barely see through the tears that were pouring from her eyes. She wasn't even paying attention to where she was going as she ran through the Insorsiled forest. All she could think about was Rhett's breaking heart. She'd stood there as the fragile, beautiful emotions that had been emerging on his soul were wiped away with one cruel stroke. And she'd been the one to deal the blow.

Liss had never felt so lost and utterly alone. She tripped over a root and fell to the ground on her hands and knees, gasping with the memory of Rhett's pain. It was minutes before she could get back up again.

She didn't hear the footsteps behind her until it was too late.

"Stop," a familiar voice commanded.

Liss reached for the dagger at her belt.

"Don't even think about it," Stone growled.

She let the dagger fall to the ground.

"Turn around," Stone said.

When she did, she felt the anger and accusation on his soul. It was there and in the furious expression on his face. He knew who she was.

Stone's hold on his sword never faltered as he strode over to her. He wrenched Liss's arms behind her back and pressed the blade of his sword to her throat.

"I hereby arrest you under the authority of the Lagonia Emperor for spying and delivering secrets to the Extended," Stone said in a formal tone. His grip tightened painfully on her wrists, and he gave her a little shake. "And for deceiving my boy."

"You're one to talk," she said with as much ire as she could muster. "After everything you've done to him."

"Everything I did made him strong," Stone spat back. "What you've done will break him."

Liss had no words to respond.

Stone kept his tight hold on her as he marched her through the woods. Liss didn't have the heart or energy to utter even a single word. It wasn't like begging or trying to explain would help her now, anyway. Stone's emotions were clear and unyielding. He felt no sympathy for her.

Liss felt her own soul fill with overwhelming shame as the familiar outlines of Ciago and Wilsean came into view. Her heart stopped at the figure hunched on the ground.

She forgot about Stone gripping her arms behind her and the way his blade dug into her skin. All of her attention was fixed on Rhett. His head was in his hands, and Liss could feel his betrayal and pain like it was her own. He didn't look up as Stone pushed her into the clearing.

"Stone, what are you doing?" Wilsean asked incredulously.

"Rhetteman," Stone said, ignoring Wilsean.

Rhett glanced up, and then, seeing her with the blade to her throat, leapt to his feet.

"Let her go," Rhett commanded. "Stone, let her go."

"She's the one we've been searching for," Stone said without loosening his hold on either her wrists or his sword.

Liss heard Ciago and Wilsean's surprised exclamations, but they were just background noise. All of her attention was on Rhett.

"Your duty dictates you bring her back to the Emperor for his judgement," Stone continued. The hard edge of his voice softened just a bit. "But I, for one, would look the other way if you wanted to spare her from the torture cage and end her life now."

"Stone, what the hell?" Ciago demanded.

"If you can't do it," Stone said, all of his attention fixed on Rhett, "I'll kill her for you."

"No one's killing her." Rhett's chest was rising and falling with the effort of keeping his emotions in check.

"If we bring her back, you know what Jaikon will do to her," Stone said. "Better for you to kill her swiftly and have done with it."

"We're not bringing her back *or* killing her," Rhett said. "Let her go."

"Rhetteman—"

"Let. Her. Go."

"Didn't you hear me?" Stone growled. "She's the spy. She's been feeding information to the Extended. She's the reason our fields are gone."

Rhett's gaze fixed on her for the first time. "I know who she is."

"It's your choice," Stone said, dragging at Liss's wrists until she was forced to take several steps back, away from Rhett. "Kill her here and now, or I'll drag her back to Jaikon."

With slow, deliberate steps, Rhett walked over to the tree where Ciago's sword was resting against the trunk.

"Don't touch that sword," Stone said, his voice a deadly calm, "unless you're willing to die for her."

Rhett didn't say anything. He picked up the sword.

"You have loyalties. Duty. Have you forgotten all of it?" Stone demanded, incredulous.

"As long as I live," Rhett said, "no one will harm her."

The regret in Stone's soul terrified Liss more than any other emotion. Stone wasn't afraid, as he might be if he thought Rhett was going to kill him. His emotions were grieving, like Rhett was already lying dead in a pool of his own blood.

Could Stone kill Rhett? Liss had no intention of finding out.

"Stop," she ordered. "Take me back to the palace."

The last thing she wanted was to be thrown in that horrible cage, but at least there, she had a chance of escape. If Stone killed her, she'd have nothing.

She looked straight at Rhett. "I don't want you to get hurt because of me."

Rhett ignored her. He spun the sword around in his hand.

"Are you sure you want to do this, boy?" Stone asked.

Rhett anchored his stance, holding out the sword in an unwavering grip. "Yes."

Stone sighed, and then he let her go.

"Run, Liss," Rhett said without looking away from Stone. "No one will try to stop you as long as I'm alive."

Wilsean and Ciago looked between the three of them, their mouths agape. Liss could tell from Rhett's emotions it would be pointless to argue with him.

She ran into the trees until she was out of sight, and then she backtracked. She found a tree she could hide behind and see without being seen. She was close enough that she'd be able to hear their every word and clash of blades. She would stay here, and if it seemed like Rhett was on the losing end of the fight, she'd put an end to it.

Liss watched, her heart in her throat, as the two men faced off. Rhett had the advantage of at least forty pounds on Stone, and he was thirty years younger, besides. Still, it wasn't enough to comfort Liss. Stone prowled around Rhett the way dragons circled their prey.

"She isn't worth it," Stone told Rhett.

"You don't get to decide what she's worth to me," Rhett replied.

Wilsean and Ciago were watching from the sidelines with a muted kind of horror. Neither of them spoke or moved as Stone and Rhett circled each other.

Stone moved so fast Liss didn't even see the strike until Rhett was stumbling back. There was a long slice down the front of his shirt. Blood was already welling through the slashed fabric. Rhett's expression and emotions didn't react, even though Liss could see the cut was deep. All she sensed on his soul was an intense focus.

Liss was balanced on the balls of her feet, ready to rush back and give herself up.

Stone struck again. This time, Rhett spun out of the way in time to avoid the blade. Every one of Stone's strikes was measured, precise, and lightning fast. Rhett hadn't gotten in a single strike of his own. Blood dripped down his chest. Liss pressed her fist into her mouth to keep from screaming.

Stone's sword flashed again. This time, Rhett didn't dodge out of the way. At the last moment, he brought up his own sword. The woods filled with the harsh sound of blades tangling. The two men stood, their swords locked together, for several seconds. They were perfectly matched. Both were immovable. And then, Rhett drove Stone back. It was only a step, but it was enough to shift Stone's balance.

Rhett didn't wait for Stone to regain his footing. He brought his sword down. The blades clashed. Rhett struck again, and again. He never got within reach of Stone's skin, but as Liss watched, she realized he wasn't trying to. Rhett was keeping up a steady attack as he rained heavy blows down on Stone. It was taking every ounce of the older man's strength and concentration to hold off Rhett's barrage. He didn't have a chance to land any of his own strikes.

The slash along Rhett's chest had widened, but he didn't seem to even know he was injured. Their swords collided over and over again. With every clash of their blades, Stone grew a little weaker.

The next blow forced Stone to his knees. With another quick strike, Rhett sent the sword in Stone's hands sailing through the air. It landed on the ground several feet away.

Rhett loomed over Stone. His chest was heaving, but his grip on the sword was steady.

Stone looked up at Rhett. "Finish it," he snarled.

Rhett didn't move.

What are you waiting for? Liss wanted to scream.

"Finish it!"

The two men stared at each other. They were having some silent exchange Liss didn't understand. She felt only resolve in Rhett's soul, and a desperate kind of frustration in Stone's.

Rhett stepped back.

"No." Stone jumped to his feet and grabbed Rhett's arm.

For a terrifying moment, Liss thought he was going to take Rhett's sword, but he didn't even try.

"If you don't kill me now, I'm going to arrest you and drag you back to Jaikon in chains," Stone said, his voice more animal than human.

Liss watched in horror as Rhett dropped his sword to the ground. "I've made my choice," he said. "Do what you have to do."

"Damn you, Rhetteman!" Stone yelled.

Rhett held out his hands with his wrists together as he faced his mentor.

Even from this distance, Liss could see the ragged, shuddering breath Stone released. She watched as Stone went over to a pair of iron manacles. Liss caught her breath.

These weren't ordinary manacles. They were Insorsiled chains, which couldn't be picked or muscled apart. They could only be opened by a single, unique key. If the key was separated from its owner when he was asleep, rendered unconscious, or killed, the key would crumble to dust, and the chains would remain locked forever.

Not even Liss could pick the locks on those manacles.

Rhett didn't resist as they clanged into place over his wrists.

"Rhetteman Loniger," Stone said, his voice tired, "I hereby arrest you for knowingly permitting an enemy of the empire to escape."

Ciago and Wilsean seemed as stunned as Liss.

"Wait," Wilsean choked. "Can't we just—"

"Leave him," Ciago finished. "We tell Jaikon he got away."

Stone and Rhett stared at each other for a long moment. Liss held her breath.

"If we don't bring him in, Jaikon will send every slaver and soldier in the empire to hunt him down," Stone said. He didn't take his eyes off Rhett. "If you cooperate, you might survive."

"But," Wilsean began.

"Your duty is to your empire," Stone interrupted. "And Rhetteman is now an enemy of Lagonia."

Wilsean and Ciago watched as Stone started to walk, pulling the slack chain until Rhett was forced to either keep up or feel the burn of the metal against his wrists.

Rhett didn't say a word as he allowed himself to be led away.

Guilt, confusion, and helplessness passed across Wilsean and Ciago's souls. They exchanged a look with each other, and then hurried to catch up. Liss didn't have to wait to see what they would do. She felt their sense of duty in their souls. She knew they wouldn't help Rhett.

Liss's mind was reeling. It would do no good to go after them; they would only arrest her along with Rhett. She needed a plan.

She forced the panic from her mind so she could think. She made herself consider the problem like it was just another one of her thieving expeditions. Rhett was the treasure. She had to steal him. The thought was a strange one, but it comforted her. If there was one thing Liss knew how to do, it was stealing.

With that thought anchoring her, she clambered back to the road. She ran as fast and hard as she could away from Lagonia.

CHAPTER 50

Rhett allowed himself to be locked into the torture cage without a word. Liss had gotten away. She was safe. It was all he cared about, and now it was done. It didn't matter what happened to him.

Rhett stood against the wall as Stone delivered a cursory report to Jaikon. There were a dozen guards stuffed into the corridor, and they were all looking from Rhett to Jaikon with clear discomfort on their faces. They knew what their Emperor would command of them, and none of them wanted to do it. With the exception of Elouicia, they were all Rhett's men, whom Jaikon had no doubt hand-selected in an attempt to break Rhett's spirit faster.

Rhett watched with little interest as Jaikon's smirk grew with each word of Stone's report. He had witnessed enough interrogations to know how this worked.

One would think the destruction of the flower fields had never happened with the way Jaikon's eyes were alight with victory. He practically laughed with glee when Stone got to the part about how Liss and Opal Smoke were one and the same.

Jaikon finally had what he had always wanted: a reason to kill Rhett that the council and his soldiers would have to accept.

Jaikon rubbed his hands together. He smiled at Stone. "You may begin."

"Majesty?" Stone asked.

"You may begin," Jaikon repeated, waving a hand at Rhett's cage. "Do what you do. Interrogate."

Rhett saw his mentor's face harden, and he knew this was what Stone had feared. It was why Stone had wanted Rhett to kill him.

Rhett felt badly for the position he'd forced Stone into, but there was nothing he could do about it. He never would have killed his mentor.

"I cannot interrogate him, Majesty," Stone said. "He was my ward. He's my—"

"I don't give a damn who he was, is, or might have been," Jaikon hissed. "You are Lagonia's Master Interrogator. I command you to extract every last morsel of knowledge from this bastard's brain!"

Stone's jaw tightened.

Don't, Rhett silently pleaded with his mentor, even though he knew what Stone would say before he opened his mouth.

"I will not interrogate, or torture, this prisoner," Stone said.

Rhett kept his face impassive, even though he wanted to shout at Stone to stop being an idiot. He was dead either way. It was stupid for his mentor to draw any of Jaikon's fury on himself when it wouldn't help Rhett and would only hurt Stone.

"Very well," Jaikon said, his voice dangerous. "Get him out of here."

Jaikon waited until Elouicia had dragged Stone away before turning to the guards crowded into the corridor. "Soften up the prisoner. I'll conduct this interrogation personally."

Jaikon didn't miss the apologetic looks each soldier gave Rhett as they delivered their half-hearted beating. Rhett saw the Emperor's expression darken with each passing moment.

"Hit me harder," Rhett whispered to the guard who was in his cage. "And stop looking at me like that."

The man looked close to tears as he hauled back and punched Rhett in the stomach.

Rhett barely felt the blow, but he doubled over for Jaikon's sake. He felt a mild frustration that not only did he need to concern himself with his impending torture, he also had to worry about his men putting their lives on the line for his sake.

"Get out!" Jaikon roared, yanking open the cage.

"If you all are too soft to give this traitor the treatment he deserves, then I'll do it myself."

Jaikon stepped into the cage with Rhett, shutting the door behind him.

Rhett could see the tiny golden key to his manacles gleaming at Jaikon's throat. It dangled there, a temptation and an invitation. Rhett didn't give it another glance. Even if he was able to take the key and unlock his manacles before Jaikon overpowered him, he'd have to get past the guards in the corridor.

Rhett wasn't sure what the soldiers outside his cage would do if it came down to it. But he knew that if any of them showed even the slightest hesitation, Jaikon would kill them. Rhett wouldn't put any of them in that position.

Jaikon pulled something out of his pocket. It was a pair of brass knuckles studded with black diamonds, which were honed to a wicked point. Rhett exhaled as the diamonds raked across his face.

"Tell me about the girl," Jaikon said. "Where is she now?"

"You should give Stone a raise." Rhett spat out a mouthful of blood. "Because you're a shit interrogator."

Jaikon hit him again, this time digging the pointed diamonds into the wound across Rhett's chest. Jaikon twisted his knuckles, deepening the wound.

Rhett laughed. "You're looking a little red in the face," he said. "If you want to take a few minutes to recover before we continue, I can just wait here."

Jaikon hit him again. And again.

Rhett knew his limits. Stone had spent years pushing the bounds of what he could tolerate, and he was far from his breaking point. As he absorbed the hits, Rhett let his mind slip away. It went straight to the cliff overlooking the flower fields, where blue moonlight shone on Liss's bare skin, and her hands and lips were on him.

He knew his body had struck the stone floor, but all he felt was the remembered softness of blankets and Liss.

Jaikon was kneeling on the ground beside him.

"This is nice," Rhett managed, his words thick with blood. "We never really get to spend time together."

"Do you truly have a death wish?" Jaikon huffed, hitting him again.

Rhett bit down on the inside of his cheek as one of his ribs gave way.

"I suppose if I was a worthless bastard, I'd want to die, too," Jaikon grunted.

The diamonds slashed across his face again.

"What bothers you more, *brother*," Rhett said, spitting out another mouthful of blood. "That you're the emperor and no one wants you for their leader, or that I'm just a bastard who your subjects respect?"

Jaikon's beating went from cruel and calculated to merciless. Blows rained down on him. Rhett willed his mind into darkness as Jaikon got to his feet and started kicking him.

Jaikon stopped just before Rhett lost consciousness.

"Tell me, *brother*," Jaikon spat, his face purple with fury. "Does it bother you that you were duped by a servant girl? Does it hurt that she used you?"

Rhett couldn't hide his reaction to Jaikon's taunt fast enough. His chest burned with an intensity that left him gasping.

A maniacal grin spread across Jaikon's face. "Don't tell me that after everything she's done to you, you're still in love with her?"

Rhett wheezed out a laugh. "You'll have to hit me harder if you expect me to start talking about my feelings."

Jaikon smiled. "It would be my pleasure."

CHAPTER 51

Liss flopped down on the road in front of the Insorsiled bike zooming in her direction.

"Help me," she called, reaching a hand out in the warlock's direction.

The warlock slowed his bike and skidded to a stop beside her.

"My dear—" he got off the bike and hurried to her.

Liss leapt to her feet and raced for the bike.

"Sorry!" she called as she kicked the bike into gear and sped away.

She did feel badly; the warlock had a kind soul. But she was in a hurry. Liss hoped with a fierce desperation that her mom would be waiting in the abandoned cottage she'd described to the Runner. It was on the edge of Insorsil farthest from Lagonia, which made it the safest meeting point Liss could think of.

As she drove, Liss worried about the problem of her mom's potion. She would need to find some way around the bargain Burk had made with the Insorsiled witchdoctor to withhold her mom's medicine from anyone except him.

She buried her fury at Burk for the moment so she could focus. She promised herself she'd come back to it when she had the time and means to do something about it…about him. Right now, her priorities were finding her mom and getting back to save Rhett. Nothing else mattered.

Liss was driving into the setting sun when she neared the cottage. She figured there was some trick of the light that was making her see things. The last time she had been here, the area had been completely abandoned.

Now, there were dozens of people milling around the abandoned field. Cookfires sent wisps of smoke blowing toward her.

Liss shook her head and blinked several times. When she looked again, the scene hadn't changed. The sunlight reflected off opal-hued skin. And on the far side of the cottage, two dozen wagons were parked.

Liss stopped the bike and got off, trying to make sense of the scene before her.

"Lissy!" Jema screeched, throwing herself into Liss's arms.

"What—what are you all doing here?" Liss asked, hugging the little girl back.

Before Jema could answer, three other familiar figures were heading toward her. Spence, Mari, and....

"Mom?!"

For the first time in as long as Liss could remember, her mother was out of bed. She wore regular clothes, not the pajamas she'd worn every day and night of Liss's life, and she was standing.

"Hello, sweetheart," Liss's mom said in a voice that didn't tremble from the effort of speaking.

Mari wrapped her skinny arms around Liss's waist. Spence gave her an awkward pat on the arm and welcomed her home in a deeper voice than he'd had when Liss left for Lagonia. Her mom hung back.

Liss's mother being vertical wasn't the only change. Instead of the crushing sadness and loss that Liss was so accustomed to feeling from her mom, there were other feelings crowded in around those. There was guilt, determination, and a fierce protectiveness.

Liss stared at her mom in open confusion. Her hair was still more gray than orange, but there was a healthy radiance to her opal skin that hadn't been there before. Liss barely recognized her.

"We were so worried about you!" Mari gushed.

Liss tore her eyes away from her mom as the caravans' Energizers joined their party.

"What time do you want us to push off?" one of the Energizers asked.

To Liss's shock and amazement, the question was directed at her mother.

"We're staying here until I know how we can help my daughter. Tell everyone to hold off on preparing dinner, and I'll hunt some game after Liss and I have talked."

The Energizers nodded and went back to their cookfires.

Liss was too surprised to speak. Her mother hadn't used a single aspect of her Huntress Extension in all the years Liss could remember.

"Mom," Liss began, not even knowing what to say, but her mother cut her off.

"We'll have time for catching up later, sweetheart. Right now, you need to know what's been going on around here."

"Burk's a bad man," Jema informed Liss.

Liss's gaze shot to her mother.

Her mom gave her a wry smile. "Even before the Runner delivered your message, I could tell Burk was up to something."

"Mari and Jema distracted him, while Nya and I snuck into Burk's wagon and searched it," Spence said. There was a brightness in his orange eyes that hadn't been there the last time she'd seen him.

"Did you know Burk wrote up a contract, which I assume he is still trying to ratify with the Emperor?" Liss's mom asked.

Spence handed Liss a thick paper marked with Insorsiled ink, which ensured the contract was binding once it was signed by both parties. Her mouth fell open as she scanned the page.

The agreement detailed Burk's pledge to share his knowledge about the Extended with the Lagonia Emperor for the purpose of tracking suspected criminals. In exchange, he'd get a home in the palace and a position on the emperor's council. It also detailed his knowledge of—and willingness to share—the identity of the infamous Extended spy, otherwise known as Opal Smoke.

The line for Jaikon's signature was blank. The place for Burk's signature was completed, with a flourish on the "k."

Liss growled. "That piece of—"

Liss's mother held up her finger, inclining her head to the younger girls.

"But Mom," Liss began, not even knowing which question to start with. "What is everyone doing here? Why are they answering to you?" *Why are you out of bed?*

"No one threatens my daughter," her mom said, a fierce expression coming over her face that Liss had never seen before. "So, the four of us put our heads and skills together to do what we could to help you from here."

"Yeah, because you're our friend and Burk's a poop," Jema piped up.

"Well said, darling," Liss's mom told the little girl.

Spence and Mari nodded.

Liss was still trying to wrap her head around the fact that her mom was lucid and on her feet.

"What seemed clear to me was that Burk's time as our caravan leader had come to an end," Liss's mom continued. "And the best way for me to help you was if I stepped into the role as caravan leader myself."

"And everyone just accepted you as their leader?" Liss asked, trying not to sound too skeptical.

Her mom gave her a little half-smile. "They didn't, at first."

"She shot an arrow between Hoki's legs when he tried to challenge her," Spence said, a grin stretching across his entire face.

"And then she threw a knife and sliced half of Bragg's moustache off," Jema added, jumping up and down with glee.

Mari said, "And then my brothers stood on either side of Nya and said if anyone didn't want her as their new leader, they'd get a knuckle sandwich." She giggled. "Those might not have been their *exact* words, but it was the same idea."

Mari's four brothers were Extended Fighters, the only ones in the caravan. A punch in the face from one of them would crush a person's skull.

"After that, the rest of the caravan fell into line," Spence finished.

"Does Burk know about all of this?" Liss asked.

Her mom shook her head. "He hasn't returned from Lagonia, but when he does, I'm sure he'll figure it out."

Spence and Mari snickered.

"What about your potion?" Liss asked, somewhat in a daze. "Burk said the witchdoctor wasn't selling it to anyone except for him. How much do you have left?"

"I've cut back on the amount I need," Liss's mom replied. "I have plenty left, and I believe I'll be weaned off it completely by winter's end."

"Mom." Liss choked on the word.

After a brief, awkward moment, Liss's mom wrapped her arms around her. Her mom's grip was stronger than it should be for someone who'd been an invalid for almost twenty years.

"Thank you for doing this for me," Liss said, overcome with a rush of warmth and gratitude toward her mother and friends.

"You've taken care of all of us long enough," her mother said. The guilt in her soul spiked. "I know I have a lot of making up to do."

Liss struggled to find words.

Her mom squeezed her and said, "Whatever happens next, I promise I'll be there by your side."

"Thank you," Liss said again, knowing the words would never be enough to express her gratitude. "But I need to go back to Lagonia, and when I return, we're going to need all the Extended we can find." She met her mom's gaze. "Can you help me?"

Her mom nodded. "I can go to the other caravans and make sure we're assembled by the time you get back."

Liss returned her mother's fierce embrace. For the first time in her life, she didn't feel like she needed to protect her mom. For the first time, she felt like her mom was the one who was going to take care of her. It made her feel strangely vulnerable.

"So, what now?" Spence asked, clearly uncomfortable with the emotional turn this conversation was taking.

"Actually," Liss said, breaking away from her mom as all her urgency returned in full force. "There's something else I need help with."

"Does it involve thieving?" Spence asked.

"In a way, I guess it does."

Spence, Mari, and Jema grinned.

Spence gave her a mock salute. "What are we stealing?"

CHAPTER 52

Rhett heard two sets of light footsteps coming down the corridor. His first thought was Liss. He tried to sit up, before remembering his body was shattered. His still-beating heart raced in anticipation.

There were soft voices at the opening to his cage. Rhett forced his eyes open. They were swollen and crusted with blood, but he could make out the two women bending over the lock. He recognized Samara and another girl who looked too much like Samara not to be her sister.

A devastated, crushing sensation settled on him that had nothing to do with his mangled flesh and broken bones. At the same time, Rhett was overcome with relief. The last place he ever wanted to see Liss was here, because that would mean she had been caught, and then all of this would be for nothing.

The cage door opened, and the two women came inside. He tried to speak, to tell them to leave before one of Jaikon's people found them down here, but his jaw was broken and he didn't think he'd be able to manage it.

The other girl—Samara's sister, he assumed—knelt beside him. She looked several years younger than Samara, but otherwise, they were almost identical. The girl was touching him and singing what sounded like an Insorsiled lullaby.

Not a lullaby, he realized. It was an incantation. He could feel the broken bones in his face realigning. It hurt almost as much as the breaking of them in the first place.

"Leave the cuts," Samara ordered her sister. "We can't make it look too good."

"You shouldn't bother," Rhett said when he had mastered the pain enough to speak. "I'm already dead, and you'll only wind up getting yourselves killed along with me."

Samara made a dismissive noise.

"If Wilsean knew you were here, he'd kill me himself," Rhett persisted. "Get out of here."

"Who do you think helped us sneak down?" Samara retorted.

Rhett wanted to argue with her, but he couldn't muster the energy.

"Damn, I'm good," Samara's sister said, marveling at her own handiwork. "Are you sure I can't fix those cuts? They're going to scar if I don't heal them now."

Right, Rhett thought. *We certainly wouldn't want them to scar.* He might even look ugly as his corpse was tossed over the cliff. It would break the court ladies' hearts.

"It grates on my nerves to leave anything unhealed," Samara's sister complained as she moved on to the rest of his body.

"This is my sister Lullianna, by the way," Samara told Rhett. "She's a brilliant witchdoctor, in case you haven't noticed."

"I appreciate this," Rhett said, "but it'll only give Jaikon more things to break tomorrow."

"We just need to keep you in one piece for a little longer," Samara said, lifting a potion to his lips. "This will make you look worse than you are."

The potion was grainy and bitter, but he hadn't been given any food or water in more than a day, so he accepted it gratefully.

"That's a kind thought," Rhett said, "but helping me will only make it take longer for this all to end."

Samara gave him an incredulous look. "And what do you expect me to tell Liss when she comes back for you, and I have to explain that I let you die?"

Hearing her name sent a stab of pain through him worse than any broken bone. He turned his face away from the women.

"I've made my peace with all of this. Don't put yourselves at risk for me."

"I'm not doing it for you," Samara replied. "I'm doing it because two people I care about love you, and because I know that if Wilsean was in trouble and Liss could help him, she would."

"Liss doesn't care what happens to any of us," Rhett muttered.

Saying the words out loud was worse than saying them in his head.

Samara glared at him. "Just because you have twenty-seven broken bones—"

"Twenty-eight," Lullianna corrected.

"—it doesn't give you the excuse to be stupid."

Rhett clenched his newly-formed jaw as his kneecap knit back into place.

"You're wrong," Rhett said, even as his vision blurred in and out of focus. "She isn't...who we thought she was."

"If you're referring to her being Opal Smoke, then yeah," Samara said. "But her love for you is more real than anything I've ever seen."

Rhett stared at her. "Did Wilsean tell you?"

Samara scoffed. "Rhett, I *am* an Empty. I knew Liss wasn't who she said she was from the moment I met her."

"And it doesn't bother you that she betrayed us?" Rhett demanded.

"Do you know what she sacrificed to keep you safe?" Samara countered.

"She lied to me...the whole time!"

Rhett tried to sit up, but Lullianna pushed him back down.

"You have no idea what she went through to protect you," Samara shot back.

"Protect *me*? You're joking, right?"

"Her scumbag caravan leader threatened her mom, Rhett. It was killing her, but she was trying to be loyal to both you and her own people. You should give her a little more credit."

Rhett opened his mouth and then shut it again. He tried to make sense of everything Samara was telling him.

"Are you sure I can't heal any more of him?" Lullianna complained to her sister. "Literally killing me."

"No, you're done," Samara told her. "And that's not the right use of *literally*."

"How would you know? I'm the witchdoctor," Lullianna retorted.

"Witchdoctor *in training*," Samara corrected, rolling her eyes.

Lullianna humphed. "Well, since my sister is intent on keeping you mangled, I guess we're done here." She held up a small bottle in front of Rhett's face. She muttered some words, passed her right hand over the bottle, and it blinked out of existence.

"I'm putting this right here," she said, placing the now-invisible potion in the corner of his cage. "Drink it first thing in the morning, and it'll strengthen your looking-like-crap illusion."

Samara gave her sister an exasperated look before turning her attention back to Rhett.

"Liss loves you more than is good for one person to love another," she told him. There was a slight edge to her voice that Rhett was too tired and overwhelmed to try to understand.

"If you need something to hold onto," Samara said, "hold ono this. Whatever is between you and Liss, it's real."

✳ ✳ ✳

Rhett woke to the sound of many pairs of boots clomping down the stairs. Most of them stopped in the corridor, but one pair came all the way to his cage. He knew Jaikon's footsteps without having to look.

"Are you dead?" the Emperor asked.

Rhett turned his head and gave the Emperor a twisted smile.

"Oh good," Jaikon replied, rolling up his golden sleeves. "After yesterday, I wasn't sure if you'd bleed out during the night."

"Maybe you don't hit as hard as you think you do," Rhett said, his voice sounding hoarse and unused.

A few of the guards snickered at that.

"Get up," Jaikon hissed.

"I'm tired," Rhett replied.

Elouicia stalked up to the cage. He wrapped his hands around the bars and stared at Rhett. The man was practically salivating.

It was easy to tell which of the guards standing by were loyal to Rhett from their rigid posture and grimaces. If he'd had the chance, he would have told them to cut it out. There was no point in being loyal to someone who was about to die.

"Get him up!" Jaikon barked at one of the guards.

The cage was unlocked and Rhett was hauled to his feet. Samara's sister had left some of the broken bones in his right leg, so he didn't have to feign weakness as he sagged against the bars.

"Where is Opal Smoke?" Jaikon demanded. "I know you told her to hide somewhere, and I want to know where."

As he had the day before, Rhett stayed silent. The Emperor prowled around him.

"You could make this so much easier on yourself," Jaikon said in a soothing voice. "You could tell me everything. You could give up." He paused in front of Rhett and smirked. "Of course, I can't promise it'll earn you an easy death. I'm rather enjoying our time together."

Jaikon continued his prowling until he was standing directly behind Rhett. He spoke in Rhett's ear, but his words were loud enough for all of the guards to hear.

"I'm really looking forward to finding your whore."

Rhett snapped his head back. He heard Jaikon's nose crunch a second before the Emperor screamed.

Five guards rushed in to restrain Rhett and get the Emperor out. There was nothing more Rhett could do with his broken leg and shackled hands, so he didn't try.

"Get out!" Jaikon yelled at the guards, one hand covering his nose.

Elouicia cracked his knuckles and stepped into the cage. "Majesty, I—"

"Don't touch him!" Jaikon shrieked. "He's mine." There was a crazed look in the Emperor's eyes.

Elouicia bared his pointed fangs and slunk back.

"You are going to regret that," Jaikon said, his words muffled.

Rhett faced Jaikon. "Do your worst."

CHAPTER 53

Go faster!"

Enraged at the old Insorsiled bike, Liss thumped its metal handle. The machine was already at its highest speed and had started to shudder. It jerked to the side, but Liss didn't slow down. Spence yelped and hugged her waist to keep from sliding off.

As they sped toward Lagonia, there was nothing for Liss to do but worry.

What if Samara didn't get her message? Pixies were unreliable on the best of days. She had paid the creature its literal weight in gold, and if it hadn't delivered her message, Liss would find the pixie and chop it into tiny pieces.

Liss had stayed with the caravan just long enough for them to hammer out a plan. Still, it had taken almost two days. She had no idea if she would even get to Rhett in time. The bike shuddered again as she tried to push it faster.

"Calm down, or I'm driving," Spence yelled.

"Remind me why I brought you along," Liss huffed.

"Because you need me," Spence replied, sounding a little too cheerful.

There was no denying it. She hated to bring anyone back to Lagonia with her, especially one of the kids, but there had been no other way around it. And Spence had been more than eager for the chance to do damage to the Lagonians. Of course, she hadn't exactly mentioned the man they were rescuing was the Viper.

As soon as the Golden Bridge came into sight, Liss tensed. If that damned pixie hadn't delivered her message, the guards would arrest her and Spence or kill them on the spot. She hesitated and the bike stuttered, but then she recognized the hulking figure of Ciago standing at the end of the bridge. She wanted to weep with relief.

She stopped the bike and ran to him. Ciago hesitated for only a moment before returning her quick, fierce hug.

"Is he—"

"Alive," Ciago replied. "Barely."

Before she could begin to wrap her mind around those words, Dannica, Rhett's soldier friend who had given Liss one of her own uniforms the first time she entered Lagonia, stepped off the bridge.

"The archers won't bother you or your opal friend," Dannica told Liss. "In return for risking our own necks, we expect you to do right by Rhett."

Liss nodded, unable to speak. She turned back to Ciago. It was then that Liss saw the dark circles under her friend's eyes. He looked haggard.

"You got my message, I take it," Liss said, forcing her mind onto more practical matters as they stepped onto the bridge.

Ciago nodded.

True to Dannica's word, the archers all stared determinedly down at the water so they wouldn't see her and Spence.

"Do you think it'll work?" Liss asked.

Ciago's expression was grim. "It has to."

✳ ✳ ✳

If you need something to hold onto, Samara had said, *hold ono this. Whatever is between you and Liss, it's real.*

Rhett clung to those words as the black diamonds raked across his flesh. The words shouldn't matter now, but they did.

Rhett was beyond trying to make sense of it all. He intended to use every minute he had left lost in the memory of their night on the cliff. He heard Jaikon's grunts as he hit Rhett over and over again, but it was just background…an illusion, like the potion he'd drunk. His reality was the cliff and Liss. The picture in his mind flickered, but he was determined it would be the last thing he'd see before he saw nothing at all.

* * *

Liss and Spence tried to keep up as Ciago strode across the Golden Bridge. Liss had known many of the soldiers were more loyal to Rhett than their Emperor, but as the one-hundred archers turned their heads and pretended not to see them, it struck her how much Rhett's soldiers loved him. If she wasn't so single-mindedly focused on the task ahead, it would have brought tears to her eyes.

"This one," Ciago hissed to Spence as a man Liss recognized as one of the Emperor's advisors came into view.

"Ciago, what is the meaning—"

The man collapsed to the ground, snoring. Spence put his hand back in his pocket.

"That's pretty cool," Ciago told Spence.

Spence scowled, but Liss could tell he was pleased.

They crossed the distance between the Golden Bridge and the outside door to the torture cage in this way. Some of the soldiers they passed turned and pretended not to see them. Spence took care of the rest.

Ciago and Spence stayed with her until they reached the door.

"This is where the kid and I need to leave you, for now," Ciago whispered to Liss. "Jaikon's got the key around his neck."

Liss nodded before turning to Spence. "Do you have enough strength for this?"

The Extended boy nodded, even though his skin had lost some of its opal sheen.

"Good," Ciago told him. "You're going to need it." To Liss he said, "Don't let Rhett die before we get back with your ride out of here."

Ciago let out a whistle that sounded just like the chattering birds that announced dawn's first light.

The door opened, and Wilsean motioned Liss inside, putting a finger to his lips. Liss stepped into the narrow stairwell as the door shut behind her.

CHAPTER 54

Rhett's vision swam as Jaikon dealt another vicious blow to his stomach.

"Does it bother you," Jaikon paused long enough to hit him again, "to know you're suffering for a girl who left you to die?"

Rhett didn't say anything.

"Wasn't some part of you hoping she'd come back here and beg me to release you?" Jaikon circled around Rhett, building anticipation for the next blow. "I know *I* was hoping for it."

"She isn't stupid enough to come back here," Rhett replied.

"Don't give me so much credit."

That voice. He must be imagining it. He had spent the last two days remembering how it sounded. Rhett knew his body couldn't tolerate much more abuse, and it didn't surprise him that he was hallucinating. He welcomed it.

"What are you doing here?" he asked, playing along.

"Rescuing you, of course."

His eyes snapped open. He wasn't hallucinating. Liss was there, outside his cage.

No.

"Elouicia, block the exits," Jaikon's gleeful command came from behind him. "This interrogation just got interesting."

"No. Liss, get out of here!"

She was standing motionless in front of his cage, staring at him in horror.

"How fortunate I didn't kill you, yet," Jaikon gloated to Rhett.

"Please, Liss. Get out of here. Get out!"

Somehow, Rhett got to his feet. He tried to push Jaikon back, away from the cage's opening and Liss. But Jaikon slammed his diamond-studded knuckles into Rhett.

Rhett forced himself to stay conscious.

Liss winced as Elouicia's hand clamped down on the back of her neck.

"No!" Rhett struggled against Jaikon. He was frantic. He wouldn't let this happen. Not to her.

"Please, Jaikon."

Rhett had never begged for anything in his life, but he was doing it now. "Let her go."

Jaikon let out a long, satisfied sigh. "What are you willing to do to save your love?"

Rhett looked past him to Liss. "Anything." His voice broke. "I'll do anything for her."

Rhett felt Jaikon's smile, even though he was still looking at Liss. She was trying to tell him something with her eyes, but all he could see was Elouicia's hand gripping her neck.

"I knew I'd find your weakness eventually." Jaikon sauntered out of the cage. He motioned for Elouicia to let go of Liss and enter the cage with Rhett. Jaikon slid an arm around Liss's shoulders.

"Get away from her!" Rhett tried to fight his way to the front of the cage, but Elouicia yanked him back.

Rhett could do nothing but watch as Jaikon circled behind Liss. He leaned in close and whispered something in her ear, never taking his eyes off Rhett. Rhett fought against Elouicia with every ounce of his remaining strength. It wasn't enough.

Liss wasn't trying to get away. *Why wasn't she trying to get away?*

Jaikon raised his diamond-studded knuckles to Liss's face. He barely touched them to the skin of her cheek, like he was caressing her. Liss shuddered.

"Jaikon!" Rhett snarled and fought like the caged animal he was. "This is between us. Leave her alone!"

Jaikon paused his perverse caresses and smiled at Rhett. "I'm going to watch you break before I toss your corpse over the cliff."

Rhett slammed his chains into Elouicia. The other man staggered back, but he recovered quickly. He grabbed the chains, yanked Rhett closer, and sunk his pointed teeth into Rhett's shoulder. There was madness in the man's eyes.

"Stop," Jaikon commanded. "Control yourself, Elouicia."

Elouicia growled low in his throat. He made a sucking sound as he ran his tongue over his blood-slicked teeth. Rhett barely noticed. His gaze was locked on Jaikon.

"I'm going to make her scream," Jaikon said softly. "I'm going to make her beg."

No. Rhett's heart felt like it was going to explode in his chest. Every part of him was straining toward Liss. He had to help her. He had to save her.

But no matter how hard he fought, he was in this cage, and she was out there with Jaikon.

"Don't worry." Jaikon smiled. "I'm going to let you watch."

"You're sick," Liss said. Her gaze kept moving to the end of the corridor, like she was waiting for something. Rhett was too frantic to think what it might be. He had to get her out of here. Nothing else mattered.

"You think Rhett loving me is his weakness, but that's because you don't understand that caring for someone else more than yourself makes you stronger," Liss said.

"How sweet," Jaikon crooned.

Liss shrugged, like she was unaware of the danger she faced. "You'll never know what it feels like to give all of yourself to someone and get all of them in return." She looked at Rhett when she said this.

It was then that Rhett knew he couldn't take the pain. He could have endured the physical torture until his body shut down, but he couldn't take this. He couldn't watch the horrors Jaikon would make her suffer.

Jaikon pulled back his arm, preparing to swing. He grinned at Rhett. "Liss!"

She didn't miss a beat. Liss ducked away from the strike in the way she and Rhett had practiced a hundred times on the sparring field. While Jaikon was off balance, Liss put her hands on his shoulders and kneed him in the groin.

Jaikon doubled over.

"Don't think that makes us even," she said in disgust, "but it's a start."

Rhett thought he saw the flash of gold in Liss's hand before it disappeared into her pocket.

Then, before any of the stunned guards in the corridor could react, Liss drew a dagger from inside her jacket and tried to drive it into the Emperor's chest.

Guards lunged forward, but not before a blue shield of light appeared between Jaikon's chest and the point of the dagger. The light originated from a tiny gold circlet attached to the Emperor's shirt. The little piece of metal was vibrating as it produced the beams of blue light.

Liss's hand shook with the effort of trying to drive the dagger through the barrier of light. Whatever magic made the translucent barrier stay in place, it was impenetrable.

The blue light pulsed again, and the dagger flew out of Liss's hands with so much force it shattered against the wall. Liss gasped as she staggered back.

For a moment, everyone stayed frozen in place. Even Rhett stopped fighting. He'd heard rumors, but until this moment, he hadn't believed them.

Elouicia recovered first. He shoved Rhett to the back of the cage and ran forward.

But before he could reach Liss, an opal-skinned boy with long, orange hair came out of nowhere. He reached out a hand and brushed his fingers over Elouicia's wrist. Elouicia slumped to the ground, snoring.

"Restrain the Extended brat," Jaikon ordered.

The guards in the hallway snapped to attention, surrounding the small boy. Out of the corner of his eye, Rhett saw the guards close in on the boy and then start to slump to the ground one-by-one. Rhett didn't spare them another glance; all of his focus was fixed on Jaikon and Liss.

"It would seem the rumors about my invincibility are true." The Emperor gave Liss his cruelest smile as he brushed a hand over the gold circlet. "I've made a powerful friend in Insorsil. This little pin protects me from mortal wounds."

Jaikon stepped forward, forcing Liss back against the wall. "Now, let's see if the rumors about you are true." His smile widened. "If you can turn into vapor or disappear, Opal Smoke, now's the time."

Jaikon moved quickly, wrapping his hands around Liss's throat.

Rhett was beating against the cage and shouting, but before he could get to her or die trying, the Extended boy snuck up behind the Emperor and put his hand on Jaikon's neck.

The Emperor dropped to the ground, snoring, along with all of the guards who had been surrounding the boy.

Liss looked down at the sleeping figure of Jaikon.

"You might not be able to die," she said with disgust, "but this should give you something to think about when you wake up."

She stomped on Jaikon's right hand, crushing the bones beneath her foot. The Emperor let out a little cry but didn't wake.

Rhett wheezed out a breath. Without his fury and terror keeping him on his feet, he collapsed. He felt, rather than heard, Liss run into the cage.

"Rhett!"

He wanted to speak. He wanted to tell her all the things she already knew. But he was so damn tired.

"You're going to be fine," she was saying as she pulled the tiny key from her pocket and fit it into the lock of his manacles. "I'm going to get you out of here."

Her face swam in and out of his view. She was so beautiful.

It seemed right that the last thing he would see in this world would be her face. He held her in his gaze until his vision went dark. Her voice was in his ears, and then that was gone, too. He was gone.

CHAPTER 55

When Rhett's head hit the ground, Liss screamed. He wasn't breathing. Liss couldn't feel his soul. *She couldn't feel his soul.* "Move!"

A girl who looked like a younger version of Samara shoved her aside and knelt by Rhett. She put her hand over Rhett's heart, shook her head, and started to mutter to herself.

Liss was sobbing and fighting against some immovable force that was dragging her out of the cage…away from Rhett.

"Let go of me!"

She had to get to Rhett…had to save him.

She couldn't feel his soul.

"Get your hands off him!" she shrieked, clawing and pushing at the thing that was keeping her from Rhett.

"Stop it, Liss," a voice commanded. She had just enough presence of mind left to recognize it as Wilsean's. "Lullianna's a witchdoctor. Let her do her thing."

Liss stilled in his arms.

There was a commotion behind her, but Liss didn't even bother turning around. She couldn't look away from Rhett's broken body and the girl touching him.

"Time to go, Liss!" Ciago's voice called. "*Liss.*"

And then Ciago's huge body filled the corridor. "We're about five minutes away from having this place surrounded by every one of Jaikon's cronies," he said. He was breathing heavily, and there was blood on his dragonhide jacket.

"The men in here won't be asleep long," Spence said. "And I'm tapped out."

"Everyone shut up!" the girl bending over Rhett commanded.

They all went quiet. So, when Rhett took his first, shuddering breath, they all heard it. At the same moment, Liss felt the whisper of Rhett's unconscious soul. It was barely there, but it *was* there.

Liss sagged in Wilsean's arms.

"Thank God," Wilsean gasped.

"God had nothing to do with this," Lullianna replied, irritated. She wiped sweat from her brow and stood up. "I'm leaving him unconscious so he doesn't thrash around and hurt himself more. There's a lot of internal bleeding that will need time to fully mend, since it would take too much time for me to do it now."

"Can we move him?" Wilsean asked.

"In a perfect world? No. But since it doesn't seem like he can stay here, just keep him as still as you can."

Wilsean let go of Liss, and together, he and Ciago lifted Rhett up and carried him out of the cage. Liss followed.

"Liss!" Samara was racing through the corridor, leaping over the unconscious bodies.

She crushed Liss in a hug. Samara let go and pressed a small bag into Liss's hands.

"Lullianna put these together for Rhett. All the instructions are inside. They'll help with the healing."

Liss was too overcome to speak, so she just nodded.

The guards who weren't unconscious pressed themselves against the wall to give them more room. Liss followed Wilsean and Ciago, who were trying to move quickly without jarring Rhett's body. It was awkward with the corridor being so small and the three men being so large, but they managed to get him outside.

When they stepped out into the sunlight, Liss saw unconscious guards dotting the grass surrounding Jaikon's enormous gold dragon.

"She's a little hard to hold," Dannica, who was straining against the dragon's bridle, warned Spence as he climbed on. "Don't let her give you any crap."

Liss scrambled up next, and then Ciago lifted Rhett into the space between her and Spence. The dragon reared, but Dannica gave the reins a quick yank, and the beast settled.

"Thank you," Liss said to the people surrounding them. She knew what they had all risked…were risking…. "I can't tell you how much."

"Consider Rhett on loan," Ciago told her with a small smile. "Lagonia isn't done with him yet."

Liss managed a shaky nod.

"Enough with the heartfelt goodbyes," Dannica said. "We need to get this dragon off the ground."

"Wait."

They all turned to see Stone, as collected as Liss was frantic, striding across the field toward them. He hadn't yelled, but she still heard him. He tossed what looked like a heavy bag at her. She caught it. The bag was incredibly light, even though it was crammed full.

"Flowers," Stone said as he came up alongside the dragon. "They were all I could get. It should be enough to keep him immune for a few months, at least."

Liss nodded, winding the strap over her shoulder so she'd have both hands free to hold onto Rhett. She was grateful for the immunity, but it didn't mean she forgave Stone.

"Will you do something for me, please?" Stone lowered his voice.

As Liss looked down at him, she saw true pain and regret in his soul. There was also more love than she had ever thought the man capable of.

"Yes?" she asked, giving a pointed look to Dannica, who was straining against the feisty dragon's bridle.

"Will you tell Rhett…I'm sorry?"

Liss stared at Stone for a long moment, and then, she nodded.

Stone's soul eased a fraction. He turned away from her.

"All of you get down on the ground and make like you're asleep," Stone barked. "The opal boy put us out and we don't know a thing. Got it?"

They all began to drop. Samara gave Liss a wink before she lay down between Wilsean and her sister. There was an audible thump as Ciago's body hit the ground.

"Ready?" Dannica asked.

As soon as Spence had the reins, Dannica let go. Liss clutched Rhett as the dragon started to rise.

"Sweet ride," Spence called from the front of the dragon.

Liss looked down at the fake-unconscious men and women on the ground. There were so many of them. It overwhelmed her how many Lagonians had come together to help Rhett. As the dragon continued to rise, Liss thought all those pretending-to-be-asleep people on the ground might be the most beautiful sight she'd ever seen.

The dragon rose higher. When she looked back again, she could no longer see anything beneath the veil of clouds. She stopped trying to look down. Liss wrapped her arms tighter around Rhett, and turned her gaze ahead.

THE END

* * *

Because reviews are so important for a book to be successful, please consider leaving a brief review on your favorite retailer if you enjoyed *Opal Smoke*. Many thanks!

* * *

Sign up for Stephanie Fazio's e-Newsletter to learn about upcoming books at:
https://StephanieFazio.com/subscribe/

Acknowledgements

I am so grateful to the dedicated group of people who helped with this book.

To Andrew Brodsky, Keith Tarrier, and Ellen Schaeffer. Thank you for being part of the team that made this book possible.

To Bob Brodsky, Rhoda Schneider, and the rest of my ARC team, for seeing new ways to bring my characters and stories to life.

To all my wonderful friends, for your enthusiasm and your belief in me. To Julie, for being the best friend anyone could ever ask for.

To my wonderful family who have given me so much, and who have made my writing possible.

To my readers. Thank you for giving me a reason to write. You make what I do possible and meaningful.

To Andrew. There's no one else I'd want to share my life with. Thank you for being you.

About the Author:

Stephanie Fazio is a fantasy author. She grew up in Syracuse, New York, and prior to writing full time, she worked in the fields of journalism, secondary education, and higher education. She has an undergraduate degree in English from Colgate University and a Master's degree in Reading, Writing, and Literacy from the University of Pennsylvania. Stephanie lives in Austin with her husband and crazy rescue dog. When she isn't writing, she's getting lost in parks, hosting taco nights, or ironically and miserably losing at word games, but having fun while she does it.

Connect with Stephanie Fazio:

Visit her Website: https://www.StephanieFazio.com
Sign up for her newsletter: https://StephanieFazio.com/subscribe/

Discover other books by Stephanie Fazio

Bisecter Series

Bisecter

Halve Human

Dusker Dark

Captain Harkibel

The Fount Series

The Prince's Chosen

The Forsaken's Choice

The Chosen Union

Opal Contagion Series

Opal Smoke

Opal Slayer

Opal Contagion

StephanieFazio.com

www.ingramcontent.com/pod-product-compliance
Lightning Source LLC
Chambersburg PA
CBHW051627180726
48284CB00006B/1627